Tales from
HIGH
HALLACK

Tales from
HIGH
HALLACK

the collected short stories of
ANDRE NORTON
Volume 3

ANDRE NORTON

OPEN ROAD
INTEGRATED MEDIA
NEW YORK

978-1-62467-273-6

Published in 2014 by Open Road Integrated Media, Inc.
345 Hudson Street
New York, NY 10014
www.openroadmedia.com

For Jay Watts and Paul Goode

CONTENTS

INTRODUCTION

A magical writer whose work has delighted me for more than sixty years, a Grand Master of the Science Fiction and Fantasy Writers of America, a friend . . . I had the honor to become her publisher at Grosset and Dunlap and at Ace, where she had for many years been published.

Shortly after becoming publisher of Ace I flew to Winter Park, Florida, to meet her in her cozy home just filled with more contented looking cats than I can ever remember having seen in one place. We spent a great afternoon getting to know each other.

When—in 1979—I was founding TOR, I again flew to Winter Park. I had the thought that wouldn't it be great if this woman who had so often been first, who had inspired so many, who had collaborated with so many, would again be first by agreeing to do TOR Books #1.

She had no need to risk moving to a small, new start-up, which would be competing with the biggest names in the industry. But she did, and so TOR Books #1 was *Forerunner* by Andre Norton.

We worked with her until she left us all in 2005. Eventually, between her new material, her backlist, and her collaborations, we would publish sixty-one of her titles.

Tom Doherty
Founder, TOR Books

Tales from
HIGH
HALLACK

AUÔUR THE DEEPMINDED
Warrior Enchantresses (1996) DAW

Here follows the true adventures of an Icelandic sorceress' search. This courageous woman appears in many sagas, but was never given her own story until now. Many places in Iceland are named for her and her search, though little is known about her outside her chosen homeland. There are many quiet heroines like Auôur in history. They do what needs to be done. Often historic accounts focus on the glitz. Remember that the less flashy people bring us closer to reality and our past.

Outside the wind was dank with what seemed an ever-present rain. Auôur did not try to pull the folds of her heavy cloak any tighter about her—the thick wool seemed to seep up the damp even though she had not been any closer to the day without than this narrow window. There was a hoarse call from behind her; it sounded twice more before it drew her attention.

Three ravens bobbed and sidled along their home perch, and seeing that they now had her attention, their harsh voices rose to a scream. She turned to face them squarely, holding out the scarred

3

wooden bowl into which they dipped bills in turn, small drops of blood flung aside by the jerking of the strips of raw mutton she provided. Odin's birds—and these were hatchlings of hatchlings of hatchlings—going far back in the past to when her father, Ketill Flatnose, had beached his longboat on the shore of the Irish and set out to reap the harvests and riches of those unfortunate enough to lie in the pathway of his force.

But he had been a prudent man, as well as a fine wielder of a battle ax, and in the end he had made a truce with one of his own countrymen who had done very well for himself—Olafur—so mighty a warlord that he had named himself king.

She had been twelve years old that summer, though sturdy enough that she had taken to far faring as well as any lad eager to win his war name. So she had made no complaint when her father sealed his bargain by giving her as wife to Olafur. She had a man to whom people pointed in pride, and he was lucky in his riving until at last his enemies (and those were of his own kind) cut him down. She had been in the great hall with her lusty babe of a son, Thorstein, on her knee when they brought her the news.

Only she had already known that ill hung over them, for it was born in her mother's clan to foreknow and sometimes even farknow.

Thorstein. Now she twirled the bowl so that the last greedy raven could strip it bare. Thorstein. Though she was his mother, she had always known there was a lack in him. He was not quite the bearsacker he wished—to rush into battle uncaring for anything but bringing death to the enemy. Though he had sworn blood oaths against those he held as his father's death givers and made them good. She had warnings that he could not hold the land his father had taken, nor survive the bloody path he followed.

But she had done her duty. He had been handfasted at fourteen to Heild, who came from proper stock and at least he had not been backward in bed. Five daughters he had sired between raidings, and at last a son. Then his last Viking raid had taken him to the land of the Scots and he had returned full of tales of rich land to bundle them all off across the sea, only to himself die before the second snow encased the wild land.

Now—Auôur turned once more to the window slit. Now it was she who must uphold the honor of the house, but she was sick of constant fighting, and only four months ago she had learned that MacMann planned to wipe them out.

How many fighting men would answer *her* war horn? She smiled grimly. More thralls (who must not be allowed weapons) than men who could swing them to a good purpose. Still there was a sureness in her that their line would not end here. Ah, no! Had she not sacrificed the fine horse which was part of Thorstein's last looting? Its smoking blood surely had drawn Odin's one all-knowing eye.

And to Freya she had also given her finest treasures, those broad gold bands of bracelets which Olafur had made her as first morning gifts. No, she was as certain that the gods would favor her plan as she was that she lived, breathed, and stood where she did at that moment.

The messages from overseas—the new lands waiting for any bold enough to claim them. With no ancient blood feuds to cut down family lines. Two of her brothers had ventured there and prospered—could she do less?

Yet the going, as she well knew, would not be easy. It must be done with secrecy since MacMann would be watching. From this vantage point she could see the screen of forest within which her thralls labored under the watchful and knowledgeable eye of Thorfin Shipmaker. A ship grew into shape there among the very trees from which it was being wrought.

There was a stir behind her and one of the ravens screeched.

"Maudlen? What is it?" She was always able to recognize the step of any of the household.

"Janor sends a message—MacMann rides!"

Almost Auôur held her breath. "How does he ride?" She schooled her voice to be even.

"Toward the Demon's Hill." There was breathless fear in her eldest granddaughter's voice.

Auôur swung around. "So. Send me the Saxon wench!"

"You would—" The fear in Maudlen's voice was ever stronger.

"What matters with you, girl? This is none of your concern. Get me Wulfra."

When the old thrall sidled around the edge of the doorway, her eyes were downcast, but Auôur knew well what red lights held in their depths.

"MacMann goes to the demons."

"So, mistress?" There was a shadow of insolence in the other's answer.

"So, MacMann is of the new faith and yet he seeks the demons. Think you what would he do with your old bones if he took us. Have you such a liking for fire to curl in you?"

"You have powers, mistress."

"I have powers, yes—it is in the blood of my mother's line. But power joined to power is even greater. Serve me well, Wulfra. You will no longer be a thrall, but have a snug seat by the fire and a girl to wait on you."

Now those eyes with their red sparks caught hers. And suddenly the thrall nodded.

"Truth you speak. What is in your mind, mistress?"

Auôur drew a deep breath. "Three days we need and then, even though it be a time of storms, we shall take to the sea. Already they load the carts to go by night and provision the ship."

Wulfra had gone to stand before the ravens, her gray head on one side. Her lips moved and uttered a cry so like those of an angry bird that Auôur could tell no difference.

The largest of the ravens bent forward on his perch so that his sharp bill struck at the old woman. Then he took wing, went out of the window, and was gone.

Wulfra now made a sound like a snicker. "A hard ride for MacMann, mistress. He'll not forget it for a time."

From the watchers who had ringed the holding came the news. A bird out of nowhere—one of Odin's own sacred flock—had flung him to the ground and those who followed him had borne him, cursing loudly, away.

Two mornings later Auôur went through the deserted great hall. Yes, they had carefully followed instructions and taken the carved pillars of the high seat. If all went as she hoped, those would be her guide to a new life. She was tired of living always with death near beside her—a new land where there was freedom for the just—

The ship was crowded. They had had to leave behind the sadly needed sheep and cattle. But they were free and driving down the bay when the steerman, Halgar Cunnersson, pointed out moving dots on the shore. MacMann had no ship in these waters, he had not thought of their escaping so.

Within two days they had near doubled their company—taking over a well-set fishing boat. The men manning her let fall their few weapons when they saw the determination of the Northmen and one of the ravens flew down to their mast to sign it so as Odin's gift. They were returned to their duties under guard, and Auôur was pleased that her *Storm Beaker* was the less crowded.

It was long, that voyage, and they weathered seas which would have turned their ships end for end had not Freya, the ever merciful, answered to the pleas of those two aboard who were of the power. Auôur the Deepminded they had called her from childhood, and now she was to prove that as she never had been before.

First they raised the Orkneys and were guested by a lord of kin to Olafur. However, still in Auôur was the need to go on. But she made a good marriage for Maudlen, who was ever sick on the sea, and took on supplies.

Beyond were seas even less known, yet there were isles to be found—the Faroes—and once again they sheltered for some months, working on their ships. Here the second of her grand-daughters was hand-fasted to a man of good name and well-worked land. But Auôur and Wulfra went to the highest point of the land, circled about by the ravens. And those flew seaward for a space, so she knew her farseeing was right—she had not yet discovered what she would have.

Only, once more asea, they found bitter going. Twice at a distance they saw mountains of ice move on the waters as if those were also ships. And each third day Auôur sent forth the ravens, but always they returned. Sometimes she moved along the crowded ship to lay hand on the carven supports of the high seat and wondered if they would ever be loosed into the sea to guide them to land. She called her grandson to her—he was still only a lad with not even full strength in his sword arm—but he listened as she spoke and nodded, understanding well that full duty must be paid to the gods.

Then at last there came a morning when the rime of frost lay like a blanket over the ships. And the ravens went forth—not together but singly in slightly different directions. That one who had been the centermost of the three did not return. There were cries of excitement then and two of the younger and more agile men made their way to the bow of the *Storm Beaker* and there detached the carefully wrought serpent head, for all knew that if a ship approached land in peace, not for raiding, such a menacing promise must not arouse the demons of the country ahead who should be offered due rights.

On the ship went with the oarsmen at labor now, and then out of the sea arose a dark hump of shadow, while out of the sky dropped Odin's bird to perch with his mates.

Once more Auôur pushed to the side of the high chair posts, and with her she brought Thorgimmur, her grandson, her hand upon his shoulder. She gave him a nudge forward so that he could reach the salt encrusted ropes which held them safe. He struggled with the knots until, though his fingers were bleeding, he had accomplished the task. But he had not the strength to hurl them overboard as the ritual demanded, and two of the oarsmen sent them into the sea, but not before the boy had laid the hand of possession upon them.

So did they come at last into the harbor of this strange land which had pulled Auôur's farsight for so long. Here they would set up their hall and prosper, that the blood of two strong lines would know many years.

Though her brethren sent for her and offered land and shelter, she took only the latter until she could set out once more, with some of her household. Inward they roved, ever marveling at a land walled with ice and yet offering springs of hot water, sea worn heights, and cliffs above fields of black lava.

In the end Auôur found her homestead, striking the end of her staff into a patch of soil. Within a year there came from her younger brother a party of thralls carrying with them the wave-beaten pillars of the high seat, and she knew then that the gods had served her well.

NO FOLDED HANDS
The Williamson Effect (1996) TOR

Jules Bearclaw watched the ant caravan move into sight down the highway. He swung his field glasses carefully about—not that he expected any of the ants to catch sight of a sun glint on a bit of glass so far above their heads that it might have been borne along by an eagle. It was just as it had been for a week now—a trail of trucks swinging along, each with its ant in charge, heading in toward the white man's country. They were always precisely in line, the same distance from each other, and they never stopped.

Now he did slide around on his vantage point and put to his lips an age-smoothed horn pipe. He blew three warn notes. And caught the very faint answer to his action.

There was a powwow to outrank all powwows back in the desolate desert lands into which the ants had not yet come. For the first time in the history of the oldest tribe, one-time enemies consorted with their most bitter foes, hands sped in hand talk between peoples of the north, the far south, the west and the mid-country—or else they used the English they had learned in school or the army to warily examine the problem of the universal enemy.

Of course some of the People argued that it was best to simply let the white man suffer from his own greed. That was before the ants moved in on Ledbetter's trading post. But it was the stories that such as Bearclaw himself told of the coast cities through which discharged veterans from the late overseas war had comem which alarmed enough of the influential shamans to consider factors, then tentatively approach their peers in other tribes until there was an interlocking system of communication from north to south.

The ants were not of this world, that had seemed a smoke tale at first, but there were enough telling it to give it truth. They had landed in great sky ships—claiming to be from the stars. Then—they had taken over the world—or were fast occupying the civilized parts of it as quickly as possible.

Not that they destroyed life. On the contrary, they encouraged it in their own smothering fashion. They built new homes for the creatures native to this planet, they produced every luxury for the asking—their one rule stated over and over was that mankind must be protected, not allowed any chance to injure itself or others. Thus they simply bound men into cocoons where they became larvae that would never come to life again.

So far they had not moved in upon the People. He wondered now briefly what might be happening in other places—Africa, or the eastern jungle lands. There was greed enough for the white man's wealth, and sloth enough for it to be enjoyed. Or were the natives there already seeing what had become of those who accepted the ants, and so were looking about for their own weapons?

The caravan of trucks came at a steady speed and was fast approaching the cliff where he lay as still now as a hump of the native rock. One—two—four—five—the sixth one seemed to have lost speed. Through the air the purr of engines developed a discordant note. So—Jim Twoknives had managed it! Bearclaw grinned, but kept an eye on the trucks that were now pulling away from the clanking one. Would they all stop? There did not appear to be any lag, and they were now a respectable distance away from that last one.

Perhaps the ants depended on each to settle his own difficulties. This was like the report delivered three days ago from a Ute scouting party. They had seen a truck fall behind, the ant disembark from its interior and set to swift work on the engine.

Yes, the Old Ones were with them this day also! The ailing truck drew to the side of the road and the ant, all in his shining armor, climbed out.

Once more Bearclaw sounded the signal, and this time he was answered from nearby. There began a steady thumping, following an erratic pattern. He poked the feather balls deep in his ears for his own defense, and his hands were shaking.

For a space the ant did not seem to notice. Then it dropped a tool, swayed nearly off its feet when it stopped to pick that up. A moment later it fell back with a clang against the side of the truck and slid down. Both of its metal hands wavered toward its round bowl of a head, and that was shaking back and forth now wildly, in broken rhythm with the hidden drums.

Bearclaw went into full action. He slipped down the slope that had brought him to his hiding place, the cliff now between him and the road. Tearing off his hat, he waved it vigorously and saw the dust of the approaching horses as the scouting party came up.

The horses were spooked by the drums, though not as badly affected as human ears. They were left in charge of one of the party while Bearclaw and Jim Whiterock unlashed the burden the one pony had carried.

They made no move to draw weapons, though two of them shouldered Uzis and the rest had sidearms well to hand. The ants *might* just be blown up with a well-placed grenade, as they had discovered some time ago. But the result had been an intense searching of the surrounding territory from which the experimenter had barely escaped. And after all, they were not to count coup on dead ants but to capture a live one for the shamans to use for an experiment.

The drums were still in force as they rounded an outcrop of cliff and saw the stalled truck. They could feel the erratic rhythm through their bodies, and it required a man's near full strength to hold steady against it.

The ant was on its feet again, but weaving back and forth, its large eyes like fire coals. It was jabbering away—some English, other words that made no sense at all. Bearclaw gave a hand signal.

The triple-woven net flew out and, though the creature took a step back, it was caught while the men around it hastily wrapped the folds tighter and tighter. It was stumbling along a prisoner in spite of its struggles as they returned the way they had come.

Bearclaw, having seen that the captive was as well secured as their preparations could make it, padded on into another jag of the cliff. The four drummers, their sparse gray hair woven with red strips of fur to give them proper warrior length, which the passing years had denied them, sat in a line. Their eyes were near buried in the deep creases of sun wrinkles but were wide open, staring at him without losing a single beat of palm against the stretched hide of hand drums. He made a swift hand signal.

As one the wrinkled hands no longer struck the drums. For a second or two Bearclaw felt slightly dizzy. It took a couple of deep breaths to assure himself that that part of the ordeal was over.

"The ant is netted, then, Younger Brother?" That was Ashdweller of his own clan who rightly broke silence first.

"It is, Elder Brother. We are ready to ride."

They were already slinging their drums and getting stiffly to their feet. One of them, the Dakota, had stiff-jointed difficulty in that, but none allowed themselves to note that weakness. Being peers in power-raising, it did not matter that their old bodies sometimes betrayed them.

There was another group of horses being led out, and the drummers made it into their saddles. Ashdweller allowed his mount to pace forward toward the waiting Bearclaw while his three late companions were trotting already.

"There will be storm soon—"

The younger man nodded. "We shall push the pace, Elder Brother, make sure of that. Those who dance the thunder will not be left without the reward of seeing what can be seen."

They had to ride single file for a while, and it was behind Bearclaw's tough trail horse that the ant was bundled along on its own two feet, which had been carefully freed for that purpose. At first it had continued to twitch and shake its head, but now it walked with confidence, showing no sign of any discomfort.

"Why did you do this?" Its voice was metallic, but not unpleasant, and it spoke English as if that were its native tongue.

There was no need either to inform or to argue with the creature, Bearclaw knew. He had scouted enough into the territory these creatures now ruled to know that each one was merely a scraping of the main enemy and had no will nor mind of its own.

He thought back over the hard months just behind—the embarkation into a city far removed from the one he remembered—new houses gleaming, set in carefully tended parklike surroundings—no haste, no noise, no clutter. It had not taken him long to be suspicious. A world was not transformed overnight for no reason. His own squad of communication experts had kept to themselves; perhaps in all of them the age-old suspicion of the ways of the white skins awoke. While the man they had fought beside seemed eager to accept the new way of life, their own body of men had watched and waited. At Bearclaw's suggestion they had spread out through the city, putting on the guise of amazed innocents. Three of them had discovered the underlying truth on the same day—

The ants ruled. Ruled not with guns, terror, and death as their strengths, but with the aid of man's own greed for the luxuries of life. But what these creatures judged good for man was sucking out of those in their nets all that was truly life. Tools were outlawed—they held potential harm for the users; most games were outlawed; men went dully to jobs where they watched a flow of useless knowledge across screens and might once in a while push a button.

And the rebels—they disappeared into the fine new hospitals, coming out as tin and alien in their thoughts as the ants.

But one could not fight the ants with weapons that were known. They apparently acted from one brain—Jim Hard had met with a lounger in the park who, after he had made well sure there was no one else in earshot, supplied the knowledge of the great sky ships that had brought them and the fact that those orders they obeyed came from an off-world source which no man could hope to reach.

Orders by telecommunication—when they had gathered that night they had centered in on that. They had been selected for the Signal Corps, as had happened in earlier wars, because they could talk in their native tongues without encoding and with any possible understanding by any listener who was not Navajo, Ute, Apache, or Dakota. They were young and somehow their particular group had been fired with a desire to use more than their tongues. There were manuals to be studied, and they had had the luck to serve under an officer who was obsessed with the possibility of new forms of communication—so they had learned.

Learned that their only true weapon against the ants was to cut the transmission that kept the creatures in control.

It had taken time. His squad had broken up and gone to their own homes. Those who had lived in cities found their families gone—back to the reservations, as a horror of ant slavery seemed also to be a part of their own heritage.

For some time the ants had not encroached on that near-forgotten wasteland that had been left to the People. And the alienness that surrounded their always busy metal bodies was a warn-off that the whites did not seem to feel. It was then that Hanson Swift began his pilgrimage.

Shamans of the past had been mighty enough that their names were remembered for generations by the Elders. But Hanson was more than a Shaman of note—he was as much a leader of men as an always-lucky war chief. From the east he had come, slipping from tribe to tribe, always talking, to the Elders, to the young, to those who would listen,· and those became more and more in number.

Once there had been a league of tribes in the east who had kept peace among themselves over many generations. Oneida sat beside Mohawk in council, and all men spoke their minds until there was agreement.

Now there was an awakening among all the tribes such as there had not been since they had been beaten to the dust by the invaders from overseas. Shamans might be jealous of their powers at first, but they were drawn into one accord sooner or later.

Now the knowledge of those wisdom keepers from nearly a dozen nations was centered in the southwestern desert land, and they awaited what Bearclaw tugged behind him, its metal feet clanging against rock. The stream of talk the thing had spouted at first had died away as they continued into a land of rocks and sand, majestic cliffs and river beds dry these fifty years or more.

That the creature could be in long-distance communication with its fellows was more than a suspicion. But they could not keep the drum vibration going throughout their journey. As it was, they picked a way already studied out by a scout in which they could not be well sighted from the air. And certainly none of the machines this enemy used were for desert travel.

He was aware of signals from the broken lands,· there had been a tight network drawn about the powwow country, and he did not believe that even a real ant might walk that way without being noted. Swift had arrived two days ago with the information that had put an end to the last challenge of the Shamans.

White men spoke of luck—the people knew that certain happenings were sent and meant to be noted and made use of by their blood. Rain was a gift of the Above Ones—but it had its dangers also. Torrents of water could in moments flood usually languid streams; the touch of lightning could set off dreaded crown fire in the forest lands. And it was that lightning which seemed to be the war gift of the Above Ones in this matter.

The rumors had come early; the proof arrived with Swift and his following of Shamans and men who had served enough with the war machines of the whites to follow the knowledge shown them by the sky itself. Lightning could knock out those controls that kept the ants about their business; not entirely—the majority of them appeared to recover after a space—but it could disconnect the unheard orders that backed their attempt to make all mankind into helpless children again.

Now they had a captive of their own to experiment with—and coming swiftly into sight was the place of proving. The Shamans had been at their conferences for days picking out a time. There had been dream fasting, ceaseless night sings, all the possible ways of summoning the attention of the Old Ones. Maybe two years ago Bearclaw would have shrugged aside the thought that there were men even among the People who could accomplish more with the full use of their minds than a weaponed and well-trained soldier could do against any enemy. Only a man never loses the blood that runs in him, can never dodge and hide from his inheritance.

Dirty drunken Indians—he had been embittered for years by such comments and sneers, ashamed for those who had become the refugees at the edges of white towns, those who had been drained of all that had given them pride in the fact that they were the People.

There were still such outcasts, yes, far too many of them. Though those who seemed to pick up the words Swift uttered spread them with nearly the same power as he could say. Men had once hidden their tattered beliefs in things beyond; now they followed them openly.

Let the ants show the white men what it meant to be help-less—comfortable after the fashion his kind held to be the proper state of mankind—but helpless—like sheep marched from one pasturage to another with no will of their own.

Bearclaw angled right, only a portion of his band following him, but there still kept up with them one of the drummers, his raw-boned range nose matching full stride with the others.

They fronted a canyon now. The bare rock in brilliant color under the sun. Bearclaw caught the scents of sage added to a fire along with other herbs—some from half the continent away. They had been purifying this slit in the rock for a week, tying prayer sticks in crannies wherever they could be thrust into crevices of the stone wall, or into the sand along the path to be followed.

The chant took life from the drum that the lone Shaman tapped with swift, expert fingers. And it sounded in three different tongues from the men about him—each giving their own accent to their petition.

Bearclaw slid from his mount, one of the younger men beside him following suit and grasping the reins of his horse along with his own. There was no word now from the ant. Bearclaw found himself almost uneasy at that smooth visage with its now dusty metal skin and its huge and apparently all-seeing eyes.

"Our duty is to serve man—" The words seemed to boom, even above the ever-forceful beat of the drum. "Ask what you will—we shall make it yours."

Bearclaw could not believe there was any note of pleading in that even, resonant voice. The ants had no emotions—knew no fears—were only here to confine, herd, change a world into something which was near actionless death.

He gave the special twist which fastened the thrice-blessed cords that had held the creature captive. Stepped back. For a long moment they stood so, man of humankind, thing born of some misguided brain on another world. A thing which had no reality in itself, only harkened to orders fed it.

"We have come to serve you—" the ant repeated. "To protect man is all our power—"

It was the Shaman who edged his bony nose forward, and his hand slapped the drum in quick time. Bearclaw raised one hand and pointed ahead.

The rhythm was a pain in his own head but he held himself erect and watched. First the creature's head swung around so it could eye the drummer. Its eyes blinked and seemed to contain a spark of fire far in their bubble depths.

Its arms clicked upward, moving jerkily, its fingers reaching toward its head. Then it turned a little and went, not with the calm swing with which it had marched, but jerkily.

Meanwhile about them the day was darkening. The horses threw up their heads and two whinnied. There was no need for any of them to look to the sky. Had there been any doubt left among them it was gone. What came was Shaman-called—called by such a gathering of power as this country had never known. Perhaps had it been possible to do so in the past there would have been no white men walking the land—though the action it was designed for now was striking at something else—at that unseen, space-spun thread which united the ants with the indestructible brain that had set them about their conquest and made prisoners, after a fashion, of half the world.

They turned their backs now on that wavering figure heading out into the open. Sand twists were rising,· they had barely time to reach the shelter already staked out—to loose the horses and to climb up into the place of the old ones, Those Gone Before,· to throw themselves down in what shelter the time-cracked buildings would afford, and wait.

Rain dances—yes—the people of the mesas had danced down the rain for untold centuries. It had become something that the white man came to watch and wonder at. But united to the rain dance now was the Calling—That Which Dwelt in the Woodlands of the North and East, That Which Climbed near Sun High, That Which was the very strength of their own bones and blood.

The shaman caressed his small drum with the sweep of his palm, but there was no way to hear its answer. For then their sound struck, from mountain top to mountain top—the brilliant flash of lightning seeming far more frightening than any storm brought before. And through all the clamor of the wind and that thunder Bearclaw could somehow feel a vibration within his own body. Yet it did not assault as had that which had taken the ant prisoner. No, instead this gave him a feeling of power as if the lightning itself flooded along his veins—that he could point a finger and scar a mountain. This was in him, of him, it fed somehow upon what it was and yet he was not consumed, only strengthened.

He closed his eyes and saw—

Was this thing like the medicine dreams of a would-be warrior? No, he was already proven on the war trail. Nor was he a Shaman with the jealously guarded powers passed from one generation to the next.

Still he saw—

It was as if he were given wings and had soared out into the furious buffeting of the storm. Yet it did him no harm, nor would it. Below him stood the ant—stood? No, its knees bent; it fell upon them. And from its head, like the line that might have taken a fish, was a thin line—extending not upward into the heavens as he had thought—traveling westward.

That which was now Bearclaw followed the line until it came to join with others. He recognized beneath him the trucks that he had watched hours earlier.

Out of nowhere struck an arrow of the same brilliancy as the lightning. It did not cut the cord. Now, rather it melted into it, speeding through those others below. The bait had been taken, now the catch was waiting.

The whirls of wind-raised sand were high, but they did not hide the truck from Bearclaw, scout in a new and different war. Suddenly the head truck went off the road. The one behind grazed it, and they all came to a stop.

That cord down which the arrow had slid so easily snapped out of sight. There was a sharp upward blaze from those still mingled on the ground. Then a thicker stem also reached ahead into a distance that the sand storm and then the burst of wind and rain covered.

Still that which had summoned Bearclaw kept him aloft—until he saw those other cords snuff out. Then he was lying, head on arm, in the place of the Old Ones with the roar of the storm heavy in his ears. Only he knew what he had seen, and surely he had not been the only one who had witnessed that. There were too many of the spirit-trained Elders who must have taken the same sky trail, though he had not seen or sensed their company. But he knew—the ants were surely tied, and those ties could be broken. At least the country claimed by the People could be freed from their snares and prisons. Let the white man sit prisoner among them if he so wished—there was none of the old strength in *him*.

Bearclaw looked at his own callused hands and expanded each finger to its furthest extent. Here were no folded hands.

AFTERWORD

There are forceful stories which make such an impression on the reader that it lingers for years. "With Folded Hands" is a classic. It is also a story which makes the reader uneasy and with a not too far hidden spark of that old fearsome feeling—what if?

It is undoubtedly taking a very great liberty on my part to turn to that fine example in the Hall of Fame with an answer. I expect wholehearted disagreement with this answer. However, it is also a deep-held belief of mine that there *are* phases of human consciousness and abilities which we have not learned to use to the utmost. And the values of one race are not always those of another. So because I have been haunted for years by "With Folded Hands," I am now daring to provide an answer—which I hope Mr. Williamson will be kind enough not to blast into the farthest reaches of space.

—Andre Norton

BARD'S CROWN
Elf Fantastic (1997) DAW

Catlin shivered and pleated her shawl nervously between her fingers. She noted that the two serving maids had crept into the corner of the small bower as closely as they could, away from the door into the great hall.

Another burst of raucous laughter reached her. There was no way she could deal with this. Kathal, like any son of Clan Dongannan, had gone to the High King for a year's service in the Guard near a year ago. Now he was back because he was the o'Dongannan, their uncle having died of a rheum. But the boy who had gone away, as reckless and thoughtless concerning others as he had been, was lost. That mead-swigging brute at rough play with his cronies out there—brother or not, she could say nothing to which he would listen.

In the meantime the whole of the valley was in disorder. There was no master to guide, advise, praise, or deal justice. And the people had learned to keep as far from the Great Hall as they could.

She raised a hand and pushed back a wandering curl of hair, anchoring it again under her hair coif. So far—so far she had largely escaped Kathal's notice, but she could not creep around forever looking over her shoulder. Being of the High Blood she could not be caught by one of those turbulent roisters out there and unceremoniously used (as two of the maids had already suffered) but there was nothing to prevent Kathal arbitrarily handfasting her to one of his drinking mates.

Even Kathal would have to learn soon that the supplies from last harvest were not inexhaustible and any yield from the new planted field was months away. Yet he had done nothing but order stored seed grains to be drawn upon. And she could feel the stir of black hate rising whenever she dared venture out to do the little she could to aid.

That high-pitched voice carried above all the clamor from the other room, somehow stifled much of it.

"Treasure, look you. 'Tis well known that Lugh's Mound holds it. The old stories are that every king who went into the Shadows took much of his treasure with him—though how much that could comfort his bones who can say."

There was utter silence now, and Catlin clasped her hands so tightly together that the bones seemed to lock on each other. Treasure—Lugh's Mound—surely Kathal would not be so utterly lost as to try for what might lie there!

"Wager! Wager!" one of the other voices rang out. "Let us see true treasure by the next moontide, and we'll shield raise you!"

Catlin's hands now sped to cover her ears. Somehow she knew Kathal's mood. He'd take up this challenge as eagerly as he would raise a sword on the practice field. There was no longer any priest to aid. Brother Victus had been ignominiously bundled out two months ago and told he was lucky he still kept his head on his shoulders.

She knew well the legend of Lugh's Mound which was raised on the tallest peak of the surrounding hills. No one went near it, but there had been those who had seen at a distance a company of riders on mounts like gray mist who circled it as guardians. Brother Victus had said they were Those of the Hills, outside human laws and duties. But the country people would leave at times a fine fleece or a bowl of honey out on the flat stone by the faint path which perhaps those mist horses had worn through the years, and were sure that luck for their households followed such gifts.

Her uncle had said it had naught to do with the People but was rather the resting place of one of those raiding lords from overseas who had been ceremoniously buried with a goodly portion of his loot when a last foray went against him. Catlin sucked in a breath. When they were children, she and Kathal, her brother had often spoken of that treasure, and now he shared the tale with those in there.

For him to venture to Lugh's Mound might cost him the rest of the ragged loyalty of their people. She could bear no more of their drunken swaggering. They were now taunting Kathal to his deed, and she knew well that her brother would take up such a challenge.

Catlin arose from the stool where she had been sitting and stepped past the two cowering maids. Closing the door to the great hall firmly, she shot the bar across it though she knew that if Kathal discovered such an act, he would have that door hacked from its hinges as being shut against his authority.

Then, turning, she went to the window and drew aside the heavy draft-defeating curtain to look out. There were no lights to be seen in the village—why would there be? Honest men and women had been long abed. But she searched through the gloom of the night—to Lugh's Mound. The moon was only a new crescent now and gave little light. All she could see was a darker shadow against the star-studded sky. She folded her hands and repeated the ward-off words Brother Victus had used.

Then she turned and signaled to the maids who saw her to her bed before they sought their own pallets.

There are dreams and dreams. Some vanish when one opens eyes in the morning, parts of others either linger on in sharp memory or shadowy uneasiness. Catlin brought out from slumber with the morning light what might be a vision—of land she knew well, having ridden and walked over it since childhood. But this carried no trim of growth—it was black and seared as if fire had claimed it. The houses were tumbled and deserted, there were no beasts in the fields. No one showing in farmyards—even the smoke of family hearths did not wreath from any chimney. A dead land!

She forced herself to wash and dress—to unbar that door and look into the foul disorder of the hall. Two men lay snoring on the floor, one was sprawled across the table—a puddle of spilled mead ruffled from his breath where his head rested.

But there was no sign of Kathal, nor the two of his companions he held the closest. There was the sound of a step and she turned swiftly. The newcomer was old Timous, once her uncle's steward, now a broken man with a new bruise on his forehead. His eyes as they met Catlin's were as empty as those of a dead man. Then there came a flicker of recognition, and he said between broken teeth, "This be black days, Lady. Himself has gone to Lugh's Mound with those to stand aside and watch that he does what he wagered to do."

"What will be the ending of this, Timous?"

"Death—and for more than those who dared this night."

His back was straightening now, and he was more the man who had been right hand for her uncle. "Lady," he protested now, "this place it not fit for your eyes. Let us cleanse it before you come within—"

"Not so, Timous. This be the Hall of my Blood and Kin. Who

26

better should set it in order?" She knew well that the old man had few to serve with him. Some shambling farm hands and kitchen boys.

With the aid of such unhandy helpers, plus her maids, they did bring order. The comatose drinkers were blanketed and stowed away, Catlin hoping, with a viciousness she had never felt before, that they would suffer the worst pangs of a morning after this drink-filled night.

It was the second of her uncle's old trusted retainers who came in before they were done and sought her out.

"Lady—the people of the valley—they have come in fear and need."

"Hew, why—" But she did not try to guess what other happening from the sottish debauch of the night before might have occurred. The knowledge that Kathal had gone treasure hunting in Lugh's Mound was enough to raise most of the villagers.

So the girl followed Hew out into a gray drizzle of a day, a day which somehow threatened that a full sun would never shine here again. The villagers were gathered waiting, from children in arms, to the elders, some of whom hobbled painfully on two sticks— with the hale and hearty in between.

Each face was pale, and frightened eyes darted from her at her coming to the gate of the courtyard and back as if they had been pursued to this haven and looked now upon her to defend them from some danger they could not meet themselves.

"Lady—" It was again Hew who was the spokesman beckoning her forward so that the throng there parted and let her through, past the outer gate into the open.

Here also hung mist, but her eyes were drawn to the ground. Down the crooked lane which was the center of the hall village, out and around, circles, arcs, lines as straight as a spear shaft, marked the ground. They were silvery and yet she was sure that they had no substance and were only prints. And they were the tracks of some mounted troop which had encircled again and again each cottage, crossed and recrossed every field within her range of sight.

"The Riders—of the People." Hew pointed to the tracks.

Already the sharpness of that sign was fading. She did not want to believe in what she had seen and yet she could not put it from her.

"Ill—ill." Somewhere in the crowd behind her a woman raised that wail. "Ill be this day and that which follows."

Catlin could feel the cold rise of fear. They might well panic and what answer did she have? She was not the Dongannan—where was Kathal?

Her silent question was answered then by other riders, substantial enough that the blowing of their horses and their own mumbling voices could be readily heard. Kathal at their head, his face flushed, his jerkin and shirt gone, and the stains of earth on his bare arms and what was left of his clothing.

"A wager!" his voice rang out. "A wager you said, Clough and Dongal. Well, have I not won it and fairly?"

He held up something, which in spite of the dullness of the morning, flashed as if for a moment he held a brand aloft. That it must be some gem Catlin was sure. His eyes held steady on it and on nothing else around.

"And there be more!" he crowed. "Richer than the hall of the Great King will be Dongannan—and all just for some delving in the dirt."

Then, for the first time, he appeared to note Catlin and he grinned at her. For a moment she thought she saw some evil mask instead of her brother's face. He leaned from his saddle, urging his mount closer, and dangled what he held over her head.

It seemed to be a spray of flowers, and yet not possessing the quick passing beauty of true flowers but fashioned from the cold hardness of colored stones. Treasure indeed—the richest ornament she had ever seen.

Kathal raised it up to his face now and nuzzled at it as if it were the first mouthful of some feast. "Ah, the taste of treasure!" Again he crowed.

Catlin and the others behind her opened a way for him and his two companions. They bore no signs of toil she saw, but neither were they in such glee as her brother showed. Instead now and then they glanced over their shoulders as if they felt other and perhaps threatening eyes upon them.

Then Catlin saw that they did have a follower. A donkey, its head hanging, plodded well to their rear, and on the spirit-broken creature hunched a misshapen lump which, as he advanced, she could make out as a man. But such a man, as gnarled and time twisted as some ancient tree. Though his back was hunched, he bent over a hand harp of some dull black wood and the strings of it appeared to be the same color as the mist about.

As Kathal's mount trotted into the courtyard, that strange rider halted. Three times his crooked fingers plucked those harp strings. However, the notes which arose from them were not of any music as mankind wanted to hear, rather gusty sighs, the last dwindling into a wail.

The harper grinned, showing yellowish teeth and eyes near buried in the wrinkles which seamed his face. Then he urged his donkey around and the animal plodded away, out of the village. Yet that which the harper left behind him moved the villagers to shrink, until some of the women and children broke and ran for their homes.

So did all peace and sanity leave Dongannan—its fields and homes, its great hall, and its peoples. The two who had ridden forth with Kathal for that ominous wager sickened and within a fortnight were dead. Their three drunken fellows rode at a wild gallop out of the holding after they witnessed those deaths.

But nothing seemed meaningful to Kathal. He sat in his high chair at the table for hours, pushing aside any food or drink offered him, playing with his treasure and talking mainly to himself, for it finally came that only Catlin would approach him, of the even greater riches to be gained when he was in a mind to do so.

The fields which had been hoof-printed were now bare of even a blade of dying grass, as were the gardens of the cottages. On the hills lay the bodies of sheep along with their tenders. The few cattle seemed to go wild, two of them horning their owners before they disappeared into the wild lands beyond.

Catlin pulled herself wearily from one sickbed to another in the ailing village. Each day she saw more of the still hale burdened with pitiful bundles of their most needful possessions going out and away from this cursed place.

It was a toll of days later that she once more saw the harper. And because she had come from the deathbed of the miller's last child, she dared to walk as quickly as she could to face him, nor did he withdraw at her coming.

"I know not who or what you are," she said in the voice of one so wearied she found it hard to hunt for the proper words. "It is plain we are cursed—Dongannan dies—and all for the wildness of a man deep in drink. If there is anything of good within you, light some hope that we can survive."

Even as she spoke, Arran, the miller's wife, came into the street. She had loosed her hair to hang in a wild tangle and she went to her knees before the entrance to the great hall.

"The curse of a mother, may it lie heavy on you for your greed and black heart. No lord of ours are you and may you die unforgiven, lie in our cursed fields, and meet with the Black Master who sent you to torment us."

Then she keened forth the wail for the dead and other pale women tottered to stand behind her, adding their voices to hers.

Catlin, however, after a first glance, kept her attention for the hunchbacker harper. And now a spark of anger rose within her and she burst forth, "For the sin of one man do you doom a village? If aught is to be done, tell me now!"

Those cavern-set eyes met hers and she held the glance between them with a fierce tightness. Dongannan she was, and Dongannan she would fight for.

"What is taken can be returned. There is no promise—you have only hope." In spite of his age his voice was certainly that of a bard.

Once more he turned the donkey and went from her. But what he had said gave her purpose now.

"Return what is taken." She thought of Kathal who had retreated to his inner chamber and barred the door against all comers, as if he feared the very thing she now knew she must do.

Hardly able to keep her feet because of hunger weakness (for she had seen supplies from the hold divided in the village) and weariness, Catlin turned back.

The keening of the women was a sobbing in the air and she saw the sullen, angry looks of the men, slowly gathering behind them before the great gate. They did not deter her from entering. In fact, they shrank away from her as if she now carried the burden of the curse on her bowed shoulders.

Catlin came into the silent great hall, now a cave of dusk in spite of the wan daylight without. She knew well where Kathal was. No food or water had passed his barred door for more than—she tried to count time dizzily—two days now. She had gone each morning to call out to him but had heard nothing in return except movement and a low muttering as if he carried on long debates with that which only he could see. Now, as she summoned up strength to pound on that surface, there was no answer at all.

The door had been readied, from the day it was hung, for a place to make a final stand in hours of peril. She certainly could not beat down such a defense.

With one hand she brushed aside her lopsided limp coif and its draggled veil which somehow had stayed with her during the past days, for she could not remember now when she had bathed, worn clean body linen, and a fresh overrobe. The door remained a barrier, but there was the window.

Dongannan had not stood a siege since long before her own birth. The single window was barred, of course, but it was her only choice. Now she made herself look around for weapons against those bars.

At length she picked up a spit still in place above a long-dead fire. So armed, she went resolutely out into the open once more. The crowd at the gate had split apart. She thought she could see a dim and ominous blot, the hunched bard, far back, though none of the villagers looked upon him.

So wearied that she saved what strength she still had to drag the spit by one end rather than lift it, Catlin rounded the corner of the inner keep until she at last faced that window.

Yes, the bars were still there. It now remained to be seen how securely they were still set. She steadied the spit, raised it, and aimed one end spearwise at the base of the nearest bar.

"Lady—" That was a ghost of a voice, but she turned her head slowly, looked at Hew. His body was gaunt, his face thinned down to mere flesh over bone.

She had not time for explanations, there was that to be done—swiftly—and she was the only one left to do it.

"In," she panted. "Must get in."

She was too wearied to know triumph as a fall of long-decayed mortar followed her first jab. Then the spit was twisted from her hands and Hew was aiming with twice the force she was able to summon and to good purpose.

There came no sound from within to answer the noise their efforts produced. And a weather-stained curtain clouded what lay beyond. But Hew kept to his pounding and prying and at last two of the bars came free.

"Leave it—I shall be able to get through," Catlin told him. She dragged off her coif. Luckily she wore the less-confining skirt of a riding dress. But the opening looked small and she feared the attempt she would make, though she said strongly to Hew, "Give me that to stand upon—"

Wobbling the man went to his knees. "My strength here and now, Lady."

Somehow she made it, clawing her way through the curtain into the darkness of the room before. The smell of death had been with her for days, but here was another more subtle stench—that which was of madness and evil.

Though the room was dark, there was a single spot of light coming from something lying on the bed. She could hear snuffling as from a beast and a hand appeared within the limits of that dim light. A hand holding a drawn dagger.

"Out—away—thief—" the three words came as three separate shouts. The knife swung viciously through the light into dark and back again, weaving a pattern over that spot of light.

Catlin swung out her own arm in a need for a weapon to defend herself. She caught at the edge of the curtain and found strength to rip it from the hangers.

Now she could see better. Kathal—no, that thing crouched on the bed, filthy, ragged, bearded, twisted of face bore no resemblance to even the drunken youth she had last seen twirling his treasure as he rode home. It was the treasure piece which had given off that spot of light and now what it emitted was growing even brighter.

Like a giant spider Kathal sprang for her and only a half-instinctive swirl of the length of heavy cloth in her hands kept that dagger from her flesh. He was screaming raggedly such oaths as perhaps even most armsmen would not know. But the cloth fell over him and brought him down.

Before he could rise, she seized from a side shelf a tankard— empty but heavy enough to pull down her weakened arm. Catlin swung it awkwardly until the wallowing thing at her feet gave a gasping cry and was still.

She lurched across to the bed, and her hand closed upon the jeweled spray. It was like grasping a coal from the fire's heat, but she held on. Backing, her eyes ever on that mound of Kathal and curtain, she reached the window and dared enough to turn around and struggle out. The jewel she had put in her bodice for safekeeping, and there also she felt its fire.

As she slipped through, there was no one to steady her to the ground. "There was only the body of Hew, still grasping the spit. Shaking herself after her tumble, she was at his side quickly. But she had seen death too many times within the past days not to be unable to detect it now.

With the spit as a staff to keep her on her feet, she went on to the open gates. Those who had been there were gone. She might indeed be in a deserted village. She was kept on her feet only by the need to do what she must do.

Catlin was not surprised when she came to the opening of the faint trace which led to Lugh's Mound to see there the hunch-backed bard. But she had no strength to gasp out any words— only the climb before her.

In the end it was the staff-spit which drew her up one painful step at a time. Until she did at last reach the heights and see the disturbed earth where Kathal must have delved.

Only it was filled in. With a broken sigh Catlin fell to her knees, and, using the spit, and then her own bruised and torn hands, she worked doggedly to scoop away the earth. To her surprise what she uncovered first was undoubtedly a shield, the metal of it half rust-eaten away.

"Iron, cold iron, Lady, and as a taunt years ago."

Even turning her head had become an almost impossible task, but she looked up and over her shoulder. Yes, it was the hunchback who sat there on his donkey, and, as she sighted him, he once more swept a hand over the ancient harp and notes of sorrow, such sorrow as even the last few days had not brought her, sent tears channeling down her grimy face.

She caught the shield with both hands and put all her strength to pulling. Since it must have been moved by Kathal earlier, it yielded to her now.

Light blazed forth and she was looking into what might be the end of a stone-walled chamber. There was a raised block in its middle and on that lay—she could not be sure what it was since the blaze was so bright. But unconsciously she brought her hands to the thing which had been searing her breast. When that was in the open, it twisted and turned and moved from her hold like a living thing until it joined with that other on the stone.

Then came such sound as entered into every part of her bone and flesh. What words beat in that refrain she could not tell, but strength was flowing back into her. It was almost as if she had become some other, apart from the earth she knew. She could remember with pity, but even that emotion was fading.

Catlin was on her feet, but she did not try to enter that chamber. Instead she was startled by a whinny and turned to see the harper. That was no donkey on which he was ungainly crouched, but a fine stallion of cloudy gray whose hooves shone like burnished silver.

And mounted in the saddle, his fingers lovingly caressing the strings of a silver harp, was no hunchback. This was a youth, and yet there was age in his eyes as if the years had no hold on him. Black his hair, held by a silver band, and his clothing was green, the green of first spring leaves—his cloak flung back a warm scarlet.

She knew him then for one out of the ancient tales—he was one of the People—those who had their own dwelling place which was not her world, though they might journey through that at their will.

His harping fell to a muted thread of sound. "No longer is the High Crown held from us by the menace of our old enemy," he was speaking and yet every word was a note of song. "Lady, of your courtesy, bring hither that which is rightfully that of my Queen."

Now Catlin did enter the chamber and her hands went out to what lay on the block. She indeed held a circlet of bright stones, pale gold and brilliant silver, formed as might be a wreath of flowers. It no longer burned, rather from it flowed such peace as filled one even as had his song.

Slowly she turned, reluctant to give to another this marvel which renewed life. But take it she did, passing the spit, then pushed aside the shield—both of the iron which legend said were deadly to what she believed him to be.

She held up to him the crown. He had swung aside his harp and brought forth what seemed a veil of mist in which he wrapped her find.

"You have held our power in truth," he said, "for this is one key to our own place. Lady, I have watched you fight that which the great cursing brought about and fight it valiantly. Come to us in all honor for already you bear within you something of that which is our birthright."

Catlin looked up into his eyes—green—or were they gold? They were pools which beckoned her to dive within. He had dismounted and now came to her, his hands empty and outstretched. Catlin took a deep breath. She was filled again, not by mist, but by a sheltering warmth of one coming home after a long sorrowful journey. She laid her palms on his. It was as if they were now one and always would be.

FROG MAGIC

Wizard Fantastic (1997) Edited by Martin H. Greenberg, Published by DAW

The puffy green-skinned body on the water-washed rock opened his large eyes. To have one's life so quickly changed could not help but disorient one for at least a short period of time. The trick was to remember who he was and what he had been, not the he of here and now.

A fly buzzed by, and his mouth snapped open; a loop of sticky tongue gathered in that brash intruder. The frog gulped, and then he shivered. What had happened was an act of this alien body, not by conscious thought of his own. He must be on guard.

"How did you do that?" The sharp croak sounded hardly more than adolescent peeping. He stared down at the speaker who clearly WAS a frog.

"As you do also," he croaked, forgetting his resolution of moments earlier to gather in a tempting offer of larger prey, a dragonfly.

"No—I mean how did you get here?" The small frog hoisted

himself up on a lower river stone and raised a forefoot to point. "You appeared, just out of the air."

The large frog sensed more than passing curiosity—there was awe in that question. Another of those too bright youngsters who were more curious than was good for their own good. Anyway, there was no time to be wasted with this insignificant youngling. But it seemed now that the small frog had lost his proper awe. Not stricken abashed by his elder's offended silence, he continued. "How do you do that—poof out of the air? One minute nothing—then you?"

"It is a long tale and one difficult to explain," the big frog was badgered into replying with almost a turtle's snappishness. "It does not matter," now he was thinking aloud, "how I got here. The question is how do I return?"

Return—how long would it take the present frog's personality to absorb Hyarmon, Wizard, Second Class, who had certainly been fatally careless today? Wizards removed enemies in this manner; they did not fall victim themselves to such snide tricks. In spite of his attempt at control, he mouthed another fly. Yes, this body would certainly, sooner or later, abort the persona of a man—unless he moved swiftly.

"Get back where?" persisted the younger frog.

Such a change included an element of time, but there was always a key. He need only discover the lock into which his fitted to be at once surrounded by familiar walls. He hoped he could deal with the problem—and later, with more fineness, with Witchita who was responsible for his present plight. His pop eyes now focused with some force on the younger frog.

"You know the river well, youngling?" he demanded.

"Sure. I've gone as far as the mill," the creature was plainly boasting, "and as far up as to where the stink water comes out by the falls."

Falls! Hyarmon had his checkpoint. Fortune was beginning to favor him now.

"A long way indeed." He tried to tame his croak with a touch of pleasantry.

"Dangerous, too!" The small frog was puffing himself up. "The stink water hole can make one sick."

Holding the frog part of him firmly under control, Hyarmon readied his body for a leap into the water. Only those four strong legs refused to obey him.

Of course. How could he have been fool enough to believe it would be that easy? It required some concentration to be able to inspect carefully the rock on which he had come into being. Frog sight might distort those lines but not enough that Hyarmon did not recognize the carvings. He hunched around to learn that he was completely netted.

The Arcs of Arbuycus. Hmmm, he might have known she would not settle for such a single step as transformation. Back again in his first position he glanced down to discover that his audience of one had expanded and was continuing to expand, as other frogs swam in to join his interrogator. The latest comer was as large if not larger than himself—and the crowd parted respectfully to let this one through.

Pop eyes centered on pop eyes. The newcomer gave a croak as loud as a shout, and the rest were instantly silent.

Hyarmon dared a probe. He encountered nothing but frog thoughts. No, this one was not to be touched by spells—but there was always the power of thought. He possessed and used that out of memory.

The large frog turned as if to take himself as far as possible from this potential rival. But Hyarmon's thought power held. The object of his intense gaze hastily submerged, but he was not going to escape so easily.

Holding onto his catch with determination, Hyarmon now tried to turn part of his attention to the frog who had first discovered him. The frog jerked, its four legs twitching, then sprang for the same rock as Hyarmon occupied. The wet green body landed with a plop on the horn of one of the inscribed Arcs. So! It could be done—now was the time to reel in his prisoner.

Sullenly fighting against the power which was drawing him, the large frog rose into sight. For a long moment the silent battle of wills continued, and then the frog came out of the water to stretch its own body over that already laid there.

Hyarmon observed the result with care. His hind limbs stiffened then he leaped, to stand for an instant on the quivering green bodies before the water enfolded him.

Upstream the younger frog had said, so upstream it would be. Paying no attention to the rest of the company Hyarmon exerted himself and then relaxed. Yes, he could depend upon the natural instinct and the rythym of this body to serve him. He kept an eye on the nearest bank. Witchita had sprung one trap; he could well believe it was not the only one—she would not want to confront him after this trial.

The hole spoken of did stink. He was not sure of the strength of frog sense of smell, but this was bad enough. It was undoubtedly a drain and surely the door he sought.

He continued to fight his way through water which was soupy with slime. The drain slanted upward, but he could find holds for his four feet. What he feared most did not happen until he was well up the shoot when a wave of dirty water suddenly showered and battered him, but he held on with desperate determination.

Though he had never explored such inner ways within the walls of his tower Hyarmon was sure he was drawing near to his goal. A dim light flittered into the way ahead, and he resumed his efforts so that fortune favored him as the scullery maid was not at work at the sink into which he crawled. He lay exhausted and panting on the hard slate of the tub unaware of voices until a name and some words made sense.

"He didn't never ride outside th' gate, I tells you. Young Master Brame said that it was all fast locked. Certain th' Noble Lord could've gone that way, but don't we all know what we hear when the gate spell is loosed?"

"Well, he ain't here, an' that one queens it in th' Great Hall as if she sits on the High Seat by rights. Gives orders right an' left this mornin'. I seed her put somethin' in th' drink she gave to Master Brame an' the guard sergeant. Now they trails behind her like they was pups and she their dam. I tell you that this here is no place to be, with that madam ruling it."

The voices were fading as the speakers moved away. But Hyarmon had heard enough. So Witchita was playing with potions now? His determination to deal with her was more than part anger. Such herbs could be used too often or in too great quantities.

It took him several desperate leaps to clear the high wall of the sink. Hyarmon could now hear movement and talking in the kitchen beyond the scullery. So he sought passage from shadow to shadow, his sleek, damp hide gathering a fur of lint and dust.

Hyarmon was near winded when he finally won to the top of the stairs and dragged himself into the Great Hall. The gleam of witch lights was plain, marking this a night hour. He searched by thought for guards—luckily in this his human persona was still serving him.

The hall was oddly quiet; no coming and going of spell-constructed serving goblins. In fact there was no table in evidence, but the High Seat stood there and toward that he made his way in weak hope.

There was no use in trying to reach his laboratory. The very devices he himself had set up for security would betray him now that he wore this alien guise. But determination won over fatigue, and he made it not only up the step of the dais but, in one last exhausting leap, to the High Seat, where he subsided, puffing.

Witchita might have changed his proper outward body, but once he was here the numbing caused by his strange form wore off and he grew fiercely alert. Wizards had tools, yes. But behind those there was always a mind which controlled such and Hyarmon now drew upon the powers of his.

After a short rest, his mind began to work furiously. He lifted one foot and then another alternately to scrape from his moist skin all he could of the debris he had gathered during his journey, wadding it down on one of the wide chair arms.

"Now!"

Hyarmon could not make the proper passes cleanly and accurately while he was in this body, but he could visualize, and that was useful now. The soggy mound arose sluggishly, thinning out into a dank mist. Two of the energy globes swooped, answering his unspoken orders, while the rest fanned out as if driven to some task.

The doubled lights swirled around Hyarmon. He could feel no change in his body—no—what he wove now was an envelope.

To all purposes a man sat in the High Chair—materialized out of that dream visitor Witchita doted on. The figure solidified into seemingly complete life and Hyarmon dispatched one globe to summon. He must concentrate on holding this shadow self together long enough to serve his plan. If Witchita were entirely alert, she might have sensed the spell in formation. She had triumphed before on her own. Perhaps she was just vain enough to believe as she was now so bedazzled by dreaming that she did not sense danger—for her.

There was the sound of a protesting hinge, and the door

opened. One of the globes appeared to light the one who entered. So—it was night. He had chosen the proper time for, as she swept forward, he could see her lithesome body more revealed than concealed by a spider silk night shift, though she had bundled a shawl about her shoulders.

Hyarmon might have smacked his lips at the appearance of a very large and succulent fly. Dream drawn she was! She had in a way ensorcelled herself and needed only a slight touch from him to seek certain pleasures.

The young man, pale of countenance but handsome of feature, did not rise from the High Seat but held out both hands in welcome, his eyes alive with passionate promise.

"Cevin!" she breathed, and her own arms came up to welcome his promised embrace. Hyarmon poised beneath the shadow he had built.

She was bending forward, having already taken the dais step, apparently not finding it strange that her phantom lover did not rise to greet her.

Still bemused as one caught in the web of sleep she leaned forward, her lips slightly parted to welcome his kiss. Lips indeed met lips but not as Witchita had expected. Her eyes widened, and she stared in terrified horror at what she had so spontaneously kissed. Yet even as her dream snapped into nothingness so did the one she had come to meet change again. The frog had vanished as had the lover. Hyarmon sat firmly on the High Seat of the Great Hall.

"You—!" She cowered, as well she might. Not only cowered, but her body was twitching wildly. The silken shift puddled as a frog, half hidden within its folds, stared at Hyarmon.

He surveyed her critically. Then, to make sure the transformation was complete, he made a quick pounce and lifted the wildly kicking frog to the level of his eyes.

"You undoubtedly make a beautiful frog, Witchita," he observed. "But I fear you shall never know the freedom of the river in which to plan a revenge."

He snapped his fingers and his wand materialized. Apparently she had foolishly neglected to break it. Still holding the frantically squirming frog in one hand, Hyarmon sketched out an oblong line on the floor. With the proper words he created a crystal aquarium. Into this he dropped the frog, who was struggling to bite with toothless jaws.

"Water—" Another pass of the wand and the aquarium was filled. "A rock for a High Seat, dear Witchita," he ordered, "and, of course, I shall see that each day you shall have the best flies to be found."

The frog had climbed to the top of the rock and now was making an attempt to leap out. However, there seemed to have also come into existence an invisible cover which kept her prisoner.

Hyarmon chuckled. "Remember your history, my dear. Frogs, kisses, and beautiful young women have met before. You thought to match lips with your desired one, but there is a different ending to this tale."

He clapped his hands and a goblin flashed into their presence.

"Smurch," Hyarman bade him, "take this aquarium to the bower of the lady Witchita. See her carefully settled and catch some flies, come morning, for her delectation. My dear, I trust you will meditate on past foolish acts. You shall be, I assure you, kept safe and secure."

If a frog could glare, the captive achieved that now. Hyarmon laughed and waved the goblin and his burden away. Now, he arose from the High Seat and stretched luxuriously, then decided to go up to the laboratory and see what mischief there had entertained Witchita during his involuntary absence.

HERNE'S LADY
Lamps on the Brow (1998) James Cahill Publishing

The Honorable Olivia Farrington on this late summer morning considered herself a singularly fortunate female as she admired her favorite view from the window of the drawing-room. Yet she was not observing a formal garden proper to the residence of consequence. Rather her gaze was fast upon an irregular rise of dark trees beyond the fields. Those marked the verge of what had once been part of a jealously guarded Royal hunting perserve, a goodly section of which now helped to make up that unbeliev-able inheritance which had so satisfactorily descended upon her some month's previously—as if she were indeed the incomparable heroine of a Marvel Press novel.

There was a dark secretiveness about that wood, but oddly she was not in the least repelled by that feeling. On the contrary she could fancy herself some high-sticker of the Ton able to challenge fate and explore at her will. Though she judged herself to be alone in this unexpressed opinion, since none of the servants had dis-played any inclination to even speak of the wood, their silence hav-ing become so apparent as to be granted the description of oddity.

She was aware from a limited perusal of the diaries of that great aunt (to whose unexpected generosity she owed her own being here) that the Lady Lettice had offered the villagers the right to take downed branches and trees for firewood, the harvesting of nuts. But it would seem that some dislike for the wood shadows was so deeply engrained in the country people they never availed themselves of such bounty.

Yet Lady Lettice had not shared in this, rather had sought out wood ways according to descriptions in the diaries (which Olivia looked upon as keys to the perplexities of this new life). She had ridden certain winding paths among the trees and Olivia had already followed her example, for she had determined from the first day of her freedom to no longer surrender to the crochets of others. For too many weary years she had been fagged near to death by family whims, and because she had had no other choice, she swallowed much without complaint.

Having endured the mortification of four seasons without an offer, her brother and his wife had refused to grossly indulge her in any farther attempts in the matrimonial field—not that she in any way wished for that to happen. Her entry into the haunts of the Ton had not given her such satisfaction as to make her long for another strained visit to the marriage mart.

She was an antidote, not even what might be dismissed as a dab of a girl. She could not play that game which seemed to easy for almost every female of her acquaintance. The matter was that she seemed unable to attach the interest of any eligible parté. Nor did that cause her any real wretchedness for she had not set eye on any of the famed catches (or even ones who fell below that level) with whom she would wish to share bed and board for the rest of her life.

Though Olivia knew better than to so express herself aloud, having faced down a number of stormy scolds in which she was informed she was insufferably high in the instep, clicked in the hob (her brother's elegant expression), one fair to give the whole family an irritation of the nerves. She knew that the plight of the unwed would be the most difficult of situations, still deep inside she felt a lightness of spirit when the fell decision was made that she would not be pushed into the London whirl again.

Being now the hopeless age of six and twenty, and having without a murmur of dissent taken to the cap of accepted spinisterhood, she had been shaken near out of her carefully cultivated calm by being Lady Lettice's heir—not only to Oakleigh Manor but also to what seemed to Olivia a handsome competence sufficient to give her a most comfortable if secluded life.

Since she was of age there could be no curtailing of her plans by her brother, and for some five delightful months she had been mistress here, in her own house, with servants (elderly to be sure) but so deeply attached to her great aunt that they accepted her without question since it was by the will of their beloved Lady that she was here.

This very morning she was about to indulge herself by making a visit to old Maudie. Maudie had been one of the duties Lady Lettice had laid upon her heir, but Olivia had not discovered it to be an onerous one. The old woman did not share the seemingly universal dislike of the wood, for her very old cottage was in a clearing set well within that shadowed territory, so much a part of the land that its stone walls might have grown as did the trees about.

Maudie had been the Lady Lettice's maid, until she had signified that she believed herself to be past the time of real service. It was by her request that the forest cottage was put in the best of order and she was installed therein. Though her Lady had made nearly daily visits, and in her own failing last days Maudie had returned to nurse her.

Now it was the established custom that someone from the manor visited Maudie twice a week bearing such supplies as might add to her comfort. Olivia had overheard one stable boy protest such a trip and so decided to take it on for herself. It was an excellent reason to ride exploring and, from her first visit, she had thought the old woman to be an acquaintance worth cultivating.

Maudie might be old but she was still very spry. The cottage was always in spotless order though there might be baskets about her hearth harboring small ailing woods creatures. Since the clearing about the cottage was wide she had room for a garden, growing not only vegetables, but fragrant herbs. Olivia had now on her dressing table a jar of soap which left the skin smooth and smelling of roses, and a bottle of lily scent she thought highly superior to any town bought perfume.

Nor was Maudie's conversation lacking in interest. For the woman spoke with authority on the ways of the wood, telling stories of animals and men in days past—though for the men she had little good to say. In particular she spoke darkly of the lord of the neighboring manor and once, when she called him by name, Olivia was unpleasantly startled.

She had met Sir Lucas Corbin herself during one of shockingly dull and over squeezed parties her sister-in-law doted so upon. And she had not in the least liked the look of him, even before gossip bore out her distaste. But that such a high sticker would be known here in this most quiet and least social of places was a surprise, until Maudie explained that it was his custom when low in funds to seek out his estate and attempt to squeeze more from his unfortunate tenants. His conduct was infamous enough to have well blackened his name, and Maudie ended her recital of his sins with the warning that he might just try to scrap a meeting with the new owner of Oakleigh since Olivia was now known as an unattached heiress. But if that lay in his mind he was not moving on it.

During her visits with Maudie Olivia began to believe that the old woman was studying her, as if weighing the new manor mistress in some fashion. Oddly enough that did not arouse any discomfort, any more than she felt any unease in the most shadowed part of the wood where she had yet ventured. Rather she had a vague touch of excitement as if something lay ahead.

This morning was one of the days to visit Maudie, and, giving a last look to the wood, she looped up the skirt of her habit and departed the house by the way of the kitchen where she came up with the cook.

"Is the hamper for Maudie ready, Mrs. Ward?"

"Yes, m'lady."

Olivia uttered a sigh. Lady Lettice's staff had arbitrarily given her a step up in rank, in spite of her protests, apparently believing that no one of lesser blood than at least an Earl's daughter could rule here.

Just as she had defied convention by setting up her establishment without some dim female to lend her respectability by companionship, so did she ride the forest paths without the grooms who, she very well knew, were so adverse to such a direction. Apparently those of the household accepted these decisions with equanimity, though Olivia knew that servants were the first to decry any lessening of propriety.

This was a morning to give one an expectation of pleasure. She had already established an excellent relationship with the gray mare, Mist. They passed at an easy canter from the wider road into the over field track which led to the wood. Olivia made sure of the fastening of the basket and enjoyed the freedom of the ride.

She was well under tree cover when she was startled by a

cry—certainly one of pain and fear. Reining Mist in a little she listened but did not halt. That sound came again seemingly weaker. Now she urged the mare on. After all this was her own land and any happening here was her concern.

Mist brought her out in one of the many glades, not as large a one as that of the cottage, but open enough so Olivia caught clear sight of distressing action.

A man with one arm locked in the reins of a wild-eyed, foam mouthed horse, was standing over a huddle of what seemed to be rags. Even as Olivia came up he brought down his riding crop in a vicious cut, the lash landing on a round of back from which a dull green shirt had already been slit.

"Devil brat," his voice was as harsh as his attack. "Gallows fruit—"

"Stop!" Olivia found her voice, and it rose with a note of command she had never had cause to use before.

The next blow he aimed did not fall true. He swung around to stare up at her, the very embodiment of reckless cruelty and ungoverned rage. His hair, for his hat lay behind on the ground dented by a hoof, was as black as the hide of the nervous horse. From under bushy brows, eyes, which seemed as yellow as new minted guineas, raked over her. Then the thin lips of his cruel mouth shaped something which was not a smile.

"Well, and what have we here." He took a step toward her, and his horse tried to rear. With a lightning swift movement he jerked viciously at the reins, sawing savagely at his mount's mouth.

Olivia's chin was up, her eyes very cold. Her own fingers tightened hard enough to give her riding crop a warning twitch.

"Sir, you are trespassing."

"Sir, you are trespassing," he mimicked her with a sneer and then suddenly seemed to recall what he might never have known—manners.

"Miss Farrington, I presume. We are neighbors and so you should have a word in this matter." His boot toe thudded home against the cowering victim. "This imp of Satan's get is poaching. As such he will answer in due time to the law, but I shall have the lessoning of him first."

"Sir Lucas, this is my land. Years ago Lady Lettice laid down the rule governing this holding. Villagers are to forage when and where they please with no hindrance."

He showed his teeth as might a wolf.

"I deal with thieves as I see fit. No miss sets my course."

She must bluff him somehow Olivia thought quickly. This man, being what he was, might well turn his anger now on her.

"My groom comes, Sir Lucas. And you are on my land without invitation or leave."

For a moment of dread Olivia wondered if he might be bluffed so. However, in his world ladies did not ride alone, and surely he was not so uncaring yet of all convention that he would brawl with her before a servant.

His face had become very set. Then he turned, swept up his battered hat, and swung into the saddle. Leaning forward a little he spoke with extravagated smoothness of voice as insulting as his slow survey of her person.

"I hear, oh, Lady of the manor," the sneering tone brought a flush to Olivia's cheeks, "and obey—for now. But the game is not done—"

What he might have added in the way of a more naked threat was interrupted by a new sound, that of a hunter's horn.

Sir Lucas' horse gave such a cry as Olivia had never heard an animal utter before and whirled, fighting the reins and plunging away, bearing its cursing master.

There came a second horn call. Mist reared as the rag bundle came to life, and, before Olivia could call out or move, the fugitive vanished into the underbrush.

She could not pursue there. It must have been one of the village children who had so dared the forest. But at least he was free now and she was certain Sir Lucas would not return to hunt him down.

Still out of temper from this encounter Olivia lingered in the glade waiting for the horn blower to join her. Those last notes had not sounded too far away. It had been particularly vexatious to have had this meeting with her shunned neighbor. Sir Lucas was not a magistrate, thanks be to fortune, and his powers were limited, but it might be well to report this confrontation to Squire Hambly who was looked upon as the guardian of affairs hereabouts. Surely the rules set by Lady Lettice for her own property would be honored.

However, no one came to join her. So, deep in somewhat distressed thought, she rode on to Maudie's.

Her relation of what had passed was listened to with every sign of concern. So much so that Olivia had to keep reassuring herself that surely there would be no further trouble.

When she spoke of the horn Maudie gave a little gasp and nodded vigorously. Then to Olivia's surprise, she spoke as one who had had some pressing question well answered.

"So it has been decided, you are free of the wood, m'lady. Just as my dear lady wished it so. As for that dark soured one, he had better make his peace while he yet can."

"What do you mean, Maudie? Who sounded that horn—in what manner have I been made free of the wood."

Now Maudie shook her head as emphatically as she had earlier nodded it. "'Tis not for my saying, m'lady. There will come a time when you do understand."

And there was a certain stubborn tilt to her chin Olivia had seen before. She sighed, knowing that Maudie was not to be moved any farther.

"I shall certainly speak to the squire—he must have power enough to make sure Sir Lucas stays without my wards."

"Do so if it eases your mind, m'lady. Squire Hambly, he is of the old blood and knows the land—" Again she spoke in riddles beyond Olivia's solving.

When she returned to the manor she sent a message to the squire, only to learn that he had gone to London on some urgent affair and could not be reached for a time. Though she made a searching endeavor to discover the beaten child that, too, failed, for no villager nor farm family would own to such mistreatment of their own. They seemed as tight jawed as Maudie the minute she mentioned the wood, until their monosyllabic answers defeated her.

Her next two visits to Maudie she made prudently, taking with her George Lankin, the coachman, a tall, hearty man with a wide stretch of brawny shoulder and fists like to send such a one as Sir Lucas a-sprawl in a hurry But Olivia noted that he rode warily, his gaze swinging from side to side, and his tramping up and down before the cottage transferred in part his uneasiness to her so that she was constrained to cut short her visit.

They entered the harvest season when the whole community outside the wood were busy a-field. For the first time the verge of the wood attracted the boldest of the children, especially when Olivia joined their company. Together they plundered the berry heavy bushes and emboldened by this sudden setting aside of their usual aloofness, Olivia organized forays to go a-nutting, taking the opportunity to load on a patient old mare wood to ease the winters of several families about whom she had become concerned.

She lost her fine lady pallor to a faint overcast of ivory brown. Which, she decided, became her much better than all the powders and creams her sister-in-law had once urged upon her. Though she still dressed in fashion within the manor, she went a-roving in sturdy homespun like any dairy maid.

The squire finally returned, but it had been so peaceful much of her apprehension had faded. He was a man of middle years, a firm rooted country man at heart, and she liked his manner. He listened to Olivia's story of her meeting with Sir Lucas and looked grave.

"The man's crack brained to be sure. We're rid of him for a space—he's gone to town. But, Miss Farrington, take care. Get some lady of quality in to live with you, see you are guarded both at home and away. He is a danger. And—" he had paused then and regarded her carefully as if seeking some hint as to what he should say. "The wood," he finally continued, "it has an odd name hereabouts. Very old some of the stories—some say it was Herne's own chosen refuge."

"Herne?" she questioned though he appeared to believe she already knew that name.

"Herne, the hunter. A very old legend of the guardian of the woods and all that lived within. Country talk, Miss Farrington, but they believe—oh, the belief lasts. And it is well not to challenge their beliefs sometimes."

She murmured something which might be taken as assent. The Herne story might well explain the attitude of the servants and the villagers, but it did not bother her, though she made a mental note to learn more if she could. However, she had no intention of hunting up some drab but worthy female to give her countenance. Lady Lettice had managed without—unless circumstances actually forced her she would do likewise.

Twice during visits to Maudie she again heard the horn. There was that about its notes which increased her longing to meet the one who formed them. Oddly enough she found it impossible to mention this to Maudie. When she had asked the old woman about the story of Herne Maudie had replied firmly:

"Naught can be hurried, m'lady. An oak grows to its own speed and there can be no pushing of it, root or branch. Wait—listen—and learn—"

What did come on her waiting was near disaster. Maudie, Olivia thought with concern, was beginning to show signs of aging. Twice she had discovered the old woman laid upon her bed, something Maudie scorned to do in daytime. She saw that strengthening wine, a good share of each baking day's produce, and small comforts were carried to the wood.

A pot of fine wine jelly from London had been added to two loaves on a bright morning when there was a certain briskness in the air, suggesting that the turn of season was approaching. As Olivia rode with her offering she wondered whether she must not urge Maudie to move to the manor before winter. Such a suggestion would lead to argument and she was marshalling her word weapons as she went. Mist had been this way so often that she knew every twist and turn of the path and need not be closely attended to.

It was not until Olivia had dismounted that she noted the green stiff curtains were still drawn across the small paned windows. But the hour was near nooning and surely Maudie would have been up and about for hours.

Mist's reins were thrown over a shrub and Olivia, grabbing up the trail of her habit, was at the door in the space of a breath or two.

She pushed into the foreroom of the cottage, near one half of which was taken up by Maudie's bed. Drying herbs hung in stings from the beams. But a portion of those had somehow landed on the floor and been trampled. It was dusk-dark, for the door had swung to behind her. Olivia could only see the bunched coverings on the bed where Maudie must be.

"Maudie!" she dropped the basket with no care for the contents and hurried to the bed.

There had been no answer except a choking cry from the direction of the window where something appeared to be struggling on the floor.

"Maudie!" Olivia turned her back on the bed to start for that moving shadow.

An iron hard hand gripped her arm jerking her back. She could not reach her assailant as he must be on the bed behind her, and his strength was such she could not break that hold.

But she fought with all the vigor she could summon. All at once the grip on her arm was loosened, but before she could pull free, she was caught a second time, swung around, and a stinging blow on her cheek near rocked her from her feet.

Breath foul with brandy fumes made her gasp sickly as she was struck a second time and forced back against the bed, her attacker looming as a dark shadow over her.

"Slut—" that name merged into such a flood of obscenity that the words lost their meaning in growls. His jaws appeared to slit in a wolf's grin. This was more beast than man, and a fear such as she had never thought to know choked her, even as one of his hands moved to her throat forming a noose of flesh and blood to strangle.

She clawed vainly, striving to tear at that distorted grimace on his face, to somehow keep that mouth from touching hers. But all her efforts were too feeble as she fought for breath.

There was a sudden sound and the light of day struck full on Sir Lucas as the curtains at the window were jerked aside and that casement thrown open with force enough to break one of the small panes.

"Herne! Herne!"

Through the panting of their struggle that cry rang, though Olivia heard it only dimly as her attacker continued to force her back on the disordered bed. She was aware as if that outrage struck another that, though he had not released the hold on her throat entirely, he was now clawing with his other hand at her bodice striving to rip apart the stout material.

"Herne!"

Sir Lucas' head swung toward the window, though he did not loose his grip upon his captive. He snarled. Then he aimed another blow so heavy that he brought tears to her eyes. However, she could at least draw a breath, for his hand had relaxed that noose hold on her throat.

She tried to scream but her voice was only a croak which was drowned out by a third call:

"Herne!"

There was a flash of green light. Sir Lucas gave a rasping cry, stumbled back from her. Olivia clawed her way loose from the tumble of covers into which she had been shoved, levered herself up in time to see her attacker turn toward the cottage door which swung open again, as if by its own accord.

Olivia gasped. From his breast protruded a shaft like that of an arrow, though it was green and shimmered like a spear of light. One of the man's hands, now swinging limply at his sides, arose as if to touch that deadly hurt. He did not fall, instead he lurched out of the door, vanished from Olivia's sight.

"Bind me in me own cloak, would he! But not sure of his knots—that one."

Still dazed, Olivia saw Maudie by the open window, shrugging off the folds of cloth hampering her. Her cap had disappeared and her white hair was pulled into a tangle. She gave a last twist of her shoulders and the stout red winter garment slipped to the floor.

Olivia swallowed. Her throat still felt as if it were half closed and she took short, frantic breaths. Somehow she managed to stand, with an anchoring hold on one of the bed posts.

"Maudie," she had to make a painful effort to shape that name and her voice was a hoarse whisper.

The old woman kicked the cloak up against the wall and came to the girl with a quick step.

"Now, m'lady, there's naught to fear. That one takes care of his own. Be at peace against all ill—Herne's lady—"

"Herne's lady?" repeated Olivia.

"Aye. Chosen you have been and rightfully so. You have been watched and measured since first you came hither. True time is not reckoned by the clocks of men. There was my dear lady before you—she was chosen. And before her another. When your own time passes you will find one who will walk Herne's wood in turn and hold his favor. For he is one of the Old Ones who did not flee the land when belief grew thin, but rather still cherishes what was always his."

She paused and held her head slightly atilt as if listening. Perhaps in direct answer came that sweet call of a hunter's horn. Yet this hunter must be guardian not destroyer.

Olivia blinked. It was hard to understand, but now small memories flowed together and fitted well. Her sense of being under eye when in the woods, the fact that the children when she was one of the party dared to venture under the trees—that horn—

"Sir Lucas—" she croaked, still rubbing her throat.

"Tush, m'lady. He was served as well he might be. Herne's arrows do not fly light but they fly well. Now set you down, m'lady. I have possets which will soothe that poor throat of yours."

She let Maudie install her in the chair by the outflung window. Herne—could one dare to believe? But why—here?

Olivia ventured a question.

"Will I ever see him, Maudie—this Herne?"

Maudie laughed. "There is a time for everything, m'lady, and when that comes you shall have no question."

"You know him then, Maudie—Herne?" She found a desire to repeat that name.

"All who dwell in his place know him. He is a good master but a bad foe, as that devil Sir Lucas discovered. Now drink up this potion, m'lady."

She had poured a golden liquid into a silver cup so old that the intricate patterning on its side had been near worn away. It tasted of honey, and of herbs, and oddly of flowers as if summer scents had been infused in it. Drinking, Olivia's last shadow of fear and pain vanished.

She smiled almost drowsily, ready to await what the future might bring—even as the Lady Lettice had lived and—how many before her?

It was not until after a night, filled with dreams which were not nightmares but promises she could not remember in detail upon awakening, that the news arrived. One of the grooms had delivered the story with gusto.

"Fell down dead, m'lady," Mrs. Beckett reported, "right before the eyes of Tom Donn who told the whole story at the ale house where our Jim heard it. Struck by the Hand of God Almighty he was, dead—and not a mark on him! They sent for the 'pothecary and he swears it must have been some weakness of the heart. 'Tisn't my place to speak ill of the gentry, m'lady, but the world is a cleaner place with such as Sir Lucas out of it."

Throughout the day Olivia kept to her role of polite if dismayed interest in the sudden demise of her neighbor. She was sure that only Maudie shared her secret of the happenings at the cottage. And since her nemesis had died apparently in his own courtyard no other would ever know.

Toward nightfall she grew restless. The latest novel posted from London could not hold her eye or attention for even half a page. She brought out a bit of work she had started with the vague idea of recovering the small chair in her bedroom the seat of which showed a sad lack of care. After she missed four stitches, pricked her finger to the extent of having to sketch in another bud of the pictured rose to cover that stain, she surrendered to the fact that she was indeed indulging in a spasm of nerves.

Or was it nerves? In her first season, before she realized how far her girlish dreams strayed from the reality kept jealously tight by the fashionable, she had sometimes felt this way before a ball. Expectation—and something else she could not define—she shrank from doing so.

Olivia did not do justice to the dinner served up where she dined in solitary state deemed suitable by her staff to her consequence. She settled at last for a peach, part of the year's crop, round and perfect, but uncommonly juicy as to the use of fingers.

The dusk had deepened so that when she looked without from the windows, her eyes still be-dazzled by the candlelight around she could not pick up any landmark until she stood blinking for several seconds.

Then—she knew! Faint but growing closer—the horn's silver call.

Turning, she raced for the stairway and her own suite above. What luck she had no personal maid waiting in attendance now. Annie, the upper housemaid who had taken over the keep of her wardrobe must have already withdrawn to the warren where the servants had their own lives.

Olivia burrowed into the great wardrobe, brushing aside the hanging clothing with no thought of wrinkling having to be dealt with. Her hands closed at last on what she sought—the softness of velvet—and she pulled out her find.

It had been her choice, her own, back in the days when her sister-in-law had kept a sharp eye on her, since it was so well known that she had no acute understanding of the dictates of fashion. The gown was very plain, no ruffles, no braid in fantastic coils, only a small stand of lace, now faintly yellow, edging the neckline.

As one who races with time, Olivia shed her house gown, pitched her proper cap onto the bed and somehow got herself buttoned into the flow of green—forest green. She surveyed her reflection most critically in the long mirror on the wardrobe door.

On impulse she raised both hands and pulled the pins from her hair. Somehow it did not look so dully brown when she let it fly loose about her shoulders. She turned to look at the back, her head at a stretch.

There was something different—she could not put name to what had appeared to have changed in her appearance but she found it exciting.

Quickly she blew out the candles, leaving only the small night light and one candle to carry with her. Holding her skirt gracefully high for greater speed, she retraced her way, not to seek out the front door but rather the side one which she knew had the faulty latch and could be safely used.

It was cool as the night wind wrapped her round, but she did not feel it. The excitement raising in her supplied a heat of its own. She had left the candle just inside the door, now she used both hands to control her skirt as she brushed through the garden gate to the road, made haste along that for the short space striving to make sure she was not sighted, until she reached the turn off to the wood.

Now she was running, the wind pulling gently at her hair, soft on her face. It was rustling the leaves in the great trees as she came into that other's kingdom.

"Herne?" Olivia called, not sharply as Maudie had summoned him, but with a softness tinged with uncertainty.

"Herne?"

Shadow detached itself from shadow. She dropped her hold on her skirt, both hands now pressed against a heart which was beating more than her recent exertions warranted.

"Herne—?"

And the welcome came—eagerly—joyfully—

"My lady."

Sometimes, there are things that one must do—even at the risk of all one holds dear.

THE OUTLING

Lord of the Fantastic: Fantastic Stories in Honor of Roger Zelazny (1998) AvoNova

Herta pulled impatiently at the hood the wild wind attempted to take from her head. Facing this was like trying to bore her body, sturdy as it was, into a wall. The dusk was awaking shadows one did not like to see if only in a glimpse from eye corner. She shifted her healer's bag and tried to hold in mind the thought of her own hearth fire, a simmering pot of stew, and a waiting mug of her own private herb restorative.

The wind howled, and within her hood Herta grinned. Let the Dark go its way, this eve it held no newborn in its nets. Gustava, the woodsman's wife, had a new son safe at her breast and a strong boy he was.

Then she slowed her fight against the wind, actually pushed aside a bit of hood to hear the better. No, there was no mistaking that whimper—pain, fear, both fed it.

In the near field there was a rickety structure Ranfer had once slovenly built for a sheep shelter, though all flocks would be safely bedded this night. She had not been mistaken—that was a lone-some cry, wailed as if no help could be expected.

Herta bundled up thick skirts, gave a hitch to her bag, to push laboriously through the nearest gap in the rotting fence. She did allow herself a regretful sigh. There was pain and she was a healer; for such there was no turning aside.

She tore a grasping thorn away from her cloak and rounded the end of the leanto. Then she halted again almost in mid-step, and her white breath puffed forth in a gasp.

There was a form stretched on the remains of rotting straw, yes. Great green eyes which yet had a hint of gold in them were on her. The body which twisted now as if to relieve some intolerable pain was—furred. Yet it was womankind in all its contours.

Herta dropped her cloak and strove to pull it over brush and crumbling wood to give some shelter. Light—not even a candle lantern. But she had the years behind her to tell her what lay here—a thing of legend—yet it lived and was in birth throes.

White fangs showed between pale lips as Herta went to her knees beside that twisting figure.

"I would help," the healer got out. She was already pulling at her bag. But there was no fire to warm any potion and half her hard-learned skills depended upon such.

She shook off mittens and into the palm of one hand shook a mixture. As she leaned closer the thing she would tend swept out a long pale tongue to wipe her flesh clean.

Having turned back her sleeves, Herta placed her hands on that budge of mid-body. "Down come." She recited words which might not be understood by her patient but were the ritual. "Come down and out into this world, without lingering."

She never knew how long she kept up that struggle, so ham-pered by the lack of near all that was necessary for a proper birth-ing. But at last there was a gush of pale blood and a small wet thing in her hands. While she who had yielded it up at last cried aloud a mournful cry-or was it a howl?

Though Herta held now, wrapping in her apron, what was undoubtedly a female child, large to be sure but still recognizable for what it was, the body which had delivered it once more writhing. Foam dripped from the jaws and a strong animal smell arose. But the eyes went from Herta to the babe and back again. And in them, as if it were shouted aloud, there was a plea.

Without knowing why, except that somehow this was a part of her innermost being, Herta nodded. "Safe as I can, I shall hold."

Her breath caught as she realized what she had just promised. But that it was a true oath she had no doubt. The eyes held to hers; then came a dimness and the figure twisted for the last time. Herta squatted, a wailing baby in her arms. But at her feet there was now, stiffening and stark, the body of a silver white wolf.

Herta's hand started to move in the traditional farewell to those passing beyond and then stopped. All living things in the world she had always known paid homage to That Beyond, but did an Outling come within that shelter? Who was she to judge? She finished the short ritual with the proper words almost definitely.

"Sleep well, sister. May your day dawn warm and clear."

Stiffly she got to her near-benumbed feet. The babe whimpered, and she sheltered it with a flap of cloak. Night was closing in. She did not know how or why the Outling had come to the fringe of human habitation, but either those of her kind would find her or else, like the wood creatures whose blood she was said to share, she would lie quiet here to become part of the earth again.

Heavy dusk was on Herta when she reached her cottage at the outer edge of the village street. Lanterns were agleam above the doorways after the Law, and she must set hers also. But luckily she seemed to have the village street to herself at the moment. It was the time for day's-end eating and all were at their tables.

Inside she laid the baby, still bundled in her apron, on her bed and then saw to the lantern and gave a very vigorous poking to the embers on the hearth, feeding them well from her store. She even went to the extravagance of lighting a candle in its grease-dripped holder.

To swing a pot of water over the awakening fire took but a moment or so, and she rummaged quickly through her supplies of castoffs, which she kept ready for those too poor to have prepared much for birthings.

Once it was washed and clad she would have vowed that this was a human child—healthy of body—born with a thick thatch of silver fair hair—but human as the one she had earlier brought into the world.

She hushed a hungry wail by a rag sopping with goat's milk to suck. It's eyes opened and Herta would always swear that they looked up at her with strange knowledge and recognition.

Briary, she named her find, and the name seemed to fit. And she had her story ready, too: a beggar woman taken by her time in the forest, who died leaving one there was none to claim.

Briary was accepted by the village with shrugs and some mutterings. If Herta wished to burden herself with an extra mouth during the lean months, the care of a stranger's offthrow—that was her business. Too many owed life and health to the healer to raise questions.

As time passed, though, Herta was hard put to explain some things. Why her charge grew so quickly and showed wits and strengths village children of near age did not. Yet, though she watched carefully, especially on the full moon nights, she saw no sign of any Outling change.

Briary early advanced from a creeping stage to walking, and

she was always a shadow to Herta. She seldom spoke and then only in answer to a direct question, but when Herta sat by the fire of an evening, a warm posset in her mug, stretching her feet to the fire's warm, she would feel a small hand stroking her arm and then her cheek and she would gather up the child to hold. Perhaps it was because she had lived alone for so long herself that she felt the need for speech, and so she first told Briary of her own childhood, and then tales of older times. But she never spoke of Outlings nor such legends. Instead she repeated the names of herbs and plants and most of the lore of her trade, even those the child she held on her lap could not understand. Yet Briary seemed to find all Herta's speech a comfort, for when the healer would take her to bed she would ask in her soft voice for more.

When spring came Briary grew restless, pacing to the door of the house and fingering the latch bar, looking to Herta. At first the healer was reluctant to let her out. There were two reasons—the Outling blood in her, which Herta tried hard to forget, and the fact that she was so forward for her age that surely the village women would gossip about it.

But at length she yielded and allowed Briary to go into the garden, which must be carefully tended, and even, walking, with one hand grasping Herta's skirt, to the mill for a packet of meal, standing quietly, sometimes with a forefinger in her mouth, listening while Herta exchanged greetings and small talk with her neighbors.

If Briary did not hunt out the children of the village, they were quick to spy her. To the older ones she was but a baby, but there were others who shyly offered flowers or a May apple. At length she became accepted; all differences denied that she was a stranger. She could outrun even Evison, who had always been fleetest of foot. And as the years passed Herta also forgot her wariness and looked no more for what she suspected might come.

Somehow the villagers came to accept, though they sometimes commented on her rapid growth of both mind and body. She became a second pair of hands for Herta, learning to grind, to measure, to spread for drying, to measure drop by drop liquids from the clay bottles on the shelves. It was she who stopped the lifeblood flow when Karl misswung an axe until Herta could come. And Lesa swore that Briary only touched the ugly wart rising on her chin and it grew the less and vanished. Herta was given credit for training so good an apprentice.

When summers reached the height of sticky weather and one sweated and slapped at the flies, hunting shade at noontide, Briary was made free of another of the children's secrets. For she had early learned that there were some things one did not blab about.

This was one mainly known to the boys until Briary had followed them. And, seeing her watching, they somehow could not send her away.

Among the ancient stories Herta had shared with her was one of the village itself. There had been a mighty lady, such as had never been hereabouts before, who had come with workmen and had built a stone house which stood now fields apart from the village. Before it was dug a pool as the lady ordered, and a spring had burst to fill it, nor had the water ever failed. Then she had built across the upper end of the pool, nearest to the building, a screen of stone.

Once that had been done she dismissed the workpeople, offering land to those wanting to stay. Later came others, odd-looking in queer garments. They, too, worked, for one could hear the ring of their hammers throughout the day and sometimes on nights when the moons were full.

Whatever they wrought was also finished at last, and they left very quickly between dawn and dusk of a single day. The native villagers took an aversion to the building. Of the lady they never saw anything again, and it was thought she must have gone with the last workpeople.

However, in time the boys used to dare each other to try the pool and, nothing ill happening, it became a place of recreation for the village in the high heat of summer. But no one ventured beyond the screen or tried to explore what stood there.

Briary seemed able to swim as easily as one already tutored, though the other girls squealed and splashed and floundered into some manner of propulsion.

It seemed that life flowed as smoothly as always, one day melting into another one, until the coming of the peddler. He arrived on a day for rejoicing for the crops, for the last of the harvest had been brought in and there was a table set up in the middle of the street whereon each housewife set a dish or platter of her best and most closely guarded recipe. They were just about to explore these delights when Evison came running to say there was a stranger on the road from the south.

Perhaps twice or three times a year such a thing might happen. It meant news to be talked over for months and sometimes things to be learned. To have this happen on the day of Harvest Home was a double event which near aroused the younger members of the village to a frenzy.

He came slowly, the peddler, with one hand on the pack frame of his mule, as if he in some manner needed support, and his face was near as red as a field poppy.

Johan, the smith, hurried to meet him, a brimming tankard of Harvest Mix in his hand. The man gave him a nod of the head and drank as if he had been in a desert for days. When he came up for air he pulled his dusty hand across his wet chin.

"Now that's a fair greeting." His voice had a cracked note as if some of the dust had plagued him to that point. "I be Igorof, trader. May all your days be sunny and your crops grow tall, good people."

"Let us help your beast, trader." Johan already had a hand on his shoulder and was pulling him toward the table. "Good feasting, Igorof." He placed him on the nearest bench while the women crowded forward with this dish or that full of the best for him to make choice.

Evison had taken the donkey to the nearby field, where two of the other boys helped him lift off the heavily laden pack frame while another brought a pail of water for the thirsty animal.

"Feast, let us feast!" Johan hammered the hilt of his knife on the table.

Briary had squeezed in beside Herta, but she noted, as she always was able, that the healer was eyeing the newcomer with a frown beginning to form between her eyes.

Feast well they did, with many toasts in the more potent drink offered the elders. Igorof's tankard was kept brimming, and he emptied it nearly as quickly, though he did not seem as drawn to do more than taste what lay on his plate.

Herta leaned forward suddenly and asked, her voice loud enough to cut through the general noise, "How do those in Langlot, friend? You have come from there—what news do you bring?"

His eyes were watching her over the edge of the tankard.

"Well as one would wish, goodwife. There be three new babes and—" Suddenly he set down the tankard so its contents splashed and his mouth was drawn crooked in grimace.

What moved Briary arose inside her as one might suddenly come from a dark into light. She skidded under the table and caught the edge of Johan's smock, pulling him backward with all her might, away from the stranger. He cried out in surprise and tripped.

The girl continued to face the stranger, flung out her arms and pushed against all those near him she could reach. "Away—away—" Her voice was shrill.

"What do you, brat!" Ill-tempered Trike aimed a slap at her.

Herta arose. "She saves your life!" she told Trike. "Stranger, what is the truth of what you have brought to us?"

He grimaced again, his eyes turning swiftly from side to side.

"No! Not the fire!" He had scrambled up from his seat. His shirt only loosely held together fell open to show red splotches on his chest. Herta's eyes widened, fear masked her face.

"Plague!"

One word, but enough to silence them all. Those nearest the trader strove to get away, and those beyond tried to elude them in turn. There had been no plague in many years, but when it struck, whole villages went to their deaths and only the wild creatures were ever seen in their streets.

Such was the role of deaths, it was said that those bearing the contagion were often hurled into fires, the living with the dead.

A wild scramble rolled along the street, each family seeking their own home, though one could not shelter with any bolt against this menace.

The man threw back his head and howled like a beast at the slaughter pen and then crumpled to the ground. Briary could see the heavy shudders that shook his body.

"Get away from him, fool!" Johan's wife showed her hatchet face at their cottage window.

Herta moved around the table to the stricken stranger. She did not look to Greta in the window, but her voice surely reached the woman, for the shutter was slammed shut again.

"I am healer sworn," Herta said, then she spoke to Briary.

"Bring me the packets from the drawer with the black spot on it." Briary ran as swiftly as in a race. But fear was cold within her. She knew the nature of those packets—they brought an end to great suffering—but also to life, and she who used them would take a great weight upon her inner self for every grain of the powder she dispensed. Yet it was said that the last moments of the plague brought pure torment, and if that were lessened it was a boon well meant.

There were two sides always to the healer's craft. In her hands from time to time she held both life and death. Briary found the packets, thrust them deep into her apron pocket and returned to the wreckage of the feast.

Herta was on her knees by the still shuddering body of the trader. As Briary came up she grabbed a tankard from the edge of the table before her and there was an answering slosh of drink unconsumed. Then she spoke to Igorof.

"Brother, you are plague gripped. There is no cure—but your passing can be eased if you will it so."

His head turned so his sweating face could be seen, and it seemed that the shudders ran also across his features. His bitten lips, flecked with blood, twisted.

"Give—peace—" Somehow he grated out the words.

Calmly Herta held packet and tankard up to eye level and shook some grayish ashes into the tankard. Then she pushed the packet back to Briary.

As if the man had been stricken by an ordinary fever and lay in her own cottage, she slipped an arm about his shoulders and lifted him, setting the tankard to his lips.

"Thanks of all good be on you, healer," he grated out. "But you have doomed yourself thereby."

"That is as it may be," she said steadily as he drank what she offered.

To Briary's eyes his passing was quick, but the body he had left behind was as much a danger to the village as the living man had been.

Herta arose and faced down the street. And her voice came high and clear.

"Show your courage now. Those who were near to this poor soul and his belongings—already, as well you know, the taint may lie upon you. Away from those you cherish until you know you are clean. Come forth and give aid for what must be done."

There was silence, no other answer. Then a door was flung open and a youthful figure half fell, half flung himself into the street. There were screams and calls from behind him as he lurched to his feet, stood for a moment as if to get his full breath, and then came forward with visible reluctance. It was Evison, who had dealt with Igorof's pack and mule. He gulped twice and turned his head not to view the dead as he approached, and his face was gray beneath the summer's tan.

His coming might have been a key turned in a stubborn lock, for now other doors opened and the wailing from within the cottages mingled in a great cry of sorrow and loss. But they came—Johan, and the others who had drunk with the stranger, three women who had taken it upon themselves to fill his plate and so had been shoulder close to him.

Johan loosened one of the benches and they brought pitchforks and staffs, to roll the limp body on that surface, carrying it into the field where the trader's pack had been left. It was Stuben who smoothed the mule's neck and, looking into the animal's eyes, said in a shaking voice.

"What must be done, will be done." And with his butcher's practice brought down the heavy axe in the single needed blow.

There was movement again in the village, though those who had come forth stood carefully away from the known cottage while doors or windows were opened. Wood cut for the hearth, a roll or two of cloth, several jugs of oil were thrust into the street.

So Igorof came to the fire after all, though it was only his tortured husk which lay there in the lap of flames. And with him burned all his belongings, the frame on which those had ridden, and the mule.

It took hours, and those who worked tottered with weariness as they pulled together more fuel for that fire. Also their eyes went slyly now and then from one to another, watching, Briary knew, for some sign of the sickness to show.

Herta oversaw the building of the pyre and then went to her cottage and began to sort out bottles and packets, Briary following her directions as to blending and stirring.

"What can be done, shall be. Gather all the cups and tankards left on the table, child, and have them ready."

The stink of the fire hung like a doom cloud over the whole village, and Briary could see those others still adding to its fury with whatever they could lay hands upon. She readied the cups and Herta came, a pot braced against her hip. The workers must have sighted her and taken her arrival as a signal, for they gathered again, singed, smoke darkened, though no one stood close to another.

"A Healer is granted only such knowledge as the Great Ones allow. I can promise you nothing. But here I have the master strength of many remedies, some akin to a lighter form of the plague. Drink and hope, for this is all which has been left to us, if we would not wipe out all who are kin to us."

Drink they did, with Herta watching that each might get his or her full share. When they had done, their weariness seemed to strike at them, and they settled on the bank of the stream. Two of the women wept, but the third wore a face of anger against fate and dug her belt knife again and again into the earth as if she would clean it well for some use; while the men, grim of face, looked now and then to the towering flag of flame.

Briary had first sought Herta, tagging at her heels as might a babe who had but shortly learned to walk and needed a skirt to cling to. Inside she felt strange and wanted comfort, but of what sort she could not tell, perhaps better than most, for she had learned of Herta's knowledge. Yet there grew in her a strange feeling that this thing was no threat to her, and that those sorrowing and damning fate upon the river bank were its prey—not she.

She still trod in Herta's footsteps as they returned to the healer's cottage. But on the very doorstep she halted as if a wall had risen past which she could not go. Yet all she could see was a string of drying herbs somehow fallen from its ceiling hook. The odor from it grew more pungent and she made a small sound in her throat—more like a whine than a true protest.

Herta swept around and stood staring at her as if she were some fragment of the plague broken loose. The healer sank down on her chair. Her lips moved as if she were speaking.

Briary heard no sound, but there came a tingling in her skin as if the briars which had been her birthing bed once more pricked at her. There seemed to be stronger smells, and some of them she found worse than those which had come from the fire.

Her hands itched and she rubbed them together and then looked down in startled horror, for skin did not touch smooth skin—rather hair. She looked to see a down appearing—gray as fire ash and certainly not true skin. Frantically she pushed up her sleeves to discover that that fluff continued, and then she tore apart the fastening of her bodice and looked down upon just the same growth.

The plague! And yet the trader had showed no such stigmata. Briary cried out her terror and from her throat there arose no true words, but rather a howl.

Despairing she held out one of those strangely gloved hands toward Herta and went to her knees, begging aid.

The healer had arisen from her seat, the twisted astonishment on her face fading. She wet her lips with her tongue tip and then enunciated slowly as if speaking to a small child who must be made to understand.

"You are—Outling!" Again she wet her lips with tongue tip. "Now you meet your true self. Why I do not know, unless what has happened this day has also a strange effect on those of your blood. But this I will tell you, daughterling: get you away. They," she gave a short nod in the direction of the rest of the village, "will wish for one on whom to blame disaster—they will remember how unlike their kin you are—the more so now!"

"But," Briary's voice was hardly more than a harsh rumble. "I—I smelled the evil—I wished to aid—"

"Truth spoken. But you have never been one to measure beside the other younglings. There have always been some who wondered and whispered. And now that black doom has descended upon us, their whispers will become shouts."

"You call me Outling." Tears gathered in the girl's eyes, matted in the fur on her cheeks. "Am I then of the night demon kind?"

Herta shook her head. "Your kind is old. Before the first of the human landseekers came down valley your people knew this land. But then you passed, as a fading race passes when pressed by a stronger, fresher planting. I do not know why your mother returned here, though her need must have been sore, for death companied her. I do not—"

Suddenly she paused, arose from her chair. "The shrine," she said. "Surely only the shrine could have drawn her hither, that she must have aid for some dire hurt!"

"The shrine—?"

"Yes, that which lies beyond the pool. None ever saw clearly the Great One who ordered its building, nor did any who worked upon it understand why it was set here—at least they answered no questions. But if it *is* a thing of power for your kind perhaps you can save yourself there—"

"But you—the plague—" faltered Briary.

"Listen, youngling, ends come to all living creatures, and the reason behind such we do not ever know. I am a healer; what I can do for these people, some I have known from their cradles, that I shall do. But I also know how fear twists minds, and I will not have you fall into their hands. Someone need only say 'Outling,' and point a finger—and the hunt would be swift and short. Perhaps your mother lost in just such a race. Go you to the shrine. You, I am sure, will find no barrier at the screen there. Go beyond and may all the blessings of seed and fruit, earth, and stream, be upon you. Go—I say—already they are on the move."

Briary glanced back over her shoulder. Those who had thrown themselves on the river bank no longer were apart but had drawn together, and Herta was right, in that their faces were turned toward the healer's cottage.

Though what Herta had said had not seemed possible to the girl, she was certain that the healer believed her own words, was moved by fear—

Perhaps—perhaps they would also hunt down Herta if they fastened on Briary as the one who had somehow attracted ill fortune. After all, she was Herta's fosterling from birth.

It was too quick, too much, Herta's words—

"Healer—" A man's voice, those by the river were standing now, moving in their direction.

"Go!" She could not withstand Herta's command after all these years of obedience. Briary turned and ran.

As she went her clothing seemed to impede her movements, her skirts twisted about her legs to bring her down—as if such were not for her wearing. But she was still fleet of foot and, though she heard voices baying behind her as if hounds had been loosed, she gained the upper slopes, cut across recently mown fields, and then the pool was before her. The pool—and the screen. What lay behind that—who knew? Though some of the more venturesome had dived in the past to discover that there was space yawning at its foot.

Now she struggled with clothes which were more and more of a hindrance, until she at last poised to dive, her small body still human in form but clad in fine gray fur.

Down she fought her way through the water, straining to reach that dark line of the screen's edge. And then one of her hands hit against it and she seized upon the edge to pull herself forward—into what? Some crevice in which her aching lungs would betray her?

Fortune was with her: the screen was less than her struggling body in length. She was still in the water but she could fight her way up frantically, until her head burst from the pool and she could breathe again, tread water, and look about her.

On this side of the barrier the expanse of water was far less, and facing the screen was a series of bars set in the stone as if to provide handholds to draw oneself out. She swam toward the nearest and pulled her body waist high into the open, her feet finding niches below into which they fitted by instinct.

Then she was fully out and facing what lay before her, what the screen had guarded all these years. It was not a large building, rather tall and narrow, hardly wider than the open doorway that pierced its side directly before her.

There was no door—only darkness—darkness thick as a curtain. Briary, not really knowing what she did, flung back her dripping head and gave voice to a call which no human could have uttered.

There was something like an early morning fog which gathered to the right of that opening, gathered, thickened, as flesh upon bone. Then she fronted a being far stranger than her known world held.

A woman, yes, for it stood on two feet, and held before its furred body a spear. Though the jaw was somewhat elongated, and the eyes set at a slight angle in the skull, which was framed with large furred ears, it was still enough like those she had dwelt among.

"What clan, cubling?" the woman guard asked.

Briary still clung to the handhold she had above the pool.

"Lady," she quavered, "I know nothing of clans."

The woman thing leaned forward a little and looked at her more closely.

"Threb's get. We thought you long dead, cubling. Neither of the People or of the Wasters are in truth, since Threb broke hearth law and lay with a Wasters to conceive you. So the Wasters have at last thrown you out?"

"No! It was Herta—and the plague—she was afeared that they would fasten on me the cause of their deaths." Somehow Briary felt she must make this statuelike figure understand and believe her.

Quickly she spoke of the healer who had brought her life and how now her own presence might threaten with harsh judgment.

"Ever the Wasters look beyond their own follies and errors to set the consequences upon others. Stupid they are—look you!"

She turned a fraction and sent the point of her spear into that dark behind her. It split and light poured out upon them, streaming from a land beyond. In Briary arose a mighty longing to race, not from what lay behind but toward what lay ahead.

"Their plagues are borne of dirt, of their rooting in their own waste." The guardian was scornful. "This land was ours before they befouled it, and every secret it had it freely shared with us. See you this?" She stabbed forward again and then swung the spear toward Briary. Impaled on its sharp point was a thing which wriggled and squirmed and yet seemed more vine section than any animal.

"This they have torn from its rooting wherever they discovered it; for to them it was nothing, and it covered ground which they wanted for their own purposes. Yet it had its duty which it did well. As other growth struggles for water to live, so this struggles for refuse and filth. They need only leaves to lay upon their ailing and aid would come. But they are fools and worse. Now, your gate is open, cubling; I make you free to the world in which you rightfully should have been born."

But Briary's eyes were on the plant. She suddenly roused herself and made a half leap to catch the vine with one hand. It rolled itself about her arm, and it was as if she had stuck her hand into a fire. Yet still she held to it.

The woman's green eyes measured her. "There is a price," she said evenly.

Briary nodded. Of course, there would be a price. But there was Herta, who knew herbs as a mother knows her children, and in Herta's hands this might yet save the village.

"If you return to the waste world"—the woman's voice was cold—"you will turn from all which is yours, and you may well pay for it with your blood. Outlings are hunted when they are seen. And it cannot be promised this gate will open to you again."

Briary huddled on the edge of the pool, her head turned to what lay beyond that doorway—a clean land in which her kind had found refuge. But between those flowers, and distant trees, and the warm sweet wind which beckoned to her, stood the vision of a sturdy woman, her gray hair knotted at her neck, her shoulder a little crooked from the many years of carrying a healer's bag.

Perhaps it was that portion of human blood which anchored her, but Herta she could not abandon.

"For your grace, thanks, Lady." She raised the arm about which the vine still clung. "This I must take to her who brought me into life and dealt always kindly with me."

Fearing that perhaps the guard might strive to take it from her, she dived once more, heading for that passage to the world she knew.

She made the journey as quickly as she could, climbed from the outer pool, and reluctantly put on her skirt and bodice though they were quickly wet through from her fur.

It was approaching dusk; that would serve her. She slunk as fast as she could from shadow to shadow. Then she saw—the cottage door was open wide—strewn outward from it were smashed pots and bottles, torn-apart lengths of drying herbs.

"Herta!" Only fear moved her now as she leaped forward. And she found what she sought, a bundle of torn clothing about bloodied and bruised flesh. But still living—still living!

Through the night she tended the healer, trying to find among the debris the nostrums she needed, not daring to strike a light, lest she draw some villager. Oddly enough her sight seemed unhindered by the lack of any lamp, and she worked swiftly with practiced hands.

It was breaking dawn when Herta roused. She stared at Briary and then her face became a mask of fear—

"Off with you! I would not have them gut you before my very eyes."

"Listen, Heart-Held." Few times in her life had Briary used those words but she realized they had been with her forever. Swiftly she swung up her arm to which the vine still somehow clung and repeated what the guard had told her.

"Bindweed, rot guts." Herta looked at her offering in wonder. "Yes, it has always been rooted forth wherever found. Cattle eat of it and die, as do the fowl of the barnyard. And now you say that it, also, has its part and the folly has been ours. Well, enough, one can only try to do one's best."

She somehow got to her feet and Briary found that the vine slipped from her furred arms smoothly as metal. Looking at that she thought she knew its price which had never been fully stated.

"I shall go," she said in her new hoarse voice. "None shall see me with you. Certainly not all of those in the village have turned mad. You have been their ever-present aid for many seasons. Let the bindweed work but once and they shall know shame at their madness. But not if I remain."

"Where do you go?" There were seldom seen tears on Herta's cheeks.

"That lies in fortune's hands. But see it is nearly light and—" The girl shivered, "I hear voices."

Herta reached for her but she slid from the other's grasp, and somehow only the bulky clothing remained for Herta to hold. Then she was running free with the rising first wind of morning around her, up and back, up and back.

She was Outling with nothing now here to hold her unless she was weak in purpose. The gate to her own place might indeed be closed by her choice, but she had the right to go and see.

Reaching the side of the pool, Briary paused once to look down to those about Herta's cottage as the morn's light made them clear. And then she dove arrow quick and smooth into the water, down and down, until the dark edge of the screen was before her. Nor did she hesitate to see what her choice had cost her but swam on, for this was the thing she had to do.

STONISH MEN
On Crusade: More Tales of the Knights Templar (1998)
Warner Aspect

I buried Osbert this morning. It was a long, hard task, my age-aching bones complaining bitterly. But as a true Templar he deserved as good a resting place as I could contrive. I am the last now, and there have been signs that the natives are growing bolder. It will be soon that they will come to this, the first and last Templar stronghold in this strange and unknown world. I only trust that I shall be able to meet them armed, and with sword in my hand as a true Knight of the Lord. Our treasure is hidden well, and I do not think it shall ever be found.

It all began with a grim hunting, leading to torture and death. I was but a senior novice of the Temple then, Owen de Clare, professed and vowed in my native England to the finest barrier Christendom could raise against the infidels—the Poor Knights of the Temple. We grew too great, too mighty, for that thrice-damned Philip of France. He wanted to dabble his hands in our treasure chests, and the fact that we owed him no allegiance—being

answerable only to that Voice of the Almighty, the Pope himself—
irked his arrogant pride and outreach for power.

They came upon us without warning. It had been subtly
and secretly planned, and the Pope himself helped in the beastly
death hunt that was turned against us. Many of us died by fire
and torture.

But our Temple, a hardly known one, was on the seacoast
and we had ships to hand. Yes, we had hunted the Infidel by sea
as well as land. I was with the Knight Commander when he saw
there was nothing ahead but our taking. And it was to me, yet a
boy scarce out of training, that he entrusted our treasure. Not the
gold and gems the king's butchers wanted, but the Casket. Sealed
shut it securely and always was, save at certain Great Days when
it was revealed only to those who were full sworn.

"Go," he ordered me. "Take the way over the rooftops. You are
still agile and sturdy enough to dare those. Get to the harbor and
the *True Spirit* and give the order to make sail at once, lest the last
of our brothers be caught in this trap."

Go I did, and that climb over the rooftops was sometimes as
perilous as a seldom-dared mountain path. But it was made, and
I carried the Casket to the *True Spirit.* As with all others of our
fleet (we swept the Infidels from the inner seas even as we had
overwhelmed them on land), we set sail.

Hope held for us refuge among the Scots, some of which wore
our device. Thus we set a course out of the inner sea and to the
north.

But it would seem that the wrath of the Dark and the Evil still
stalked us, for we were caught in the greatest of storms, our small
fleet scattered.

The winds drove us hard. Three men were carried overboard
by the waves. But the power of that which lay within the Casket
brought us through—though our course the sailing master could

not guess. In the end, when we were lacking in water and food and might die aboard our craft, land was sighted to the west. To that we headed, coming at last into a narrow inlet between shores that sloped sharply upward and were crowned by the greatest trees I had ever seen.

We came to anchor there—forever. Our ship had been so battered that we dared not turn again to the sea. This was the edge of the world itself, and perhaps we were the first of our kind to set foot on it.

There was a sharp, steep climb using a narrow ledge to the cliff top, and we stood wonderingly among the trees. Not far away a deer raised its head to look at us inquiringly, as if our kind were unknown to it. Osbert, my sword brother, was quick of eye and ready with bow, bringing it down.

So we filled our bellies, and drank from a stream seeking the sea. Thus we became wanderers, ever seeking a place we could hold.

For there were men after all in that forest: strange, half-naked of body. They would have brought us down. However, their stone-tipped arrows, the flint-pointed spears, made no dents in our armor, which we had worked hard to keep at its best.

Thus using the stream as a guide, always aware of the need for careful watch, we traveled westward, seeking a resting place. For each of us in his heart knew that there would be no returning.

With us went the Casket of the treasure, each man being honored to carry it in turn. It gave a core of strength that banished our despair, for we believed that it was indeed our leader in some way.

Ever we sought a place that might be easy to defend. Two of our company we had lost along the way. One was brought down by a huge bear that only the ax of Wulf could end. And Piers ate some berries that were the seeds of a demon that racked him into the quiet of death.

Then we found what was our goal—an isle in a wide river. There were rocks on that river island; and we labored, knight, novice, and seaman, to build our crude fort. The heart of it was the place of that treasure that had been given us to guard.

Years passed; the commander died of a coughing rheum, two who went hunting in the woodlands never returned. We were a handful, still faithful to our trust. By the Blood shed by our Precious Lord, we so held to our faith and honor.

So we dwindled, and today I have buried my sword brother, who was as dear to me as blood kin; and I stand alone—to wait for the coming of the savages who have showed more and more boldness. There will be none to bury me, yet I hold my honor to the end, for that which we guarded is safe and in a place where no naked savage can find it. Perhaps in time—all things are ordered by our Lord—there will come one fit and needful to take up the task again.

They were a small party to dare the river, though recent reports had not suggested that hostiles had made forays in this direction. Somewhere ahead of their clumsy craft, which rode the current erratically, was the outpost of Deerfield. Three of them were aboard: Galvin Rodder, rafter, trapper, guide, or whatever he chose to turn hand to, had been wary all morning, sniffing the air like a hound on trace. He spoke to his companions, Matthew Hawkins, man of God, and his son Owen:

"Preacher, we-uns may be in for trouble. An' I'd like firm ground under me when it comes. Maybe that there isle up ahead. That there they say is a ghost place. The Injuns swear it was held by the Stonish Men."

Matthew Hawkins was alert at that moment more to Rodder's hint of legend than to what might be behind them. Though he was pledged to bring the Word to heathen souls, he could not always restrain his own private hobby of gathering all the queer stories and legends that seemed to abound in this land of trees hardy enough to resist only the most determined of invaders.

"Stonish Men?" he now queried.

Already the raft was heading toward the island where ledges of rock broke through the general green.

"They was supposed to be hereabouts. The Injuns swear as how they had stone bodies—no arrow nor spear could bring them down. I tell you, Preacher, we-uns were not the first white skins to travel west—there's a capful of tales like to this."

Behind him Owen Hawkins was listening, but he was more intent on watching the shores on either side. His hand tightened on his rifle. Maybe it wasn't proper for a man of God to go armed, but nothing said his son, who had taken no such vows, could not make himself well acquainted with the best weapons he could afford.

He had little interest in the old stories his father liked and sought. Most of it must be rubbish. This land hid far more forceful dangers, and that odd feeling he always had as a warning was stirring.

From the cloaking of forest behind them came the boom of a shot. Galvin grunted as a red splotch appeared high on his shoulder.

"So they's nosed out our passin', an' now they is ready to make their move," he gasped. "This here raft ain't no place to make a stand—it's gotta be th' island. We got no chance in Hell . . . pardon, Preacher . . . of outrunnin' them. An' in the open, they can pick us off just as they please."

"The island will prove a shelter, then?"

"I ain't sayin' yes and I ain't sayin' no—it's a maybe thing. But I sure don't want to lose what hair I've got me left!"

He poled their unwieldy craft at a faster swing, the red spot on his shoulder glistening in the sun.

"Head to the right, behind that point there." Owen found himself saying those words as if repeating some suggestion from another.

Galvin's bushy eyebrows lifted as he demanded: "How come you knew there was this here place waiting?" They had slid behind an outstretched hook of rock stretched like a beckoning finger and were certainly, for the moment, no longer clear targets.

Owen flushed. "I didn't know," he protested.

But Galvin had no more time to ask questions as he swung the unwieldy craft into what did seem almost like a pocket-sized harbor. They united to pull the raft halfway up the bank. Then his father insisted that Galvin have his wound, not a deep one, tended. As much as preaching, Matthew Hawkins knew something of the healing art.

However, once the task of transferring their stores ashore was accomplished, Owen had to yield to that which had pulled at him stronger and stronger from the moment he set foot on this isle. He headed inland with the skill of one who knew exactly where he was.

Rough stone walls confronted him. No redskin he had ever heard of did that kind of building. Most of it had tumbled this way and that through the years, but enough remained to mark out a square. He jumped one of the fallen walls and stood in that square. For a moment he was giddy, as if something had struck him on the head, and then he turned—someone might have caught him by the shoulder to urge him so—to the one portion of the wall that sturdily resisted the attacks of time.

When Galvin and his father caught up with him, Owen was down on his knees, running his hands back and forth to brush away moss and reveal the lines deep graven there.

It was a cross slightly different from any he had seen before. A grave? It might well be. Then his father's shadow covered the patch he had cleared.

"What have we here?" Matthew Hawkins went on his knees beside his son. "Spanish? Never heard they came this far north—"

But that same force that had brought Owen here set him now to digging swiftly—and with all the strength he could summon—at the edges of that crossed stone.

Galvin had loaded all three rifles and had them well to hand.

"Good-enough place," he observed.

There came the call of a jay, and he stiffened. "Seems like that there old story isn't goin' to help us, Reverend. You and the boy better get to the guns. We've got the best cover in this part anyhow."

The stone moved at Owen's tugging and then fell to the ground, barely missing his knees. The space within was small, but he could see the box inside, and eagerly he pulled at it.

"Well, I'll be!" Galvin gave the find a long glance, and then his head snapped around as a birdcall came from some rocks.

The trailing party was slow to show, or perhaps some last remnants of superstition kept them from charging. Owen hefted the heavy rifle. The box was between his feet, and now in the full light it gleamed and sparks of light made patterns at the corners of the lid.

There followed no time for treasure hunting. Their trackers suddenly took heart and came leaping into view. There was one among them who wore a tattered hunting shirt, and whose greased-back hair was a dirty red. A renegade.

Perhaps they never had a chance from the very start, but they took out two of the attackers before they were pulled down in turn and looked up into wolfish faces dabbed with paint. Better dead than captive, Owen knew, and shivered.

"Wall, now." It was the renegade who stopped and caught up the box. "Got yourself a pretty, boy. You won't git no chance at it now. I, Hawk Haverage, gits this."

They were already pulling that about. Galvin's eyes were closed, and there was a thick smear of blood down the side of his face. Owen could see only his father's feet being bound with rawhide thongs.

"Let's see what's in this pretty of yourn." Haverage swung it back and forth by his ear, listening. Perhaps for a rattle of contents. Then he applied the point of his knife to the edge of the box, prying it up on all four sides.

The Indians had stopped their own looting to draw closer. Finally the lid rose, and Haverage looked confounded.

"Old sandal. Look, it's old enough to be just dust." He turned the box upside down and shook it. Dust did come out, but it did not fall. Rather, it spread and thickened—thickened enough to form bodies. Bodies bursting from that fog. There was a shrill screeching as the Indians took off, scrambling wildly over the broken walls.

Haverage was of stronger stuff. He flung the knife he still held at the nearest figure. It struck true enough, and Owen was sure that he heard the ring of metal against metal before it fell.

They were no longer things of shadows, those who gathered here, but rather like some of the pictures he had seen in those books his father sometimes found to borrow. Knights!

Knights from a different world and time. The leader had reached Haverage. A sword as solid as any normal steel swung up and came down. Though his body showed no visible wound, the renegade collapsed and lay still.

Then that silent company out of time gathered around the box. They knelt, holding their swords by the blade before them. Owen could see their lips move, though he caught no sound, and he believed they were praying.

Slowly they arose and then they marched into the fog that had been hanging like a curtain. There was a feeling of withdrawal, as if something utterly precious had come to an end.

The fog was gone, and with it the knights. Haverage's body lay unmoving by the wall, but his father said sharply:

"Owen, that knife, can you get it and cut yourself free?"

It was an effort, but he achieved that at last and, making a wide circle about the box, went to free his father. Galvin groaned and struggled up on one elbow with his bound hands, which Owen quickly freed, to reach his head.

Once more Matthew tended a wound that, as the blood was washed away, proved to be less serious than they had feared. But instead of watching his father's labors, Owen kept his eyes upon the box that lay by Haverage's inert body.

Finally he made himself move to pick it up. Its interior was clear of dust, but there was writing engraved on the lid. He knew a little Latin, all his father could drive into his head on occasion when there was time for schooling.

His father came up behind him. "Now that has the look of a Popish thing—"

Galvin was sitting up, and now he said weakly: "What's it for, Reverend? Looks like gold, don't it?"

"They were used to hold holy things—bones of saints and the like."

Owen pushed it into his father's hands. "There's writing on it—Latin, maybe."

His father studied the engraving, carefully brushing away a film of dust from the lines.

"Where His Holy Feet pressed let all remember the courage of Our Lord." Then Matthew pointed to a last symbol. "A Knights Templar seal. They were always thought to have found great treasures of the spirit in the Holy Land, and guarded such to the end. . . ."

"But Haverage said there was only an old sandal inside. . . ." Owen said slowly. That odd sense of being one with someone else grew stronger and then was gone.

" 'Where His Holy Feet pressed.' Remember your scripture, boy. When Our Lord was sent to the cross, did not the soldiers on guard throw dice for His robe—and perhaps His sandals? Only our Holy Father knows the secrets of this world. Templars came here fearing the wrath of those roused against them. They were the Stonish Men in truth, keeping guard until death. But today we saw them return, that their treasure not fall into evil hands."

His father knelt, and Owen followed quickly. With the ease of long practice his father spoke those lines intended to ease the passing of those who died in the Light—far from home—deep in time.

Owen did not even realize that he was moving until his hands closed about the Casket and he was kneeling, to set it in its old hiding place. He fumbled with the heavy stone and urged it back into position. It was empty, but it had once held very much. It, too, must not be any longer troubled by the greed of men.

CHURCHYARD YEW

A Dangerous Magic (1999) Edited by Denise Little, Published by DAW

"Yes, yes—well—I'll see—"

It was very plain to Ilse Harveling that her hostess was between irritation and embarrassment, fighting to break into the flow of speech on the other end of the phone line.

"Yes." That came with sharp firmness—Louise was losing control. "I shall let you know." She snapped the phone back on its cradle forcibly. "People! Really—"

Ilse waited for her to return to the small table in the bay window where they had been sharing a leisurely breakfast. *"People!"* she exploded for the second time.

"So—we have people, my dear. And it is plain that something you dislike has been asked of you." Ilse slid the jam spoon back into its pot. The morning sun was bright across the table, it was a good morning—yet—there was a shadowing which was not that from any cloud.

Louise plumped herself into her seat, beginning to fiddle with the dishes before her, moving a plate, a cup and saucer a fraction. So far she had not met Ilse's level gaze. Then her lips pursed as if she tasted something sour.

"It is an imposition. I will not allow it!"

Ilse waited. Louise was more upset than she had ever seen her.

"Marj Lawrence—she wants you to come to lunch at Hex House."

"And this is an invitation which you find so very upsetting. Why is that?"

"Because Marj—she thinks they have a ghost—or something wrong. Of all the stupid things! It's my fault. I'll admit that. I told Marj once about the time in Bradenton when you helped old Mrs. Templer. Jack always does say I talk too much and this time it's caught up with me. But you are not going to be pulled into anything. Of course I feel sorry for Marj and Tom—they invested most of their savings in that place. There were some old stories—but goodness knows that James Hartle lived there all his life and there was never any trouble. It was only when they bought the place and turned it into a bed and breakfast and that lawyer died of a heart attack. Then people began talking—"

Louise planted her elbows on the table, supporting her chin in her cupped hands.

"People," she continued, "have heart attacks all the time in all kinds of places. It was just hard luck for the Lawrences that this Mark Walden had his in one of their bedrooms. The doctor said there was no question about the cause of death. They could just have shut up that room and forgotten about it for a while. Only all the talk started. Just a lot of gossip which should be laughed at. Maybe some of it was even this Walden man's own fault—he was poking around asking questions—seems he thought he had some roots here—of course, with that name—but it's been over a hundred years!"

Louise paused for breath and Ilse took the opportunity to ask: "So there was indeed a story. Why was the house given such an unlucky name in the first place?"

"Well, it was called the Hartle place when the Lawrences bought it. But Marj is a local history buff, and she started to trace its history. So—there you are," Louise said triumphantly. "It is partly her own poking around which must have started the talk. She thought what she found out was romantic! Ghosts!" Louise uttered a sound which was not quite a snort.

"And there was a recent death—it is this, then, that has started talk?" persisted Ilse.

"A man died of a heart attack. Now most of the valley is talking about it and the Lawrences are not prospering. But they are not going to drag you into this, I promise you, Ilse! You came here for a rest, and we have things to do which are cheerful and fun. Tomorrow there is that auction at the Brevar farm and the old lady is said to have just trunks and trunks of stuff which have not been opened for years. We could find some real treasures."

Louise's mouth turned up. She was a collector of vintage clothing and the thoughts of what might be found in those old trunks drew her attention momentarily away from the woes of Marj Lawrence.

"There ought to be some old beaded things—just what you are looking for, Ilse. Mrs. Brevar inherited from her mother and her great-aunt, and her grandmother, and none of them ever threw anything away."

"An outing to be enjoyed, Louise. But for the moment, please, satisfy my curiosity concerning this affair at Hex House."

Louise frowned. "It's about the oldest house around here. The story is that it was built on a direct grant from the king in the old days. You know that the south end of the valley was settled by some odd church people from Austria. Not Amish—but something of the same order—very strict but excellent farmers.

"In that day Hex House was rather like an inn—travelers stopped there. The church crowd would have nothing to do with anyone from the inn. In fact, there was bad feeling. Honestly, Ilse, I really don't know much of the story. It had been forgotten until Marj got her certainly unbright idea of capitalizing on its history. You would have to ask her—Only you are not going to! She is not going to bother you."

"I do not think that the term 'bother' enters into this, Louise," said the other slowly. "It might be well to lunch with your friend and hear what is troubling her so greatly."

"No! Ilse, she has no right to ask you—"

"That is not the truth, Louise. I did not hear your friend's side of that telephone conversation, but I think you were speaking with someone deeply distressed. I do not believe that there is any thought of publicity in Mrs. Lawrence's desire to speak with me."

Louise was shaking her head.

"You know, dear friend," Ilse continued, "that I have been granted certain gifts. When one is so favored—or burdened—there is also a duty to use those for the relief of others. I think it is wise that we do accept this invitation. Perhaps it is all nothing as you believe, but on the chance that my talent is needed, I cannot say no. And—" Ilse hesitated. She was not watching Louise now but looking beyond her into the garden. There was a strangeness about her stare as if she could sight something of importance if she would try hard enough. "And, if that invitation was for today, then I think it best we accept."

Louise's face was flushed. "I am more embarrassed than I can tell you. I do talk too much and so I am caught—and you with me. All right."

She got up so abruptly from the table that it rocked a fraction and a spoon fell to the floor. Paying no attention to that, Louise went to the phone, dialed with an impatient flick of the finger, and relayed their acceptance.

"At least you'll get to see some of the southern valley," she said when she put the receiver down, though that thought did not appear to cheer her much.

The southern end of the valley did have its appeal as Louise drove slowly along the narrow back roads, ditches on either side, the verges thick with the berry-shaped flowers of red clover and the tall lace-crowned stalks of Queen Anne's Lace. Wild morning glories with their pallid blooms patched the strangling vines clumping on the old fences. Here and there could be sighted a red barn or a low-roofed house.

"Stuben land," Louise waved with a gesture wide enough to include most of what they could see.

"Stuben?"

"That's what the north valley calls it. I told you about those church people who settled here—they kept aloof from everyone, did all necessary communication through one man—Johanus Stuben. So everyone thought of them collectively as Stubens. Oh, here's their church—looks more like a barn, doesn't it? That was part of their beliefs: no steeples, no ornamentation."

Louise stopped the car before a building now sagged of roof, its narrow windows shuttered by weathered boards nailed to shut out time and life. It did resemble a barn but lacked the usual quaint appeal of those structures.

"The sect has died out?" Ilse studied the sober, grayish block. Even the common field flowers appeared to shun its vicinity. Only sun-browned tangles of grass grew sparsely about.

"Oh, a long time ago. The younger generations broke with the strict rules and most of them left. I think there are one or two of the old families that still have descendants hereabouts, but there are no more Stubens. I'll turn back on the highway here, and Hex House is only a short distance on."

It was exactly on the stroke of noon when they pulled into the parking lot of Hex House. Save for a dusty van and a small, aged Volvo, theirs was the only vehicle, which made the space seem almost deserted. Once outside the car Ilse stood for a long moment surveying the structure facing her.

The present parking lot was cobbled, perhaps a restoration of its former paving when this building might have served as a stage station. There were smaller outbuildings on either side, all constructed of the same gray native stone cut from a nearby quarry. The main house was two stories high with deep-set windows flanked by newly painted shutters. A door, which had a shallow overhang as a weather guard, showed the glint of gleaming, well-polished brass at both knocker and latch. There were certainly no signs of dilapidation, but rather of careful and knowledgeable restoration.

Yet it was also apparent that the house was very, very old and had settled well into the land which formed its foundation. Ilse's head was up, and more than her eyes were questing. Time, as she well knew, could encase and even nourish that which was not of the daily world. Disturbances of the kind she had met in the past flourished in such places.

"Oh, Louise!"

That polish-enhanced door had been flung open before they had advanced under the overhang of the half porch. The woman who stood there was of middle years but as well kept up as her surroundings—in a discreet manner, so she made an appearance neither brittlely smart, nor dowdily out of fashion.

Her fine hair was a silver cap cut very short, and she wore a black-and-white-checked shirt crisp from laundering, with well-cut black slacks. Her skin, however, had a yellowish tinge and there were dark shadows beneath her rather prominent blue eyes which even the large-lensed glasses she wore did not conceal.

"Dr. Harveling!" She hailed Ilse in the same nervously enthusiastic voice as that with which she had greeted Louise. "It was so very good of you to come—so very kind—" For a moment she paused, her lips tightened as if she were fighting for control.

Ilse knew fear when she saw it eroding another. She smiled and held out her hand, closing it about the nervously fluttering one of her hostess.

"I am Ilse Harveling, yes. And you are Mrs. Lawrence who has brought this old place back to life."

"Life!" the other interrupted her. "No," it was as if she gave herself an order, not addressed her guests. "We shall have time— Oh, but I am so glad you could come! Eliza is ready to serve us what this locality calls a 'spread'—she has a wealth of old recipes—her mother was from a Stuben family and, if they did not allow any pleasures for the eye or the ear, they did not stint at the table."

She led them on down a short passage into a long room which had once been the kitchen. The huge fireplace still had its spit and pot chains in place. The door to the brick side oven looked ready to be opened for instant use.

There were two chairs at the deep arch of the hearth opening. A long dresser with an enticing wealth of old blue-and-white wear stood against the wall. But the larger part of the room was occupied by half a dozen small tables each covered with a blue-and-white-checked cloth, the attending chairs bearing matching cushions.

Ilse and Louise were firmly steered to one of the tables, urged on by the hostess as if they were famine refugees who must be fed at once. As soon as they were seated, Mrs. Lawrence vanished through an opposite door, probably to summon the "spread" before they could really adjust to their surroundings.

Louise's eyebrows rose a fraction. "Well?"

Again Ilse had been studying what lay about her. "Your friend is a badly frightened person. She is not like herself today. Is she?"

Louise shook her head. "I never saw her this way before. And I have been here a number of times. Jack and I often have Sunday dinner here. They've been open for almost a year. It's a treasure house, really. I can't believe that—"

She was silent as Marj Lawrence returned, pushing a table cart on which there were a number of dishes.

It appeared that Mrs. Lawrence was determined to play the part of hostess—during her time away she had once more gained full control—and as they lunched (and very well), she kept her flow of subject matter away from any problem. There was no mention of a shadowed past, and certainly not of any fatality within these walls.

As they lingered over coffee, Ilse quietly guided the conversation with simple questions concerning restoration problems, and she mentioned their having seen the deserted Stuben church. Marj Lawrence plunged in, into what was undoubtedly one of her deepest interests.

"Yes, the Stubens are all gone. Their settlement really lasted only for a couple of generations. Johanus Stuben was a prophet of the old school, and his successor, Rueben Straus, tried to carry on but they turned against him. Rueben was a queer mixture. Look here!"

She jumped up from the table and went to a ledge running across the mantel, to return holding an object she set down before Ilse.

"Now what do you think of that?"

It was a carved candlestick of aged wood, worn a little by years of handling. But its thickly patterned display of intertwined vines and leaves was still in strong relief. As Ilse picked it up and turned it around, she could see minute additions to those vines and leaves which were only visible to the seeking eye. Here was a face peeping from under a leaf—a face which was subtly nonhuman; there a weird insect was in half-hiding.

She cupped it with both hands and closed her eyes for a moment. No, she was not mistaken. Though it had never been used as she first feared, the skill which had shaped this had known secret things. As it was, it held no menace, but that menace could have been called forth.

"This was made by Straus—the pattern is foreign, perhaps Black Forest, perhaps Austrian."

"Rueben Straus made it right here." Marj Lawrence's hand swung perhaps to indicate this room. "He wasn't one of the first Stubens, though they say he was related to old Johanus. He and his sister, Hanna, came later. He was a hunchback and couldn't farm, but he earned his way as a carpenter and by making things like that. Only that one he made specially as a gift for Gyles Walden, the man who owned this house.

"Hanna Straus came to be cook here. By all the old gossip she was more than a cook. Gyles had a roving eye, but no wish for a wife. Only the Strauses did not believe that. Hanna worked on filling the dower chest Rueben made for her, and he did what he could to provide her with a dowry.

"But when it came down to the actual calling in of the preacher, Gyles went off on a trip. He came back from the east with a wife— a rich widow—and she soon sent the Strauses packing."

Suddenly Mrs. Lawrence's flow of words slackened. "But all that ancient history can't have anything to do with—"

All her animation vanished as fear again showed in her eyes.

"Please," Ilse said quietly. She pushed aside the candlestick and put her hand gently on Mrs. Lawrence's wrist as the other woman stared at her with an almost childlike plea. "Tell us what you know of the past. It may have more bearing on your trouble than you think."

"But it can't. After all, people who died more than a century ago—"

"And who were those dead?"

"The story is that Hanna drowned herself—she was going to have Gyles' child. And Rueben buried her in the dower chest he had made for her. He quarreled with the Stubens, and they threw him out, saying that he had dealings with the devil. He was found dead in the woods, and they said he had fought with Gyles. But no one ever tried to find out.

"Oh—" she was flushed and it was plain she was even more upset, "—maybe it is all my fault! I thought it was so clever to go hunting down all the old stories. I wanted to make a booklet, you see—just like those they sell at the old English houses open for visitors. There was the curse rumor, too—"

"A curse?" The quiet question stemmed the flow of words for a second. Marj Lawrence had dropped her eyes and was looking down at the crumbs on the plate before her.

"There was an old letter—we found it while we were cleaning out the long attic. That was a mess, and it took us just days—but the things we found—!" She touched the candlestick. "It was like a treasure hunt."

"The letter?" Ilse drew her back to face a subject it was very plain she did not want to discuss.

"Yes, well, it was sent to Gyles' wife after she had gone to New York. It was almost a threat—all about how her husband had paid, but the price not enough. It warned her against coming back here, but she did—only long enough to sell the house to the first of the Hartles."

"And the price Gyles was supposed to have paid?" persisted Ilse.

"He died—very suddenly—in his bed. Probably a heart—" Mrs. Lawrence's eyes went wide, and she stared at Ilse. "A heart attack," she finished in a voice hardly above a whisper.

"And the Hartles—they lived here for several generations, did they not? Was there any trouble recorded in their day—any stories?"

Marj Lawrence shook her head. "There's been nothing wrong. And we've been here for nearly two years. There have been workmen all over the place since we opened and after—and nothing except the things which always cause trouble: plumbing, heating, leaks.

"I—I didn't go ahead with the booklet idea; somehow I didn't want to. But we did give it the name people called it before the Hartles took over. 'Hex House' was so different. And everything was going so well until that Mark Walden showed up!"

"Mark Walden—Gyles Walden—there was a connection?"

"Maybe. He said something about wanting to see some of the older places around the valley. He was pleasant enough, but there was something about him—he was very reserved and stayed to himself. The police asked questions afterward, they and his partner—where he had gone and what he had done—but nobody had really paid any attention. The partner said he had been engaged in a big law case which had been before the court for a long time, and after it was over he decided he needed a rest. Somehow he ended up here." Once more her gust of speech died.

"Mark Walden . . ." Ilse repeated slowly.

"You know him?" Louise demanded.

"*Of* him. He was a criminal lawyer of standing in some circles. So Mr. Walden died of a heart attack?"

"Yes. He had left a note on the hall desk to be called at seven in the morning, as he wanted an early start to return home. The church fair was the day before, and I saw him there. He bought some old books and a cane—something he certainly had no real use for. When he didn't answer Tom's knock on the door in the morning, we waited a while, but he had been so insistent that we call him that Tom finally used the pass key. He was lying across the bed—dead. Tom called Dr. Albright, and the doctor got the police. They asked questions, but the autopsy proved it was his heart."

"You question that?" Ilse was aware that this volatility had been born of fear. Those hands twisting together, the eyes which no longer met hers, were reactions she well recognized.

"His—his face—" Marj Lawrence swung around in her chair as if to elude Ilse as much as she could.

"The face?" prompted Ilse.

"I—I saw—but Tom says that I just imagined it. I was afraid to say anything afterward to the doctor. By the time he got here it was—changed. Maybe—maybe I did just imagine it. But then why do I keep on having those horrible dreams?"

"You have dreamed? But first tell me what was it in Mr. Walden's face which frightened you so?"

"It looked—he looked as if he had been caught by some kind of monster. Oh, it does sound stupid. But he looked so afraid. And one of his hands had clawed at his own throat. That cane he had bought at the fair was in his other hand, one end of it caught at the top of the bed. But by the time the doctor came the horrible look had smoothed away. Only then the dreams began."

"Yes, the dreams," Ilse said. "What about the dreams?"

"Always the same thing. I am standing in the hallway right outside the door to that room. I have to open it, although I am afraid." She shivered. "It is dark inside, but still I can see. It isn't a room anymore at all but like a wood of trees with their limbs moving back and forth—reaching—I've managed to keep quiet about it, especially around Tom. He'd think I had lost my mind. But I can't keep on!" Her voice arose shrilly, sliding into hysteria.

Ilse was out of her chair, leaning over the woman, holding both those hands in a firm, restraining grip.

"Louise, in my bag—the small bottle with the silver top." Her tone held authority enough to send the other scrambling to obey.

"Twist off the lid and hold the bottle under her nose!"

As Louise obeyed Marj took a deep breath—half choked, as a strong scent filled the room.

"Again." Ilse kept her grip on the woman's wrists. "Take a deep breath and hold it as long as you can." She watched sharp-eyed as the other followed her instructions. The taut body began to relax. Some of the flush faded from the other's cheeks. The moisture which had gathered in the corners of her eyes formed tears.

"I'm—I'm all right." She jerked to free herself from Ilse's grip. A moment later she added, "I guess you think I'm an idiot—dreaming dreams such as that."

"Mrs. Lawrence," Ilse returned quietly, "you were moved to ask me here because of a danger which your spirit sensed, even if your mind cannot identify it. This is a troubled house, and the heart of that trouble must be found and cleansed. You spoke earlier of a curse—such are often a source for scoffing these days but, as with all things, there is often a kernel of truth at the heart of such stories. I wish now to see this room which is the center of your evil dreams and which has already sheltered death."

Without another word, but as might an obedient child, Marj Lawrence pushed away from the table and led the way into a hall from which a staircase led up past paneled walls polished into life. There was another hall above, and the shut doors of what must be a half dozen rooms faced each other across a strip of tightly woven rag carpet. It was to the last of these that Mrs. Lawrence brought them, throwing open that door but standing aside so that they could enter the room or not as they pleased.

It was not a dark room, nor did it look in any way threatening. The walls had been papered with a pleasing design of green vines, showing here and there clusters of pale lavender flowers. There was a framed sampler on the wall and what might be authentic old engravings of European style, picturing ancient houses and forest-bound castles.

One wall gave center room to a tall, free-standing wardrobe of pre-closet days, the mirror door of which, though polished, was slightly misted by age. A more modern chest of drawers flanked the doorway. By the window in the right wall, which had short drapery repeating the vine pattern, was an inlaid table on which stood a lamp, and a chair, the arms and back of which were heavily carved, cushioned in green plush.

There was also a small bedside table with a very modern reading lamp in place beside a pile of books. Another chair, less impressive than the first, with chintz cushions promising more comfort, was drawn up by the second window, which broke the wall against which the head of the bed had been placed. At the foot of that piece of furniture itself was a dower chest painted with an age-faded pattern.

However, the bed dominated the room. The head, though well above six feet in height, was not solid. Instead, wands of dark wood had been woven like wreaths or vines. Yet there were thicker places where a number of those entwined by some freak of pattern and those portions showed evidence of carving.

The foot was not so tall but was of the same workmanship. And the wood, which showed no evident dust, still appeared overset with a filmy cast.

Mrs. Lawrence made no effort to join Ilse and Louise. And Louise herself stepped in no farther than just within the door.

It was Ilse who advanced to within touching distance of the bed.

"You didn't have that here before—I didn't see it at the open house." Louise's voice was almost accusatory.

"It was one of our finds in the attic. We had a hard time cleaning it up. It had just been jammed back in the corner and was covered with dust."

"It is made of yew," Ilse said as if she had been paying no attention to them. " 'Churchyard yew' they used to name it, for it was mainly planted there."

Delicately, as if her touch might disturb something better not alerted, Ilse's fingers continued to trace the curves and hollows of those wands. Her head came up a fraction; she might have been questing as a hunter for a scent.

"There is something here, yes. Rage, hate, fear. But it sleeps."

Suddenly she drew back the hand which had rubbed the ancient wood. "By the same hand—this was also made by Rueben Straus. His mark is graven into this wood even as it stamps the candlestick and—something else—"

Ilse moved now to the head of the bed. It was made up ready for use with an intrically patterned quilt for coverlet. Ilse slipped off her shoes and climbed close to that billow of quilt marking the hidden pillows, bending her head very close to the carving. Once more she raised her right hand and finger traced a path of weaving.

"A wedding bed." It was more as if she murmured to herself than addressed those with her. "Symbols for good fortune, for fruitfulness, blessings—all here." She shook her head. "This was meant to bless, made by one who had knowledge, old, old learning. This," she moved a fingertip across one of those knotted spots, "is the moon waxing, bringing life. Here is the heart wish in full. Yes, this was meant to bless, not to blast."

She moved back a little but still knelt facing the headboard. Now she raised both hands to her temples, her eyes closed, her body tense. Then, as if a finger's snapping had aroused her she turned to the two at the door.

"A blessing which is poisoned by a curse—so twice potent. There is something locked here which I cannot reach without deep seeking. Mrs. Lawrence, is the room exactly the same as it was on that night of death? What changes may have been made?"

Marj Lawrence came reluctantly into the chamber and looked around.

"Everything is the same—except his things are gone, of course. And the bed linen, that was changed." She gave a small shiver. "That quilt I bought at the Kellermans' sale last spring, and it was the right size, so I put it in here. We had not used it before."

"Otherwise all is the same?" Ilse persisted, sliding down from the bed.

"Quite the same."

Ilse's right arm moved; her hand, palm flat, was held out before her as if to sense some energy arising from the floor. She had reached the wardrobe and stopped, in mid-step, her hand swinging as if it had been ensnared by a cord and jerked in that direction. In a moment she had the mirrored door open and was looking within. Then she went down on one knee to feel along the floor. There sounded a rattling and she brought into light a cane.

The length of most of its surface was smooth, but the top had been carved into a twist of vine. As Ilse swung her find into a patch of full sunlight they could all see a small head which was nearly concealed by a curve of that carven vine.

"Made with love," Ilse said softly, "made for a gift with love and admiration. She who wished it loved deeply. Then—" she frowned. Her finger pointed but did not quite touch the shaft immediately below that carved head, "This!"

"What?" Louise pushed forward to look over her friend's shoulder.

"Something of the dark—perhaps meant as a warning—or a threat—"

"But that is the cane Mr. Walden bought at the fair—at the white elephant table!" Marj joined them. "How did it get here? I thought we packed it with all his other things. He was quite taken with it—told Tom it was a real bargain. It must have fallen down in there and been forgotten."

"This was in his hand when he was found?"

"Oh, yes. The top of it was caught in one of those twists of vine on the headboard. He must have been looking at it when— when—" her voice dwindled.

"Yes—when. Now I must tell you this, Mrs. Lawrence. In itself there is only a hint of darkness about the bed, in this cane. Together—together there could be a change. So—we shall see. I must spend the night here and, with what I know, try to find the core of this evil."

Louise protested at once and, more slowly, Marj Lawrence offered some token opposition which Ilse swept away. It was decided that she would return later and check into the disturbed room.

"Tom wants to just shut it up," Mrs. Lawrence said. "But it is better to know the truth, isn't it?"

"Evil is as a spot of rot upon an apple," returned Ilse. "Unless it is cut away, it will spread. You do not want to merely lock the door upon something which may taint your whole house."

Louise continued to protest as they drove back to her home until Ilse said firmly: "I told you, my dear, those who are gifted must return what is asked of them. Now, if you really wish to be of service to me, let me ready myself for what is to be done."

She helped herself to the contents of various herb containers, many of them her own gifts to her hostess, and brewed a pot of a dark liquid which she strained and drank at intervals during the afternoon. She chose only a small portion of fruit for her supper before she refused Louise's offer to accompany her back to Hex House. Marj Lawrence welcomed her eagerly.

"We have no guests tonight, and Tom is at a lodge meeting. I'm all ready—"

"No, Mrs. Lawrence," Ilse spoke with authority which could not be questioned. "This I must do myself. If you wish, you may remain in the hallway, but otherwise it is not safe. This is a force which is malign—it has already killed."

She turned on the lamp by the bed, focusing it directly on the pillows where she folded back the quilt. On the sill of each window she placed a small packet. Then, from her overlarge tote, she brought out a pair of blue candles which she set in holders Marj Lawrence provided and placed on the dower chest at the foot of the bed.

Having made a minute inspection of the now-bared sheets and pillows, Ilse lifted the cane which she rubbed for its full length with a rank smelling cloth. Now she again busied herself with the bedclothes. The pillows she put in a straight line lengthwise down the bed and then pulled the sheet up over them.

The cane was laid carefully beside that semblance of a body. From the tote Ilse brought out a small tightly closed flask. She wet her fingertip with its contents and brushed across the top hump of pillow which might be a head.

"By the White Way, The Light Way, the Right Way, here rests one Walden. So be it by all that stands against the Dark!"

A snap of light switch and the only illumination now came from the candles. Yet it was enough to give full sight of what was happening.

Ilse had withdrawn to stand at the foot of the bed squarely between the candles. She could only improvise, and she had. But now she centered all her inner consciousness on what lay before her. Almost in the subdued light it did seem a body rested there.

She shut out the thought of time. Time was born from the acts of humankind—it might mean nothing to what lurked here. *Lurked*—yes. She was right—there was building that feeling of another presence, of age-tattered but still-strong emotions: fear, rage—hate?

The cane sprang like a piece of iron seeking a strong magnet. Its head clicked against one of the knots in the headboard. Then—down that connecting rod speared a thrust of darkness— as thick as one of the wands from which it had been born.

It struck against the top pillow and at the same time there belched forth a stench of old rottenness, a wave of unhuman menace beyond all bounds of sanity.

Ilse's lips moved in words as old as time's meaning could be measured. With both her hands she raised the old christening flask to her teeth and worried out the stopper. Then, holding the bottle in a fierce grip of fingers laced tightly together, she threw its contents at the heaving mass on the bed.

There came such a burst of flame, such a roaring in her head, as if not only in the room—such a scream of heart-piercing anger as made her sway with its force.

That threshing on the bed stopped; the cane lay across the rounded covers. What had been here was gone.

"What was it? Will—will it come again?" Marj Lawrence crouched by the door.

"It was the murderous will of one who had black knowledge and sought to use it in revenge. Rueben Straus made these: the bed for his sister's wedding, the cane perhaps for her gift to her lover. But since Rueben had some glimmer of mistrust in him, he put in also a demand for justice if there was any sorrow for the one he loved. Instead of gifts these became curses. Mark Walden could indeed have been blood-related to Gyles, or else perhaps he only shared some deviousness of spirit. So Rueben's hate made a trap . . ."

"But—but it is gone?"

"I only banished this manifestation." Ilse was very tired. "Fire cleanses best. You must see that this bed, the cane, are burned and the ashes well scattered. This doorway must be so closed."

"Yes, oh, yes!"

Ilse, looking at the other woman's drawn and haggard face, believed her.

ROOT AND BRANCH
SHALL CHANGE
Merlin (1999) DAW

The character of Merlin is a very complicated one, entwined in such a weaving of various legends that the searcher can find many Merlins, each alike in some manner of power, yet unlike in the use of it. In one of the sage's guises, he uttered dire prophecies of the wild wrath of both elements and stars, foretelling that, in the future, the earth would exact from humankind payment for its befouling.

With Arthur, Merlin failed, and we are given several reasons for that failure. In some accounts, it is hinted that he was too impatient in striving to bring about what was necessary to achieve ends foreseen along one future path, and thus his power turned against him.

Was Nimuë, his disciple and comfort, in truth a traitoress and one who chose a dark path? We cannot be sure of the wisdom of accepting such a direct answer as legend has presented. Certainly, though, she was the woman with whom Merlin could share his dreams and desires, and the mage—in all accounts—stood alone until her coming.

Yes, they list—the seekers-of-legends—a number of Merlins, sometimes sundered by centuries of time. Perhaps, then, the prophecies uttered by one of these wizards of the past may also lie ahead. We are told that Arthur was, and is, the Once and Future King; surely, then, Merlin is the Once and Future Master of Powers.

Thus there might come a time when such a tale as this could shape itself into reality.

How fares a survivor whose world has collapsed, leaving no firm refuge or retreat?

First came the dreams—wisps of action in which I was caught, but which I could not understand. Yet, in a way, such visions were better than waking; and with each dreaming, reality also became stronger. I awoke to find myself talking to the air about me, not only arguing with one I could not see, but repeating strange words and phrases. Strange, yes, and yet—once they had a strong meaning.

After a space, when I awoke from one of the dreams, I could not put a clear name even to myself. I was no longer Ninan Tregarn, once teacher to the young in a dull gray city where the debris which humans had made cluttered the breast of the long-suffering earth. *You see,* I would tell myself unhappily, *you now stand apart, having left the company of your own kind.*

The visions had begun even before the breaking of the peace of the world. True, men had troubled their own peace for generations, but now earth and sky, sea and stars, left their appointed patterns and changed, sweeping away most of the humans who had failed.

The meteor showers, the tumult of the oceans, those dark shadows across the moon, the fatal plagues—HE had foretold them in his time.

His time! But Time folds upon itself when Nature strives to throw away a past. Could there begin anew anything—anything?

It was cold, and it had hailed, battering my half-starved body. The ragged blanket I drew around me now as a shawl was heavy with damp. Only a small spark of defiance had kept me moving the past few days.

But, for the first time, my need was clear. I was no longer Ninan—no, I was again that other who had once gathered to her all she could hungrily grasp. Then there had been a parting, and thereafter ill repute had been cast upon me. Through the centuries, I was remembered as a traitor, a woman who had brought about the death of the only one who had ever tutored and—yes— cherished her.

However, Time was not finished with either of us, nor was the earth ready to take us into itself, to part flesh from bone, from— soul? Spirit was a gift, a loan from Her who rode the heavens at this hour, and it was surely She who sent me stumbling on my way.

That new-old part of me, which was growing stronger with every breath I drew, was my guide now. My head was no longer bowed; instead, I listened, perceiving something not heard as sound but rather felt as an inner trembling of the body.

The forest my budding other self remembered—that was long gone, swallowed up by the lava-tide of relentless human expansion. Nonetheless, as I moved ahead, trees rose about me, tenuous shadows of themselves at first, then strong, sturdy growths, complete. And that trembling within grew ever stronger, urging me on.

Suddenly I no longer moved alone, for there came another, well-shrouded in a tattered robe. Memory stirred. In the days just behind me, some had arisen who had, in their anger and fear, sought stern gods, turning fiercely against all who did not believe as they had come to do. This man was one of their Speakers. His face was as gaunt as if the flesh had already departed from the sharp bones, and it seemed to me that his eyes were mere pits of fire in a skull.

He raised his hand high, pointing toward me, and I could see that his taloned fingers held a curved carving like unto the bowl of a bell; this object he also swung, yet there was no clapper within its throat. Nonetheless, I knew that the unheard sound which had drawn me hither issued from that tongueless bell.

"Well do you ring! Wait you upon an answer?" I asked, realizing as I did so that I spoke a language long dead to men, yet to me strongly alive.

"No answer," the ringer grated a harsh reply. "Get you hence, woman of ill fortune, betrayer, thief of power never meant to be given to any female!"

Suddenly it seemed that he spoke in jest, for the way of his imagined god had never held any truth for me. I found laughter I had not known for many days upon my lips as I moved determinedly toward him.

The Speaker wore a mask of sheer horror now, as though his features in their warpings and wrinkles pictured all the evils his beliefs held that womankind had brought upon the world. "Begone—into darkness, begone!" he spat.

Fearsome the man might be, but he was only a final adversary, worn out by centuries of waiting. Knowing what must be done, I put forth my hand and snatched the bell from his grasp.

It was as if I had plunged fingers and palm into a cold that ate. Then the ice became fire, as violent in its burning as the meteors which the death-days had spilled upon the earth. Still, I held to the bowl; and for the first time I dared to summon, from those memories that had only recently regranted me the ancient tongue, a lilting song of Power. Once I had been taught to guard so, and now I stood, battle-engaged, once more.

The one who faced me gave a sharp cry, spittle bursting from between the stretch of his thin lips. He strove hard, and the pressure of his will was nearly enough to silence my own call for strength. Tearing through the air with his claw-fingers, striving to regain what he had lost, he tottered forward as though about to throw himself full upon me and snuff out my life with the weight of his body.

But what he had held was now mine. I raised the bell high, and it moved smoothly and well. As before, no sound for the ear issued from its empty half-round, yet that trembling which reached into the body grew and grew.

He whom I had so confronted—false priest of a human-created god—began to darken, seeming to draw upon shadows in an attempt to rebuild himself. Such, however, was not to be his fate, for darkness instead swallowed him, and he was gone.

A glow brightened within the walls of the enringing trees, as though the orb that is Her own hung there now, and the silent song of the bell drew me on until I came to the foot of a jumble of rock such as could be found in many places since the shaking of the earth some seasons past.

Once, I well remembered, a proud rise of stone had stood there—a haven-fortress which he whom I now sought had made his place of peace and study. Within had been stored and safe-guarded ancient slabs of stone patterned over with symbols of power; books so great and weighty as to need both hands to shift them; flasks; coffers. And I had known them, too, drawing knowledge and skills from that which they held.

Now only a shapeless mass of rubble was to be seen; however, I would not accept that I had been brought here only to confront a sterile and futile ending. At first I thought to lay aside the bell and strive to remove the pile of rock piece by piece, using my hands. Then I noticed that, when I fronted the heap directly, the tremors I felt inside my body seemed also to resound in some fashion within its substance. Shivering free from their resting places, the stones rolled down the mound by the force of no touch save the call of the tongueless bell.

By the moon's silvery light, near the crest of the hillock so swiftly dislodging itself, a dark spot could now be seen—an opening made larger by the fall of every rock. In a few moments I faced a door, and then the stones ceased to tremble and tumble.

It was small, that entryway, and I had to stoop to enter. Before me was only all-swallowing darkness, but, taking one cautious step after another, I went forward.

The radiance of the forest-filtered moon seemed to rest fingers of light upon my shoulders and to make clear what lay before me. I saw shelves deep-carven into the walls of what had once been a cave and, upon those, the heaped remains of weapons of *his* kind, long since come to dust. All that lived now was the knowledge which was a part of me and which had been summoned from the past.

Against the far wall lay what seemed part of a great log. I stood gazing at the vast trunk, and tears filled my eyes once more, even as they had nearly overcome me when I had last paused in that spot to take a silent farewell.

I had come so far to do what must now be done, yet somehow I could not make the final gesture. Here—even in this very place—I had stood, tricking my love for his own sake, in the hope of saving him by defeating Time itself.

Time . . . yes, that had passed, and I had been caught up in a chain of many lives. I was a seeress, a dreaded woman of strange knowledge, whose body had been given to the fire by those who had feared her. Then, as the Old Beliefs had failed, so I, too, had faded, losing those abilities. I had toiled in fields, and—equally a slave—in the machine-filled pens of later ages. And never had love warmed me, for I had betrayed it, seeking in my pride to master death. Despite all such strivings, I had died, more often than I had any wish to remember—and lived again, in each new form withdrawing farther from that which I had been.

Yet I had been brought here and my memory reawakened; and that She had some use for me I was certain. Had I not come across a starved and dying land, living on what roots I could find, and pushing forward always against great weariness to crouch now in this place of sorrow?

Now I put aside the bell, for this spell I would break was one of my own setting in the long ago. Leaning forward and placing my hands flat on that seeming length of log, I called up the binding as it had been laid. For even as the ensorcellment was wrought, so it must be rescinded word by word, gesture by gesture—a thing which I alone could do. I began with great care, lest my tongue twist and give some fatally-wrong accent to a word. Gradually, with increasing confidence, I ordered the phrases, remembering the swing of the chant, the proper movement of the hands. Thus, and thus, and thus—

I had stepped out of time as humankind knew it. My body swaying to the rhythm of the incantation, I became only a voice, fueled by what was left of my strength. As was required in such a casting, I now closed my eyes upon that which lay before me; rather, I built and held to a mind-picture of what it was needful to bring forth by my wreaking here.

The flow of words slowed. I reached once more for the bell, and its weight seemed to draw my hand toward that tree-not-tree which had been shaped and set here to guard a most precious spirit. In answer to the bell's call, like the stones that had sealed the mouth of the cave, the illusion of bark covering began to slough away; and with the fall of each flake, a portion of my remaining inner power was lost, as well.

My last bespelling, this enchantment had once been. Now it was finished yet again, and I felt nearly as spent as I had with its making. The vibration from the bell died as I crouched down to see what I had uncovered, not truly sure that my will could be undone as it had been done. There was not now any threat from Morgause raised against him, such as had lent me strength beyond the might of mortals to send my teacher beyond her grasp. That jealous queen had had her day and place, as well as her hatred, which had been so strong it had led her to a murderous act. No, here there was only myself, and—

Light arose from the interior of the loglike coffin. The radiance blazed, and I held out my hands to it as one coming in from bitter cold would seek a beckoning fire.

I looked, and gave a little cry; then I stared fully down at what lay there. It had been majestic age I had sealed so against death in that far-off time; but—

—here lay a child. The hair, to be sure, was still silver, but the locks were vibrant with young life. The features likewise were as yet untroubled by time's passing. I had left an oldster, one who had lived longer in the world than many of his kin-blood; but it was certain that I now looked upon a youth of middle years.

Around the body was still wrapped the Master's cloak. Over its surface played rippling lines of color, each of which expressed the inner secret of some mystery not revealed to humankind unless such knowledge were hard fought for and the proper rites enacted.

On the quiet breast, the folds of that enshrouding garment had shifted aside. Lying there against the ivory of the skin was a length of substance I had never before seen. It was not the steel of a blade, nor any safe-ward I could understand.

Nonetheless, though the thing had no place in my past, I knew what had to be done. Clutching the bell-bowl tightly in my left hand, I reached out with my right and raised the object from its resting place.

I held a cylinder measurable by my forefinger yet thicker than that, a rod not smooth but rather deeply graven. I brought it closer to eye level. This was very ancient—so old that it reached far back beyond any memory I could summon. The carving showed a woman's lush figure, heavy-breasts and wide-hipped—a shape such as an artist might craft whose purpose was not to show the real but the ideal. Though I had seen its like only once, and that many lifetimes ago, I knew what lay in my hand.

This was the Great Goddess as the earliest of our race had known Her: the Earth Mother in all her fertility and strength. Hardly conscious of what I did, I put the bell and this new found clapper together. The sound which shouted forth was no longer mere vibration; now it smote the ears like the brazen clangor of a mighty gong.

The closed eyes of the child-man opened and stared up into mine, neither blue nor gray in color and fiery with life and barely-leashed power. It was true, then—he who lay here in such strange guise was, indeed, restored.

The just-wakened one raised himself slowly, drawing the overlarge cloak about his body.

"So . . ." His voice had not the piping lilt of the youth he seemed but rather a stronger tone. "Welcome, Nimuë. *'Root and branch shall change places, and newness will come to all things, as is the measure of the Power.'* Greatly must the earth have altered since last we met here—so much indeed, that, as I forespoke, the place of the trees and the very land is changed. As once you learned from me, so now must I relearn from you. How fares this world into which you have drawn me?"

I did not answer him in words; instead, pictures passed through my mind of vast sufferings—evildoings and bloodletting by men and the uprising of nature itself against humankind. And he also, I knew, read my recent memories, viewing what I myself had seen and, beyond that, perceiving through me knowledge far wider and deeper than any I could offer him.

He shook his head when I was done. "Dark are the roads trodden by mortals, for a host of ills are shaken from the garments of those who travel there! The Great Mother cannot be denied forever."

"Yet," I ventured to question, "what can any do, if the skies, seas, winds, and the earth itself rise in battle against us, as they have done?"

"We must make a beginning," he answered. "I shall draw from you in full all that lore I once freely gave. Thereafter—together—"

My master, now my pupil, hesitated only a moment; then his fingers reached out and touched the wrist of the hand with which I held the bell. A charge tingled through my flesh as though I had grounded lightning, and in that instant I, too, might have uttered a prophecy. Great, in truth, had he been, but it was in him to be greater still, and under Her tutelage he would become the mightiest of Her servants.

Pulling the cloak tighter about him, he rose up, freeing himself from the shell of the tree trunk. Again he put out his hand to clasp mine, and I understood that in partnership we were to bring new life to a ruined world.

Thus—Merlin and Nimuë once more—we stepped forth into the open of that strange forest, and the ring of the bell was in rhythm with each purposeful step we took in company. Out of the shadows came a great gray wolf with whom my lord had once walked in harmony. From over our heads sounded the harsh cry of a raven, and ahead of us, waiting majestically, stood a horn-crowned stag, king of that woodland court to which Merlin had paid homage long ago.

And Time turned, even as the stars move in their appointed paths, and Hope was born anew to light the Dark.

WHITE VIOLETS

Marion Zimmer Bradley's Fantasy Magazine
(1999) Issue # 45

Dilly was busy making flower-and-leaf bonnets for her two favorite dolls. She was also where she was not to be—in the garden alone. But Mackie, who had ruled her world almost since she was born and Mother had gone to Heaven, had a headache—one of her very bad ones which meant lavender-water cloths on her forehead, a dark room, and *no* noise. And Simpson, her sister's maid, who was supposed to be keeping an eye on her, was busy with Violet's gown to be worn this evening at the big ball.

Dilly pinned two leaves together with thorns and examined the effect. She had been told directly *not* to go into the garden, but here she was, which gave her a sense of adventure. However, she had not ventured far from the Manor—the garden was too large, and besides, Old Buskins, the head gardener, would soon be through with his elevenses. It was best to keep out of sight, which was why she had squirmed back into the bushes.

Only, suddenly, there were voices—one of them quite loud and angry and the other sounding nearly just as sharp, as Violet could speak when she was upset. Dilly dared to pull aside, though for only an inch or so, the branch which hid the newcomers from her.

Yes, it was Violet, though she was supposed to be resting before the ball tonight—the important ball when Papa would announce that she was going to marry Colonel Sir Christopher Hale. Dilly's lips shaped soundlessly that very important name, which Violet and Papa shortened to "Chris."

"It was entirely open to the understanding of everyone at tea," he was saying in a harsh voice she had never heard before.

"Are you calling me a flirt?" Violet snapped back. She had picked a rose and was now pulling it to pieces.

"You were wrong to allow him to pay you so much attention, and you know it!"

"Now Clarissa is speaking through you!" Violet stamped her small foot, though only a twist of her wide skirt suggested the angry gesture.

Dilly's mouth shaped a big O. Violet was angrier than her little sister had seen her since Bruce had broken her perfume bottle last Christmas.

"We'll leave Clarissa out of this!" Chris returned. "She has only the best wishes for our happiness —"

"Does she?" Now Violet's face looked white, almost as though she were going to be sick. "I was warned about her. She isn't going to give up her brother willingly —"

"Shame, Violet—that is not just. Clarissa has been very kind and would be more loving if you let her. But she has nothing to do with your encouragement of Ridgley in such a public fashion —"

Violet was tugging at her wrist. The bracelet she wore there was caught in the lace of her sleeve.

"As well I learned in time, Colonel Hale, just what kind of suspicious tyrant you are! It is plain we don't suit and never will if you can take some harmless fun so seriously. I don't like your ordering me about, and I don't like you anymore, either! You can give this back to Clarissa as a trophy to prove her dear brother is free from the toils of the seductress!"

"Violet, you've gone beyond reason!" The outraged man's face was red, and his small mustache seemed to bristle.

"No, *you* have!" Violet tossed at her erstwhile lover the bracelet she had at last freed from the lace. The ornament fell to the ground just beyond the edge of her skirts. He made no move to retrieve it, as Violet, gathering up the same skirts a little, blundered away from the small clearing. Nor did she look back.

Chris stood very still. He looked, the eavesdropping child thought, like Papa when something at the Manor had gone very wrong. Not stooping for the bracelet, he turned and marched in the opposite direction as stiffly as if he were on parade before the Queen herself.

Dilly waited until she could no longer hear any footsteps from either direction. Then she squeezed through the screen of foliage so that her hand could close upon the bracelet. Since Violet had thrown it away and Chris had not taken it up, then neither of them wanted it, and she had found it. She had never seen it really close, for Violet had only had it for a few days. Chris's sister, the one who had fallen from her horse and couldn't walk anymore, had sent it to Violet when the engagement had been known to their families.

Now Dilly turned the ornament around and around, admiring what seemed to her to be a true treasure. It was formed of gold links holding together ovals, every one a little picture set in a gold frame. And the designs were all of flowers made of small bits of white and green set into black, each forming a white violet.

The little girl closed her hand tightly upon the bracelet. No one wanted it; they had just left it lying there, so it was going to be hers. She had heard it had come all the way from Italy—Simpson had told the first housemaid that. Now she had a precious thing of her very own from far off! Pushing back under the bushes, she retrieved Rosamond and Lucy and, with them under her arm, she started back to the house, keeping hidden as best she could.

There was the sound of hooves on the circle drive, and Dilly saw Chris riding off.

Back up the second stairs to the schoolroom the child padded and hunted out her own secret place, which not even Mackie knew about. Dilly had discovered it herself one rainy day when she was tired of the doll family and the many-times-read books and had gone poking about, running her fingers along the carvings on the wall. There were a lot of these, because this was the oldest part of the Manor and the rooms here had once been important.

The child had pushed on a rose that day and been amazed when there had come in answer a creaking and the opening of a very small cupboard built right into the wall itself. Then, there had been nothing but dust inside, but Dilly had cleared that out and afterwards used the cubbyhole for secret treasures. There were the sixpence from the Christmas pudding and the little tarnished silver heart she had found back in a drawer, and now the bracelet joined them.

There was a great bustling in the house. Dilly dared to creep to Violet's room and, even through the thick door, she could hear her sister crying hard and Aunt Susan's voice sounding almost as sharp as Chris's had been.

Of course, no one ever told Dilly anything, but she listened as she always did, and Mackie was not around to keep her in the schoolroom. Papa came up the stairs—the child could hear the heavy stamp of his feet in spite of the hall carpet—and went into

Violet's room. Then he roared, and Dilly heard all sorts of things about her sister's behaving badly, shaming the family, and being an unfilial daughter with no feelings for anyone but herself.

In the end, all the preparations for the ball stopped right in the middle, leaving the servants whispering in corners. Then Mackie had found Dilly eavesdropping, and she, too, had been told she was a disgrace for listening.

The family never really let her know what happened, but, three weeks later, Violet and Aunt Susan went away. Papa spent most of his time shut up in the library, while all the servants kept as much distance as possible from that room.

It was autumn before Violet came back. She looked quite different—more like a grown-up lady. She always spoke in a sharp way and mostly ignored her little sister, but she had a new ring, and Dilly was going to have a new brother—Lord Ridgley. The child did not like him very much, for he acted as though he did not see her, was stiff, and had hard eyes.

Dilly was allowed down for tea on the afternoon that the news came about Chris. Lord Ridgley had brought in a paper from London and read it out loud: Colonel Sir Christopher Hale had fallen in battle with the Sepoy rebels at Lucknow, way off in India. Lord Ridgley looked at Violet right after he read that. The child saw her sister's face go very pale and her hand shake so that her cup clattered on the saucer as she set it quickly down, but her lips were very tight together, and she raised her eyes and looked back at Lord Ridgley, saying:

"He was doing his duty; that meant much to him." Dilly thought she heard a quaver in Violet's voice, though her sister did not move even a hand. But Aunt Susan began to cry and, catching sight of the child, sent her back to Mackie.

One season followed another. Dilly had a governess now, though Mackie still ruled her life. She was growing up, Rosamond and Lucy had been packed away, and she had lessons, not only from books but also in dancing, manners, and how to act in company.

Violet did not come home often. Lord Ridgley had a post in the government, and the couple lived in London where, Dilly was told, her sister entertained a great deal and was considered a fine hostess. No one ever mentioned Chris, and there was no visiting between the Manor and the Hall. Sometimes, though, Dilly saw Clarissa out riding in the carriage. The young woman looked away quickly on such occasions, for there was something in that gaunt, sharp-featured face which made her shiver, though she never knew why.

Dilly herself rode along the paths, but she kept away from those which were close to the Hall. Then she met Clement. For a moment, when she first saw him, she had been startled—he looked so much like Chris, only he was young. Clement was a soldier, too, but only a captain. He was also a "Sir," because Chris had died and he was Chris's brother's son. He had come to spend his leave at the Hall because his Aunt Clarissa wished it. Dilly heard Mackie and Miss Johnson, her governess, talking, and Mackie declaring that Miss Clarissa was "fair daft" about Clement, even as she had been about her brother.

"Never wanted to share that one." Mackie put down the petticoat she was hemming. "She tried to keep him away from Miss Violet, only he had a will of his own. But I have always thought"— she hesitated before she continued—"that she had a hand in breaking that engagement. Miss Violet—it was like she had been somehow witched. She stood out against all of us, saying she never wanted to see him again. It was a pity —" Mackie shook her head.

Though there was no visiting between the Manor and the Hall, the girl did meet Clement, and in the most proper way. She had ridden to the vicarage with some special herb receipts

Mackie had promised Mrs. Trevor, and Clement was walking in the garden with Mr. Trevor, who came forward at once to greet her and introduce his visitor.

Dilly felt an odd breathless sensation when she looked into his gray eyes. Chris's eyes had been blue, but Clement still seemed so much like his uncle that she almost called him Chris. He was very polite and asked if he might accompany her when she left. She had John, the groom, with her, so it was indeed proper, and she had not the least desire to say no.

They met again and again in the weeks which followed. The young woman always had John with her, and she felt there was no harm in doing this. Somewhat to her surprise, Clement never mentioned the past, Violet, or Chris, and she wondered if he knew about what had happened more than a dozen years ago.

At length, greatly daring, she invited him to tea. When she admitted to Aunt Susan what she had done, her aunt looked shocked, and Dilly had to hurry on to explain that the couple had been properly introduced by the vicar.

"Captain Hale never speaks of Violet or Chris," she said quickly. "Perhaps he does not even know."

"He must." Aunt Susan sounded almost grim. "But, since you have been forward enough to ask him, he will be our guest. It is a pity that your father is in London—I do not like this situation in the least."

The tea, however, was pleasant; Clement was most attentive to Aunt Susan, and Dilly could see that he was winning at least her approval. Nor was that their last meeting at the Manor.

When Papa returned, Dilly was summoned to the library— a fearsome place in which explanations of behavior were always demanded and punishments announced. By now, though, the girl was so sure she *had* done right that her shivers as she entered were but slight ones.

"What's this your aunt tells me about young Hale?" Her father was plainly not at his most yielding. "I wonder that one of his family comes near to this house!" He slammed his hand flat on the desk so hard that one of the pens jumped out of its holder.

"He—he never mentions Violet—or Chris." Dilly summoned her courage. "He has been most proper—Aunt Susan will tell you."

Papa just sat staring at her. "Hale's a good enough youngster," he said at last, "but why —" He stopped short.

"Papa —" The girl decided to risk all upon one throw. "The fête in the garden next week—may we send him an invitation?"

Again her father did not answer at once. "Well, that can do no harm, I suppose, though I think perhaps Miss Clarissa will arrange matters so that he does not come. She is a very bitter woman, Dilly. If you continue to see this young man, she may make trouble for you. She never wanted Chris to marry—they were twins, and she was fiercely jealous of Violet. I have always wondered . . ." He shook his head as though trying to dismiss some unpleasant thought. "Just be careful, child. You're not as quick-spoken as your sister; see you keep on in that way and guard your tongue.

The fête was held, and even Papa unbent when Aunt Susan introduced Clement to him. Nor did he ever give any more warnings during the long summer days when Dilly felt she was caught up in a dream. Then came the time when the Captain found her alone in the rose garden and asked if he might speak to her father about an engagement. That was the dream come true!

There would not be a ball this time—Aunt Susan said something about tempting Providence—but instead only a gathering of friends at dinner when the momentous announcement was to be made. To her aunt's obvious surprise, the invitation sent in courtesy to Miss Hale was actually answered in the affirmative.

On that afternoon, Dilly wandered into the old school-room. Though it was kept in general order by the housemaids, no one came here much anymore. The young woman opened the chest drawer and looked in at Rosamond and Lucy. The sight of them made her think of that long-ago day in the garden and, on impulse, she went to her hiding place.

There was the bracelet, gleaming never more beckoningly from the dark pocket. The girl drew the ornament out, put it on, and fastened the catch. It was pretty, too pretty to be hidden. Certainly no one would remember it after all these years, so—she would wear it this evening! That decision seemed to come out of nowhere almost like an order.

Dilly had a new dress of the palest green, and Sally, who now acted as her maid upon occasion, coaxed her red-brown hair into the most orderly waves, with a curl to lie across her shoulder. She then endured the twitching and turning of the modified-crinoline-supported skirt which was the latest fashion. And, for the first time in her life, she looked into the mirror and decided she *was* attractive—as attractive as Violet had been.

"Come along with you." Mackie stood just within the door. "The first of the carriages has turned in, and you must be ready to greet the guests."

This evening, Dilly appeared to have laid her usual slightly-timid and retiring manner away with her daytime dress. Her hand sought the bracelet, turning it around and around on her wrist as she descended the stairs. Young ladies mostly wore a modest pearl necklet like the one she also had on, but there was nothing worldly or showy about her other ornament.

Papa held out his hand to her as she took the last step down and, beyond him, smiling welcome, was—Clement. The young woman blinked and blinked again. These past two months, the Captain's face had become as well known to her as her own mirrored features; but his gray eyes now—they were somehow unpleasant, as though she had committed a social error. And there was a quirk to his lips as he smiled which made him look almost disdainful and caused her to feel like a country girl intruding among her betters.

Then she was standing between her father and Clement with Aunt Susan in line, greeting neighbors and distant members of the family. Violet had sent a civil refusal—this was the night of an important dinner which Lord and Lady Ridgley were helping to host. Oddly, no one had thought her refusal strange.

Dilly's arm, wearing the bracelet, hung down beside Clement. Twice he had crooked his own arm in invitation, but for some reason she shrank with a real sense of aversion from his touch. She could not understand why her intended seemed suddenly such a stranger, and she tried to tell herself it was because she was uncomfortable at being the center of attention as she had never been before.

Most of the guests had arrived when there was a small commotion at the doorway, and an unusual procession appeared. First came a chair which was mounted on wheels and was being pushed by a brawny footman in full livery. There was no mistaking the sharp-featured face of the woman who sat bundled in several shawls in that strange conveyance. Dilly heard a startled "Hmph!" from Papa; then he and Aunt Susan moved forward to greet Miss Clarissa Hale, whose penetrating glance had already shaken Dilly. A moment later, the Captain took a grasp on her arm and pulled her forward too.

However, the woman in the wheeled chair had another attendant. Dilly, trying to forget that unpleasant stare pinning her, gave a little gasp.

The stranger presented a complete contrast to the dark figure huddled in wraps to whom he paid patient attention. He—he was the Knight! Dilly saw him as plainly as if he had stepped from the pages of the *Idylls of the King,* which the girl had dreamed over ever since Papa had given her the volume for her last birthday. Somehow she was able to take her eyes from him long enough to greet Miss Hale, whose stretch of thin lips was anything but a cordial smile.

"Since we are family, or about to become so," Miss Hale spoke directly to Aunt Susan now, "I knew that you would not mind an addition to the party. An extra young man is always useful." She laughed, and to Dilly that mirthless noise sounded exactly like a crow's harsh call. "This is Gerald Langley, dear Clement's cousin on his mother's side, who happened to be passing through the shire and had the good manners to renew family bonds with a visit."

Both Aunt Susan and Papa had on their set "social faces," but the young woman was sure they were not pleased; only one could not turn the guest of a guest from the door.

At that moment, Hawkins came to announce that dinner was served. Aunt Susan looked around a little wildly, as if she wondered how they were to conjure up a place for this unexpected addition to the party, but Hawkins favored his mistress with a certain look which suggested that the matter was well in hand. Nothing ever seemed too difficult for that pillar of the family to manage.

"Foster, you may go now." Miss Hale was abruptly dismissing the footman who had pushed her in. "Sir Clement knows well how to manage for me."

And Clement did move obediently to the handle at the back of that chair. Dilly watched him, not a little nettled. By all the social laws, he should have taken *her* in himself, but it was plain that his aunt had him well "under her paw"—a saying Mackie often used.

"Miss Manners, may I have the pleasure?" It was the Knight, coming to her rescue before the eyes of the company, just as was fitting for the occasion. Dilly looked up at him. Yes, he was just like the Knight. Was it Lancelot or Galahad? She could not remember now; however, she felt a warm glow as she put her hand lightly on the arm he offered. At least she would not be trailing behind Captain and Miss Hale like a charity child summoned in for inspection!

There was something of an undignified scramble at the table where Miss Hale's majestic chair had to be accommodated. The result was that the lady sat on the right hand of her host with Clement still in close attendance on her left. As the minutes passed, Dilly's irritation grew. Her intended seemed altogether occupied with seeing to his aunt's comfort, answering various questions she addressed to him between statements to Papa concerning affairs in the world at large. She would say such things as, "Now, you are a military man, dear Clement—what is the Army's reaction to this?"

Dilly found that, in a curious way, he seemed to be fading— that he was not her bright and happy friend or, yes, lover anymore. She had a growing feeling of shadows stretching out to overcast the future drawing near. Would Clement expect her, after they were married, to *live* with Miss Hale? The estate belonged to him, but he constantly deferred to his aunt, saying that she had run it ably for so long her advice was needed.

For contrast, she allowed herself to be amused by the light chatter of her seatmate, Mr. Langley, who seemed to be anything but "under Miss Hale's paw." The girl found herself laughing at his amusing comments about his travels in the shires.

Suddenly the older woman shot a question at her, completely interrupting a story Mr. Langley was telling. "It is somewhat unusual for a young lady to wear much jewelry, but that is a very handsome bracelet you are displaying this evening—certainly fine mosaic work. Italian, is it not?"

Dilly flushed. She knew Clarissa had recognized the bracelet. What would that sour spinster say next? Clement was frowning at his intended as though she had, indeed, broken some rule of good breeding. Defiantly, she held her hand out a little further so that the candlelight brought the ornament in question fully into view.

"It is an old piece, Miss Hale. I really do not know much about it, except that I found it in a drawer. The pattern is quite pretty, and I admit it tempted me."

Miss Hale was smiling once more. "Just so. Violets are modest, maidenly flowers and quite suitable. Clement, I think my chair needs some adjustment —?"

There had been something about that exchange which made the younger woman feel a small shiver. She wanted to pull the bracelet off as Violet had done in the rose garden on that day a dozen years ago, but she could not make a scene. Now, though, the mosaic piece seemed very cold, and the flowers looked faded and far from pretty. She turned abruptly to Mr. Langley with the first remark that crossed her mind—something about the rose garden. Rose garden—she must not think of that!

Fortunately, in moments her interest was caught and firmly held by his description of his visit to the royal gardens at Windsor and his subsequent presentation to His Highness the Prince of Wales. Clement and Miss Hale could be forgotten—Dilly was determined it would be so.

Only at last the dinner, which felt as though it had lasted forever, was nearing its end, when Papa would be giving the toast in honor of the engagement. How, at that moment, she longed for the Knight beside her to see her safely away! It seemed to Dilly that tonight Clement had revealed himself as an entirely different person—one she did not know and would not like even if she did.

Deep within her arose a little quirk of wonder at why she felt that way, but it quickly vanished.

Somehow Dilly managed to sit and smile through the toast, blush in an appropriately-demure way, and accept the good wishes of the company without catching Clement's full gaze again. Mr. Langley was all consideration and once actually murmured something about time making him a loser which she hoped only she had heard.

Then the girl was free. By now, her head was pounding, and she wanted nothing more than her bed and Mackie's soothing hands stroking her hair. She glanced about in near desperation, but knew that neither Aunt Susan nor Papa would countenance her withdrawal—no, she had to go inside, stand by her betrothed (who seemed bound by an invisible tether to his aunt's chair), and present the proper appearance. Mr. Langley still watched her, and now and then their eyes met. It almost seemed then that he understood her growing confusion and need for escape.

Finally the party began to break up. Clement turned to her with a suggestion that they go out onto the terrace, but Miss Hale's harsh demand that he guide her chair into the hall summoned him away. Aunt Susan and Papa were busy saying farewells when the Knight appeared beside her.

Dilly was not aware that she had raised the hand backed by the bracelet, but she found it clasped in his and felt the unnerving brush of his mustache as he raised her fingers a little to kiss them. At the same moment, Clement appeared in the doorway. His face looked hard and set, and he summoned Mr. Langley with a wave; nor did he come to Dilly but left with his aunt and cousin without so much as a goodnight.

The young woman's head was bursting now, and she wanted to cry. She got by Aunt Susan and Papa, she never knew how, and back to her room. Once in that merciful refuge, she sent Sally away and dropped into the big chair by the window, not caring how her skirts were being crumpled. Holding her head between her two hands, she tried to understand what had happened to her.

"Child—" The familiar endearment from Mackie brought the tears, hurting tears, which Dilly tried to wipe away.

"I knew that one would make trouble." Mackie drew her close in soft, comforting arms; then, suddenly, the nurse's fingers closed tightly about her wrist and turned it into the light. The girl heard, even through her sobs, the hiss of the old woman's breath.

"Where did you get this?" Mackie gave a jerk hard enough to bruise Dilly's wrist and waved the bracelet before her charge's tear-filled eyes.

"I—I found it —"

"This was Miss Violet's, sent her by that woman."

Dilly managed to get out the story of that long-ago afternoon in the rose garden and what she had seen there. "The bracelet was so pretty, and they did not want it, so I took it." Her voice sounded childish even to herself.

"Pretty? Aye—about as pretty as a viper!" The aged nurse was holding the now-dangling band as she might well hold the reptile in question. Now, moving away from Dilly, she lifted the ornament close to the nearest candle. She was looking, not at the flowers, but rather at the back of the oval gold pieces which framed them.

"Yes—as I thought all along when Miss Violet acted so. This is a wicked, bewitched thing! That woman—she knows more than anyone mortal has a right to do. I wonder she can set foot in church of a Sunday!

"But where there is darkness, there can be light. Where is your prayer-book, child?"

Completely amazed to the point where she was no longer crying, Dilly went to the bedside table and took from its drawer the worn, velvet-bound book which had belonged to her mother and which she had carried to church more Sundays than she could remember.

Mackie had pulled aside the curtains at the closest window. Now she carefully placed the book, opened to a certain page she had hunted for in the full moonlight, and across the flattened volume she laid the bracelet.

"Darkness and hate, spite and harm—what is within this thing of evil, may it be brought forth. In the Names of the Father Above, the Son Whom we cherish, and the Holy Spirit Which awaits the call of any in need." She said the words slowly and solemnly, and then she added certain other ones which Dilly did not understand at all but which had the sound of an urgent summons.

Did she see a mist gather over the bracelet? The girl was always sure afterward that she had. Then that mist passed on out through the window and was gone, and she felt as she had when she was small and was recovering from a bad illness. Now all the events of the night appeared utterly strange and unreal. Clement—Clement was strength, and warmth, and loving—

The young woman rubbed her hand across her eyes. "Mackie—do such things happen? This is real life, no fairy tale! Did Miss Hale wish some kind of bad thing on Violet and Chris and try to do it again with me, until you sent it away?"

"Child, there are many powers in the world, both good and evil. Belief makes either one strong to help or hinder. This evil is gone —"

"But I do not want that ever again." Dilly looked at the bracelet. "Put it away, Mackie, in one of the trunks in the attic. Let it stay hidden forever."

Clipping from the Obituary column of the Lincolnshire *Times:*

The sudden demise of Miss Clarissa Hale was a sharp and sad

surprise for her family and friends. She bore her infirmities with dignity and courage and was an outstanding example of the best of a fine old family.

From the same publication six months later:

The wedding of Delia Lucinda Manners, daughter of the Right Honorable Robert Manners and his deceased wife, Lady Pauline Dervant Manners, was celebrated in St. Richard's, the bride's parish church. The happy couple are about to set sail for India, where Captain Sir Clement Hale will join his regiment, the Bengal Lancers. The Hale family has a long history of service to the Crown in that country.

Among the guests were—

Advertisement in *Antique Guide 1995:* Estate sale. Unusually fine example of 1840 Italian marble mosaic bracelet. Unique pattern of White Violets.

NEEDLE AND DREAM
Perchance to Dream (2000) DAW

Dwelling in the pocket of fertile earth that lies walled by the rise of Mount Tork to the south and the Sleeping Hills to northward, the villagers had little knowledge of the outside world. They did, however, have dreams; and, through the centuries they had been isolated from those who had once been their own kind, such night visions had become their one link with the Power Beyond.

The village folk did not dream often these days. Thus, when man, woman, or child spent sleeptime in a dream, they made haste to report it in the morning and were hurried off to the cottage of the Keeper. There, that guardian of the Old Ways would question them rigorously, noting down in his record book their descriptions of things they had beheld, of actions in which they had had a part.

Many of those sleep-seeings would prove a reliving of normal doings, though sometimes the daily round was admixed with irresponsible behavior in scenes which the sober Keeper had to shake his head over. But dreams of true foretelling had been sent, as well, and those were entered into the charts and carefully consulted at need.

There had also come images from the Dark, and those were like a poison in the body of the village. Hanker, the smith, had dreamed of plague—and did it not strike their valley from out of nowhere within two tens of days thereafter? The folk who Dark-dreamed were shunned by their fellows and forced to stand apart, and they were given potions by the wisewife to make sure they did not follow one such nightmare with another.

It was a cloudy dawn when Krista awoke. Sweat beaded her forehead, and her nightshift clung to her spare body, which shook uncontrollably. She huddled, drawn in upon herself, as though a monster padded about the bed preparing to seize her if she put forth so much as a foot.

The girl could not forget even a portion of her dream, though much of it was strange beyond her understanding. At last, mechanically, she dragged herself from her narrow bed and dressed for the day, but once she had braided her hair she could delay no longer. All the rules she had been taught to live by pushed her to duty now. She had never dreamed before, yet she knew well the course that lay ahead for her. Luckily, no sounds could be heard within the cottage—she alone had waked.

Fog swirled around each of the small houses along the lane, dimmed them to hulking shadows—forms that, for the first time, Krista found menacing. The girl shot wary glances left and right as she hurried to the last cottage at the very end of the village. There alone a lighted lantern hung, for it was the rule that any dreamer must seek the Keeper at the end of his or her seeing, even though the time might still be night. Raising fist against the door, the newest visionary smote its surface with what force she could.

Though Krista had been beckoned in by a wave of the Keeper's hand and sat now on a stool by the fire cradling a tankard of hot herb drink between her shaking hands, she still shrank from speaking. The lore-master, meanwhile, made ready the great recording book and set out a pen and a small cup of soot-black ink. He performed these tasks with great precision, as though he, too, were reluctant to break the silence. At length he turned his head to survey Krista, and the girl gulped, while the tankard threatened to douse her with some of its contents.

"Master Keeper," her voice sounded high and shrill in her own ears, "I have dreamed."

"And what have you dreamed?" he asked calmly.

His visitor set her drinking mug down on the raised hearthstone, then twisted her freed hands together in agitation, but there was no escape.

"Of the Dark—it must have been of the Dark!" The words burst forth in a near scream.

Krista expected her host to frown, to draw back in aversion, to order her from his hut with a curse, but the Keeper's inquiring expression had not changed. He was still merely expectant, not judgmental.

"Tell me, from the beginning," he said, as though he were greeting her in the village lane.

Her listener's attitude was soothing. Even though the young woman was still cold with fear, she found that she could, indeed, recount her vision from its start.

"I—I think I was at the inn. It was market day, and an outlander had come with a wagon filled with wares that were rich and strange. He did not cry aloud these goods—rather, he stood to one side and let the people look for themselves, with no pointing out of this or that item. Yet even without merchant's patter, the folk took many things, bringing out long-stored savings so that they might deal with him. But they did not need such monies, for the trader's prices were small—too small for what he had to offer. With each sale he made, I saw that his eyes looked like—" Krista took a swift breath, "like a hunter's watching a fook-hare nose at a trap!"

Shivering at the memory, the girl continued. "Most of the goods had soon been taken from the cart. It was as though no one thought the cost was set too low—they seemed not to wonder."

"But you did—and chose nothing from this wagon of strange wares?" the Keeper asked.

The dreamer shook her head vigorously. "I wanted nothing of what I saw; truly, I would have gone away, but I seemed to be held there."

Taking up the thread of her tale once more, she continued, "Soon all the money was gone, and the people had to bring items for trade to do their buying: hides, jars of preserves, lengths of weaving. At last the wagon stood filled once more, this time with the work of our neighbors' hands. Then the trader turned and started onto the mountain track. Yet none watched him go—they were all too busy comparing their bargains, boasting of their good fortune. But—" The young woman shuddered, raising hands to cover her eyes as if she could thus blot out an evil sight before her.

"But—?" the loremaster prompted gently.

"It was as though all they had taken from the stranger had been dipped into the blackest of shadows, and those shadows had passed into the folk themselves."

Krista halted, but her host continued to look at her, evidently awaiting more.

"What was then shown to you?" he asked.

"I—I went after the merchant up the mountain trail: again, something made me act against my will. And I found myself holding," the dreamer stretched forth her arms, gazing down on them as though they still held a burden, "my marriage quilt, the bride-piece I have stitched on ever since Gregor spoke for me before he went to the summer pastures. The quilt—or all I have done so far—is of patchwork. It has red in it, and yellow, like to those flames yonder." The young woman gestured toward the embers. "And it seemed that, when I held up the fabric, the colors blazed as does a fire newly fed. The quilt twisted in my hands; then it tore away from me and floated toward the trader and his cart. He and the wagon together turned black as a dark o' moon night until the cloth flapped down upon them both.

"There came fire at that touch, not the clean blaze of a home-hearth—this was black in flame. But it did not consume the quilt; rather the quilt smothered it. Then I woke, but a terrible fear was with me that that shadow-stuff had taken me prisoner also. This was a dream of evil, Keeper," the girl finished in a low voice, no longer daring to look at her host, and waiting for his judgment.

However, instead of accusing her, the loremaster asked a very unusual question. "Of what, Krista, is your bride-quilt made?"

His visitor shifted on her stool, relieved and also irritated—why ask about matters that had nothing to do with the coming of Evil?—but she answered.

"Because I am the only girl of our house, my mam and my aunty opened an ancient chest, long stored, for my use. They brought out odds and ends of fair finery and of other bride-pieces stitched long ago. Then my mam drew forth a pattern, clearly drawn, which she said my grandmam's mother had lined because she had seen it in a dream—"

Startled by her own words, Krista stopped. For the first time she remembered mam's tale. As she pondered what it might mean in the light of her own dream, the Keeper pushed the ink and pen a little away and began leafing through the record book. Shaking his head, he arose quickly to reach down another such volume from a nearby shelf, then began flicking through its pages.

"Your great-grandman was Mistress Magda." He put down the book, opened to a mid-point page. "That was in the time of

Keeper Whitter—near to a hundred year-lengths ago. He noted her vision carefully, for he was certain it was more important than it seemed. Indeed, it must have been a true foreseeing."

Setting the record aside, the Keeper turned directly to Krista. "You have dreamed of evil, yes, but you have also been shown a weapon—"

"A *quilt?*" she exclaimed.

"All defenses are not arrows, swords, or axes, maiden," he replied, smiling at her bewilderment. "The Powers Beyond at times use other tools. How near done is your bride-piece?"

"I have the backing of the patchwork side, then the quilting itself to finish," the young woman answered. "There is still much to do—it is my rest-time work, you see."

"No," the loremaster shook his head. "It is your true work, and from now on you will sit to it every day. Through you, we have again had a fore-glimpse of the future, though that may not run in the same path shown in your dream. The Powers have granted us a warning, and we must abide by it."

Nothing was told to the village concerning the subject of the latest dream to visit the people; yet Krista had, each day of her work with thread and needle, an audience that came and went. A few of the men paused to examine her labor, and, while they could see no sense in what she did, they did not gainsay the Keeper that it should be done. However, all the women and girls, down to the smallest tot holding to her mother's skirts, came and watched, went and came again. There was always a cushion close to hand full of ready-threaded needles, and most of the womenfolk who viewed her work would add to that supply.

Each stitch must be set by her own hands—that Krista some-how knew without being told. Hers was not the lighthearted task that a bride's work should be—in fact, the girl no longer consid-ered that her quilt was destined to serve any purpose of her own.

Still, the design was bright and cheerful. Shades of red formed the hearts that promised joy to a new-wedded couple, and bright gold backed those symbols of love, each set into its proper square. The quilting lines themselves, though, were strange, and the young woman had to concentrate intently on the placing of nearly every one. The pattern was like no other she had ever tried, and several times she saw Mam and Aunty shake their heads over those swirling lines made up of tiny stitches.

The dreamer kept at her task, though her shoulders grew sore from continual bending over the frame set up near the hearth of the cottage. Sometimes her head ached, too and, when she closed her eyes for an instant, those lines appeared before her once again, running red as threads of blood. At first she expected to dream again, but when she stretched wearily onto her bed at night she slipped quickly into a sleep that was untroubled.

At the second seventh day after Krista had begun to work at her stitchery full time, from overmountain came a curious arrival—not the trader's wagon she feared but rather a ragged straggle of folk. Mothers trudged along, gaunt from hunger, striving to nurse infants who seemed close to the Lasting Sleep. Here and there among them limped a man held up by a crutch, or one who stumbled blindly, guided by a woman or a half-grown child.

Nothing of the Dark clung about these unfortunates—indeed, they were so far spent that they could not remember what had happened to them. But it was plain that an action of the Shadow Power had driven them into the valley.

On the twentyday after she had begun her work, the girl at last overheard one of the strange women, to whom Mam had opened the door, stammer forth some of the story. Beyond the mountains, the newcomer said, disease and death had ravaged the earth and all who walked it. Hope was at its lowest ebb when a fine lord had come riding into the town with many liveried men in his train. He had offered true gold for land whereon to build a dwelling, and he had been very free with his riches.

Joyfully, the men, and the women as well, had gone to labor on his walls and towers. When they had finished, a feasting had been appointed. To this, too, they had gone eagerly—only—

The woman who spoke shook now, holding close her silent baby. To that celebration had also been summoned Something *Else.* The fair nobleman had become foul, drawing about him black clouds, and from those—though it was the height of summer—fell pellets of ice. The trees drooped and died. Then his underlings had come among the people (who had found they could not escape) and sorted out all the men who were hardy. Meanwhile, monsters issued forth from the unnatural darkness to torment and herd all the other folk over now-blasted fields, past dead horses and cattle, to the very feet of the mountains. And the lord himself came to the place where the townsfolk huddled and laughed hatefully, boasting that more power existed in the world than those dolts could ever know and that he had seized such might and made it obey his will. He then pointed to the mountains and swore that not the rocks themselves would hold from him what he wished.

As the fair-foul one rode away, his shadow monsters moved in once more, and the outcast people strained to climb above the sad twilight that held them. Thereafter they had wandered, for how long none of them could count.

This tale was, indeed, the meat of an evil dream, but it did not contain the mysterious merchant and his wagon. Krista raised her voice: "It was a lord who used you so? Not—not an outland trader?"

The woman started, as though the question had pierced through a mist in her mind and a memory had suddenly become clear. "There *was* a merchant, but in an earlier season," she answered hesitatingly. "He brought many fine wares and was eager to trade—so eager that he asked under-price for what he offered. He took, in the end, bags of grain from the fields and fruits dried and preserved. Those goods he loaded into his wagon and was gone with the dawn, and we never saw him again."

Now she frowned, sitting up straighter, and fixed Krista with an oddly compelling stare. "He had strange eyes—" She paused, then added, "So did the evil lord and his men. Why do I think of that now?"

"Strange eyes?" The Keeper had come in and was standing behind the woman, listening. "In what manner were they strange?"

The speaker shook her head. "I do not know why—that is gone from my recalling."

The loremaster turned to Krista. "How near are you to your task's completion?"

The young woman surveyed the frame-stretched quilt. "Perhaps—yes. I shall finish by tomorrow's eve."

"I think." he said then, "that our time grows short. Why this Dark One hungers for land I cannot tell, save that the Shadow, which is lifeless, is ever greedy for what can bring forth things truly living. I doubt that these who have already suffered at the hands of the fair-seeming lord were meant to reach us; yet perhaps the Great Power wrought their fate so, even as It forewarned us with two dreams, separated by ten tens of years. Stitch well, Krista—the weapon must be ready when the enemy appears."

There was much stirring in the cottage after he had gone as the woman from overmountain was pressed to tell all that had occurred. Her audience grew and grew until they threatened the quilt-frame. Then Krista's mother came back inside and stood looking down as the girl set one precise stitch after another.

"You dreamed," the older woman said after watching the work for a few moments, "and the Keeper has said your vision was a foretelling. We know of old that such night-seeings can be hard to understand, for they seldom show what *must* be—only what *might* come to pass. In truth, I know not how a maid's stitchery can aid against a great servant of the Dark, but—" Laying her hand gently on Krista's head, she ended, "do what must be done, daughter. You have the skill to do it well."

But do I? the young woman asked herself silently as she straightened shoulders stiff from bending over the quilting frame. Her many-times-pricked fingers were sore, as well, yet she dared use no ointment on them lest it stain the cloth. Her bride-piece. Krista pushed her chair back a little and looked at the design measuringly. Why had she thought the pattern so fine? Now the colors seemed to clash, and she knew she would never want so gaudy a spread of stuff across her marriage-bed. Marriage . . . she did not seem even to remember clearly what Gregor himself looked like, how his speech sounded—it was as though *he* were a dream long past. (Take another threaded needle between thumb and finger; place another stitch with care.)

That night Krista worked as long as she could by the light of the five candles her mother had brought; and, just as her tired eyes blurred, she knew she had achieved her goal. Save for the edge-binding, which was the last and easiest task of all, the quilt was finished.

The same heavy sleep that had followed each day's labor on the bride-piece descended upon her, and once more she slept with no troubling dreams. When she awoke, she found her workday clothes gone from the chair where she had left them; in their place was her feast-day finery. She was starring at these rich garments blankly when mam came in, a cup of new milk in her hand.

"The Keeper has sent word," the woman said breathlessly. "Two of the outcast folk who built a hut up-mountain have seen what we await. The trader comes!"

Krista half staggered to her feet. "The binding—"

"It is ready, dear heart, save for the last stitches. Drink now, and dress in your best, for this is the day toward which you have labored."

And the binding did go forward smoothly—even the pain in the girl's fingertips did not delay those straight and simple stitches. She put in the last of them just as the noonday sun placed a golden patch of its own on the floor within the edge of the open door.

That light was eclipsed as the Keeper came swiftly in. He did not seem to see Krista but had eyes only for what she held. "It is done? That one is coming past the mill—"

The young woman began to fold the quilt, trueing up the edges of the bulky square.

"It is done." she answered, hugging the bundle to her and stepping toward the door and the waiting lore-master. If the merchant was as close as the mill, then it was certainly time they were gone. Mam had assured her that the overmountain folk had all hidden themselves well out of sight so the trader would see only what he expected—a small village busied with its own affairs.

Then the girl was out in the sun, caressed by summer air. Her back straightened as she moved away from the cottage with her mentor; somehow she was sure of the worth of the work she held.

There was, indeed, a tall canvas-topped trader's wagon just pulling to a halt before the inn. The beasts that drew it—four of them—were certainly not the oxen that the villagers knew, nor were they true horses. These creatures had rust-red coats now matted with road-dust, and horns sprouted from their heads, short, stubby, and black—black as the hooded cloak their driver wore.

Though the day was fine and warm, the new arrival had wrapped that cape about himself as though he felt deep winter's bite. But the hood shifted a little as he moved to the rear of the wagon to loose the ties of the canvas and open to sight his wares.

The villagers surged forward as if they had been summoned by hunting-horn, fully intent on what was now on display—and that which lay within the cart seemed truly a hoard of treasures. The merchant stood to one side, merely watching the people as they milled about, pointing, reaching, urging each other to look at this wonder or that.

Fighting the pull of a strong desire to join them, Krista broke free of that surge of folk and moved nearer to the trader. Then she might have called to him, for he swung around and faced her directly. His *eyes*—At once the girl recalled what the exiled woman had said. Neither blue, nor brown, nor gray, nor green was orbed there—rather it seemed as though two coals, black save for a spark of fire in their hearts, had been set into his skull.

The young dreamer did not know what was expected of her, but she shook the quilt out of its folds, and the gold and scarlet blazed in the sun, even as did the outlander's coals of eyes.

Two strides he took toward her, then stopped abruptly as the heavy length of cloth unfurled, dropping a corner at his feet. For the first time, he shrugged the cloak away, revealing a jerkin and breeches the dusty gray of wood-ash. About his waist was a broad sash-belt divided into pockets. With his eyes still fixed on the girl, his fingers sought one of those compartments, fumbled within (for he did not look down), and withdrew, a-glitter with gem-hung chains of silver and red gold.

The outlander did not speak but dangled these baubles at eye-level before her; however, when Krista made no move to take his bright bait, he abruptly dropped the necklaces into the dust of the road as if they were worthless trash. Again he opened a pocket in his sash, and this time—

He seemed to have caught the end of a rainbow and tossed it out onto the air. So fine was the substance of the shawl-scarf he now displayed that a goodly length had been folded into the belt-pouch before being freed to expand and float in the breeze.

The young woman gasped before she could control herself. This web was out of dreamland itself! The trader whirled the stuff closer, wordlessly urging her to take it—and this time he also made clear his own desire by pointing with his other hand at the quilt.

This time Krista found her voice. "No—this is not for trade."

The glowing embers of the merchant's eyes flared, and his lips twisted in what was close to a snarl. Loosing the scarf to the pull of the wind, his hand sought yet a third pocket.

What he drew forth this time was neither gems or fine fabric but a book. The girl's gaze was drawn to the scuffed hide that served as its cover, the symbol set thereon in dark metal—a design like to, yet unpleasantly unlike, the one graven into the door of the Keeper's cottage. Though her tempter made no move to open the volume, the young woman drew a deep breath.

Dream power—lore long forgotten in this land! She knew without explanation that this was the gift he was offering her now: such might as a great lord—or lady—could wield to gather all the world into an iron grip.

Krista swayed, her body striving to betray her. An unseen force was cloaking itself about her, pushing her closer to—

"NO!" She spoke her denial aloud, and in the same moment she was aware of new knowledge. This one—no true trader—was here to play on the greed of the village. Indeed, those of the company surging around the wagon (though some few had stopped, torn themselves away, and were watching the two who stood apart), looked like folk completely overcome by desire.

The outlander was smoothing, almost stroking, the cover of that noisome book, which seemed to Krista to waft forth an ever-growing foulness. Again she braced with all her spirit's strength against taking what he had to offer. The volume of vision-lore use was truly the most valuable thing he possessed; but by offering it to her, he had, in his arrogant assurance that she would be unable to resist, resummoned her dream—

Again Krista moved, not to step toward the merchant but rather to shake free the quilt that hung limply before her. Strength whose like she had not known she could summon flooded into her arms in that moment and, even as the scarf had lifted weight-lessly into the air, this far heavier work of her hands rose. The red of loving hearts, the gold of good fortune flashed brilliantly in the sun. She whirled the bride-piece out, fearing suddenly that she might not have the agility to make it reach to where it must go. But—

The trader, who had opened the foul book, snapped it shut again as the cloth reached him. From its pages puffed up a black dust—and the girl knew that he used, now, his ultimate weapon.

Even as that murky powder thickened, the quilt tugged itself loose from the last fingerhold Krista kept upon it. She heard fear-stricken cries, answered by harsh orders barked by the Keeper. The villagers turned as one and stumbled away as fast as they could, women dragging screaming children, men waving staffs and walking backward as though to put themselves between the merchant and their kinfolk.

Red and gold—warmth of heart and truth of soul—the two were mingled together as the quilt found its prey. So brilliantly did the colors blaze that Krista's eyes were dazzled until she was near blinded.

The bride-piece settled. Through its bright expanse nothing could be seen of the outlander. Down, down, it fell; then there was no sign of any wandering trader—or Dark One.

Fire flared, leaping to the canvas of the wagon with a roar of what might have been vengeance. In the same instant vile odors arose, and tendrils of sooty smoke coiled out, seeming wishful of trying to reach those who watched.

There was a last burst of raging flame, and then the fire was gone. Where the wagon and beasts had stood was nothing save withered grass, but where the malevolent merchant had paused to confront the maker of the quilt lay a circle of scorched earth.

Krista sank to her knees, her face buried in her oft-pricked hands. She had trifled with a great Power—and, by the traditions of her people, payment would be demanded for this day's work.

Then hands were on her shoulders, supporting her and drawing her to her feet.

"Have no fear, daughter—you have destroyed the Dark in one of Its guises. True foretelling, Krista, a true foretelling dream!"

The girl turned her head a little so she could see the Keeper's face. In it, she read concern, but also pride—pride in her and her ability with the needle.

She summoned a wan smile and, within her, peace and belief were warm. Then she glanced to where the work of her hands had become a weapon, and she said, with a small catch in her voice,

"It seems that I must needs set to work again, or there will be no bride-piece come oathing-day."

Another quilt, yes—but one born of a dream of heart, not head.

PROCESSION TO YAR
Guardsmen of Tomorrow (2000) DAW

The Guardian lay belly down on the sun-heated rocks, as flat as if his yellow-furred skin held no body. In the wide canyon below, the intruder crawled at an even pace, seemingly undeterred by the rough ground. There were no signs of any legs below its oval bulk, no other signs of propulsion. It might be a Fos beetle swollen to an unbelievable size.

Almost directly below the Guardian's perch, it halted. Sound carried easily as a portion of the nearer side swung up. Movement there, then first one and a second creature emerged to stand beside the crawler, pointing to the rock wall and uttering loud noises.

The Guardian froze. It could not be true! For all the generations his breed had kept watch, there had been no such coming. Still, on the wall below were carved, painted, set so deeply that time had not erased, representations of figures akin to these invaders.

One of them ran back to the beetle, returning with a box. Holding that up with forepaws, the creature made a slow passage before the wall from one end of the procession to the other.

The Guardian's muscles tightened as he gathered his feet under him, rumbling a growl deep in his throat. What did they do? Was this offering a threat to the Far Time? Might they even be trying to wipe away this message of the Great Ones?

He edged backward. Now he could no longer watch them, but it was time he followed orders. These intruders looked so much like the pictures he had seen from cubhood.

Following a trail worn by countless generations of his kind, he pushed between two spurs into the opening behind. His claws were well extended, searching for holds as he passed into darkness.

It *had been four seasons since* the last inspection, but there had seldom been trouble with rockfalls. He dropped into a long chamber. Though the right-hand wall seemed intact, there were concealed openings that emitted enough light to serve a race with well-developed night sight. In turn, those offered spy holes.

He could hear sounds, meaningless to any pattern he understood, and sensed rising excitement. Two strides brought him to the nearest spy hole.

The invaders were just below him, and he studied them carefully for the report he must make. Like the Great Ones, they walked on their hind legs and were tailless. Their forepaws easily handled objects. But they were not altogether alike—the fur on the head of one was grayish while the other had a fire-red patch.

He began to understand that the constant sound was their form of communication. They would not—or could not—touch mind patterns in the proper manner. But perhaps—

One could contact a spas, though the winged ones of the heights were certainly not People, and those of the waterways also used mind touch. Dared he try such with these?

He centered his full attention on the one with the red fur and tried to channel. It was the only way he knew to understand who—or what—they were, or from where they had come.

The thought pattern he touched was alien—like a fast-flowing stream ready to swallow up any mind thrust. Red Fur stopped his spray of sound, swayed back and forth, his paws holding his head. His companion caught his shoulder to steady him, uttering louder noises.

Instantly the Guardian threw up a screen. Even if he had not been able to truly contact the others, there was no reason to believe that they did not have power or powers like enough to his own to strike back.

Instead he sent a warning back to the Caves, addressing the duty officer. Only seconds later he was locked to Yinko and giving a report.

"They are somewhat like the Great Ones in appearance. And they are studying the Procession to Var."

"Have they sought out the Gate of Retrieval?"

"Not so. They have only viewed the carvings. But could it be"—it might be blasphemy to send that thought—"some far kin to the Great Ones have returned after these tens of tens of seasons?"

Yinko did not immediately reply, but when he mind touched again, it was an order.

"Keep watch, report if they do more than look. We shall come."

Red Fur was on the ground leaning against a rock. His companion reentered the beetle. The Guardian studied that carrier as much as his angle of sight allowed.

It was well known that the Great Ones had servants not of their own species. Once, before they had left, they had chosen to instruct the People in many strange things. For a while after they had left, the People still controlled things of metal which could eat out new caves and make life easier in many ways. In time, those had died, though some were kept in memory of those days.

The second intruder was returning with a container he placed on the ground by Red Fur. He pushed something into the mouth of the younger one who then drank from the container. But he still sat with his head supported by his hands, hunched in upon himself.

The Guardian was bemused. It was evident that Red Fur's plight had been brought about by the attempt at mind touch. So—these could not be any far kin of the Great Ones. They had been masters at such contact.

Thus the People had a defense without having to descend to claw and tooth. If his mild attempt had so brought down Red Fur, what would an all-out thrust by the Elders do? He relaxed as curiosity overcame wariness. What did the beetle riders want here? They had appeared greatly excited by the wall paintings, one of the last rock messages remaining. But it was not those faded carvings which had stationed Guardians here so long.

Those only pointed the way to what the Great Ones had put in keeping for a return which had never come. They had stored secrets beyond secrets. This was the outer shell of a storehouse and the warning had been impressed upon the People that only the Great Ones should ever seek its inner heart.

"—sun—"

Galan, Histechneer, Second Class, steadied his head with both hands and somehow managed to answer Narco.

"Not sun—" With an effort he raised his head. His sight was misted at first, but after a few moments he could see the anxiety in the other's face.

Galan drew a deep breath and tried to make sense of what

had happened—not only for Narco but for himself. There was no reasonable explanation.

"In my head—something—from outside—"

Narco sat back on his heels. "An attack? But what—how?" He continued to survey the younger man closely. "All right—the old rule holds—to each world its powers and secrets. A mental invasion?" He slewed around to look at the wall. "A protection? But this is very old. Could any security device last so long?"

Not waiting for an answer, he went back to the crawler and returned wearing a shock helmet and carrying a second one for Galan.

The eye screen cut out some of the punishing rays of the sun. Wearing it did give a sense of security though Galan still felt shaky.

Narco had gone to stand before the wall at midpoint, his eyes sweeping from right to left and back again.

Perhaps it did conceal some secret, but the pictures were plainly meant to represent a journey. Only nowhere else during trips out from the survey camp had they found any indication of such a civilization as these pictures suggested.

There were a number of platforms apparently hovering above the ground unsupported in any way, each carrying heaped-up cargo. Scattered among these floating platforms were people: humanoids.

To have carved and painted this wall would have taken a long time, yet in their own sweeps of exploration they had not found any trace of settlement on this world. Of course the Zacathan head of their expedition might have information he had not yet shared.

"Who—what were they?" Galan staggered up.

Narco shrugged. "Guess. It always comes in the end to guessing. But this is a major find—will surprise some people." He grinned.

That was true. There had been grumbling in the camp lately, though Galan was sure no one yet had said they were wasting time—at least not when the Zacathan was within hearing distance.

Narco retrieved the recorder and was reciting into it a careful description of each section of the wall.

Yes, the time-blurred figures in that Procession were certainly humanoid. They walked erect. Unlike the floating platforms, they needed the support of the ground beneath their feet.

But no matter how hard he tried, Galan could not clearly distinguish any features. Their elaborate headdresses were as secretive as masks.

As Narco went to signal their find to base camp, Galan began to pace along the line of carvings. He noted now that the parade was led by a single figure several lengths ahead of the rest. All of them were wearing tight-fitting garments, each having a belt from which dangled a number of unidentifiable objects, The leader, however, carried a round ball breast high, resting on the palms of both hands. And that ball appeared to be of some substance not native to the cliff, dark gray in color.

The Procession ended just before a fault in the cliff wall itself. Instead of a smooth surface, there was a fissure, triangular in shape, one angle pointing skyward. This was packed tightly with rubble, thoroughly corked.

Tomb? Treasure chamber? Temple? Galan approached that matting of stones cautiously. There had always been a pattern in Forerunner finds on other worlds. Those had varied from the remains of cities to what might only have been temporary encampments. And there were many different races, so these finds had varied to a striking degree.

If something did lie behind that packing of rubble—Every seeker of the past longed to make the GREAT discovery. The

Forerunners had spread through the galaxy, ruled a mighty stellar empire, only to vanish in a sea of time where his own people could not hope to venture beyond the shallows.

Stepping back several feet, he continued to survey that triangular mass from bottom to top. But, as Galan's glance reached the tip, he stiffened. Crowning that point very near the lip of the canyon was—

A carving? But one far more clear-etched—it could have been finished this very day. A head! But not that of any humanoid. The features were almost hidden in a full bearding of red-gold hair or fur. While the broad nose and jaw appeared to resemble a beast's muzzle, the eyes were very large and a startling green, making one think of sun-touched gems.

Galan could not remember sighting that image during their previous close study. Suddenly, there was a grating sound and, from a point not far below that head, a detached stone fell. Galan's hand went to the stunner at his belt.

As his fingers closed on the weapon, they seemed to freeze in a rock-hard position. He struggled to call Narco, only to discover that he was not only held by invisible bonds but also unable to speak.

The green eyes continued to study him impassively for a long moment and then the head withdrew, leaving a dark hole behind. As it disappeared, he found himself free of the strange paralysis that had gripped him.

"Narco!" He felt he dared not turn his back on that hole, and his stunner was out and ready.

"What?" His companion stopped short when he saw the weapon.

"Up there—" Galan used the stunner to indicate the hole as he told what he had seen and how he had been helpless when he thought of trying to defend himself.

Yinko slipped back to where the Guardian and his own escort of scouts waited.

"Weapons they do carry, but against the Power those can not act. They are certainly not of this world." He paused and looked to the Guardian. "Since touch sent one into helplessness, it may be necessary for us to unite and open their minds, to discover what they would do here."

What he suggested was against the First Law and they all knew it. But there was also the oath by which the People had been bound. That which they guarded must not fall into the hands of invaders.

"Upon me," Yinko continued, "the debt of such an action shall fall."

Yinko's words were interrupted by an odd sound which none had ever heard before, a sound that seemed to come from out of the air. A "thing" crossed the pale green of the sky. Not a spas—infinitely larger and moving without any bending of wings.

Instinctively, the party on the cliff flattened themselves down on the rock. The sky thing coasted along above the canyon to where it widened at the northern end. There, the object dropped until it settled near the beetle and sand sprayed out.

As had happened with the beetle, a side opening appeared and more invaders disembarked. However, these did not resemble those from the beetle. The first was humanoid, the body covered with a form-fitting garment not unlike the hue of the rocks. A tight black cap covered all but the humanoid's facial features. High on its shoulders the newcomer wore a bag; from this projected a second head, much smaller and furred.

This first comer moved a short distance away, in a manner which suggested wariness to the watchers above though there was no weapon to be seen. Another figure emerged from the flyer. This one was taller and not of the same species, for all its visible skin was scaled. The hairless head was backed by a fan of skin which rose like a bristling mane, the forepart lying about throat and breast like a collar.

There was an added oddity to this stranger. The left arm was shorter, ending in a hand far too small for the size of the rest of the body, and the appendage on the right was hardly larger.

The scaled one raised that stub of a right hand and started to join the earlier invaders. However, his companion swung around suddenly, as if his body must shield the other from the carved wall, while he also signaled.

Black Cap faced the cliff squarely while the creature he carried in the backpack rested its chin on his shoulder to stare at the carved wall.

On his way to join the newcomers, Galan halted also—half expecting to see a furred head appear aloft.

Naturally, the Histechneer Zurzal had come at the first report of their find. Ranking very high among the Zacathans, he had supplied the backing to assemble this expedition. This planet, for some reason of his own, had been his first choice for investigation.

Black Cap was a Shadow, a professional guard, the Zacathan's constant companion, formally oathed to his service. It was well known that Zurzal was on the Black List of the Thieves Guild, having ruined one of their long prepared missions, and it was well he did travel with one of the formidable Shadows.

The small creature was a Jat. No one had ever been able to discover their full intelligence. However, when one bonded with a human it supplied an ever-present awareness of trouble—an alarm system of flesh, blood, and bone.

His guard's warning had halted the Zacathan. He folded his long legs in a sitting position facing the wall. The Jat, freeing itself from the bag, dropped to join him. But the guard remained standing, positioning himself so he could view both his employer and the cliff.

With the arrival of Zurzal, authority passed to him. Galan's hand went to the strap of his helmet, half expecting another bolt to strike at any moment. It did, but this time the thrust did not find him defenseless. The pain and disorientation were less, heard through the helmet's warning signal.

Blinking his eyes, he saw that the Shadow had wavered a step or two from his position but otherwise did not seem much affected by the attack. The Jat and the Zacathan showed no signs of discomfort.

Jofre, Oathed Shadow, swallowed and swallowed again. As much as he had been trained in the inner Power, he had to meet that pressure with full strength, which aroused the fear of deep brainwash, a rumored weapon of the Guild. Zurzal continued to stare at the carvings, seemingly at ease. Yan, the Jat, had laid a hand-paw on one of the Zacathan's mutilated arms as if in protection.

"The scaled one," Yinko thought-linked. "That one has power—as does the small, furred thing. Not our power, but like to it."

"Great Ones?" The question expressed doubt. These were too alien to People memory.

"Like—unlike," Yinko shook his maned head. "But I doubt we can control these." Once more he looked down at the three who seemed to be waiting—perhaps hoping to discover what defenses the People had.

"We wait," Yinko decided.

Time no longer had any meaning; neither party made a move. At last, the two from the beetle joined the others.

Galan saluted. "There is—" He paused, wanting to explain with care. "It must be some security device. But where? We have not been here long enough for a full search." He glanced at that dull globe carried by the leader of the procession.

"Mind touch," the Zacathan returned calmly. "Hit you hard, did it?" He indicated the helmet.

"But—how? It's all just stone and paint!" He had heard of mind touch, mind speech. However, as far as he knew, he had never encountered it before. That had not been a touch but a stab, one he felt had been delivered with intended malice.

"That is what we see, yes," Zurzal nodded at the wall. "But no, there is no instrument set on guard here. Only living minds can reach so."

"What is to be done?" Narco joined them.

"It lies with who or what watches here." The Zacathan was scratching behind the Jat's large ears. "Wait for a space—"

But time was against them, for again the whine of a flitter echoed arrogantly from the heights. A flitter? But the only one known here was just behind them.

This was larger, and Jofre, well trained, caught sight of those threatening tubes pointing fore and aft. It was armed! And there was no Patrol Star to be seen on the dirty brown of the cabin side. That paint was meant to fade against the mountain lands and desert around them.

The warning came from the Zacathan. "Down—! This is—"

His hissed speech was drowned out by a roaring voice from above.

"Halt! Stand! See and fear!"

A lash of fire flicked out of one of the fore tubes, striking the cliff face. The tip crossed the rubble in the triangle to touch the globe carried by the leader of the procession.

Galan reeled, saw Narco fall, curling up like an insect touched by flame. The Shadow was on his knees, his head shaking from side to side. The Jat plastered itself tightly against the Zacathan's body, its mouth open as if it were screaming, though Galan could not hear through the roaring that filled his head.

Where that flash had fallen was dark—black—as if the very substance of the rock had been consumed. But the globe was alive—vivid ripples of blue, purple, and green were circling out from it. Galan found himself unable to raise his hands to push the helmet closer over his tortured ears. He was locked in place and unable to turn his head.

And now—

There was other movements beside those ripples. Not among the party in the canyon. Nor had anyone descended from the rogue flitter. Long, flattish bodies, the same color as the rocks, were slipping down from the crown of the cliff, hard to see except by their movement.

They avoided the curling streamers of color given forth by the globe, coming to ground to crouch in a defensive line before the Procession.

The black spots were spreading outward in patches as if the entrances to a number of caves were being revealed. In spite of his streaming eyes and painfully roaring head, Galan could not look away. Was this indeed the opening of some treasure-house?

There was a second ray from the enemy flitter—aimed now at that furred line waiting in what seemed to be a pitiful gesture of defense. The thrust did not touch, rather it turned in midair, flashing back toward its source.

The Zacathan and the Jat did not move, only stared ahead. Now the Shadow had crawled to them and raised a hand, though no weapon, so he also might grasp one of the mutilated arms Zurzal held out to him.

Before that deflected blast touched the flitter, it was gone. But the flyer itself bounced upward, steadying well above the cliff top as a hovering warning.

"This is surely of the Great Ones!" The Guardian broke the united mind hold. "Those—they gave to us Power—" He stared at the invaders, still quivering from that strange inflow of force he knew originated with the scaled one and his two companions.

Yinko mind sent in a way that commanded an answer. "Who are you?"

"Seekers of knowledge."

"And those above who would destroy?"

"Those who fear true knowledge. But do not hold them lightly. They are a part of a great evil which has spread from world to world—"

Yinko interrupted: "They turn what they find to their own use?"

"It is so—On guard!"

The flitter had been moving away, only now to circle back. There was an opening in its belly, though if these jackers had come for wealth or knowledge of the past and used even a gas bomb, the effects of which might last long in this canyon, they could defeat their own purposes.

Yinko looked to the Guardian. The order he gave was one which had not been used for a thousand years or more. With a burst of speed that seemed incredible to the watching invaders the Guardian threw himself as if to crash against the wall. That wall which Galan saw was cracking as the circling light of the globe appeared to bring destruction farther and farther out.

Into one of those enlarging cracks the Guardian plunged headfirst. He was now back in the gallery from which he had earlier spied on the strangers. Speeding across it, he slammed his metal-sheathed claws into a spot on the inner wall and exerted all his strength.

The door he attacked gave reluctantly. Those without would buy him time if they could, but how strong was the power of the others? Could their weapons be held for a second time by the united effort of the People and those who had voluntarily aided at the first attack?

He was looking down, not into some dimly lit cavern but rather into a very large space where at intervals along the walls were set rods emitting light. Nearly all the floor was covered with large, topless bins, packed in turn with containers of all sizes and shapes. The Guardian turned left, finding footing on a narrow ledge.

Outside, the jackers seemed in no hurry to press an attack. They must know that the offworlders below knew very well the threat of that open hatch.

"You gave power—"

Zurzal still held the Jat and had drawn the Shadow closer. "We gave power," he corrected

"Why? Are those not of your kind?" Yinko pointed upward.

"Not so," Zurzal's denial was quick. "They are enemies who seek the destruction of many. My people came here to learn of the Forerunners, those Great Ones of the past. That is the work of my life. For knowledge is the greatest weapon and defense that any life-form may have."

"Are you of the Great Ones? They had, we know, many forms." Yinko watched the Zacathan closely.

"We cannot be sure that long ago they did not give us life. But they were long gone before we rode the starways."

"Still you seek—for what—new weapons—treasure?" persisted Yinko.

"For knowledge such as you have guarded here."

"Much has long been forgotten. Those who come know not even what they seek. Unless—" he glanced overhead, "it is for gain, for death. Surely, these deal in death."

"I have said they are enemies of ours as well as of your people. Yes, they are death dealers."

"Yet they came not until you did. Therefore, perhaps you were their guide."

"Not knowingly. You have met us mind to mind. These have not mind speech," he indicated Galan and Narco. "But they are allied in our searching. Those," he glanced up, "may have followed, yes, but we knew it not."

Galan wondered why the jack flitter did not move in. They must be well aware that those in the canyon—at least seemingly—had no visible weapons of defense.

His answer came from the sky like the growl of some great predator.

"Down on your bellies, all of you! Or be crisped!"

The flitter was again on the move, slowly and with visible precision, as if those on board had a task needing great care.

Yinko's head jerked up as did those of his following.

"Though it has been forbidden, it must be done. We must use the great blanking—and from it there is no escape." His thought was as sharp as a knife thrust.

In the depths of the cracking cliff the Guardian had reached his goal. Never had this action been carried out, but all those who had held this duty during the years had been well drilled in what was to be done. He dropped from the ledge to land in front of a large screen. Staring at it, he flexed his claws.

"Galan! Narco!" They had guessed that the Zacathan had been in contact with the creatures by the cliff, but now he used normal speech. "There is only one chance for us now. These are about to draw upon mind power. You have not had the training, nor perhaps the inborn talent, but—there remains one small hope. Discard your helmets, open your minds. Think of yourselves as channels and welcome what comes. I cannot promise you survival, but this I know. We have no other hope against what the Guild will do."

Galan fumbled with the clasp of the helmet. This—It was beyond all reason, but one could only trust. If Zurzal thought they had a chance, he would try it. He closed his eyes as the helmet thudded to the ground beside him, not even looking to see if Narco had made the same choice.

The Guardian felt as if the whole of the mountain had come, shivering, to life. He jerked under the power of the order which came, bringing his claws down to depressions not made for the fingers of his kind but into which he could force them. He was no longer—no longer anything. Color, light, waves of darkness closed about him. He was—not!

Galan cried out as that which he could not see, only feel as a growing torment, filled his head. Then—then there was nothing at all.

From the cracks in the wall of the Procession came something. It could not be seen with blinded eyes, it could not be heard by deafened ears, nor answer to any touch. But the strength of it was beyond belief.

The jack flitter had released an oval object, yet it did not fall as it was meant to. Rather, it hung just below the opening through which it had come. None of those below saw; all of them had been woven into a single purpose.

With a jerk, as if it had been seized by a giant hand, the flitter spun and then was released. With the weapon still dangling below, it headed westward out over the wasteland. And, as it went, it sped far faster then its designers had ever intended. Then, there came sound, sound which broke through the concentration of the defenders. Near the far horizon arose a fiery cloud.

For those in the canyon it was as if they fell helplessly from a great distance. Pain—such pain—Galan could not see! He felt as if there was terrible pressure trapped within his skull battering a way out.

He never knew how long he was encased in that hell of torment. On opening his eyes he noticed there was still a web of mist about him. There came a touch on his head. It did not add to the pain; rather, the torment began to fade. He cared only for that touch and the ease it brought. At last, he could make out the Zacathan bending over him. There were no stones or sand under him. But as the pain lessened, he became aware he rested on something soft—fur? The—beast things. As he turned his head slightly, still fearing a return of pain, he could see the furry face, closer to him than the Zacathan. The alien must be holding him.

"Rest," he was ordered and, even as he slid into waiting darkness, he was faintly aware that the order had reached him in a strange new way.

Morning brought full sight of what their defense had cost. Great cracks, slices of fallen stone lay against the wall. There was nothing left of the Procession to Var. But it was before the site of that irreparable loss that most of the People held conference with the offworlders.

"This shall be promised and sworn to by the First Law," Zurzal's thoughts came slowly as if he found it difficult to shape them.

Galan's hands were at his head again. There was pain; there would be for some time, the Zacathan had told him. But he had awakened something he longed ardently to use—that he must learn.

"Sworn to," Zurzal was repeating. "Our report to those who sent us shall be that there is no evidence of any Forerunner remains here. And that is now true."

"True," Yinko echoed. "Knowledge is worth much, but life is worth more. You have not asked what may lie within," he gestured to the riven cliff. "By your aid you have bought the right to know."

"No. There is this. I am a marked one. Those who attacked us here are my enemies. In some fashion they discovered that we were coming to your world to search. It is not my right to uncover secrets which should only be known by those left to guard them. This I promise you. There will be no report of what has happened. We shall destroy what records we have already made. Nor shall we speak of the People. This shall be an aborted mission and a forgotten world."

He got to his feet, the Jat moving from the crook of his misshapen arm to lean against his shoulder. The Shadow was also on his feet, but he wavered a little until he raised his head with a look of grim determination on his drawn face.

The battle was not over for those three, Galan knew. Would it ever be?

Yinko lingered for a moment. "You serve the Power well. Truly the Great Ones must once have touched your people. Our People will guard until the stars change and those who once were shall come again."

The furred ones were already climbing the battered cliff. Galan searched for sight of a single figure, a carved curve of stone or a faded sweep of paint. It was gone, all gone. Suddenly, fiercely he longed to see it again.

This had been a major find. Yet, with the mind touch still with him, he knew that the Zacathan was right.

He could not guess what had been here, but he felt that it was something his species should not find. And if, by trying to discover more, they would again bring in the Guild—no. Let them raise ship and go.

"Galan," the mind touch could still startle him. "There are many worlds and many finds to be made. And a greater one may be waiting."

Zurzal started for the flitter, and Galan entered the crawler where Narco was already at the controls.

On the cliff top Yinko and the others watched them go, one set flying, one crawling. Then he turned and saluted with both forepaws.

"To you, Guardian, rest well in the place of peace. You have fulfilled the duty set upon you."

SET IN STONE
Far Frontiers (2000) DAW

If some mad god had deliberately set out to create a planet utterly alien from all that was normal to the crew of First-In Scout S-9, he or she could not have been more successful than with this one. A man had to force his offworld eyes to report matters that brain patterns found too grotesque to believe.

A dull throb was spreading down from Kannar's temples, reaching out for room in neck and shoulders. This place was just *wrong*; yet, along the starways, one could never rightfully judge anything, no matter how it appeared—

"Get scruffing, you Gart!"

That sharp mind-beam smote like a blow, though it was a prodding he had come to expect during the past three years. Yes, he was a Gart. Not many of them could be left by now, as Garthold had long since been wiped from the maps. As for his kind, they were the least blessed of all their kin. Kannar no longer grasped at memory, which grew—mercifully—ever fainter with each recall.

Fifteen planet years ago . . . The young man plodded along through the dense gray sand, weighed down by his heavy pack but careful to avoid the thick pad-patches of yellow-green growth. Fifteen cycles past, he had been at Herber, a child selected by rigorous testing intended to prove his fitness for special service to Garthold's need.

Two hellish days and a burning, blood-filled night had put an end to that life, though some Veep among the invaders did think to keep Kannar and some of his fellows alive for use in "experiments." More trials were visited upon them by their new masters, during which many died, while others were rendered mindless and thrown into the Pits. What quality the alien overseers believed Kannar possessed had brought him into the Quasing Exploration Service—not, of course, as an equal, but rather as a living test-beast for the unknown perils of distant worlds.

The boy's thick gray skin itched now, as it had ever since Captain O'ju had ordered him to gather a liver-red growth for the science officer using his bare hands. His masters had given Kannar no treatment for the fiery result; they had merely watched its progress detachedly, as yet another investigation.

"You damned dirtworm—gun it! We want to get this crawler going before dark!"

As that order rang in Kannar's head, he could see below him the land vehicle in question, its curved nose almost touching one of the standing rocks. No trees graced this world of Henga, or at least the Scouts had observed none during any of the preliminary flybys; but rising upright in rough circles which, in places, clustered thick together, were the stones.

Those formations had presented the planet's first great mystery. Though to the eye they were only crude pillars of a granite-like stuff, they could not be touched, nor even approached closely enough for any to attempt to set hand upon them. They were, it seemed, impregnably shielded by some unknown force against close examination.

Kannar did not quicken his pace. He knew too well that nothing he could do might protect him from the vicious attentions of O'ju waiting for him down there. The accident with the crawler would, of course, be blamed on him, and then . . .

Overhead, the green-fired orb of the small sun was now close to the broken line of the horizon, and the slate-colored sky had begun to darken. Even as no trees grew here, neither did any birds or flying things soar aloft—in fact, the sole life-form that seemed to have been grudgingly bestowed upon Henga was a variety of malignant vegetation.

The youth drew up beside the land transport and grounded his pack on the sand thick underfoot. The captain, always careful of his tools (human and otherwise), waited until that storage bag was safe; then, wielding his laser like a club, he aimed a blow at its bearer.

Kannar dodged as best he could, stumbling back toward the stone against which the crawler was now nuzzled. He struck against something he could not see that gave a little on contact with his body, then pushed him away. The combination of that shove, the irritation of his skin, and the throbbing in his head broke through the control he had held so firmly. For a moment, the scene around him wavered; then he could clearly see the weapon threatening him in O'ju's heavy-gloved fist. No longer was the gun held for use as a bludgeon—now it faced him muzzle-end first, the inescapable death-dealer it had been cast to be.

The laser grew in the boy's sight, looming larger as his superior approached. Why didn't O'ju simply fire? Certainly his captive slave possessed no defense.

Defense—?

Through the pulsing pain in Kannar's head a thought struck. The fear that had held him motionless, an easy target, suddenly gave way to a clear memory of his half-forgotten life and the training that had protected him in the past. He was *Gart!*

Moving in one of his old defensive tricks, the youth landed belly-down in the sand, partway under the stalled crawler. Blinding fire burst around him; then there was darkness.

"Scout Six, to the fore!"

Kannar lifted his head an inch or so. The effort was almost more than he could sustain.

"Scout Six, report! "

The order was a further goad. That voice from the impenetrable blackness—the Scouts must be on night maneuvers.

"Scout Six in, sir," the boy mouthed through the grit that masked his face. He tried to lever himself higher and pierce the stifling night by sheer force of will. Unable to see, he tried to listen, to catch more speech or any identifying sound.

Then he began to cough. It was as though the dark had invaded his throat and was striving to reach his lungs. One bout of the chest-racking spasms left him weak and gasping until he felt that no more breathable air remained to him. Kannar flailed out in near panic, fighting to beat away the smothering blackness, but his weak efforts were futile, and he ceased to struggle and sank into oblivion once more.

Yet even his inner night was without peace, lit by a fitful lightning of dream-flashes and broken bits of memory that skittered away whenever he tried to focus upon them. The boy whimpered and huddled in upon himself, seeking forgetfulness again.

When the young Scout roused the second time, it was into real night-dark, not the curtain that had been drawn across his mind before. The first of Henga's three pale moons was climbing the sky, and there were stars—*stars!*

Though still aware of a heavy stench that made him gag, he had awakened clearheaded enough to know where he was and to realize the source of his lungs' torment. He managed to drag himself upright. Within arm's reach was one of the thick patches of moss, and in the reduced light, he could see the sparks that arose from the mat of vegetation.

Even that poor illumination showed Kannar more: a body— or rather a portion of body, for the head and shoulders of that sprawl of flesh and bone had been reduced to blackened rags melted into the sand on which it lay. O'ju. But—who had turned a laser on *him?* The boy clenched one of his own scaly hands reflexively. A gun was lying on the ground almost within reach, yes, but *he* had certainly not dropped it!

Suddenly the Scout froze. There had been movement close to him—the motion of something small, perhaps only a little larger than his two hands clasped together. As it neared the phosphorescent plant-stuff, he could see its form more and more clearly.

The creature had eight legs, the two at its fore-end being held aloft and tipped with large claws. Its body shared the puffy plumpness of the moss and was a dull gray, near the color of the sand across which it was scuttling. It made a detour around the dead, but seemed to be following a purposeful course.

Then it halted by the laser. Both fore-claws swung down and fastened upon the weapon, which was raised until it rested on the round back of the thing. Task apparently completed, the being swung about and headed back the way it had come.

Kannar drew a deep breath, wrenching his mind back with an effort from the curious action he had just witnessed to the ugly scene at hand. He could do nothing for O'ju, and repair of the crawler was beyond his skill. No Gart had ever been allowed knowledge of Quasing technology. But the youth was aware that the land vehicle sent out some type of signal to guide searchers, and that sooner or later the surviving Scouts would make a flyby from their camp. They would find a dead man, the second-in-command of their mission, an inert crawler, and—a *Gart*. To them, the answer would be very simple.

The boy licked dry lips then spat grains of sand. Many ingenious forms of death had been invented by his masters—even death-in-life. He could not hope for a clean ending if he remained to be found.

The creature with its perilous burden could still be seen, heading toward a wider space between two of the rocks; it was plainly seeking what it considered a safe place. The Scout made a swift decision. What might be a haven for one born of Henga could be a lethal trap for an offworlder, but perhaps the ending he could find there would be quick. The youth was bleakly convinced that a death of this world was infinitely preferable to any the ship's crew would deal him.

The native had crawled between a pair of the stone pillars, keeping an exact distance from both. The off-world boy was considerably larger than his guide, and the field of power generated by the rocks might well repel him. He could only test it.

Doggedly, Kannar moved forward on his hands and knees, his out-suit crunching on the sand. With every breath he drew, he expected to be smitten by some force beyond his comprehension.

But the opposition he feared did not come. Instead, once he had passed completely through the portal-pillars, he came into a place where there was more light and a feeling of freshness in the air. The boy reached what was roughly the center of that uneven circle and hesitated. At last he hunkered back on his heels and strove to scan all the surrounding rocks with a slow turn of his head, a crouching shift round and round. Nothing he could see differed from what was before him at every view: the silent stones deep-rooted into the sand. But the being he had followed, though the weight of the laser was plainly sapping its strength, was still going purposefully forward.

Now it faced the most massive of the rocks, and there it laid the weapon upon the ground, seeming to have accomplished a set mission. As Kannar watched, unsure of just what was taking place, he saw a movement at the foot of every stone within his range of sight. More of the puff-bodied creatures rose from the sand in front of those pillars. As the first native stood a little to one side, each of the newcomers advanced in turn. None of them attempted to raise the gun, but rather scraped their forelegs across it length- and width-wise, the tips of their claws grating on the metal of the offworld weapon.

The late arrivals trailed away discreetly and vanished as they had appeared; however, the creature who had delivered the laser remained where it was. The young Scout saw no signal given, heard no sound break the ever-noiseless night, but the burden-bearer now began to dig. Throwing goodly clawfuls of sand from side to side, it worked with such speed that, in a short time, a hole appeared. Into that opening it purposefully tumbled the laser, then covered the weapon with the same haste. An instant later—

Kannar caught his breath. The stone before which the gun had been entombed began to glow, and—though he was certain nothing like this had been there before—a line of some sort of crystals appeared, zigzagging down the rough side of the pillar. The glittering bits shed a soft light, too, and their radiance grew brighter with every second.

The creature gave a sudden spring forward, plastering its full body-length against the rock and across the crusting of crystals. The watching boy became aware of a new scent in the air; unlike any he had encountered on this world, yet the odor was pleasant, and deep memory stirred within him. *Holiday—feasting—well done!* Why did he now think of a trophy award?

His hand reached forward instinctively, but he was not close enough to touch the pillar, even if such contact were allowed. The native being had dropped from the stone, and the vein of mineral formations was fading fast. Then the limited light around him began to fail, as well, until the dark ruled utterly. Unbearable fatigue descended upon Kannar, and he slept.

The Scout awoke suddenly. Light had come again—the light of day—and—sound. A flyby. The search pattern might not take the ship directly over this stone circle. A flyer had gone down during the first general exploration, and the theory had been offered that the protection surrounding the rocks might also extend into the air above. But, if that hope failed, the rock ring afforded no place to hide.

The boy swallowed, painfully aware of a dry throat and the pinch of hunger. The others need only leave him where he was, and their purpose would be fulfilled: another Gait would be accounted for, and with very little effort on their part.

Kannar could see between the stones clearly. The crawler still stood, nose pressed to one of them, and nearby lay the splotch that had been O'ju. The flyer was setting down well away from that point. Three men emerged from the cargo door, rendered clumsy by heavy protect-suits. Each carried not a laser but a blaster, and they advanced in a broken pattern as though to discourage or evade attack.

There was nowhere to run now, the youth knew. The strength that had sustained him through his years of being a Gart in bondage was gone. He could do no more than wait and hope he would die quickly.

A crackle sounded in the earphone he still wore. Captain O'Lag had reached the land vehicle and looked upon what lay beside it. The harsh stridency of his voice seared Kannar as his commander voiced the filthy destiny due a Gart.

"No laser." That was O'Sar, the science officer.

But O'Lag was no longer studying the stalled machine and the corpse at its base. His bulging eyes burned yellow with rage as his gaze swept through a gap in the stone circle, pinning the boy to the spot like an insect specimen on a board. The captain stopped his volley of curses almost in mid-word, and his blaster shifted as he sighted through that opening at Kannar.

On impulse, the Gart abandoned his hugging of the sand to pull himself upright and face his superior who stood outside the ring of rocks. It did not become one who had been Second Cadet Officer at Herber to cower before the enemy. Sometimes how a man dies matters, and death would be swift and sure when O'Lag pressed the button—

Fire came. So blinding was the flash that Kannar staggered back, though he did not fall. He heard sizzling in his earphone, then such cries as brought back nightmare memories of the invasion of his own world.

Fire had come—yet he was not consumed! The youth blinked, fought against the brilliance that seemed to cloak his eyeballs. Though the shrieks had died away, he could now smell the stench of cooked flesh, the acrid tang of metal heat-seared. But he still stood—*lived*—and soon he began to see again, at first as if through a mist, then without hindrance.

No blaster-burn was visible on the stones facing him, between two of which O'Lag had fired; no reek of death any longer poisoned the air. Without the circle, however, lay two crumbling forms, their ash mixing with the sand, and the crawler with a great hole melted into it. It looked—Kannar rubbed the back of one hand across his eyes and cleared his vision enough to see true—it looked as if the captain had aimed not at a trapped Gart but had rather turned his weapon against his own men and their machine.

Noise again; the flyer was taking off. The vessel was equipped with out-mounted blasters. Did the pilot now intend to avenge this disaster with air-to-surface fire?

Yet though the vessel made a circuit of the standing stones, it did not approach closely, nor loose any deadly bolts from its belly. It did not linger long but winged away toward the camp.

He was still alive: Kannar accepted as fact something he would have thought impossible. Yet Death was not far off, for so great was his thirst that the dryness in his throat choked, and hunger gnawed him like a beast. Because there was no more need to make a parade of pride, the boy allowed himself to slide to the ground, facing the opening in the rocks so he could still view the carnage that lay beyond.

What he saw there was as much beyond reason as his own survival, if he could believe what dimming eyes told dulling mind: both the near-consumed corpses and the blasted crawler were sinking steadily into the sand. But even so strange an event meant nothing to him now. The last link with humankind—for the Quasings had to be deemed at least physically human—had been broken. The youth turned his head slowly and stared up at the dense gray-blue clouds that showed Henga's green sun through their drifting mass like matrix rock revealing a precious jewel.

Time seemed to have stopped for him. His memory had been buried even as had the dead Scouts and their vehicle, and he was being consumed by hunger and thirst. A man could not take long to die thus. . . .

It was as though a hand had been laid on his scaled cheek, moved to touch his lips. Kannar raised his head to follow, to hold that touch—and then he was crawling toward the stone pillar before which the laser had been entombed. He gasped and coughed rackingly as he dragged himself forward, barely able to breathe or see; but though all other senses were nearly gone now, he could still smell, and there was a *scent*—

His fingers touched the roughness of the rock, and for an instant he hunched his shoulders, waiting for a blast of defensive energy he would be helpless to counter. When no attack came, he looked up again. Then he saw it—a glow welling up from a crevice in the rock between his hands. Those crystals with the radiance of gems—they gave forth not only light but that scent, which promised help ever more strongly.

The boy's painfully swollen tongue touched the bubbling stuff. It gave—No words existed in any galactic language he knew to describe *this!* Warmth, comradeship, all he had lost long ago were restored to him in a moment, more richly than before they had been torn away. He licked the feast, which did not cloy, until he was thoroughly sated.

It appeared that Kannar had partaken of a true banquet. First his body had been tended, and he was not tired anymore but refreshed and avid to enjoy what might be offered next. That was the main course. And for the after-sweet? A gift to mind and spirit: thoughts were what he drank now. This planet was indeed more strange than any he had seen or heard of.

What his kind had taken for pillars of lifeless stone were the Old Ones, who stood rooted in the very flesh of their world, who had seen stars be born and die. To them knowledge came, though some of that a human could not understand. With them in partnership lived the skaat, the creatures who served as hands when such aids were needed. And even the winds and the clouds brought messages, for what any thought became a part of all the world.

Old Ones—?

Welcome, star son. The words rang as clear in Kannar's mind as if he had heard them with his ears. *You are now blood of our blood, substance of our substance.*

The boy had been minded of a prize awarding when the gray creature had claimed its crystal-feast after burying the laser. He felt so now. Everything that had been Herber in the days before the ending of Gart was here, and he was entering the great Gate of the Victors where all his comrades waited to greet him.

Kannar knew that he had much—oh, so much!—to learn, but those of this place were anxious to share. And he did have something of value to offer in return: his memories of Gart, his knowledge of other worlds, different beings.

A flurry of activity commenced in the space near the Old One who had made him welcome. The skaat—a number of them— were digging speedily, and a hole of some depth soon appeared. Without hesitation, the youth took two steps forward, then lowered himself into the scooped-out place, which engulfed his body to the knees. Sand was shifted quickly back to cover him.

Rest now, star son, the stone-born voice rang in his mind. *When the Change is done, we will have all the time of the stars to learn from one another.*

A gentle night closed upon Kannar as though curtains had been drawn, and a sudden drop of sweetness dewed his lips. He drew it in eagerly, then slept.

RAVENMERE
Historical Hauntings (2001) DAW

"Heard as how they has sold Ravenmere—to foreigners. Have to be such."

I had nearly reached that portion of the general shop sacred to Her Majesty's mail before the two women at the other end of the crowded room noticed me. For my part, I paid no visible heed to the silence that ensued as they did; in the small towns of my American homeland, strangers were equally suspect.

Mrs. Jones propelled her considerable bulk around the end of the counter. "You was a-wanting your package, Miss? Jimmy the Post brought it in last night." She produced a box from a pile of parcels and slid it toward me.

"Mighty lot of stamps on that," the proprietress observed. Though her delivery duty was concluded, she did not turn away but stood watching. The little eyes in her broad face flitted from me to the box and back again.

I decided that, the sooner I gave my new neighbors something real to discuss, the quicker I would be accepted as relatively harmless.

"Yes, there are," I agreed; then I took my first step toward acquaintance. "Some children collect stamps. Do you know any youngster who would like these, Mrs. Jones?"

The shopkeeper nodded. "If you'd be so kind, our Jamie does that, miss—Miss Tremayne."

Out of nowhere a pair of scissors appeared, and I carefully cut out the much-bestamped corner of the parcel's wrapping. Enid had certainly made sure of a safe delivery of my order, I thought as I passed the scrap to Mrs. Jones.

Encouraged by this minor ice-breaking, I voiced my real concern. "Could you direct me," I asked, "to someone who could help in the house?"

Silence again, except for a kind of hiss from the other customer, who was now looking at me intently. The shop's owner retreated a step or so, and her mouth pursed as though locking itself on any answer.

"I can post a notice if you want," was the curt reply. The woman nodded toward the door, where a small board hung to which a few tags of paper had been pinned.

"That would be most kind," I answered. "I would like help every day but Sunday—just general cleaning."

Mrs. Jones nodded once more, then abruptly turned back to her other patron. "More o' them cream biscuits for you today, Missus Calder?"

I had been dismissed but accepted the fact without irritation. I was far from certain I would be here very long; however, though I am not a gregarious person, there are shades of loneliness that even I did not wish to darken my days.

As though bodying forth my thought, the overgrown trees and shrubs on the path leading back to my lodging cast their own darkness over me. It was most apparent that this was not a well-traveled way, yet its budding promised an early spring that I longed to see.

A few minutes of travel brought me into an uneven clearing that contained my temporary home: a cottage larger than those in the village. When Ravenmere was in its glory, this place must have housed the bailiff. But what, I had wondered from my first sight of it, had it been in the very beginning?

Two slabs of rock resembling menhirs flanked either side of the door, and stones even larger and apparently more ancient formed the base of the walls. The structure had been created by additions—quite a number of them. Each succeeding century had left its own mark here.

The great house of the estate was now merely a tumble of stone half-hidden by vegetation long out of control. I had no desire to explore that area; none of the locals had warned of snakes, but such a miniature jungle seemed a place where snakes might well set up hole-keeping. What the present owners intended to do with the long-deserted estate they had not yet decided, but meanwhile I had settled here at their invitation for an indefinite stay.

On so promising a day, my chosen workplace was not inside. I set the box I had just acquired into the top of my handy wheeled tote, then pushed past bushes that clutched at my jeans, heading for the discovery I'd made on my second day of residence.

They were called "follies" two centuries ago, such fantastic small buildings placed in formal gardens. Some, of which I had seen pictures, were modeled after classical temples or hermits' caves, and a few were large enough to be used for sheltering picnic meals or staging amateur theatricals. This one, set to front a weed-choked lake, must have indeed been a folly where money was concerned. Its shape was that of a square tower, as though to suggest it had once been part of a now-vanished fortress. Fortunately for my needs, real windows, not arrow-slits for the convenience of castle defenders, had been built into the four sides of the structure. All gave good light, but that was best at the side where I chose to set up my worktable in the single room: facing the water.

The lake was framed by coarse reeds that formed an oddly-precise ring about its murky liquid. One could easily imagine strange life going about its own affairs beneath the surface; yet, while I had been drawn several times to study it, I had never thought of menace.

I unloaded my tote with the ease of long practice, setting out assembly trays, then glass bottles of beads, boxes of threads, and a container of tools—needles and the like. Next I took out my pattern sheet, which I had fastened to stiff backing. At last I was free to deal with the contents of the parcel.

I lifted away the packing material, and what lay within came to life with color. For a moment I simply feasted upon those many hues. Enid had been more than generous. Glowing ember of garnet, molten lava of ruby, noon sun of gold—bands of fire appeared to pulse across the beads dyed with the warm tones of the spectrum. Farther along, the colors cooled to water-tints of green and blue, then chilled to silver, gray, and black. Every nuance was present, from the lightest to the darkest.

Yesterday I had set up the embroidery frame. Now I rose and pulled it from the wall, untied the protecting cover, and drew it into the strongest light; the casters on its legs would make it easy to move as the sun shifted. Finally I arranged the pattern, creasing it so it might be readily consulted. When I had subsided again into my chair, I let myself relax and become absorbed in studying the lines marked on the long banner of gray silk tight-stretched before me.

This was an old art. Exquisite examples had been brought into being in the far past but were now only to be marveled at in museums; however, such "painting" had recently been reborn to enchant beadworker and beholder alike. Considering the challenge of the craft, I flexed my fingers nervously, so much in doubt of my own skill that I almost shrank from threading the first needle.

I continued to gaze at the waiting fabric, picking out the lines I had set there as guides no more than an afternoon ago. But—quickly I pulled my chair closer, reaching at the same time for the large magnifying glass I kept always at hand—*No!*

I snatched up the paper pattern with its intricate markings. Leaf and branch were gone! A drawing remained there, right enough, but it no longer showed the picture I had so carefully designed in days of planning. The glass tilted in my shaking hand.

There was no possible way this could have happened. The new lines had obviously been set down by someone experienced in such work; however, I could not believe that what I had created with such labor had simply vanished—or rather been exchanged for this alien motif which bore no resemblance to it.

Shaking with anger fast growing into such a rage as I had never known, I lifted one hand to rip the cloth from the frame. All my limited time—wasted! And by whom? In this small village, which person could have the expertise to do such a thing—and why?

With this thought, my hand fell again to the table, and I cowered in my seat. The unnatural—impossible—nature of the act had smothered my fury with a fear as icy cold as the anger had been hot. Such a thing could *not* happen!

Every movement was an effort; still I forced my head around and twisted my body so I could view the room without trying to get to feet I did not believe would support me at present. I listened, too, though I could hardly demand an explanation from emptiness.

Then an answer came. Like a hand gripping me by the nape of my neck, some compulsion forced me to bend forward, examine again those marks I had never made. As I did, I began to understand the meaning of this and that traced line. They formed a picture, yes, but one very unlike what I held in mind. The more I studied the artistry of that unknown hand, the greater grew my fear. The only word I could put to the feeling of what I detected in the new pattern was—*Power.* My fear became awe, then envy. This was masterwork, as far above my own labors as they would be beyond the stumbling stitches of a clumsy child.

I laid down the magnifying glass, pushed out of my chair, and stepped through the door, leaving all behind me unprotected. A wind, not yet more than a breeze, had arisen. Careful to keep away from the edge of the reed-bed, I stood for a long moment facing the lake.

The rising air was light, but it drew ripples across the surface. As I watched, though without truly concentrating on what I observed, I saw colors moving wave-wise in my mind: green of standing water, blue of sun-touched shallows, gray of shadow-play.

Thus—and thus—and thus—

I swung around and ran back to the workroom. Throwing myself into the seat, I faced the smooth stretch of waiting background. *Yes!* There could be no mistake: the design had been altered to represent the pond. But by whom had it been drawn, and for what purpose?

Curiously, those questions no longer troubled my mind. It seemed enough that the scene without had been brought within. I might be caught up in a mystery, but fear had departed.

Touching the fabric, I gasped. My probing finger had been stung with a sharp burst of force like that of an electric shock. I felt filled with energy, consumed by the need to bring to life the image I could now see on that expanse of cloth.

When I looked up from my labor, the light had moved; the hard jewel-glitter of the beads had softened to a stained-glass glow. For the first time, I was aware of the ache in my hands, my shoulders, and I felt dizzy as I straightened up. My mouth was dry, too. I had never worked thus before, so utterly absorbed in what I was doing.

I glanced away from the small section on which I had been concentrating, then back again—a device I used to sharpen sight dulled by fixed gazing and to catch any error.

I saw the green of velvety sod, the blue of liquid unclouded by murk and laced with a silver glint that expertly created the illusion of breeze-wakened ripples. And at the nearer edge of that body of water was the outline of a pacing bird.

Close-mown grass, not the rank growth I knew to exist outside my window; water of such freshness that it might be rising from a clear spring; a bird in stately pose. The deft shading and setting of the beads made it alive—all of it. I drew a breath of wonder. I had prided myself on my work, but *this*—this was perfection such as I had aspired toward but never before attained.

Thus began my bondage, for imprisonment—and forced labor—it came to be. Luckily, the cottage had been stocked with provisions when I moved in, as I begrudged any time away from my task, even the brief length needed to prepare a simple meal. I sustained myself by oatmeal made in quantities and swallowed speedily when I came out of bed; then by soup and crackers, or a mess of canned vegetables, heated up at dusk when the light had faded too far for me to put in even one more bead. I did not break my absorption for any midday meal.

During the hours when I was not occupied with needles, beads, and tiny stitches, muscles I never knew I owned protested their hours of being pulled as taut as the threads they had sent into the silk. However, while I labored, I felt nothing but excitement, a relentless drive to accomplish as much as I could. That in itself was new, for it was clear that I was now somehow able to complete far more work at each sitting than I had ever done before.

On the third day I was interrupted. Without warning a shadow fell across the backing of the bead-picture, and I glanced up, startled, to see someone standing at the window that faced the lake. At the same instant, the passionate desire to continue my crafting vanished.

The woman was tall, and her body was concealed in a dark garment so that only her face was visible. That was an ivory mask in which the eyes alone showed life; but once I had raised my own to look into them, I could not turn away. Out of that muffling cloak emerged a pale, long-fingered hand, and she beckoned.

Nor could I delay my answer to that gesture. I rose and went to the door and, as I opened it, found myself facing my visitor through the window in another wall. Again her gaze held me mute and waiting. She herself was in no hurry to speak; instead, she shrugged almost lazily, and her covering slipped from her. That garment never reached the floor—suddenly, it simply *was not*.

The dress she wore beneath fitted far more snugly and was of a now-familiar green-blue shade touched here and there among its folds with a flick of silver. Her hair had been divided into a pair of heavy braids, one of which fell across her left breast while the other disappeared behind her right shoulder.

By now I was shivering—this *lady* (she surely owned no lesser title) could not be anyone from the village come in answer to my note posted in the store. Not by the greatest stretch of imagination could I envision her wielding broom or duster, or bustling about a kitchen with cooking pots!

She ceased to hold me with her measuring stare but rather advanced boldly so that I was forced to move aside as she strode past me. When I turned, she was standing before the frame and tracing with her first finger a pattern in the air, at a few inches' distance from the patch of completed work. Now and then she nodded, as though with approval. I was still trying to summon the courage for a question when she spoke.

"Nimuë ever chooses well. You are truly of her service, Maid of the Needle—"

Nimuë . . . that name . . . Deep within me, a memory struggled to awaken.

At last I succeeded in speaking. "Lady—who are you?"

My visitor smiled enigmatically. "Who am I? Well, I have borne many names in my time: Traitor, Challenger, Destroyer, Dealer-in-Death. How like you such titles?" Now she laughed, on a mocking note. "You will find them told in chronicles long kept, but said to spring only from bards' fancies and to have no force of true life in them."

I backed away, believing by now that the woman was not only attempting to frighten me but also that she was working herself up to an act of violence. Clearly she was insane.

"No," she replied as though she had read my thoughts. "I am not twisted of mind—I am, in truth, more sane than this world with all its strains and stresses. But this work," she indicated the bead-picture, "will alter that. For you there will be payment, when the labor is complete. And that must be soon."

I began to shake my head. The gesture of negation grew ever faster, until I could hardly see and only the supporting wall behind me kept me on my feet. Still I could not voice the denial that seemed dammed behind frozen lips.

Now my legs, too, obeyed orders that were not my own, carrying me to my seat and planting me firmly in it. I twisted my hands together, resisting the pressure that came next to pick up a needle, choose another bead.

The woman had likewise moved, and I could still see her.

That she was enjoying the sight of my resistance—and relishing my grinding-down into subordination—was very plain.

"What name do you bear in this age, Maid of the Needle?"

That query swung a lash of force against which I could not stand.

"Gwen—Gwen Tremayne."

Once more the water-gowned one laughed, and her gaze swept over me slowly from head to feet, as though she were appraising me in some way.

"This time is not so fortunate for you, is it—my Queen?" she drawled, her tone close to insolence.

What she said had no meaning as far as I was concerned—or so I thought.

"So you are yet lost; still, you can make yourself useful." My captor held out both hands brought together to form a cup, and into that improvised vessel liquid began to splash, though from where I could not tell.

This meeting had passed so far beyond the bounds of reality that I closed my eyes. Had I labored with such intensity during the past few days that I was hallucinating?

"Nine we were . . ." intoned a voice, one so distant that I heard it only as a whisper. *"Nine we divided the Great Wheel . . ."*

And then I saw—though with some sense of the mind or memory, for my physical eyes were still shut—that there was, indeed, a Wheel. Lines of silver crossed, overscoring one another to form a disk, and adorning it were nine glimmering stars of argent light.

"Turn with time!" the voice ordered crisply.

One of the stars moved forward, expanded, and eclipsed the Wheel. It formed a frame that enclosed the head of a woman. Her piled gray hair supported a crown, or what seemed the ghost of such a diadem: a tarnished circlet pocked with empty settings for now-lost gems. Her face was near as hueless as her hair.

"Greetings to thee, Dindrane, Queen of the Wasteland," chanted the speaker.

"Greetings to thee in turn, Mistress of the Wheel," the gray woman answered, "but I am not for your summoning again. What we wrought, we wrought, and that is long past."

With that speech, she vanished. The silver-traced disk became visible again, though briefly, for another star flung out of it to front me. Once more a woman appeared; however, this lady had free-flowing black hair beneath a crown of clouded silver, and she wore a countenance as deeply tinted as her predecessor's had been wan.

"Hail," the voice greeted her, "Dark Woman of All Knowledge."

The answer of this high one, too, came swiftly. "The Storm Winds blow no longer; I am not for your calling."

So they came and went. Some were young, others in the fullness of life. Each was crowned, and every one was saluted by the speaker as a woman of Power. However, when the seventh star swung outward and grew, the frame it formed was empty, save for the likeness of an apple behind which hung an argent branch.

"Aye, you still linger." The voice rendered no formal greeting but a curt phrase chill with anger. "Yet your power is long since wasted, Flower Queen, and the Wheel has thrown you off—though not so far that I cannot bring you to my service. For I am Morgan, and the Wheel answers to me in this world, which I once lost, as well as in Avalon!"

The frame vanished, and the nine-sectioned disk once more appeared—but one of its blazing stars was gone.

"Look—with the eyes of the body!" The speaker sharpened those words into a compelling order.

I opened my eyes. No Wheel any longer hung before them, but the dim light of the setting sun made of the window another sort of frame for the woman who had intruded. Now she took several long steps that brought her to me, holding out her still-cupped hands. That chalice of flesh she presented to me with a command I dared not disobey:

"Drink!"

Lowering my head, I sipped. The liquid was cool, and from it rose the scent of ripened fruit which, as I mouthed it, I knew for the juice of new-pressed apples.

I drank—and I understood—but part of me still refused to believe.

"I am *not*—" I began to protest.

"Remember—do not deny memory!" Morgan gave her third order.

A tapestry of doings and dealings that were certainly not mine in this life unrolled in my mind. So fast it happened, and so galling were many of the recollections, that I covered my face with my hands and felt them wet with tears.

Fingernails dug painfully into my shoulder as the witch-woman brought me back to the present. "May Queen you no longer are," she declaimed, "yet you remain the key that will open the door. I have not lost my power but have gained more while I slumbered. Mistress of the Wheel and of Time is Morgan, daughter of a king, wife of a king, sister and first love of a king!"

"And," I answered bitterly, "one who brought about the destruction of a world that might have been." For the past was now mine, though I wanted none of it.

Yet somber legends of an age agone seemed no more unreal than the waking nightmare of my present imprisoning. Dusk had now sealed the window behind me; however, light still lay all about within the room—it might have been flowing from the walls. As I fronted the frame with its stretched silk, I found I could see as well for my work as though the sun were standing at full noon.

And labor I did, without hesitation and untiringly—needle and bead, green of this shade, blue of that hue. The picture before me grew magically, but in the border only—the very center of the scene being created remained blank.

Time no longer had any meaning. All that mattered was the place I was bringing into existence; yet with the only part of my mind that remained my own, I did not forget the one whose predatory-bird gaze watched my efforts and whose power kept me at them.

Those of the Wheel—those women I knew, as well. Queens they had been, and priestesses also; and in a time so distant from this that no mind could rank up the years between, they had held the rule of this land which had, in turn, mothered that of my birth.

Dindrane . . . Kundry, the Old One of Death and Knowledge (the lore of both being intertwined). Enid, Lady of Joy . . . Ygraine, the Hallows Queen, bearer of Him Who Was, Is, and Will Be. Nimuë, holder of the strength of Merlin . . . Dame Ragnell . . . Argante, who dwelt beneath a lake and gave the world's most famous Sword to the greatest of champions . . . Guinevere—

Like a finger that touches flame, my whole being drew back from the last of those. With fierce concentration, I centered my mind wholly upon my task. I wanted to deny that I had ever answered to the name of that Queen who had compassed the destruction of another Wheel, the Round Table; but the same mystical sense that forced me to own that truth revealed what I now did—though in spite of myself—as another act of betrayal.

Completed, the work I labored upon would, I knew, be seized by Morgan, and for a second time an act of mine would change the world. It was a world already deep-stained with blood and heart-gnawed by evil, true; yet the release of Morgan's full power would transform it from a place merely shadowed to one utterly enshrouded by the Cloak of the Dark.

That must never come to pass—not, at least, through my hand, my needle, my beads. Still I sewed and could not stop.

Save for the empty space at its center, the picture was finished as the dawn's rays touched the window, warring with the witch-light about me.

"Done—well done!" The praise was not meant for me; it was my captor's pleasure in her own accomplishment that she was voicing.

Morgan had stood by my side as I labored through the night. Now she stepped in front of me, gripped the beading-frame, and swung it to face herself. A large needle gleamed suddenly in her hold, and she leaned forward until the point of that implement touched the fabric. There was a flash of pallid fire, then another, a third . . .

When the sorceress stepped back, her contribution to the design was revealed: the Wheel, web of a spider freed once more to spin her nets of shadow. Yet the labor was still not complete, for she issued an order to me, her gaze still fixed on her work:

"Crystals—"

Again her power held me, moving my hand against my will. Crystals . . . yes, a small tube held such clear mineral spheres, part of the treasure Enid had sent. I laid them out in a line, eight in number—but a ninth I grasped tight in my hand and did not add to that gleaming row.

This time I did not need to thread the needle I had set upon the edge of the sorting tray. Once the crystals had been released from their vial, they arose of their own accord and, flying toward that nine-pointed web, fitted themselves one by one to each star on the Wheel. Hidden in my palm, the remaining bead, icy cold, was stealing all sensation from my flesh. Still I clutched it close.

Morgan gave a near-purr, a sound like a cat well satisfied; she seemed to have forgotten me. In that moment I took my chance. Clenching my left hand to match my right, I raised both fists and brought them down onto the work table with all the force I could summon. Under that assault, a rich shower of color geysered up as beads by the hundreds, the thousands, filled the air like a shattered rainbow.

I heard words screamed out like a curse but paid no heed—I was intent on something else. The ninth crystal I held must be meant to center Morgan's own star—the topmost on the tapestry—and I saw nothing but that. Groping without looking, I closed my free hand about chill metal: a pair of keen-honed scissors.

The fist crimped round my own bead had numbed to the point of uselessness, yet my left hand still obeyed me. Leaping to my feet, I slashed down at the unfinished picture with the open blades. But I had leaned forward to aim that blow, and now I overbalanced and—*dropped.*

Water closed about me—water, such as had ever been the medium of Power for the Sisters of Avalon, the Women of the Wheel.

I fought as slime-laced liquid surged up to draw me down, hearing as I did so the thwarted sorceress screaming as a raven might screech above a battlefield. My right hand a weight dragging me to the depths, I flailed with my left, kicking my feet to keep my head above the surface. Knowing that I must open the clenched fist or be pulled to my death, I forced its fingers apart with a desperate order from my mind. The crystal, loosed, tumbled away. But now my other hand was a dead weight!

Morgan was coming, striding across the surface of the water. Her features were twisted into such a malevolent mask that she seemed a very demon.

Somehow I was able to raise the lifeless thing my left hand had become. As it moved up through the water, I could see a gleam of metal; but when it lifted into the air, that glimmer became a light. Yet I did not hold my work shears, as I believed; instead, I clutched a clump of reeds, each darkening fast, and growing heavy—oh, so heavy.

The witch-woman was almost on me, no longer voicing a battle-bird cry but rather keening sounds in no language I knew.

I made my last and greatest effort, swinging my leaden arm up to meet the blow she aimed my way. I was not even certain I had touched her, but she flinched away and bent over, nursing one of her own arms against her body. Then her mouth opened to show pointed teeth, and she howled, maddened and dangerous as a wounded beast.

I was sinking, the noisome waters rising past my shoulders to neck, then chin. My resistance grew feebler as the last of my strength ebbed. Yet still Morgan made no move to slay me— instead, she retreated a little, mouthing words.

"*Sisters.*" I could understand her now. "*To me!*"

Did seven shadowy faces show for a moment behind her? And from whence came the cry that I myself choked out, fighting to keep my lips above the liquid?

"*Iron, cold iron!*"

I lost myself in darkness.

Pain found me all too quickly and brought me out of that friendly nothingness; every bone in my body ached. But I was content to lie as I was for a space, eyes closed, for nothing threatened now— of that I was sure.

Slowly, as one might assemble scattered pieces of a puzzle, I strove to understand. I opened my eyes. Above me rose the cobweb-curtained ceiling of the folly. By the light it was near to noon. My back protested, but I managed to lever myself up in spite of even greater discomfort in my palms—strange sharp stabs. My throat was painfully dry, and my head swam.

Swam—

In a rush, memory returned.

Morgan! I scrambled up, catching hold of the edge of the table, and somehow got into my chair. For some moments I sat brushing beads from my clothing and dusting them from my hands, where many had left small bleeding pocks. At last I looked toward the tapestry.

The picture showed a great rent scoring its center, and caught in the frame hung a streamer of green that, even as I watched, crumbled into gray ash.

The wreckage in this room might be thought proof of my victory. I must accept it as that—accept it, yes, but never let it be known. Though how I had done it I might never understand, I had won my way from the Wheel—

Wheel! On the floor near my feet lay an object bright enough to attract my attention even now. A crystal star, its symmetry marred by two broken points. Steadying myself in the seat, I stamped it ruthlessly into dust.

Had my actions destroyed those others—the Ladies of the Lake? I do not know, but I remain free, and of this I am sure: the triumph I gained was not a passing thing, but for all time, and perhaps, also, not for me alone, but for all the world.

THREE-INCH TROUBLE
A Constellation of Cats (2001) DAW

Tailed banners, bearing the codes of many trading companies, snapped in a brisk wind over the booths jammed together. A constant din of voices, raised in argument or in praise of this or that ware, assaulted the ears.

Raven tightened his claw-hold on the perch where he rode with the ease of long practice. As a crew member of the Free Trader *Horus,* he had experienced such gatherings before. Cargo Master Grospar was in no hurry. Once the main cargo was aboard, the star-sailors combed these fairs for personal gambles of their own, a tradition going far back to a time when ships were borne on planet-bound seas and men never dreamed that the next port could be another world. Fortunes had been gained from more than one lucky private deal.

"You choose, Raven. Or are you more eager for offerings to satisfy the innards?"

Raven butted his black-furred head against that of the man on whose shoulder he rode. Such a crude suggestion! He'd provide an answer to fit. Languidly, he drooped his tail to one side.

"Ros-rats? You're losing it, mate!" Grospar sneered, but, disdain notwithstanding, he pushed through the crowd in the direction the cat indicated.

Ros-rats were nasty vermin, but even they had value: they could clear alien wildlife out of a cargo hold in a very short time. As a result, every warehouse had cages of the creatures.

However, a booth to one side displayed distractingly exotic offerings. A pile of furs lay heaped there, with two other spacers arguing over prices. Cages of brilliant-hued flying things hung on display chains. Raven spat at a hand-sized dragon from Kartum as it flickered a forked tongue at him. Transporting live cargo was twice as hard as hauling nonliving wares, and only a few large ships could do it successfully; but even reduced to bundles of bright plumes, lengths of scaled skin, mounds of sensuous fur, outworld creatures would attract buyers.

A woman squeezed around a booth and stepped directly into Grospar's path. "Moon be clear for you, Cargo Master."

Martin Grospar laughed. "You here, Lasseea? I hope fortune favors you, as well, and I trust your moons are clear indeed."

The tall, thin female was not in space uniform, but rather wore a colorful flowing robe. Her hair was hidden by a glitter-sewn scarf, and the breeze played with the fringes of twin shawls about her shoulders. Lasseea was a star-reader, and justly famous: several of her important predictions had been accurate.

The seeress leaned forward and tapped Raven between his golden eyes.

"Greeting to you, brother-in-fur." Feline eyes and green human ones locked in a deep gaze. "Sooo—" Now she spoke directly to Grospar again. "There will be work for this little one soon, and then he will prove the worth of all the cargo you have checked into your ship."

The cargo master's smile faded. Lasseea may have insisted, planet-years ago, that Raven shared an important birth star with her and was a bringer of good fortune, but Grospar prided himself on being free of the superstitions that spacefarers could collect. Star-voyaging brought much that was difficult to believe when experienced, and the unusual—even more so than for other adventurers—was the usual for Free Traders.

"He's already earned his rations several times over," the man answered gruffly. "What will we have to thank him for now?"

"One sees ahead but little." The star-reader pulled her top shawl closer about her. "Watch and wait."

Then she was gone.

Grospar and Raven continued on to the booth that had attracted the cargo master. As they arrived, the dealer was occupied with a sale, bargaining with two spacers who wanted the shining furs of Arcalic Night-Bats. The *Horus'* officer took advantage of the chance to survey the wares. He was attracted first by a string of small bone carvings hanging against a display rack. Then his eyes shifted to a box below them—a container that looked vaguely familiar. Grospar picked it up. The clasp proving loose, the box opened, and man and cat looked inside.

Within lay six slender bottles, or maybe "vials" was the word. Each was frosted down its length, except for a space at one tip, but those areas were so small that they afforded no glimpse of the tubes' contents. The cargo master caught sight of markings on the nearest and held the box closer. Raven nearly lost his shoulder-seat as he leaned down to sniff.

The Free Trader glanced at the dealer, who was now collecting credit slips. Grospar did not know him, but that was not to say he was a jack dealing in stolen goods. The fact that he had openly displayed this container meant he believed he had nothing to fear. On the other hand, both box and contents were stamped

"SURVEY PROPERTY," and such artifacts were usually strictly guarded.

"You have an eye for a mystery, Cargo Master?"

The booth-keep, Grospar guessed, was a fellow Solarian— from Mars, to judge by the brown skin that nearly matched his thinning hair.

"Mystery?"

"That there—" the dealer jabbed a showman's finger at the vial-holder "—come in 'bout ten days ago. Ast'roid miner found it hooked on the belt of a floater who'd got caught in the rocks he'd been blastin'."

Grospar pointed in turn. "That's a Survey stamp," he said. "The law is—"

The hawker's laugh interrupted him. "Laws! They don't hold much, 'cept when a gov'ment man's there to back 'em up. Who's gonna make an extra flight to Jason or Silenea to turn in somethin' that little? Gimme ten credits, *you* can take it, and," his eyes narrowed shrewdly, "maybe get yourself a reward."

"Eight," the Trader countered, then automatically turned his head. "Worth that, Raven?"

The cat gave a small chirp of encouragement. There was something decidedly interesting about their find.

"Eight an' a half." The merchant fell into the natural rhythm of a sale.

The haggling went on for a few moments. When the cargo master left the booth, the box and some of the bone carvings were tucked into his shouldertote.

As the partners made their way back to the ship, Grospar stopped now and again to examine other offerings. Raven, however, paid no attention. He was keeping an eye on the bag that held his companion's selections and striving to pick up the thread of a very strange scent. Nor did he go off on his own when they were once again in the *Horus* but instead kept close to the cargo master's heels after he had leaped from his moving perch.

Grospar opened a chest built in under his bunk to stow away his most recent purchases, but before he closed the storage place, he opened the box again to view the six vials.

"*What—!*" The cargo master grabbed for a hand light and shone it into the interior, full on the transparent portions of the tubes. A—head? Some kind of carving?

There was no time now to make sure, for the liftoff alert had sounded, and that meant strap-down. He paused to boost Raven into the cat's hammock, then made his own preparations for ship-rise.

Raven wriggled until he could still see the box, which Grospar, for some reason had never placed in the chest. His lips shaped a soundless snarl. What was it? His feline senses were strained to the limit, but he was still frustrated. There had been no movement, no increase in that curious scent—nothing to sound the alarm, yet his inner warning system was clamoring ever more loudly.

The cargo master held the box with both hands, peering within. Carvings? No, he was seeing heads, with staring eyes— heads hardly bigger than his own thumbnails. Well, Survey often brought back samples of strange life—insects, plants—and this container bore their seal.

Found on a space-suited body . . . how long had its owner floated in the void, cast to a lingering and horrible death by some starship disaster? If the vials had once contained specimens living at that time, they were surely dead by now.

Once more Grospar inspected the tubes, tilting the chest to see their tiny clear windows. One of the half dozen had somehow worked loose. Before he could push it back into the padded crevice that had held it, the vial broke completely free and rose in the now-gravityless air of the cabin, moving upward with surprising speed.

The cargo master snapped the box shut and wedged it under his own body, lest another tube escape, then swept up a hand to snatch at the floater. It seemed to jerk, as though eluding his fingers.

But it did not escape Raven. Claws hooked, swung, and dragged the prize to the feline.

"Hold it, mate!" Grospar ordered. "Don't bite it through!"

As if Raven had any intention of doing *that*. Man's four-legged companions in space had been chosen because, among other traits, they possessed a well-developed sense of caution. The cat simply pressed the vial against the webbing in which he rested, summoning more strength to hold it there.

But the tube rolled, as though it had a will of its own and was fighting to escape. Raven stared into the unfrosted portion. Now he was sure he saw eyes—eyes that met his own. He blinked. They were—*no!* He would not—he would not!

Yet his warding paws moved against his wish, and the vial gained near-freedom even as the cabin was weighted once more with the partial gravity of ready-flight. As he fought to keep his trophy captive, his forelegs, insanely, did just the opposite of what he wanted: they opened. The tube spun lazily down to the floor—and met Grospar's metal-soled boot.

Raven snapped the safety catch of his hammock and leaped, only to pass through a puff of greenish vapor that burned his eyes and brought a squall of pain from him. He landed on the cabin floor and rebounded a little, dazed and limp. The cargo master caught him up, but seconds later the man began to cough with a force that made him drop the cat to gasp and clutch at his own throat.

The feline hit the floor again. Rubbing a paw at his smarting eyes, he let out another cry as Grospar continued to hack, collapsing back onto his bunk. The Survey box joined Raven on the floor, and a second of the vials was jarred loose.

Out of that tube's green gas skidded a reddish blur, an occurrence of which the sickened cat was only half aware. Then the blur made a scuttling approach to the container and its remaining vials. Raven strove to raise a paw but found himself unable to do so. However, while his eyes still hurt, his vision had cleared, and he could see what was happening around the mysterious cache.

The cargo master lay flat on his bunk, coughing in deep, racking bursts. But the tubes were all out of the case now, pulled free by the thing—no, *two* things—that had got out first. The breaking of each vial released more of the breath-stealing vapor to torment the rightful occupants of the cabin.

Those . . . creatures. The cat squinted. They were as large as his human partner's longest finger, and they had four appendages, but they moved so fast it was hard to see more than that they used an upright position as well as scrambled on all fours. He sprang toward them and, to his utter astonishment, missed.

The cabin door signal sounded a note. Grospar's head turned, and he tried to call out, but a strangled cough was the only sound he was able to make. However, it was a sufficient summons, and the door opened.

Raven squalled again—not in pain, this time, but at the thwarting of his performance of duty. Those elusive beings, avoiding Captain Ricer's booted feet, vanished past him into the corridor. Determinedly the cat started after them, but his steps wavered, and he did not get far before the captain scooped him up.

Thus began a reign of, if not terror, at least fierce frustration for the crew of the *Horus*. The creatures from the Survey box seemed not only uncatchable but unseeable as well; but the wrack and ruin they appeared to deliberately cause was more evident every day.

Some cabins had their furnishings nearly wrecked, while smaller treasures were either bashed beyond repair or disappeared altogether. Across the bunks where off duty crew members were attempting to rest, the things began to scuttle—and worse. The medic treated several nasty bites as best he could.

Raven grew thin, apt to hiss warningly when approached by even his favorite shipmates, and always he hunted. At last, however, he managed to corner one of the enemy in Supply Storage, while it was busy tearing at some packets of the captain's treasured Larmonte tea.

The cat had gotten his paws—or rather one paw—on the entity, only to be leaped upon by two of its kindred who had been devising devilment on a higher shelf. The impudent brutes had no fear of him but bit and snatched at his fur, tweaking tufts of it out of his skin. His battle cry soared into a yowl of pain, but he fought to hold his prize.

"What the—!" Rasidan, the steward and cook, loomed suddenly above the fray. Raven's prisoner bit, hard, into its captor's right front paw, and he snapped back, his teeth closing about one of the creature's forelegs. Then a smothering cloth descended upon feline and foe as they fought, and the warring beings were lifted into the air. Tenaciously the cat held his grip, even when the knot formed of himself and his keening captive was dropped onto a hard surface, and the fabric loosened to fall free.

They were in the captain's cabin, with crew members crowded around the pulldown leaf of the desk. Raven's prey went abruptly limp, but still he did not release his hold. It was Grospar who reached down for the small body. His furred partner growled, body tensed to spring away. He was going to finish this catch!

That's what he was there for: to make sure that the ship—*his* ship—was free of such intruders.

"It's all right, Raven," the cargo master assured him quickly. "Let me have it."

The cat held on, studying the situation. He mistrusted Grospar's ability to keep a grip on the thing. It was far from dead, and he was sure that if he released it, it would vanish again. These invaders had already proved that they were too swift, too small to be managed by men.

"Raven!" Captain Ricer spoke now, and he held up a square of cloth. "I'm going to wrap this around it—then you let go."

That was a definite order—a captain's order—and even he had to obey. He ducked his chin, relaxing his jaws. As he did so, the being came to furious life, but the captain had it bagged. The cat edged back. His numerous wounds burned, and an evil taste filled his mouth; however, he had set his own mark on the menace. He moved forward again to lend the weight of his forepaws to the control of the heaving bundle, though his superior continued to pin it also.

"In that lower cupboard." Ricer was giving Grospar directions. "Yes—that's it!"

The cargo master had stooped and risen. What he placed upon the desk was equipment from his commander's own private hobby. The captain, when the *Horus* had time in port on a lesser-known planet, hunted flying insects, then studied them in holding boxes of his own design. Since some of his captives had not only been large in size but equipped with menacing jaws, claws, stingers, and whatever other defenses nature had chosen to give them, the cages were indeed right and tight.

The one Grospar held at the ready was a cube of heavy netting with a thick metal floor. Into this the captain now transferred the frantically-wriggling contents of the improvised bag.

The cargo master instantly slammed down the top of the box with force enough to make it catch and lock—and just in time, for the creature sprang, only to be knocked back by the lowered flap.

"Now, then—" Ricer beckoned forward those who wished a closer look at one of their miniature nightmares of days past. Those of the crew who had gathered in his cabin closed in, staring at the cage and its inmate. For the first time, since the things moved with such speed, they could all view a specimen as it tugged and hurled itself against the wire-net walls that now enclosed it.

The body was covered with what seemed to be matted brownish-red fur, but the front paws, shaped not unlike human hands, were equipped with pointed talons that were now hooked into the screen barrier. An open mouth displayed similar armament in the form of a set of needlelike teeth, which were dripping a green liquid. The nose was flat and the face hairless about the jaw, cheeks, and eyes.

Its first battle rage was stilled, but the small nightmare still clung to the wire. Glittering blood-red eyes were fixed upon Ricer as he knelt down to bring himself closer to the surface of the flap-desk. Without looking, he groped along its top, brought out a magnifier, and swung that circle of view glass between himself and the now-quiet prisoner.

Raven approached the other side of the holding box. He snorted at the musky odor that was so strong, then stopped, growling, as though he had come up against an unseen barrier. He sensed from the being an intense malignancy. He could pick up no fear whatever—only a raging fury.

"I—don't—believe—it—" Captain Ricer accented each word he spoke, apparently wanting to deny the report given by his eyes.

"Don't believe what?" questioned Medic Lothers as he pushed Raven to one side to better view the cage and its occupant.

"That," Ricer declared slowly, "is a *monkey!*"

"A what?" Lothers asked the question for everyone.

"If that beast were about a hundred times larger—" The captain let his sentence trail off unfinished as he swung away from the table. He opened a cupboard and reached within, emerging with a reader-tape from his personal library. This tape he slapped into the viewer that shared the desktop with the cage and its captive.

The cat paid no attention to his commander's behavior, not even to the picture that appeared on the screen as Ricer triggered keys. He was intent on what was happening before him.

The entity had released its clutch on the wires and dropped to the floor of the box, where it curled itself into a ball. All at once, Raven shook his head vigorously, feeling as though both his ears had been invaded by loudly-buzzing insects. After a moment, he realized that the creature was mind-calling—and in a manner he had never encountered before.

The feline could not interpret the sense of the message being sent, but he was certain that it was either a warning to the being's own kind to take cover or a plea to them for help. The thing turned its head, staring at him. Again Raven could sense no fear—only a consuming rage.

In any grouping of wildlife there was always a leader. Even in an assembling of ships' cats, such as occurred at times when a starport's fields were crowded, one or two would take precedence, and the others would accord them room, as was required. This angry alien was not such a dominant one, but it seemed to believe that its mental broadcasts would reach its fellows. And perhaps that vast hatred had, indeed, reached a level of force in its projection to where it would bring aid. . . .

The men had moved away from the cage and were concentrating on the reader. Raven closed his ears to the argument that seemed to be rising among them—something about a comparison between the information on the tape and the size of the thing in the box. The cat was entirely intent on its broadcasting of near-insane anger.

Suddenly he made a move of his own. A sweep of paw struck the cage to the floor of the cabin, and an instant later he was beside it. A hand grabbed for the holding box; a second caught one of his own feet in a trap-tight clutch.

"What you trying to do, Cat?" It was Grospar who held and questioned him.

No time! Raven bit—hard. The cargo master yelled and loosed his grip. His furred partner offered no more aggression but rather jumped for the cage, sank teeth into its netting, and dragged it out into the passageway beyond.

The prisoner's kin-ones were coming—the cat could not see them, but he knew. He yowled, standing directly before the box, which he was using as bait to draw the rest of the creatures out of hiding. Then a pair of space boots grazed his tail as Grospar stopped just behind him.

"Stun him!" someone yelled.

"No!" shouted the cargo master. "He's got some sort of plan—I'll swear to it!"

The feline heard this exchange as though it were a rumble of distant thunder that had no meaning for him. He bobbed his head and gave the box another shove.

Within its enclosure there was no stir; the tiny intruder was still enwrapped upon itself, concentrating on its call. Not for the first time Raven wished he could communicate with his human crewmates. True, he could convey broad outlines of feelings or ideas to Grospar, but not detailed ones such as he needed to share now. He could only—

The cat crouched between the men and the cage. Should these invaders turn away from the summons and seek hiding places, it might be a long time before they would be found and routed out. Let them come into the open to free their fellow, however, and any member of the crew with a battle-stunner might take them.

"By the Last Ray of Corbus—look—they're coming!"

The cargo master had apparently sighted one of those scuttling shadows Raven had already sensed, though he was keeping most of his attention on the entity in its pen. The cat raised his still-bleeding forepaw and shook the box back and forth. The reaction was instantaneous—a fresh burst of defiance struck at him, revealing that the little brute was still both aware and angry.

The men had been exchanging a rapid-fire volley of suggestions, but a single word from the captain brought instant silence.

"Stunner—"

"Here?" challenged the medic immediately. Use of a stunner within the narrow confines of a corridor ran counter to all the never-questioned rules of ship safety.

The creatures were all in view now, though spread well apart. Once more Raven rattled the cage, then almost at once shook his head again. The original broadcast of wrath seemed a love pat compared to the silent waves of killing fury that now crashed into his mind, causing actual physical pain.

Through the red haze he forced himself to think: *Get behind the ones who would rescue their fellow—cut off any retreat.* But how could he achieve that position—and how would his own crewmates snare the things still loose? These were monkeys, with the intelligence of all their kind, but incredibly small in size and able to move at a speed too fast for eyes, human or feline, to follow—

Raven gave a last bat of his paw to the box, then turned around. As he had hoped, the cargo master was right behind him. With a swiftness rivaling that of the aliens, he leaped upward, hooking claws deep enough into Grospar's ship suit to pierce skin. The man gripped the cat and ripped him free.

For a second time. Raven bit the hand that held him, thus achieving part of his desperate plan. He was hurled away (a spluttered oath loud in his ears) to land some distance ahead, well past the pen.

Perhaps what the cargo master called "luck" was truly on his side, for the cat by his actions had now placed the invaders between himself and the crew. The creatures scrabbled frantically, but escape was impossible from the section of corridor into which the mind-call of the captive had brought them. One tried to dart in Raven's direction, and the feline responded with the hunter's reflexes of his kind: he did not try to pin this being down but swatted it, straight back at its companions.

The men of the *Horus* had spread themselves across the other end of the passage where they stood forming a barrier, space boot to space boot. Once more Captain Ricer spoke the word that told how he would deal with this situation, but this time, as he turned to exit the corridor, he was not inviting debate:

"*Stunner!*"

Raven uttered a yowl of agony. The free monkeys were not attacking, but the beat of rage inside his head from the confined one was almost enough to knock him down. Almost, yes—but not quite. A stunner, though—the cat knew what such a weapon might do if fired at close quarters.

Retreat? No. That was a very fleeting thought. This was his ship, his territory, *his!*

The crew members on the other side of the cage drew back a fraction, and the creatures, who had seemed frozen in place by wariness, suddenly stirred. Raven felt a thrust of anger that was purely his own. Were Grospar and the rest going to give the enemy a chance to escape again?

But it was the captain for whom the men were making way. And he was carrying a tube that the cat had seen borne in action planetside only twice when lives had been threatened.

Instinctively he braced himself. There would be no sound, no visible shot fired—there would be—

Blackness swallowed him. The dark was painless, but it carried fear. He was in bonds, and he could not escape—not even open his mouth to cry out a protest! Panic had almost overwhelmed him when a familiar scent reached his nose, his brain. Grospar—? Yes, the cargo master had picked him up, was cradling him.

"Raven! Come on, li'l shadow—"

A quick sharp stab in his shoulder, and the helpless weakness began to fade.

"That ought to bring him around—"

Those words broke through the blind bondage that no longer held so tightly. Raven opened his eyes. Medic Lothers was watching him, and behind him stood the captain. Grospar gave his friend a last hug and laid him down on the softness of a bunk. His returning senses registered the odors of the captain's cabin.

"Got 'em—every one o' the buggers!"

Fortunately, because his head still felt too heavy to lift, Raven could see what was happening from where he lay. First the cage containing his "bait," then Ricer's insect-capturing net were being placed on the desk, and the bug-bag was bulging with inert bodies.

"Dead?" The cargo master, his hand still poised above the cat's head to touch him gently now and again, had asked that.

The captain gingerly inserted fingers into the insect-net. Bringing forth one of the small bodies, he held it out to Lothers for a medical verdict.

"Well, it can evidently survive being stunned because ifs still breathing," was the doctor's reply. "Can't tell whether it's damaged, though—too alien."

Ricer produced another collecting cage, then a third, and into these the creatures were placed. With the three miniature brigs lined up before him, the commander could finally perform a careful examination of the inmates.

"Survey can certainly have you," he at last declared to the entities who might or might not awaken from their enforced slumber. Then, his prison inspection concluded, the captain swung around to Raven. Standing at attention, he lifted his right hand and touched his temple in the formal salute offered only on state occasions to valiant beings in the Star Service.

"Ship's Guard," he said solemnly, "well done."

Grospar smiled, giving the cat a second, more intimate reward in the form of a rub behind the ears. "Lasseea was right, fur-friend," he said with a sigh of relief. "Your lucky star was our luck, too."

The weary feline lowered his head and closed his eyes. These attentions were very flattering, but right now he just wanted his shipmates to clear out and let him sleep. What nonsense humans talked, he thought. Suns in the heavens an influence on fate? Better the light-of-mind that was his kind's common sense. Were he to attempt such a farseeing as Lasseea's, though, he felt sure he could predict that Grospar would never go salvaging Survey-sealed material again. He, Raven, Ship's Guard of the Free Trader *Horus,* would personally make certain that there was no more such—what was the expression the men used for foolhardy activity?

Ah, yes (the cat wished he could smile)—*monkey business.*

THE END IS THE BEGINNING
Oceans of Space (2002) DAW

The two kits settled in front of the Teacher watched the unroll-
ing of a tape so old that it was, in portions, dim, while the front
of the machine's screen was scratched beyond any possible pol-
ishing. Most kits believed that the instructional device was one
tool used by the now-vanished Smoothskins to spread what the
Commander often called the Great Lie. However, the tapes could
still provide some degree of entertainment, and one could think
up many questions based upon the actions witnessed therein
with which to baffle both Big Ones and other less-observant
Littles.

"Why the Great Lie, anyway?" Marguay muttered, watching a
scene wherein some type of creature supposedly—impossibly!—
raised itself high into the air.

"Because of the Far Flight," Porky replied in a bored tone, as
he lifted his right hand and licked the fur on its back. Then he
began to recite, and Marguay joined in the ritual they had learned
by rote from the time their eyes had fully opened and they had
started exploring beyond the nest.

"The Smoothskins went out to the stars,
And the People went with them.
Long and long did they travel.
Among them were those who were close to the People,
And wished to draw nearer,
Desiring to share speech and duties.
Thus they used magic taught by the great Machines
And strove to make the People as they visioned.
So did the People learn to walk as the Smoothskins,
Use forepaws as hands, and—"

"What are you doing here?" demanded a voice from the doorway. "You two are on duty—why this hiding away and looking at parts of the Great Lie?"

Mam Sukie stood in the entry port to the compartment. Marguay hastened to shut off the machine, thinking ruefully that there was probably no trip to the Lookout for them now.

"Scat!" The ruler of the kits smacked each of the truants hard as they slunk past her. "You for litter-box duty—right now!"

Marguay waited until he was (he hoped) beyond hearing distance before he hissed; then he glanced quickly back over his shoulder. A Little must not forget that the Big Ones were able to walk very softly, and never more so than when about to bring a kit "to order," as they called the meting out of such discipline.

"There are no Smoothskins anymore," Porky huffed, panting a little as he strove to match his brother's pace. "I wonder where all of them went?"

"Don't be a weanling!" rebuked his companion. "You've heard Harvey often enough—they all up and died, and then they were shoveled into the converter."

"But—Father Golden says that when we die, we go out to the stars. Where did the Smoothskins go—to the stars, like us?"

Marguay hissed again. "Those clunkpaws? Hardly! Maybe that's just another part of the Great Lie. You want to meet one of them?"

Porky rumbled out a growl. "NO! My mam, she says they sometimes kept kits in *cages,* and other times—" the tubby Little's voice dropped to a near whisper, "—they did bad things to us. It was only because more and more of them died, and they did not have many small ones of their own to learn their tricks, that we People at last were given all *this,*" he threw wide his furred, clawed hands to encompass what lay about them, "for our own selves."

"Hey, you!" Ahead stood Wilber, and he was mad. He was almost Big in size, too, so the Littles felt it wiser not to tangle with him, even though they were two to his one.

They hurried on to the smelly place. Tippi, a small gray, she was already tilting a pan into one of the waiting cans. Her whiskers twitched as the he-kits joined her, and Maggie, her companion, snarled:

"What were you doing that mam sent you along?"

"Looking at tapes," Porky answered before Marguay could stop him.

"Waste of time," Wilber commented, "all the Great Lie—never could be stupid stuff like that anywhere. Get to work, you two."

As he cleaned under Wilber's sharp eyes, Marguay thought about what he had found the last time he'd gone roving. There were many compartments where the People did not go very often, and a few of them held fascinating things. Some of the unknown objects were amusing to roll around and jump at when one was very small, but when a kit grew older, he could make even more interesting finds.

Not all the People were able to do as much as the Smooth-skins, though more and more kits now being born were able to use machines easily and think harder ideas. Marguay's own mam,

Knottail, had been able to open the box-things that had many pieces of paper fitted inside them. Lines of black dots marched in rows across those sheets, and a kit could learn to tell what they meant. A lot of the marks—most, in fact—dealt with the Great Lie, and some told their tale so convincingly as to make one believe the past had happened in just that way. And there were instructing devices, too, almost like the Teacher except that they unrolled different stories. Marguay had every intention of going back to the last compartment he had found only yesterday and tinkering with the machine in that chamber—one of those pages with the Smoothskin-scratches told how to make it work, and the determined Little had almost been able to get it going.

Tippi was using a brush and catch-tray to sweep up crumbs of spilled litter; not much of the pan-sand remained anymore, and what might be saved must. Careful as the cleaner was, though, the job could not be spun out to excessive length, or Wilber would march the duty-doer off for another job. Marguay *had* to get away before then!

He and Tippi were out of the older kit's sight now, and the she-Little stood up, brush and scoop in hand, and looked at her partner.

"You going to the play-place?" she asked.

The Big Ones might call the room set aside for amusement "the play-place," but they themselves were always there, and thinking up tasks for Littles to perform—mostly the jobs no small kit wanted to do. Before he thought, her striped companion shook his head.

"Then will you go sneaking again?" she persisted.

Marguay's ears flattened in annoyance. What did Tippi know about him—and why? He had never noticed *her* very much; shes had their own affairs.

"I don't sneak!" he retorted.

"No?" she shot back. "Then what were you doing up on the top level yesterday?"

How had she found out where he was?

"Get to work, you two!" Wilber roared.

Both the Littles started guiltily and speeded up their labors. Marguay glanced at his fellow helper as often as he dared, wondering. How much had she learned? If he slipped away when they were through here, he must be careful she did not follow. He knew he wouldn't have to worry about pursuit by Porky—that well-rounded yellow fellow would be on his way to the mess hall by then, ready (as always) for a snack.

When the pair had finished their nose-wrinkling job and Wilber had reluctantly told them they might leave, the would-be explorer did not shoot away in the direction he wanted to go. Instead he followed Porky for a little way; then he slipped into one of the side passages, listening intently and looking back now and then. Luckily, none of the other People, Big or Little, appeared to be coming to retrieve him; so after making two more way-turns, Marguay went for his goal.

Less light shone up in this high passage. The inquisitive Little had overheard several full-growth kits talking about whether the illumination in some parts of their home was eventually going to fail. He was also aware that Commander Quickpaw had Big Ones working with him all the time, hastening to learn more about the objects the Smoothskins had used long ago.

Marguay shoved aside the compartment door and jumped up to the seat before the long shelf on which stood a machine with a dark screen. The box-thing—*book,* he corrected himself— that he had found yesterday was still open, and it was held outspread to the page he wanted by a Lie-thing. This was a figure, very heavy for its size, of one not unlike himself. But when had any of the People ever sat so, a ring in one ear, and—the he-kit pushed the offending object away from him a hiss—wearing a *collar!* Except for those adornings, though, the statue was not altogether of the Lie—the Little knew three of the Big Ones who were colored like this. But he could not let that problem trouble him now. Giving the false-kit-figure a final shove off the book, Marguay settled down to find out what he could manage to do with the silent machine.

What, he mused as he pored over the scratch-filled page, if he were able to make a *real* discovery—and the Commander were to learn that it was he, Marguay the Little, who had performed the valuable deed? Suppose—

"What are you doing?"

His reverie shattered, the striped kit reared back and nearly slipped off the chair onto the floor. No longer did he hiss, as he had done to the statue—this kind of scare deserved a real spitting.

Tippi paid him no attention. Crouching slightly, she launched herself and leaped to the shelf that held the perplexing device. She then nosed against its blank front as if, by so doing, she could smell out its purpose.

The fur rose along Marguay's back, and his tail expanded and lashed. "Get out!"

His work-mate continued to ignore him. Seating herself in a calm curl, she patted the face of the machine; if she had any fear of it, she showed none.

"New Teacher?" she asked, as conversationally as though they were both in learning-Utter. "You had better tell One-Eye. Remember what happened to him when he was a small kit and started up that chittering box? He was never able to shut it off either—and his eye got hurt." Still paying scant attention to her companion, Tippi bent her head intently and began to study the row of buttons below the blank square.

The hero-in-his-dreams could stand this insolence no longer. Wanting to do battle, or at least chase the intruder off, he slapped at her, claws out. She dodged the blow with ease, but Marguay's hand struck against three of the buttons.

Sound answered the blow. Tippi jumped back as they both heard a hum—the noise the Teacher made when coming to life. Two of the buttons the he-kit had bumped now showed green, not in a steady glow but a pulse that flickered very fast. The last one in line was red, and it did not move.

Down the machine's face-front now scrolled lines of the Smoothskin words, but these were gone too fast for Marguay *to* puzzle them out. And then, almost as *strident* as the battle-cry of a Big One, a *voice shouted:*

"Mission accomplished! Destination located! Assuming orbit!"

The two kits crouched together, for not only did the device repeat its message over and over, but a change was occurring in the compartment itself: the very walls were echoing the hum made by the machine when it had awakened. Then another call commenced, reaching even above the double din of voice and hum:

"Orbit alert—landing in twenty-five hours! Orbit alert, orbit alert! All systems go, faults negative—"

The noise in the walls continued. Marguay hurled himself down from the seat, Tippi following behind him so closely that she nearly bowled him over when she landed. Both intrepid explorers streaked for the door of the chamber.

They got no farther than the next deck down. On that level, the two found themselves in a most un-People-like crowd and confusion. Big Ones were racing for the section in which, it was said, the Smoothskins had sat in council when they were here. Other full-growth kits were also gathering; and mams were trying to catch Littles and having a hard time doing so.

Marguay and Tippi had been separated in the ever-growing press of People, and the he-kit shivered as that loud voice began to boom its announcement again.

"Orbit alert! Orders obeyed! Landing in twenty-five hours—"

Unable to pull free, the young adventurer was borne onward into the assembling-place of the Smoothskins. Bright-hued lights now flashed from many of its surfaces on which few now hurrying in had ever seen any life before.

Marguay squeezed himself as small as he could, trying to escape being stumbled over by Big Ones. Certain of those full-growth kits were standing by the machines and, as the Little was pushed forward into the room, he heard Commander Quickpaw roar a series of orders that sent them all into seats before the newly lit screens.

What were they trying to do? Marguay saw clumsy-appearing hands press down on buttons. Below some screens, lights burned red, and the commander leaped from one to the other of those machines, shouting at the Big Ones stationed there.

More hand motions, and the red lights disappeared. Commander Quickpaw watched closely for a short time; then he turned his head to hiss at those crowded in behind.

"Out. The ship is landing."

Ship? That was part of the Great Lie!

"Come," Father Golden waved his arms, urging the mass of People toward the door. "Our Learned Ones must be left alone now. There will be Cries to the Stars in the Great Assembly Place. Come!"

Slowly they obeyed. Mams carried very Littles in their arms, herding larger kits before them. The Big Ones came after. A husky full-growth routed Marguay out of his crouch, pulled him to his feet, and kept a hand on his shoulder until the group was out of the hall of many machines.

They regathered in the large compartment where the Big Ones always met to decide what was best for their kind. Now, however, the room rang to the voices of kits from the new-weaned to the white-whiskered.

"The Lie!" Marguay heard over and over again. "The Great Lie!"

Father Golden held up his hands and fairly war-screeched for their attention.

"Brothers—Sisters—we who are the People! The She-One of the Stars has remembered us, for we have come to the end of our far-faring such as the old tales foretold would be. Strengthen, then, your hearts; arouse in your inmost beings the courage of our kind—"

"This is the Great Lie—the lie of the Smoothskins!" A cry that ended in hissing interrupted him.

"Those who littered us," the father continued, unperturbed, "and those who brought them forth, birthing upon birthing beyond memory-reach—yes, they named as falsehoods the say-ings of the Smoothskins. Yet if they—and we—lulled our fears asleep, as a mam quiets her kits, with the belief that story was a falsehood, then the fault is ours. Yet I say to you that the mighty Star-She whom even the Smoothskins once served is with us still, and that there will be a new life for us all. It may be very strange, but we are the People, and we will survive!"

Overcome with shame, Marguay hunkered low, hoping to avoid Father Golden's sweeping gaze. The young kit wanted fiercely to close not only his ears but his mind in some way so that he could neither hear what was happening here nor remember what he and Tippi had done.

The crowd began to disperse. Certain kits drifted away with frown-creased brows, as though they strove now to make them-selves believe a history long firmly denied. Others drew near to Father Golden and began the Cry to the Stars, the Plea to the She Who ruled them.

Under cover of the movement, Marguay slunk as far away from the rest of his kind as he could. A Lie that was truth—and he and his playfellow had *made* it so!

The erstwhile adventurer concealed himself in a storage place that looked empty, but something stirred in the shadows there, and Tippi mewed softly. Then she was beside him, her tongue touching the spot between his flattened ears, smoothing his fur. The two kits curled together, taking comfort from the warmth of each other's bodies; yet in spite of this reassurance, whenever that booming voice proclaimed another measure of time as the hours passed, they shivered.

At last, though, Marguay decided that it was better to look forward and not back, and he spent the rest of that longest of nights trying to recall the many wonders that had appeared on the old worn tapes. "There will be many things we have never known," he mused to his curl-mate, "and some we could not even dream."

"Those creatures in the air," Tippi agreed, catching his enthusiasm. "And all that green stuff outside—someone must have planted a very big water-garden!"

Both kits summoned from memory all they could, not only of what they had learned from the Teacher but also from the stories that had been told them about the old days of the Smoothskins. Some of the tales were less than pleasant.

"If the Furless Folk are waiting," the he-kit said, "we must hide. The People are free now, not slave-ones to be caged as the Smoothskins used our litter-sires."

He felt Tippi's shudder of sympathy. "Yes—hide," she agreed.

All too short a time later came the call for the People to assemble. When the two youngsters joined the rest, they were led to another compartment where a weblike substance was being woven across the floor. The netting, they were told, was to keep them safe while the ship landed. Marguay reflected that parts of the Great Lie must not have been taught to all kits, for he had never heard of this hold-fast, though the Big Ones in charge seemed very sure that such must be used.

The he-kit could never afterward remember that landing. He roused, sensing Tippi not far away. Cries, mews, and hisses filled the air as those about the two also wakened; then came Big Ones to free them all.

Hand in hand, Marguay and Tippi joined the crowd growing around the port that had never been opened. All watched apprehensively as the Learned Ones struggled with centuries-glued seals. To one side of the door stood Commander Quickpaw and a group of warrior-People who carried curious metal rods. The young he recognized those—one had been pictured in the bookbox he had pored over. Such weapons could make a being fall down and be still—sometimes forever.

When the port was opened at last, the commander and his soldier-ones were the first to exit. Alien air flowed in after them, and Marguay lifted his head high to sniff a heady mixture of odors—unfamiliar, but enticing—mingled together.

Time passed, but the remainder of the People were forced to wait and wait. At last came the word that they might go, but they were warned to stay together, with the rod-bearers keeping guard abut them.

This place had no—no *roof*, was Marguay's first discovery as the kits stepped down a tilted walkway to the green flooring ahead. And that material was not flooring, either, but a substance that was soft underfoot. Then something moved, and a nearby he-Little grabbed at it. A moment later he raised a hand that clutched a small creature, near as green as their footing, which kicked until the kit crunched it.

Tall green-and-brown plant-things stirred when the breeze blew against them. The stalish atmosphere of the ship was gone now, and the People, ever sensitive of nose, reveled in the myriad fresh scents.

Five suns later, the ship's passengers and crew had established an outdoor living area. Scouts had discovered water that ran freely in streams. It had also been learned that the small beings in the grass (that, Marguay learned, was the name of the floor-growth) could be safely eaten. Two of those who explored—though all the People were under strict orders not to venture far from the camp, no matter what intriguing phenomenon beckoned for their attention—sighted much larger animals. And there were, indeed, living things—*birds*—that traveled through the sky itself!

Commander Quickpaw might have designated his Big Ones to reconnoiter this new world, but once again it was Marguay and Tippi who made the great discovery.

The youngsters had undertaken to follow for a little way the stream, in which yet another kind of living being moved swiftly about. A day earlier, the he-kit had managed to get one out with his hand and had taken it back to his mam, who pronounced it excellent eating—better, even, than those tiny furred beasts that ran squeaking through the grass. Two of the other mams had then asked him to catch more of the water-wrigglers if he could.

Marguay had already flipped one of the creatures out of the stream. Now his companion, belly-down, was attempting to equal his skill, when a high-grown bush on the opposite side of the water began to shake. The kits glanced at each other, startled. Could this be one of the bigger animals the scouts had reported?

A moment later a—beast?—fell, rather than worked itself, out of the shrub. It scrambled on two hind legs down to the stream, then thrust its head in, gulping and choking. Though it bore patches of unkempt reddish hair on its body in places, far larger areas of bare skin were visible; and its head was not shaped as were the heads of the People.

Marguay and Tippi edged back from the water. Though they

were not yet frightened enough to run, they had no idea how fast this creature could follow. The young he-kit longed for one of the weapon-rods.

Suddenly his companion caught at his arm with one hand, and with the other pointed excitedly at the drinker. Marguay saw what had caught her eye. Around the thing's thick throat ran a bright red band, and from this collar stretched a heavy leash that trailed back into the bush from which it had emerged.

The young explorer had no more than sighted that controlling device before the shrub once more rustled, then swayed. The leading-line snapped up and tightened, jerking the creature back out of the water. The patch-haired brute was held captive so, pulling at the prisoning collar and clasping both hands around the leash, but it was not left long to its struggles.

For around the shrub stalked a Big One—a very Big One, taller by far than the largest full-growth the kits knew. His fur was a tawny color with black spots in bold contrast. He, too, wore something about his throat, but his neckpiece was no slave-collar. It was a broad band of metal nearly the hue of the pelt on which it rested, and it sparkled in many places with bits of bright color. Encircling his forearms were a pair of similar glowing-and-glinting bands; and in one of his ears gleamed—a gold ring!

Marguay's mouth, already opened in astonishment, drew in a pleasing spicy odor from the stranger, borne across the water upon the wind. But the newcomer had halted abruptly to stare back, and he was now looking at them so intently that the small he-kit felt as though he had been lifted up by one of those clawed hands and was being turned round and round for inspection.

The two-leg beast that the stranger held in check raised its head. Matted and tangled hair covered most of its shoulders and blunt face, but there was still something about it—

"*Smoothskin!*" Tippi shouted.

The brute was not really one of the ancient aiders-of-the-People; yet it was similar enough that Marguay could see how his companion might make such a mistake.

In response to the she-kit's outcry, the one who held that half-beast in check called back to them. Nothing about his voice or stance seemed threatening as he did so, and slowly the two Little explorers advanced once more to the water's edge. They had not understood what he had said, and he was *very* tall indeed, yet all their senses told them he was kin.

Pulling his unwilling captive with him, the alien Big One entered the stream to splash across. Both kits waited courageously. Their noses wrinkled at the smell of the brute-thing he led; still, his own scent, beneath its exotic spicy tang, was as familiar as their own.

Again he spoke. Marguay shook his head but answered in his own language: "Come—see our commander, the Big Ones—come."

The stranger obeyed, giving frequent jerks to his charge's leading-line as he moved; and in this manner the pair of junior adventurers brought him to the encampment. Several of the guards fell in around their prize and his "pet," but those soldier-kin offered no raising of rods.

Thus Antimah of the Tribe of Rammesese, in the service of the Great Goddess Bast Herself, came to sit at a council meeting with the People from afar. Some of the attendants drew sketches with sticks in the dirt; others returned to the ship and brought out maps of the star-ways, pictures of their vessel's interior, drawings of the Smoothskins.

Marguay, however, slipped away from the crowd that stood watching the momentous meeting in wonder. Once more in the ship, he ran unhesitatingly to the compartment he had discovered, and there he caught up that statue-representative of his kind who wore golden adornment much like that of this splendid new-comer. When he had hurried back, he held high the figure and dared to interrupt the commander himself.

"Look!"

All heads swung toward him, and look they did. For answer, the stranger moved first. Coming to Marguay, he lifted his hand, palm out; and, fixing his eyes on the statue, he bowed his head.

Then he turned. Tossing to one of the guard-kin the leash of the Smoothskin-That-Was-Not, the living model of the figu-rine opened his arms wide in a gesture that could only mean full welcome.

Above them shone Sol, and underfoot was the soil of Terra. The far-farers as yet had that to learn; but for them, the end of their flight was also the beginning in a world that the Smooth-skins, in their time of power, had near destroyed. For the People, sent forth without their consent, had touched the outermost reaches of the heavens, and now their years'-lost home had received them once again.

THE FAMILIAR
Familiars (2002) DAW

The west wall was breached two hours after dawn, for the invaders had their own magic, of a sort—a powder that could crumble stone, no matter how thick or well-laid. I knew, then, that my chances for continued existence were limited to almost none.

My greatest shortcoming—as my elders and betters had so often pointed out—was indolence. Years of lazy drifting, of quieting my conscience with the reassurance, "She is too young; there is time," lay behind me. As a result, my familiar had never had her innate talents honed as they should have been. True, I had tried to begin this wit-sharpening last year, but the minds of the people of this world became less easy to work with as they grew older. And now—?

Now I must make do. Thinking it was fortunate that I knew much more about this merchant-house than the humans living here even suspected, I gathered my true strength and let go a summons.

The girl was in the lower hallway, sensibly resisting the screaming of a maid who was urging her to flee the house, to run to the castle gates. Evidently the servant did not know that those portals had been closed and barred at dawn, preventing either entry or exit, or perhaps terror had carried her beyond sense.

My familiar had thrown back the lid of the massive chest that stood in that corridor. Now she knelt and reached in, stripping away the layers of cloth stored there until she came to the cloak that had been folded over me. A moment later she brought me forth. I could feel her surprise at those actions, which I had directed: why should she place herself in peril to retrieve what she saw as a toy? Then, as I had done many times since she was small, I exerted the invisible bond we shared, and she hugged me tightly against her breast.

"Fossi, Fossi, what can we do?"

I noted with satisfaction that "we" in her speech; our link—a connection I had been strengthening through dream-touch for some nights—was tight. Now I exuded warmth, security, projecting those emotions as strongly as possible. Again I gave orders, and once more she accepted them without question.

The master of the house had been lending aid to the defense of the walls, and when I sent a seek-probe to find him, he was gone. The fear-maddened maid who had been caterwauling below had taken her own advice and fled into the streets. Only my familiar was left in this place.

Young and beautiful by the reckoning of her kind, the girl would be welcome prey for any invader who sighted her. We would have to work fast. Still holding me tightly, she stooped and caught up the cloak she had uncovered earlier; then she moved quickly down the stairs and into the kitchen. There she set me carefully on the edge of the large central table and spread out the garment beside me. As she did so, she staggered slightly, lifting her hand to her forehead. I felt a sag in our bond and straightaway tightened it.

Bread of yesterday's baking, a round of cheese, and a jar of dried fruit were heaped atop the cloak, which was gathered to form a provision bag. Lastly, two sharp knives were thrust into her belt, and she had garnered all she could here.

"Now what, Fossi?" My familiar was looking intently at me, and our link was now firm enough that I dared to reveal a little of my true nature. When I had first located the girl, she had been so young she believed my stuffed-toy disguise, and that was the beginning of the bond for both of us. However, as she had grown older, her perception of the form I wore in her world as that of a mere plaything had grown more strong. Could I, in time to save us both, convince her of what I truly was?

The clamor in the streets without, which could be heard even through these thick and long-laid walls, had been as a rising wave to sweep us onward. Now, above its muted roar there sounded the shriek of a woman, laden with such horror and pain that my familiar's hand flew to her mouth and her eyes went wide. Into her mind flashed the thought of what she might do with one of those knives to prevent such agony being wrung from herself, and she shuddered so we were both shaken. Quickly, I moved to take full command, intensifying my mind-send to break her trance. At last she moved, taking up the bundle of food in one hand and me in the other.

We hurried through to the head of the cellar stairs. A lantern hung on a hook there, witch-fire blazing at its core. Such magic would supply light for as long as we had need of it, and that might well be long indeed. I tensed; it was time now for the next step. Squirming in the girl's hold, I freed one of my toy-body's arms and pointed at the lantern.

My companion paused, indecisive again. She was noticing too much of the here and now. I added to the link. So goaded, she placed me on the cold stone of the first step, then tied her bag by the ends and slipped its circle over her shoulder.

"Fossi?" She spoke my name on a questioning note, peering down as though seeing me for the first time. Then, as though coming to a decision, she took me up again and reached for the lantern. Thus we went down into the dark chill depths beneath the house.

It was not yet time for me to take the final step to cement our bonding, to let my familiar see all I could be and do on this plane of existence. I held firmly in place that last thin veil between us as she made the descent step by step.

The cellar was made up of storage rooms, filled with barrels and chests. From one wall had been hewn an alcove, and in this niche wines were laid down. A mighty woodpile was carefully stacked in yet another area, awaiting a cold season this place might never see. My companion was familiar with this part of the house, but a few minutes' walk at the near-run we were keeping brought us to the end of the ways known to her.

Once more she addressed me, her voice that of the lonely child she had been when I had first moved myself into her life. Then she held up the lantern to the stone wall that ended our journey and murmured in a dull singsong, "No door—no more—"

Swiftly, simply, I fed my companion the knowledge to solve this problem. As though controlled by the strings of a dance-doll, her right arm lifted until it pointed to the blank barrier before us. With her forefinger, she next outlined a space up, across, and down the stone, that finger seeming to jet fire as a blue line followed its path. Finally, coming close enough to touch the surface, she set hand against the section of wall defined by the lines—and pushed.

If the girl had expected movement, none came. I gave an inward sigh—it was plain that she still had far to go. But the wall before us was hardly a slate for lessons now.

Again I loosed power. At this, my friend pulled me roughly away from her and held me up so that our gazes met.

"What—!" No bewilderment clouded her green eyes now—instead, fear fought rising anger. Frustrated, she swung my toy-form forward so that its floppy forelegs struck the stone where her palm had rested a moment ago.

I pushed those stuffed paws as hard as I could against the barrier, regretting bitterly all the wasted hours when we might have perfected what we carried. Such a gift had to be nurtured by both its possessors or it would bear no fruit for either.

Our first answer was not motion but sound: a bell-like chime I knew of old. The stone blocks within the square she had traced suddenly shone blue. When that color had whirled away as a mist, they were gone, and what lay behind them was opened.

A narrow passage, broken by no door, ran for a short distance. At its end lay a room not unlike those that made up the house above. A table stood in the center with a chair at each end, while to one side was placed a chest like a housewife's hutch with crowded open shelves above, cabinet doors below.

Dropping her bundle onto the table (and thereby raising a cloud of dust), my companion sank into a chair, but not before she had set me directly before her, keeping me upright with both hands. She began to stare.

She was waking, this girl I had chosen—and been chosen by—in her earliest youth, and her newfound sight was piercing the cloak of illusion in which I had been so long enwrapped. The hour had come when I must take the last step. Carefully, I loosed my hold on the appearance of a body filled with straw and covered by short reddish fur through which patches of skin showed where time (and love) had worn it away.

My companion let go her grasp, for I stood erect without support. Now I settled myself on the table, forepaws crossed, sneezing as I disturbed more dust, and waited.

A question came almost at once. "What is your name?"

Speaking aloud, I answered slowly, as if my friend were still the child of years agone.

"By your calling, I am 'Fossi.' And you?"

To exchange names is to set seal upon bonding. The girl held me with her eyes for a moment longer; then she seemed to arrive at a decision.

"I," she spoke briskly, chin high, "am Jeseca, daughter to Welfrid of Crask, merchant. And fear must have driven my wits from me utterly, for I believe an old toy can speak and its paws push aside a stone wall. Fossi, who—and what—are you?"

"What I have always been," I replied. "Your kind is not born with the Sight to see me in my true form, yet such power is now within your grasp. Your mother was Roseline; she was born of this house, but she had not the Talent strongly enough to warrant training. Before her was Aloris, who truly bore the Gift; and before your mother's mother were Catheral, and Vinala, and Darlynn—" I recited the women of my service-roll. To my delight, I saw my newest pupil nod twice at two of those so named.

Then, though the girl's hands no longer touched me, I felt them tremble where they rested on the table. "Those women—" her voice faltered, but she forced herself to continue, "—it is rumored that they were *Wyse*."

"And what does *Wyse* mean to you, Jeseca?"

"Having strange powers," she whispered. Fear was rising in her again, like the dark vapor lifting from a marsh. I wished I might gently coax her free of its clutching tendrils, but there was no time.

Turning, I gestured with a flick of paw at the cupboard; then, to test her a fraction more, I mind-sent a picture of what I would have her do. Slowly she stood, glancing from me to the hutch and back again before she went to obey.

The upper shelves were filled with small pots and sealed jars. Much of what was stored there had doubtless had its virtue leached away by time, but we had no need of salves or simples. At my direction, Jeseca opened the doors below, and from that area she brought forth a flat disk of dark glass which she placed on the table between us.

I glanced down to see myself reflected in its surface. My disguise of the hugged-to-shabbiness plaything was gone; my red-brown fur, living now, was not even dusty. The form I had been given upon first emerging into this world was mine once more: rounded head, large eyes as green as my companion's could be, long hard-muscled body, and two pairs of limbs on which I could either walk erect or take to all fours when the need arose. Yes, it was good to be back, but I needed no mirror to tell me so; and in any event the polished round on the table had not been intended as a tool for physical vanity. I spun the object about and pushed it before Jeseca.

"Think," I ordered her sharply. "Think of someone you know in this city, on this day!"

The girl gasped, bent low over the table. The disk she gazed upon now supplied a window giving onto the outer street. Its circular frame held a grim picture—one that grew ever sharper as I added my own power to its shaping. On the cobbles lay the maid who had run from the house, clothing torn from a body scarcely out of childhood, blood painting flesh and stone alike.

"Ursilla—oh, gods—"

Just then an armsman rose up between us and the slain servant, mercifully blocking her figure from view. As he turned away, we could see that he had a rainbow-hued scarf wound about his bandoleer.

"He must have been in the house—into my things!" cried Jeseca. "Robyon gave me that scarf on my nameday!"

"Yes," I said quietly, watching her. The anger was mounting in her eyes like a tinder-fed flame.

The soldier had stopped and was now peering at something low down. Then, across the muddied and gore-streaked stones, there came creeping toward him—and so into the circle of the viewing disk—a child, scarcely more than an infant.

"Minta! No—*NO!*"

The invader reversed the matchlock he carried, preparing to use the heavy gun as a club. At the same instant, my companion pulled the larger kitchen knife from her belt. As the stock of the weapon swung down toward the child's skull, the point of the knife hit the mirror.

The explosion of power that followed, released so wildly without my ordering, nearly threw me from the table. The farsight-glass itself cracked down the middle, but we could still see the baby, wailing though unhurt. The musketeer had not fared so well; he appeared, curiously, to have been stabbed through the heart. A moment later he fell in a fountain of blood.

"See!" Jeseca's voice was a carrion bird's shriek. "See what I did—and shall do! Let me clear Quirth of all those demons!" Knife still in hand, the girl caught at me, commanding, "Show me more of them, Fossi—*now!*"

For answer, I lifted a paw toward the blade. Jeseca gave a cry of pain and flung the hilt from her as though it had suddenly become too hot to hold; and indeed, it had left an angry weal on her palm. We faced each other as she nursed her hand against her breast. The redness faded from her skin as the flush of rage paled from her cheeks.

"You hurt me." The voice was a child's once more, sullen at a scolding.

I gestured at the glass disk, and the out-sight vanished. "I am sorry, but it was needful. Yes, the Wyse power can do much—very much. But it must only be used with a cool head and a warm heart, for there is this—" Rising, I fixed my eyes on hers and held them there. "Use Wyse-wiles in wrath, for revenge, and in the end the Power will turn upon you."

My companion blinked in surprise. "But you made me look upon that which would rouse my anger," she protested.

"Because," I explained, "your rage unlocked the talent within you, something that had to be done now."

Her hands curled into fists, though it was plain the right one still pained her. "I will *not* throw blood-price away—I shall have it for poor Ursilla and for all the other innocents in Quirth."

"Then learn," I answered. "The dealing of death is not always the best way to pay a score. A wielder of Power can kill, true, but he—or she—can also heal; and for the truly Wyse, the binding up of the world's wounds is a far greater task."

My companion had seated herself again while I was speaking. All the child in her had been burned away by that last flame of heart-heat, and the Jeseca who now faced me was a woman, eager to learn what she could, and should, do.

Then a shadow clouded her bright face. "But what can we do here?" she asked, spreading her hands to indicate the small dingy chamber. "We are trapped." Her voice trailed away uncertainly.

"Not true!" I returned with feeling. The doubt, so deadly to any Wyse work—or wielder—was stretching out its icy tendrils toward her again. At all costs, she must begin this business by believing in herself; but how to make her do it?

After a pause of thought, I had an answer. "Give me your hands," I said, extending my paws as I spoke. My companion looked puzzled but held out her hands, palms up, to cup them.

"Only an hour agone," I began, "I—we—could not have done this, making fur meet flesh in a living touch. At that time, too, you still believed me a small one's night-friend—and yourself a helpless maid. But in that same turn of the sand-glass, all notions have been shattered, even as that mirror—" I indicated the look-round with a nod of my head, "—was cracked by Power. Out of 'traps,' as you would call them, have come freeings: I to my true form and strength, and you to womanhood and knowledge. Littleness and youth are only cocoons, safe places to shelter—like this chamber—till wings are grown."

My friend's smile had returned—this time no mere quirking of the lips but a soul-deep joy. And from the years of our association, I knew her mind to be as quick, as open, as her feelings. Praise was in order. "When your wings of learning are full-fledged," I told her warmly, "who knows to what heights you may—"

"—Wyse?" she finished, and we both laughed. That was my Jeseca. She was, and would be, a familiar beyond price.

RED CROSS, WHITE CROSS
Knight Fantastic (2002) DAW

The land was the same. Below the hill upon which Michael lay, it stretched golden to the edge of the orchard. He strove to see any evidence of neglect, but none could be sighted from his resting place. Locksley-on-the-Marsh . . . he had worked in its fields during his novitiate, had ridden forth as a squire from the cluster of buildings half-ringed by the arms of an orchard. And here he was once more, spying upon a land that now might well be a trap set to close upon such as he.

Yet he had sworn upon the cross-hilt of a broken sword— a weapon not even his own. Fortunate indeed had been the brethren who had died at Acre in all honor, defending to the last a Christian hold against the infidels in the Lord's Holy Land. Michael was too late to march in that company, even as the least of fighting men.

The scene that lay before and beneath him wavered as though wrapped in shifting mist. He was feverish—his healer's training was enough to tell him that. And the pain had been with him always since—Michael forced himself up, nursing his right wrist, its bindings now filthy, against his breast. Wrist? Naught but a crushed stub answered to that description. Right hand—sword hand—wild laughter bubbled to his parched lips, and he held it back only with an effort. A handsome jest *they* had thought the deed: no sword hand, no sword! But some men in this world wielded blade with the left hand, as well, or even both with equal ease.

How many days had passed since Sir William, Senior Knight Commander of the Convent of Locksley-on-the-Marsh, died in a rough nest of grass among the bushes? Sir William, betrayed by a mob of villeins in a stinking huddle of huts, his white robe with its blood-red cross torn from him. At least the old Templar did not die at the hands of that rabble who shouted for a fire to send to hell such a son of Satan. Those muck-crawlers had thought Michael dead from the wound he now nursed; but his commander's sword, caught up in his left hand, had driven them off. Then one of the wretches had sighted men-at-arms approaching from the castle, and the rabble had taken to their heels.

Michael had made no move against the soldiers of the castle guard, aware as he was that all hands were now raised against the Templars. Instead—he would never be sure how—he had managed to get Sir William down to the river and into the skiff he had earlier noticed there.

From the boat, the young knight could see the party from the castle heading toward the village and knew that he and his precious charge could be seen in their turn. As he paddled the unsteady craft out into the current, he murmured one of the prayers he had learned from much repetition: a plea for aid. The True God had answered, for the two men had crossed the stream without being sighted. And, once ashore, Sir William had been granted enough strength to work his way into a thick maze of brambles that grew near the water's edge.

Michael had not dared to try a fire, even when the chill from the river reached them. Fevered by the great gash on his head, Sir William rambled, repeating orders once issued in battle, fragments of the Divine Office, or mere wordless mouthings, and it was necessary at times to lay fingers across his dry lips as he raised his voice. His subordinate could offer no more ease to either of them than to apply crude bandages, torn from their shirts and wetted in the stream, first to his commander's gaping wound and then to his own wrist, lifting the latter to his teeth for knotting. Michael seriously questioned whether the older knight would ever raise himself out of this hole.

Sir William, standing tall, his hand resting on his sword hilt, the spotless white of his cloak making a frame for the great red cross . . . that was how the young man had seen his superior on the day he took his own vows. The Commander was a man of honor and a mighty fighter, yet at times—even as did the lowliest of the Brotherhood—he had tended the injured and ill, cared for the homeless and poor. To be his squire had been—Michael fought against a darkness that seemed to be rising about them both in spite of the coming dawn. Sir William, who had stood witness in his own hastily-held initiation and had thereafter been as much mentor as master . . . Sir William . . .

As if he had spoken that name aloud, the man he supported spoke, not in a mumble of half-consciousness but with the strength of the past.

"Michael?"

"Brother!"

"You must do it . . ." The voice faded.

"What must be done, sir?" Michael prompted gently when the other did not continue.

"The safekeepings—for others." Again a pause.

"At Locksley?" Michael guessed.

"Yes—widow of Lord of Lauchon—needs funds. King Philip and Hospitallers must not take—*no!*" The old knight coughed heavily with his vehemence. "You must get—to Lady Gladden—what is hers." The next silence was unbroken.

Wordless, too, Michael cradled the cooling body against his own. The Templars had served not infrequently as custodians of the funds of merchants and nobles; in London, they were wardens of even King Edward's treasures. It was greed that had brought about their destruction—not the knights' own, but the gold-lust of Philip of France, who wished all the wealth they guarded—as well as their holdings—in his own hands. Vile lies had been fostered to achieve this end, some by the very Church that had once trembled before the Infidel and clamored for aid to the Brotherhood of the Red Cross.

But persecution did not justify the dereliction of duty to God—or men. The Templars had acted as faithful stewards, and such service must continue to be rendered even were the Order to be scourged from the Earth.

Michael's heart felt numb, but his mind was clear, and so was his way. Groping in the brush, thorns tearing at his flesh, he grasped the broken sword.

"Brother," he whispered, "it shall be done." Then he swung its cruciform hilt into the air and, as the morning light blessed it with gold, added fervently, "Upon this Cross I swear it!"

That same oath had brought him here. There had been no reverent burial within the shadow of any Temple for Sir William; maimed as he was, the young Templar could only heap a mass of leaves and drag loose branches over his commander's body. Prayers—yes, that much else he could do; but he was no priest to give rest to his dead master. Surely, however, that Lord whom both served, knowing the truest treasure coffered in a faithful soul, would accept this warrior long in His service.

Now Michael himself was near the end of his task. Three days it had taken him to reach Locksley since Sir William's passing. Hunger gnawed him like a beast, its pain near as bad as that tearing ever at his ruined hand. So far he had seen no sign of life below him; the convent might well be deserted. Doubtless— he grimaced at the thought—when the soldiers had swept in to arrest the brothers, they had done some looting. The safe-room, though, was always well hidden. When he had been here with Sir William during the months of danger, he had been shown the secrets.

It was common knowledge that King Edward and those descended from the families who had given rich gifts of land to the Order in the past opposed the Church's recent command that Templar holdings be yielded up to the Knights Hospitaller. But this convent had been hardly more than a grange, and as such it would be under the care of a custodian who visited it only at intervals.

He knew he must move, and soon, or he would not be able to move at all. Noting ahead the bushes that might afford him cover, Michael started down.

No noise could be heard of cattle or horses, and no watchdog gave tongue in warning. Crouching low, the knight approached the enclosed farmstead. At last he pulled himself to his feet, aided by the gate of the wall that encircled the main buildings.

The door of the inner one facing him had been beaten in, and nothing had been done to repair it. Michael drew a deep breath and lurched forward. Did its damage betoken plundering? He could only believe that it must. But who had wrought the ruin— king's men, villagers roused by a priest, or mere outlaws emboldened by the news that the Templars were to be taken?

Staggering to the broken door, he worked his way inside. All the simple furniture of the large meeting room had been smashed into kindling, and from the fireplace rose a greasy reek where half-bare bones had been thrown—the remains of a pig's carcass.

Food—the first in three days! Michael bent to twist free a bone that still held blackened flesh and clutched it possessively. However, the need to discover what had happened in this place was a stronger hunger than an ache in the belly, and, without eating, he moved on to the other rooms.

The chamber where Sir William, nigh on a year ago, had written his reports to the Grand Master had been stripped of all furnishings save a broken chair. Beyond lay quarters for knights or visitors; the dormitory for the sergeants was on the second floor.

At the door that led to the chapel, the young man hesitated. It was closed, and no signs of assault were evident; but creeping from within came a strong and evil odor—the unmistakable stench of death.

Entering, Michael pressed his shoulder against the right wall to steady himself and so made his way into the sacred chamber that was the center of every Templar dwelling. As he reached the altar, he stopped, rooted by shock at what he saw, unable to believe that any born in Christendom had committed such foul sacrilege.

He wheeled around, unable to fight down sickness, but though he heaved, there was nothing left in his stomach to void. Sliding down the wall that had supported him, the knight lay too weak to move, closing his eyes tightly to shut out the abomination around him. Then a deeper darkness mercifully veiled it from him.

"May they be damned into hell for this!"

Sharp as the sword that had severed his hand, the curse cut through the inner night that had held him. Michael was forced to open his eyes. Light from a torch struck them, flaring and fading, but enough to show him two men standing close by and to glimpse others in the shadows behind.

The companion of the torchbearer drew a step closer. Fire glinted on well-kept mail, though much was hidden by an over-garment. A cloak, a cross—not white with a blood-scarlet sign, but rather black with white. Hospitaller! Come to see what the Church had declared now belonged to his Order, was he?

The Templar's lips flattened against his teeth. Let them cut him down here and now, he thought savagely; to the end he would keep the oath he had taken. And he would not die like a cringing slave. Bracing his arms to raise himself up, he struck his mangled wrist against the floor. Agony lanced through the wound, and he screamed.

In the moment it took for the fiendish torture to subside, Michael found himself fronted by the cloaked knight, who knelt swiftly beside him and steadied him with a strong arm. Then the torchbearer came forward and, in spite of pain-blurred vision, the young man had clear sight of the mail-framed face now close to his own. "Ralf—?"

Perhaps no one heard that whisper save himself, or what he saw was but a cruel delusion born of the fever he carried. Yet new-kindled hope made him strive again for an answer:

"Ralf—brother—"

"Michael!"

The arm about the injured man tightened, holding his body more securely than before; but the wave of weakness and relief that washed over him swept his mind away into darkness once again.

"Michael—here!"

A whisper, then a tug at his hand. He was back in the great hall at Colmount, and someone was striving to draw him into the shadows near a tapestry that hung on the wall behind the high table. Ralf, of course.

"What—" he began, realizing as he spoke that a strange glamour seemed to be holding them both. Ralf looked as he had the last time they had been alone together—a boy in a rumpled smock. And he—he was in the same state.

"Be still!" commanded his brother. There was only a year between them, but Michael was the elder and did not take kindly to such orders. He had just opened his mouth to protest when he heard another voice—one he hated. Scowling, he edged still closer to the dais and the tall-backed chairs that held and hid the speakers.

"Have you thought upon Stephen's advice, my lord?"

"Yes." The single word was a grunt.

A moment of silence followed. Michael could hear his brother's quick-drawn breaths as the two rubbed shoulders in the small space.

"You would be choosing well, my lord." The first speaker's light voice carried a trace of impatience. "They would bring honor to themselves and their house, and you have another son—"

Michael wanted to spit. Oh, yes—Udo!

So he and Ralf stood and listened to the decision that would change their lives forever, removing them from the world they knew and taking from them all they had, to favor the half brother they despised.

That their father was under the will of their stepmother the boys had learned even before the marriage. With the birth of Udo, they had also become aware that the Lady Anigale wanted the heirship for her own stupid cub.

And her scheme had borne fruit true to its seeding, for Michael and his brother were separated. Ralf had gone to the Hospitallers; he, to the Templars.

"Michael—"

Faint and from far away came that voice, but it was enough to break his dream. He returned to himself enough to sense that he lay not on stone now but on a softer surface.

"Drink!"

A rim of metal was pressed against his lips as his head and shoulders were lifted. Unwilling to open his eyes, he drank, and his mouth filled with a taste of blended herbs; then he was allowed to lie down again. The darkness was waiting, but this time he made no return to the past.

When at last he roused completely, Michael found himself staring up at a white ceiling like a cloud, cleft by the lightning of a jagged crack. This was not the chapel—it was one of the rooms of the infirmary, his torpid memory supplied that much. Two burning torches were thrust into rings on the wall. By their light, as he slowly turned his head, he was able to bring into focus the back of a man who stood by a table, counting liquid drop by drop as he held a small flask above the mouth of a larger.

As though sensing his patient's gaze, the other turned; then, with one long stride, he was beside the Templar and on his knees. Again Michael was looking up into the face of his brother.

"I am meat for the sheriff." He was able to think clearly again, and his voice was stronger. "Best let me go—"

Bound as Ralf was by the Hospitallers' rules, could he—or would he—do otherwise, or did too many years lie between them now?

"*No!*" The word was spoken with force. "How came you here, and—"

"—why?" Michael could readily guess that second question. "'Tis simple enough. I am under oath to the Senior of this holding, which is now—" he strove to keep his voice free of passion, "—sealed by Church and King to your Order. But what brings *you* to this place? Is not Rhodes the land where the White Cross holds sway?"

"I was on caravan," began Ralf, then paused at the bewilderment on his brother's face. "Oh, yes—we are now wedded to ships, but a scouting voyage is still deemed a 'caravan.' Our vessel was dispatched out of the Middle Sea to London on matters of the Order—" Once more he fell silent.

Michael thought he had a good idea of what such "matters" might be. "You and your brethren are to survey your new properties here."

"You have the right of it," said Ralf, looking relieved at not having to speak a painful truth. "But, know this, Michael—" He leaned closer over the pallet and spoke in a near whisper.

"In the past there have indeed been times when the White Cross has differed in creed or deed from the Red. But the foul lies that have brought low the Knights of the Temple—have sent them to torture and death—those we do *not* believe. Some of your brothers have even taken refuge with us, have changed their white cloaks for black. Our Order still battles slavers; the blood of Turks—and not all who are of that cruel mind dwell in the East!—is drink for our swords. Yet we also labor to heal those struck down by either steel or plague."

" 'Put not your trust in princes,' brother," Michael quoted. Then he added with a bitter smile. "Or in Church fathers; perhaps your day of doubt, too, will come.

"As to why I am here," he continued, "I gave oath to my leader, even as he died, to carry out a mission. You know that we of the Temple have had safe places wherein merchants, lords, and even kings have stored their treasures. These riches are not ours, yet much has lately been seized, and the true owners fear their wealth is gone beyond recovering."

Ralf straightened a fraction. "Men's worldly goods pass not through our hands!" he retorted hotly. "Lands we will do with as the Church decides, but we claim nothing left in trust; we are sworn even to refuse those charges ourselves. You now seek such an object of safekeeping?"

"Aye—there is a lady very needful of what lies here. The Lady Gladden—"

Ralf stared, then drew back a little. His mouth set in an expression of truculence his brother knew of old.

"What mischief roils the kettle now?" Michael repeated the question that had been so often aimed at them by Dame Hannah, their mother's nurse, in those lost days.

Ralf ran tonguetip over his lips as though to open them for the passing of words that were hard to utter.

"Our father died six years ago."

"What of that?" Michael made answer to this news. "I have no thought of seeking out Colmount again. Udo may sit in the high seat there until his beard turns white, as far as I am concerned! Too well I know that the countess stands always behind him, quick with her suggestions—"

"Udo died of a putrid fever," Ralf cut in. "Our late lady stepmother gained nothing in the end from Colmount; she had to satisfy herself with another lord—Gladden! And *he* met with the Scots, to his swift undoing. She is now without lord or land; yet you say she has some treasure here."

Michael lay very still. His eyes met those green ones, so like his own, set in his brother's face, and saw them suddenly become hooded, withdrawn.

"I know what Sir William wished of me," he said at length into the silence, "and to that I must hold." He struggled up, Ralf doing nothing to help him, until he was sitting on the rough bed of cloaks and time-tattered blankets. "I *must* hold," he repeated, but he made the vow only to himself.

The Hospitaller rose to his feet and, once erect, gazed for a long moment down at the Templar. "A man does what his honor demands," he said formally. "Lady Anigale may be the witch we always deemed her, but she will still have your service, it seems—"

Michael had known the blinding pain of having his hand severed, the withering of spirit brought by the knowledge that his life had been shattered beyond mending. Those sufferings, however, diminished to nothing when compared with the thrust Ralf had just delivered.

"I have heard nothing of Lady Gladden." Ralf spoke slowly, giving each word more than its usual weight. "I have found one set upon by outlaws, and to him I have given aid, as my Oath demands. We await Sir Jean de Averele, the leader of our party, who is to meet us here. I have seen no Templar, only a wayfarer—perhaps a merchant. Who and what you are you must decide for yourself. Understand this."

"I understand."

Ralf turned on his heel and was gone. And so their first reunion ended.

Nothing was left to him except, as Ralf had said, honor. After his brother had left the room, Michael crawled on hands and knees to a table close by and used its sturdy trestles to pull himself to his feet. At least he knew this building and the exact place of his goal.

Suppose he did bring what he had sworn to retrieve out of its safekeeping; how could he return it to—*her*? During the past few days, he had never thought beyond opening the cache. He did not even know how much was to be transported. And there was none to turn to—his younger brother's parting words had made it plain that there was little in common between them any longer. It was small comfort that no amount of planning could have prepared him for the ironic twist this tale had taken. He was now severed from everything and everyone more surely than he had been in that hour when the rabble had held him down to maim him in body and soul.

The windowless hall beyond the door was deep in darkness.

Michael judged that day had passed into night, though he could not depend upon his perceptions, being unable to reckon how long he had lain unconscious. However, the Hospitallers had not ridden out, and they might still be in the process of evaluating their new holding. Yet, as the Templar scraped his way along the wall, he heard no sound and saw no further dance of torchlight. It might be that Ralf, knowing now what had brought him to Locksley, would be waiting to use him as a guide and thereby discover the safe-room without difficulty or danger.

Rounding a corner, he came to the entrance of the chapel. Even in this place, he heard and saw nothing to suggest that others were still present under this roof, though there could be no service here. Those who had despoiled the chapel had also desecrated it, and it would have to be cleansed before the Host could once more be brought within.

But there was light—moonlight; a portion of the roof had vanished not far from the altar. Michael took step by wavering step until he caught at the massive block, then used it for support as he steered himself around to the other side.

Once more on his knees, he sought the wall behind it. The effort to arrive here had winded him, but he breathed as shallowly as possible to avoid drawing in the air about, fouled as it was by what had been nailed to the Cross: the body of Nigar, Sir William's hound. The space behind the altar was pitch-black, and Michael, shuddering, had to run his hand down the besmirched stones, counting the mortar seams between them.

Twice he made that tally; then, certain, he spread his left hand flat on the block he had selected. With all the force he could summon, he set his weight against it. Again he placed his hand, this time at another section of the same stone. Four times, all told, he repeated the action—one he had performed before under Sir William's eye.

At first Michael thought he had failed; then the blocks gave a little. With renewed hope, he put forth the last of his strength, and suddenly the whole wall grated loudly and swung forward. Stumbling to get out of the way, the young knight fell again and lay gasping.

After a moment, he rolled over awkwardly and got back to his knees, an effort that made moisture run down his face until he tasted salt on his lips. Half-crawling, he pulled himself to the doorway, then through it. Just inside he hunkered down, breathing in stale air scented with unidentifiable odors, some of which surely arose from what lay in the chamber.

And where among its contents was he to find what he sought? This ignorance seemed, somehow, the final defeat. With its realization, Michael cast himself prone on the dust-carpeted floor. Once more he murmured prayers—not the ritual entreaties of any service, but broken phrases wrung from a soul near to the mortal sin of despair.

Then came the sound of boots, and fingers of torchlight probed within the treasure place. Those who approached had the glow at their backs, so Michael could not see their faces until one swung around and reached a torch into the room.

It was Ralf—and he was not alone in wearing the cloak of a sworn knight. As he brought the light closer, Michael could see his companion. The other man was much older, and his face was graven with the same lines of authority that had seamed the countenance of Sir William. Here was surely the superior of whom Ralf had spoken.

"Be this your invader, brother?" the elder knight asked. "It would seem that he is also a master of secrets—which is a curious thing, since the mighty among our brethren of the Temple were not wont to share hidden knowledge beyond their own tight-held circle."

Michael braced himself up on the elbow of his left arm.

"I am Michael of Colmount, Knight of St. John of Jerusalem, and now prey to any enforcer of the law. Take me in to Dorchester and get the glory of it! I came here at the orders of the Senior Knight of Locksley-on-the-Marsh, but I have failed. There is no more to be said."

Sir John de Averele stood beside him now. The two men were pressed close by the number of chests and coffers crowded into the small chamber.

"Sir William de Vere—you served him?" he asked. "He is with you, here—?"

The Templar's throat was thick with grief, but he forced himself to reply.

"He is dead," he answered shortly.

"So?" the Hospitaller glanced around at all the wealth that had been concealed in this place. "Your leader being dead, you came to fill your pockets? Such tales are now told of your kind in the courts!"

This offense against his honor gave Michael a last strength to front his accuser. He threw his maimed limb over a chest beside him and pulled himself upright; then another arm—a strong one—was about him, and he was held on his feet by a body solid as the neighboring stone in its aid. Ralf!

"Sir William died, yes, pulled down by the scum of a village," the young knight answered evenly. "I gave oath to complete his mission."

He wanted so much to strike that face, framed in its shining mail-coif, with his wounded wrist, to show what it meant when all the world turned against a man—one, moreover, who had sworn to protect that same world from the ravages of evil.

Sir Jean now tried another tack. "You name yourself of the House of Colmount. Another of that House stands beside you— does he speak for you and your presence here?"

"Ralf and I be brothers indeed by birth," Michael replied carefully, "but we have known naught of each other since we were children. What is warded here is no affair of his, nor is my purpose."

"Which is to plunder—"

"*No!*" the Templar's voice rose to a shout. "I take no man's goods for myself! There is a treasure here that does not belong to the Temple but was sent to this place for safekeeping. Sir William heard that the rightful owner was in great need and promised to find and deliver it to her."

The senior Hospitaller gave a strange smile. "This lady is also known to you, Sir Michael, and not happily. Oh, yes, Sir Ralf has told me a curious story, one almost too hard to believe; yet proof exists that it is true. Can you now find this so-precious thing? If you can, and it proves to be, as you say, the property of another, then it will be returned without any report to that owner."

The Templar turned his head a fraction to survey the chests, the boxes, the bags. He had no idea as to the nature of what he sought; he could only hope that the Lord in Whom he had placed his trust for so long would guide him—it might be for the last time.

He would have moved unaided in his search, but Ralf resisted his efforts to tug free and instead matched steps to his. Sir Jean, taking the torch, walked behind, keeping its gleam on the storage containers as well as he could.

Then there came an answer. The light showed it plainly: a small coffer, resting on a second, larger chest. And on the carven lid—an owl. The Owl of Colmount!

Michael did not hail his discovery by voice or touch, merely pointed. Sir Jean called, and the sergeant still at the door strode forward to take the torch, while the senior knight stretched hand to the wooden box. "We shall examine this in more suitable quarters," he announced, motioning to Ralf, Michael, and the others to follow.

The Hospitaller looked to the Templar as the group emerged into the gloom of the chapel. "You can close what you have opened?" he asked, indicating the door.

Michael nodded. "Swing it shut again and press three times on one block down from the opening at the top, then at the left edge and the right." He watched, fearing that his instructions might not work. They did, however, and the knights proceeded without hindrance to the room that had been Sir William's chamber. No chairs had been left there by the vandals, but saddles had been brought in to serve as seats. Ralf lowered Michael onto one and stood behind him to keep him steady.

Sir Jean pried up the lid of the coffer. Then, as though the age-bitten wood had been dead ash to be swept from living embers, a glittering fire was revealed at its heart. Jewels, as Michael had expected. The older man lifted every pendant, bracelet, and hair-band, examining each in turn.

"A fortune for the lucky, yes," he commented as he worked.

But when one necklet was drawn forth, Michael blinked. The ornament was a chain of silver, hung with what seemed drops of frozen moonlight. That was a Colmount jewel only by default, thought the Templar angrily; their mother had worn it once. He remembered, and, by Ralf's sudden clutch on his arms, his brother did, as well.

"A fortune for the Lady Gladden—"

NO! Michael wanted to howl. The fingers of his left hand balled into a fist. For a long moment, he fought within a battle such as he had never faced in the field—perhaps his personal Acre. But this time there was victory.

"Sir William deemed it her right." He thought the words would choke him.

"Very well, then, it shall go to her." Sir Jean closed the coffer. Then his full attention returned to Michael.

"And what will you do, loyal Knight of St. John of Jerusalem?"

"I can die like the rest," the Templar made answer, "and I shall if any take me. They have not yet laid heretic fires here, but God alone knows what will happen." With this final defiance, Michael felt as though all the strength that had upheld him through his ordeal had seeped away. He no longer cared for his fate, except that he wished to have it done.

"Brother—" Ralf was speaking to his superior. "Others who wore the Red Cross have turned to the White."

"They were not cripples who would be pensioners." replied Sir Jean.

The maimed Templar was too worn to resent that truth. No, he would not appeal to be put into a hospital for, though his body might be tended in such a place, his mind and soul would shrivel for lack for purpose.

"Brother—" Ralf again, "—he is left-handed."

Sudden as lightning, the Hospitaller's sword appeared over Michael's shoulder. Instinctively, the Templar seized the hilt with his remaining hand. Ralf half-loosed his hold upon the blade, and it swayed for a moment, then straightened up.

Michael's head no longer drooped in defeat.

"Take me to your practice-field, if you will," he said, his voice firm, confident. "I was blooded in Spain against the Moors, and I won my cloak with the consent of the Brothers in assembly, as is the custom. I was also trained to fight two-handed, a swordsman right or left. I can be so again."

Sir Jean studied him. "I cannot speak for the Masters," he said quietly. "But ride with us, and we shall see."

Thus, as had been perhaps ordained long before by a Power beyond both, the Red became White, and heart sworn to one Cross found service beneath another which was, in truth, the same.

SOW'S EAR—SILK PURSE
30th Anniversary DAW: Fantasy Anthology (2002) DAW

*It is an accepted fact that, if a maiden is to prosper in this world,
she must possess the gift of beauty. If she can claim that blessing,
then fortune, fame, and illustrious marriage will surely follow in
due time. This "fact," however, is seldom true.*

*And if a young lady is not born with a mien of exceptional
comeliness—a treasure more precious than the silver-spoon-in-the-
mouth of proverb—then ways exist, albeit laborious ones, whereby
she may acquire at least a modicum of the desired appearance. No
one turns willingly away from the chance to show a radiant face.
Or does she?*

In the fifteenth year of the reign of King Karl the Sluggard, the
town of Yerd boasted several families whose wealth was considerable enough to make them the equals of minor gentry. These
prosperous folk were fully aware of the importance of their standing: the Sorens, the Wassers, the Rhinebecks, and the Berdmans
had hats doffed and curtsies made to them whenever they chose
to go abroad.

Marsitta Wasser had recently made a most fortunate marriage with a knight who held a position (albeit very minor) at court. That he was both threadbare of cloak and empty of pocket mattered not in the slightest when his shield bore the quarterings of four noble families. The young woman's dowry would soon repair any lack in her fiancé's fashions and fortune, and, in any event, the title "my lady" discreetly covered such embarrassments.

Some weeks after this world-altering event, Master and Dame Soren were returning from a visit to the home of the knight and his new bride. Not only had the Wassers still been very full of the wedding—they were now projecting a visit to Court. The Sorens felt thoroughly out of sorts and made their way home in silence and dark thought. Not until the maid, Jennie, had opened the door and Master Soren had stepped inside the hall did he speak.

"You have a daughter—" he barked.

Ingrada Soren bristled and caught him by the sleeve to pull him into the parlor, away from listening ears.

"WE have a daughter!" She spoke with the firmness born of many years' peacemaking in small family wars.

Margus Soren made a sound close to a grunt. "We have a milkwater miss with a body as skinny as a *darem* bush when the leaves are gone, a face as freckled as if one of the carriage team had blown bran at her, and a fat-pudding brain so dull it cannot tell madras from silk!"

Dame Soren was stung by this sorry litany. Certainly Feliciana was no great beauty, but she was biddable and deft with her needle—both desirable traits in a wife—and one lone mistake in the cloth-mart did not mean she was lacking in wit. True, she had to be watched lest she dawdle away hours with those books the rector's wife had lent her. Perhaps it would be best to see soon to breaking off that particular friendship.

With a shrug of his shoulders, her husband moved to one of the long windows that fronted the square. Sweeping the heavy drape to one side, he glanced out as the thunder of the iron-shod wheels of a traveling coach abruptly drowned out the usual street noise.

"The Boroughmaster's nephew must be in trouble again." Margus continued to watch the activity below and did not turn to his wife as he spoke. "Here he comes once more, to wait time out until Rhinebeck mends matters with Lord Gargene."

The arrival of Yerd's most notorious—but well-connected— rascal was hardly of great consequence. Such was Dame Soren's first thought, but it was swiftly followed by another. All knew that Hilda Rhinebeck had chafed at the amount of attention paid to the Wassers' wedding, being always eager to promote her nephew— no matter his reputation as a good-for-naught. Of course, he *was* grandson to a baron, and he *did* rub shoulders with the noble youths—the ones fond of gaming, at least—at the court. (Dame Rhinebeck reveled in the bits of scandal he reported and would arrange her entertaining accordingly.)

" 'Tis near the beginning of the hunting season," Ingrada said slowly.

"Aye," replied her husband, his voice still gruff, "and then half the lay-lazies of the shire will roister in our streets! Rhinebeck will be well out of pocket paying extra constables before the end of the month. That gangrel of a nephew will have to be watched. For has he money or no, depend upon it, a flock of fools will crowd about him to bet their sires' silver—money already owed to honest guildsmen. We could do without that!"

Dame Soren made no answer; her mind was already busied adding this new information to its picture of Feliciana's future, like a thread of gold added suddenly to a drab weaving. Men, she reflected, never really understood the finer points of marrying off a daughter to be a credit to her family.

Ingrada began listing the names of a few prospects as she headed for her chamber upstairs to lay aside her visiting finery—elegant clothing donned all too rarely, as Yerd was sadly lacking in festive occasions. She continued to be thus absorbed as she passed the closed door of the chamber where the object of her musings sat sewing, but the heel-clicks of her best shoes gave her away.

Feliciana's head jerked up. Swiftly she made sure that the letter she had been reading was safely stowed in her work-box. As she heard the door of her mother's chamber open, then close, she gave a sigh of relief—no visit, with the inevitable scrutiny of her limited charms, seemed likely now.

The girl rubbed her eyes tiredly, wishing that she might as easily escape from the mocking memories that had been with her ever since Marsitta's wedding. Ingrada, she knew, would be spurred on by that social slave-auctioning to market her own daughter. Feliciana had no hope of escaping more of those nightmarish, shaming hours of sitting uncomfortably to one side of a ballroom, waiting until one of the "gentlemen" present was drunk enough to ask to partner her in a dance. At such times, she invariably either stumbled or committed some equally-unpardonable offense that she would hear about for days afterward.

She gulped, feeling physically ill with such remembrances, but she forced herself to set another stitch in the linen stretched over the frame before her. In the distance a door opened. Her mother *was* coming, after all! It had been too much to hope that she would not come in—she had been at the Wassers' that morning, and what she had probably heard there would not be such news as to leave her in a good mood.

As Dame Soren entered the sewing room, Feliciana rose awkwardly to curtsy, but Ingrada waved her impatiently back to her seat. She herself remained standing, the better to view her daughter from head to foot, then back again.

The girl, she observed, was dressed well enough, her gown of that rather odd hue of red that was neither copper nor rust but a shade between, and one that truly suited her. There was no denying that she was plain, for her angular body lacked womanly curves. However, at least her eyes were stronger than those of the Berdman maid's and, for all her foolish preoccupation with books, she did not squint. But her hair had always been straighter than a string—

"You have not used the curl-rags!"

With a guilty gesture, Feliciana pulled at a typical lock of lank, dull-brown hair. "The knots hurt so I cannot sleep," she said miserably, "and when I comb it in the morning, it all just goes straight again."

Ingrada set her lips. "Then Jennie must bring the iron."

Feliciana forced herself not to shrink back. *Jennie* and *iron* meant *burned ends* and *nasty smell*—and, again, curls that did not last long.

Dame Soren strode toward a large chest set to one side of the chamber and opened the coffer with such force that the lid banged against the wall. She began to pull out lengths of linen, satin, and patterned silk—the finest such stuffs to be found on the shelves of the Soren shop. As she held up each in turn for inspection, Ingrada glanced from the cloth to her daughter with no lightening of countenance.

"We shall have Dame Roslyn in—and we had best see to that at once, as her work will be in demand."

Then, closing the chest, she was gone.

No—no—and *no!* The denial Feliciana dared not utter aloud rang in her head. She clasped her hands together until her fingers cramped. They would dress her in milk-and-water colors, as became a maid, choosing a modest style of gown, as suited the daughter of a Guildsman of the Council. But, as ever, she would be the object of smirks and titters.

Resolutely, she forced herself to concentrate on her needle-work. Sometimes when she bent her mind wholly to her labor, she could, for a time all too brief, forget what lay ahead.

Jennie arrived, bearing not the curling iron but rather a tray of food; Feliciana was, then, to eat her noon meal in private. There was a plate heaped with gluttonous servings of several dishes; beside it stood a tall mug of milk and an after-sweet of rich cakes. This was her regular fare in double portion! So her mother was going to try to stuff her in the hope of producing curves where Nature had shaped her form with a miserly hand.

"Th' Rogue do be back." Jennie had put down the tray, but she was lingering.

"Is he?" Feliciana had little concern for this development; everyone in Yerd was used to Master Rogar's comings and goings.

"There's goin' t'be mighty merrymakin'," the maid continued, ignoring her mistress' lack of enthusiasm in her own excitement. "Dame Rhinebeck—she's been lookin' to outshine th' Wassers. An' th' hunters'll be comin' soon!"

When Feliciana still showed no interest, Jennie smoothed the edge of the tablecloth with elaborate care. Plainly, there was more she wanted to say.

The girl indicated the cakes. "'Take one, Jennie," she urged. "I'll never eat so many, but I'll hear about it if they are not all gone."

"Thank ye, miss." The servant bobbed her version of a curtsy and picked up a sweet but showed no sign of leaving. At last she burst out:

"Th' Mistress—she's a-makin' plans again!"

To this ominous statement Feliciana said nothing. Jennie, however, took her silence for encouragement. Dropping her voice to a dramatic whisper, she revealed, "That Wasser girl, 'tis said she went to the *Green Hag* and got her luck there."

Now Feliciana did take notice. "Why would Marsitta need to do that?" she mused, bitterness edging her voice. "She was born with all the bounties."

The maid frowned with the effort of unaccustomed thought. "Sometimes one wants t' make sure," she said slowly. "Maybe she just wanted to make *real* sure. Though I'm a-thinkin' maybe she'll find as how she didn't do so well for herself—that knight o' hers, he had him a mean-lookin' mouth."

"I don't want to get married!" The protest wrenched itself from Feliciana, strident as a battle cry.

"Maybe not," said Jennie sadly. Then she shrugged in resignation and repeated, "But th' Mistress—she's got plans."

Feliciana drew a deep breath. Too true, but—*no!* She set down her fork, feeling the familiar wave of nausea at the idea of being exposed yet again to humiliation. In fine clothes that made her thin, awkward body look even more clumsy . . . with hair curled by force but too soon straggling down raggedly . . . powdered . . . painted. . . . She would feel a perfect fool, yet to some man, the girl knew, she would still be acceptable. The only way to escape would be to become so utterly ugly that no buyer would offer a beggar's bit for her in die marriage mart.

Feliciana tensed. Ugly—grotesquely hideous. Could she bring herself to such a fate? She glanced toward her sewing box, in which rested the leaflet that Dame Kateryn, the rector's wife, had given her.

Places existed, the broadside told, where an unsightly or crook-shanked maid could find refuge out of sight of the family to whom she was a source of shame. There she could do fine needlework, learn herbcraft for cooking and healing, or freely read and write. The women who lived in the haven of which

Dame Kateryn knew taught the daughters of even the high nobility.

"The Green Hag," said Feliciana suddenly. "Tell me about her, Jennie."

Pleased at being invited to such an intimate confidence, the serving girl leaned close and spoke in a hushed voice. "They say as how she comes with th' full moon, an' she'll give ear to the maid or man what takes her a gift she fancies. Them as is brave enough can seek her out near the Ghost Trees—"

Feliciana forced a laugh. "I fear *I* would never be so bold," she said with careful indifference. "But thank you, Jennie." Reaching out to draw her embroidery frame closer, she turned away from the barely tasted meal—and from her recent confidante. The servant hesitated a moment longer, then ducked a curtsy and left.

At the full of the moon—that was only two days hence. As she resumed her needlework, the young woman considered the perilous path of invoking the Wild Magic and the dire fate that might befall one who did so. It would be easy enough afterward—always supposing the tales were true—to say that she had fallen afoul of the Hag and thus had been undone. Feliciana did not like to think of the pity and scorn she now endured being multiplied a hundredfold if she were given a repulsive appearance, but—she stabbed at the fabric viciously—*nothing* could be worse than to have her mother try yet again to marry her off.

So far had she speculated when a sharp knock sounded on the door. A moment later, her father tramped in to plant himself before her with only the needle frame between them.

"Got news for you, girl."

Feliciana scrambled up and curtsied. "Yes, sir?"

"Received an offer for you—most respectable one." Margus Soren cocked his head to one side in a gesture of triumph and waited for his daughter's reaction.

Suddenly the girl was truly afraid. She cast her eyes down, as was modest and fitting, and asked no questions, but her father was watching her closely, and she was sure he could see the pounding of her heart beneath the bodice of her gown. *Who . . . ?*

"Big a surprise as I ever had, mind you," Master Soren went on expansively. "The Boroughmaster himself sent the offer. He would have you wed with his nephew—the grandson of a baron, no less! True, that House has had a run of bad luck—lost most of their holdings, they did—but naught can take away their standing.

"Yes," the guildsman concluded with satisfaction, "Fortune has certainly smiled upon us. Be getting at your bride clothes now, for it's a soon wedding they want. Marsitta Wasser can be a lady, but you'll be a greater one—your dowry will be the Panfrey estate as came to me for debts five years agone. They'll do well by you, girl, and so will we."

Feliciana's father was smiling benevolently at her, but his eyes were narrowed as he waited for her reaction. The young woman forced a shaky smile. "You have done all a daughter could wish, sir," she said. That reply was the only one she could manage, but it was the truth by the standards of Yerd.

He nodded, satisfied, and left. The bride-to-be sank once more into her seat before the embroidery frame and stared at it, unseeing. The Rogue! His conduct had ever been ill, and many lurid stories were told of his exploits. He was rumored to consort with the red-wigged women on the north side of the town, and he was known to be a gambler, a liar, and a taker of pleasure in the evil plight of others.

The girl wanted to scream. Now the only hope left was to acquire an ugliness so appalling that it would outweigh the prom-ised dowry.

For the next two days, Feliciana somehow bore the burden of her parents' joy and the congratulations from members of the household and friends. In a hand that she forced not to shake, she signed the marriage contract under her father's boldly written name. As yet, her betrothed had not made his appearance, and to that fortunate fact she clung, for if he saw her with her present homely-but-not-unwholesome face, any change would be laid to the meddling of Master and Mistress Soren.

For the next two evenings, the Rogue's unwilling fiancée endured the twisting of her hair in the ritual of torture with the curling iron. But if by night the torture was inflicted with fire, by day it was performed with water, or at least an unending flow of speech from her mother, mixing instruction and admonition. There was also a sticking with pins, as though she were a curse-poppet, though this pain was not intentional: it was the byproduct of long sessions of gown fittings. The girl felt added guilt at the cost of these rich garments that would never be used.

At last the night she awaited came. Wearied by the tryings (and tryings-on) of the day, but more than ever determined *not* to enter the life her parents envisioned for her, Feliciana crawled into bed. Jennie drew the curtains, shutting her off from the unwanted world.

When she was sure the maid had gone, the girl pushed off the covers and sat up. She feared to close her eyes, not only because she must not sleep but because her dreams had become nightmares that showed a death dance of ghastly faces. Finally, she could wait no longer.

Wriggling off the tall bed, Feliciana moved once more into the room. By the feeble light of its night-lamp, she dressed in the simplest gown and the oldest cloak she owned. Before Master Soren had risen in the Mercers' Guild and prospered in the world, the family had lived with far less show, and she knew the town well from walking a number of its cobbled streets.

Yerd had not been threatened for many generations; in consequence, the city gate had stood open for so long that perhaps now it could no longer be closed. A constable was supposed to be on duty after dark, but he seldom stirred out of his shelter.

Keeping to the shadows, Feliciana slipped into the outer world. The Green Hag, she had learned, held rule not far from the ruins of the old Illet Abbey in a pocket-sized wood, the remains of a once-great forest. The way to the forsaken holy place was nearly grown over. She pulled her cloak about her as closely as she could, but every few feet she walked it was caught by a thorny claw from the walling brush.

Too soon, however, she reached the open ground about the abbey ruins. There the moon shone very bright. The girl felt for the small bag held in the breast of her chemise. She had no way of knowing what the Wild Witch would want in payment, but she had brought the only treasure that was truly hers: the pearl necklet given by her godmother at her christening.

It was so quiet. Instinctively, Feliciana went at a slower pace, even though the way was open. To the left, extending from the edge of a crumbling wall of stone, stretched the wood. At one time its growth of trees had been more close set, but now a tall upright stone could be seen, the first sentinel of an ancient shrine. To follow those stones would lead a seeker to where the Green Hag sheltered.

Feliciana passed the first of the towering markers. The silence continued; no cry came from owl or other night-hunter, no rustle of wind brushed leaves. She began to hurry a little, wariness rising in her. Would it be wiser to retreat?

Abruptly the girl stepped into a second open space, a smaller one. Here the moonlight fairly blazed, a fire not of red-gold but of silver. The shrine was open, and One stood in the doorway.

A woman, her white body striped with living vines. Beneath

that scanty covering lay nothing but skin, shaped in lush curves that any woman would envy. About her shoulders hung thicker twists of the growing stuff—but none hid her face. That showed a pig's snout, a gaping mouth from which green slime dribbled, eyes that lacked either lashes or brows save for a dried lichenlike crusting. The body of a goddess; the face of a demon.

Feliciana did not hesitate but continued forward; she had the feeling that she was being tested in some fashion. At last she paused at a little distance from the One who stood as still as a statue.

Fear had stolen the girl's speech but not her wits. The being before her might be of no mortal kind, but one could never go wrong in offering courtesy. This she did, gathering cloak and skirts into both hands and dipping graciously as she would have to any of her parents' friends.

Those eyes, which had been dull and unfocused a moment earlier, now centered on the young woman. A purplish tongue flicked out over protruding lips.

"You come as a seeker?" In yet another mad contradiction, the voice that spoke from that monstrous face had the musical lilt of a bard's.

Feliciana summoned her courage, which was already threatening to desert her.

"I—I do, Lady."

The Hag made no immediate reply. After a moment, the girl pushed back the head-folds of her cloak.

"So," came the response then. "You human females are all too easy to read. A fair face, a well-shaped body—those gifts, you believe, will make all your dreams real. You have no doubts of that, ever—"

The Wild Witch paused. Though the nightmare visage showed no change of expression, the singing tone now held a sting of disdain.

ANDRE NORTON

"No!" the girl said hurriedly. "I do not want beauty, I wish to be ugly—"

"Now *that* I have never heard!" The Hag laughed, and the sound was no cackle but a noise of honest amusement. "You must be hard-pressed indeed to crave such an ill boon. Why do you wish to change yourself?"

"I—" The seeker hesitated, then hastened on before she could think further of the bargain she sought to strike. "My father has signed my betrothal contract, I do not care to wed. I would be free."

"Is your swain, then, so foul of person or habits?"

The girl shook her head. "His world is not mine. If I am forced to enter it, I shall fail, over and over again, at all I should be expected to do."

Now Feliciana brought her hand into the moonlight. The pearls of her christening necklet shimmered, not with the hard glitter of diamonds, but with a muted beauty that rivaled the moon's own.

"I have only these," she said, feeling compelled to explain the modesty of her offering. "My father is but Mercer Guildsman."

"Be this your dowry?"

"Nay." Now Feliciana could speak without shame. "That is to be the Manor of Panfrey."

"Your mercer father is most generous. One might guess that the groom is of fairly high estate?"

Why did the Green Woman keep her talking? Feliciana wondered. She seemed to be probing for a certain piece of information.

"He is the nephew of the Boroughmaster," the young woman answered, "and his grandfather is a baron."

"Ah—the Rogue is to be wed willy-nilly, is he?" Again that silvery laughter rippled forth, but it changed swiftly to the sober tolling of a warning bell. "You are indeed stupid, girl. There is

276

often far more to life than what humans call 'love.' Consider: you will be mistress at Panfrey! And think also on this: my gifts, once given, can never be undone. Would you truly be an ugling all your days?"

Feliciana swallowed but stood firm. What did one's outer person matter? Veils could shield the unlovely. As for the great manor, she had no rights in her dowry; and the Rogue, who knew well the beauties of the court, might wed her, but he would surely cast her aside as soon as he could.

Bitter though it was, the girl forced herself to pursue the thought to its end. Better that rejection should come now than after they were bonded for life, for there would be none to whom she could even appeal. However, should she be cursed—and the families might well name her fate such—then they would wish to be rid of her, and waiting was that retreat of which Dame Kateryn had spoken. No, she would not be bound to a round of duties she would shrink from more each day. Between the two fates, she would choose this.

"Such is my desire, Lady." Feliciana was proud that she could speak so steadily.

That monstrous head shook, setting the green vines a-rustle. Again came a liquid trill of laughter. "A little threat will be good for the Rogue," the Wild One murmured, as though speaking to herself. "He is entirely too certain that life owes him his every good thing. I am minded to send a message—"

The girl was surprised at this speech. Did the Hag *know* the Boroughmaster's nephew—and, if so, how?

The Green Woman was speaking once more to the supplicant before her, and her tone was grave again. "Remember, human youngling, you cannot come crying for my aid a second time. But if you are heart-set on this course, give me that trinket of yours, and hold up your head—then we shall see what we shall see."

Feliciana stepped closer and dropped the pearls into the waiting hand. The Rogue's betrothed was sure that Witch would not take kindly to any wavering of resolve now. She hoped that the transformation was not to be a painful one—a possibility she had not considered—but no. No hurt of body could equal the searing of soul she had undergone so often. With that thought, her resolution was set.

The Hag twined the necklet about her wrist, then beckoned her seeker even closer. Now she lifted both hands to frame the girl's face. Feliciana felt a soft touch that started at her forehead and slipped slowly down to *her throat. Three times then did* the Wild One serve her.

To her great relief, the young woman felt no wrenching of *bone or skin, as she had* half expected. When the Green Woman *withdrew* a little, eyeing her critically, she dared to *raise her* own hands to touch cheek and chin, but she could feel no change.

"I am no different!" she burst out.

"Nay!" retorted the Hag sharply. "Sight and touch are not the same. Never in your own eyes will there be any change you may behold—only by others may your transforming be seen. Mind you—" She paused, holding Feliciana's face in her gaze for a long moment—and doing more, the girl knew, than viewing her own handiwork. "You must live with what has been given. It is for you from henceforth to make the most of the boon you asked."

The moonlight seemed to flow about the Green Witch like a mist, veiling her completely. A moment Feliciana stood transfixed; then she came to herself, sighed, and sought the path of the pillars that would bring her out into the world again.

The bargainer with the Wild Magic found it as easy to return to her bed as it had been to leave the chamber. However, she did not seek sleep under the thick quilt; rather she sat upright, still patting and stroking her face. All she could think of was how she would appear to her parents and the rest of the household at the coming of day.

Before dawn, though, the girl slipped into restless slumber, threaded by dreams that brought great distress. In them, she wandered endlessly through rooms thronged by women of great beauty and well-favored men. On sighting her, they drew back in revulsion, pointing fingers and mouthing cries. She could not make out the words, but it was plain that she was held in horror, a figure to be shunned.

"Feliciana!" That voice she could hear, and it brought her out of the last of those contemptuous crowds: her mother was standing outside the curtains of the bed. As in the hour she struck her bargain with the Hag, the girl steeled her resolve. She had done what she had done, and there could be no more delay; the "gift" must now be shown.

The young woman lifted the bed-drape and waited for the storm to break. Ingrada Soren wore an expression of astonishment, yes, but the look was overlaid not with disgust but with—*delight?*

"What—what—" The woman put out a hand as if to touch her daughter's cheek.

Feliciana called upon all her courage. "I went to the Green Hag that I might be a pride to you. But I angered her, and she cursed me with this—" The girl gestured hopelessly at her face.

"*This!*" The joy in Mistress Soren's own face was now beyond denying. She snatched up the small mirror that hung from the chatelaine at her belt. With a rough pull, she freed the polished disk and held it out.

"What do you mean you are 'cursed,' girl?" she demanded.

Completely mystified, Feliciana took the mirror and gazed at herself. What she saw was the image that had always greeted her; but her familiar appearance was what the Wild Witch had told her she would see, while all others would perceive her as loathsome.

The Hag had played with her, then; as had the folk of human society, the Green Woman had made her a laughingstock. But in what way? Taking a steadying breath, she said, "To me, Mother, I seem to be as I ever have. What do you see?"

By now she was shivering. Had the previous night been a dream? Yet it was apparent that *some* change had been wrought.

"Has the transforming turned your wits, you foolish child? Cursed? You should ever praise the Green Lady for such a bane! What do I *see!*" Ingrada paused, breathless from both speech and excitement.

"I see such fairness as is seldom granted a maid: a face of ivory with the faintest touch of color on the cheeks, brows soft and winged, eyes blue as summer pools. I see a lush fall of black curls, lips that are luminous—"

Feliciana could stand no more of this catalog of her charms. Her "luminous lips" shaped an anguished cry. Indeed she was accursed, undone—and she alone would ever know! Too well she remembered the warning of the Hag before this sorry trick had been played.

Her mother's smile opened into laughter. "La, Feliciana, but they will gasp and roll their eyes when you appear! Master Roger should be grateful all his days that his uncle was so thoughtful for his future. Now get you dressed in haste—your father is fortunately late in leaving for the Guildhall. He will be as thankful for this miracle as am I!"

When Mistress Soren had whisked away to share the wondrous news, Feliciana gave her feelings free rein. Weeping, she stumbled to her dressing table, and in its mirror she beheld again the plain, lank-locked self she had always known—and would always know. Taking up her silver-backed hairbrush, she slammed its heavy head against the surface until the old glass splintered. The world was mad, and she could not put it right again.

She sank down onto the bench before the cracked mirror and began the painful business of preparing her hair. At first she could not understand what was wrong. Finally she pulled a long side section around to the front where she could see why it felt so odd. It was a curl, right enough, but it did yield now to her painful tweaking. Again she remembered the Green Woman's foretelling that she would never behold any of the changes in herself.

Huddling miserably, she wiped the tears from her "color-tinged cheeks." One of the sayings she used to be set to copy when she practiced writing as a child seemed to imprint itself on the air before her: *"Beware what you wish for, lest it be given you."*

And so it had, in its way. She had wanted a change—and the Wild Witch had found amusing the act of altering her life thus. Feliciana sat up straight.

"No one," she vowed in a grim whisper, "will find me a thing to scorn or pity again. I shall learn to play their silly games, but I shall always know who and what I am."

It was said in later years that the Baroness Gargene, for all her great and long-lasting beauty, was strong of character and keen of wit beyond most noblewomen. She drew her lord away from court follies and made a man of him; and never did any plain maids sit unhappily in her hall while their more comely sisters enjoyed themselves but she would welcome them into any merrymaking. In spite of much urging, she never permitted her portrait to be limned; and that this was no show of false modesty was proved by a most curious act. Beneath an empty picture frame, holding a blank canvas, she caused this motto to be set:

"Maledicta sum"—"I am accursed."

THE COBWEBBED PRINCESS
Magic Tails (2005) DAW

It was going to be a good day—a couple or sniffs of such breeze as managed to find its way through the narrow windows of the princess' chamber told me that. I jumped to the floor, rattling through the drift of parchment-dry leaves that had blown in last fall, and paid my respects properly to the Lady Bast with forelegs extended to the limit and head bowed.

The large chamber was dim; three of the windows bore a double curtaining of rich brocade within and tapestry-tight overgrowth of vines without, while the fourth had been sealed with a branch that had been driven into it by a winter storm. However, I had no difficulty in making my morning inspection.

Maid Mafray still snuggled atop the pile of linens she had been carrying when the magic had struck so long ago. Under a veiling of dust and more leaves she had grown no older, of course; that was part of the spell. Diona, Lady of the Wardrobe, had not moved either. Her head still rested on the folds of the gown she had been about to present for the princess' approval at the moment the curse had cast its word-web over the castle.

I padded back to the huge curtained bed and leaped up onto it. My charge lay there as comfortably as I had been able to dispose her, the covers made as smooth as I could arrange them, with patting paws and cloth-tugging teeth, under her chin. Her silver-fair hair fanned out to form a net, living but motionless, over the satin-covered pillow. Yet, even as I watched, her eyelids flickered.

Tensing, I crept closer with the same care I took to hunt one of the skittish wildfowl that landed in the courtyard below. A line appeared between my lady's arched brows, and I began to purr; turning on the soothing rumble I hoped would banish what could only be an evil dream. Now her head turned and, with the movement, swung one of the strands of hair across the chain of the amulet she had ever worn about her neck and snagged the lock so that it was pulled painfully.

Crowding against the girl, I touched her lips with the very tip of my tongue. I knew of both the bitter spell that had reduced her to this state and the sweet kiss that would revive her from it, and I had long ago begun to wonder whether perhaps it were up to me and not some dream-born stranger to perform that act. I had tried it twice before when her night was troubled but had met with no success; never had the sleeping shape shown that it was more than an effigy of the Princess Charlita of Fallona—

—until now. Was the third time, indeed, the charm?

The princess' lids fluttered, then opened, and her eyes stared into mine, recognition at once evident in their violet-blue depths. I retreated as she sat up. Dust puffed forth from both the pillows and the heavily embroidered coverlet as she pushed them away; she sneezed vigorously and shook her head, and with the gesture caught sight of Mafray. My lady frowned and, lifting a hand, brushed it across her eyes before glancing at her maid-in-waiting again. Charlita might have just returned from the ensorcelment of decades a-dream, but her wits were perfectly clear.

"The curse—" Her voice, loud in the silence, broke off suddenly. She was shivering. I crept forward and stretched my neck so I could lick at her arm, but I did not gain her attention by that small gesture of comfort. Instead, she rolled halfway over, then sat on the edge of the bed, which was raised on a dais two steps above the floor. More dust rose, and she coughed and waved her hands before her to fan it away.

"Mafray?" The princess slid down from the bed. She nearly fell as her long-unused feet skidded on the platform, but at last she stood on the stone flags. A few more steps, each increasingly sure, brought her to the side of the sleeping girl; Charlita's death-in-life might have ended, but her serving maid's had not.

Jumping from the bed, I padded over to her. To be sure, I have certain talents, and they have been well proven; however, I could not communicate directly with my charge, and this restriction would, I feared, cause difficulties. The girl looked at me and frowned, and I strove to reach her, mind to mind. If she possessed any Gift, it was limited; yet it was not wholly absent, for she sensed the intensity of my focus and stooped swiftly to gather me up into her arms. She knew how to properly lift a cat, placing one hand under my front legs and supporting my hindquarters with the other.

"You were there when—" Charlita hesitated, then began again. "Urgal wielded the rod—the Silver Rod—"

I stiffened and must have put out my claws in my surprise, for my charge gave a little cry, and I hastened to sheathe them again. What had she just said—how could she know? The Sleep should have held her too deeply to dream of—*that!*

The princess shifted her hold on me so that our eyes met, and she said firmly, as though by forceful utterance she could make her telling a truth, "You are Cobweb, my birthday-fairing from Granddam Foreby—but you are more than any mere cat." She gathered me closer so that my head was again near to her chin, and once more I gave her a quick touch-of-tongue.

Still carrying me, Charlita moved across the floor, carefully avoiding Maid Mafray, and headed for the nearest window. There she lowered me to the wide sill while she herself wriggled forward to peer through an opening in the curtain of vine.

Her gasp was almost a cry. What lay below was enough to shock anyone whose last memory was of a castle filled with life and light, not a gigantic mausoleum where time itself was held in check by a spell set working by evil witchery. The girl retreated from the view, her face pale.

"It is true, then, Cobweb—the curse has indeed fallen upon me, and through me upon all these innocent folk—" She paused and turned her head to gaze first at Mafray and then to Diona. "Yet I am now awake, so why not they also? Why not they?" Her chin quivered.

I knew as well as she the conditions of the curse, its why and wherefore, and its birth from the jealous spite of the Great One who had come late to Charlita's christening. The princess appeared to be reviewing those terms, as well, for now she studied the forefinger of her right hand.

"No sign remains, Cobweb," she murmured, then lifted her eyes to me once more. "I remember, dear furred one—you tried to stop my taking up that spindle!"

I bowed my head, for I, too, remembered. Like all my kind, I was proud of my quickness of movement, deft play-of-paw; but in that far and fateful hour, that skill had either failed me—or *I* had failed. My mistress had taken up that tool of labor she had found lying on her bed, and it had turned in her grasp as a serpent might writhe, so that its point had struck deep into the first finger of her right hand. Then the dire enchantment had fallen on her, and on every being beneath this roof save myself. And not only had sleep overwhelmed those within the castle, but forgetfulness of the Kingdom of Fallona itself had spread like a poisoned mist throughout the adjoining lands. It was as though the most potent Older One had wiped the very memory of our realm from the world.

"Yet do all indeed still dream?" Charlita queried of the air as she stepped towards the nearest of three tall wardrobes. "Perhaps not all; let us see!"

The girl had taken the Sleep in her chemise and her belaced underskirts, for she had been about to try on the dress which Diona held ready just as she sighted the spindle protruding from beneath a pillow on the bed. Now she tugged open the door of the wardrobe before her and pulled out the nearest of the gowns within.

Thus Princess Charlita and I went searching throughout the castle for some sign of waking life, though I knew she was as certain as I that our quest would be fruitless. She hailed sleepers, sometimes going so far as to pat a face, pull gently on a shoulder, an arm. Nowhere did her touch evoke a response—a lack that grew from the merely frustrating to the nearly unbearable when we reached the palace library. There my mistress beheld her mother, resting not ungracefully against her embroidery frame, and her father seated at his desk, his head pillowed on a pile of parchments. Charlita did not intrude upon the king and queen but instead subsided into a high-backed chair placed just inside the door and sat twisting her hands together, fighting sobs. I jumped into her lap, and again she hugged me. Slowly her weeping quieted; then she spoke.

"Everyone but you, Cobweb. How did *you* escape?"

How I longed for the gift of speech, or at least mind-touch, so that I might tell her! The answer was that I had fought then with the full strength of that talent which was my birth-gift from Bast.

Soul to soul I cried to Her, the patroness of home and hearth: *Let me not fall into slumber, Lady, but remain awake to watch and ward, for this human one was mine to cherish, and I did not succeed in keeping her from harm.* My recollection of that plea was interrupted as the girl tightened her embrace.

"There was to be a prince, Cobweb, who was to awaken me with a kiss. Goodness knows, the curse and its cure were told me over and over from the time Nurse Ardith thought I was able to understand words. So—where is my royal rescuer?" She laughed harshly, then hiccupped as though holding back further tears.

Perhaps would-be saviors *had* visited throughout the years. However, the hedge of thorny brush that was the outward sign of the curse had grown dark and dense around the castle until it was more forbidding than a barrier of stone. Had any high-minded youth come seeking my mistress, perhaps in an attempt to prove a legend true, he had neither found nor fought a way through that living wall.

The belief grew within me that I had failed once more in my duty—that what I had done, if I were indeed responsible for the princess' waking (as I grew ever more certain I was), had been wrong.

Once again the girl's hands tightened grip on me, lifting me up until I was eye to eye with her.

"What do I do now, friend-in-fur? We alone are awake—we . . . alone! Do I play 'hunt-the-spindle' again—return to sleep? *Tell* me, Cobweb!"

Charlita's voice held a near-hysterical edge I did not like, and I cared even less for the way she shook me as she posed her questions. I wanted to strike out with a claw-spread paw but, knowing that fear and not cruelty caused her to handle me roughly, I contented myself with hissing.

All at once I caught movement at the desk where the sleeping

King Ludoff dreamed on his parchment pillow. The library windows, which were the only ones in the palace to contain glass, could admit no breeze to stir the papers that lay there, yet a small cloud of dust had just risen. Now I distinctly saw the topmost sheet of parchment quiver, then one corner roll up.

We cats depend upon sight to hunt, whereas most dogs rely upon scent or hearing. Thus it did not surprise me that the great warhound, Briser, still lay behind the king's chair as deep in slumber as his master, for, whatever its nature, this intruder moved in utter silence.

The page beneath the king's fingers set to wriggling like a living thing, working its way to freedom. I heard the princess gasp, felt her move to rise. However, I could spare her no attention, for at that moment I only wanted to know what creature, hidden from my sight, was making itself free of this room. I leaped to the floor, crouched, and launched myself upward, aiming for the top of the desk. Claws came to my aid, and I scrambled over the edge safely, to see the paper floating above me, motionless. I heard a snort like a suppressed laugh. Briser moved his head, and the spikes on his thick collar rasped against the stone flooring. I expected him to awaken, but he did not.

To my amazement, Charlita was the one who acted. Two strides brought her to the desk. Her hand was already out, and now it shot forward and her fingers closed firmly about the edge of the parchment. However, the sheet did not yield to this persuasion but strove to wrench itself free; plainly whatever—or whoever—held it would not surrender its prize without a struggle.

Once more I crouched and sprang, and it came as no surprise when one of my forepaws raked on cloth I could not see, tearing it, while my claws caught in flesh and a smell of blood followed. I strove to turn my body as it hung in the air and strengthen my hold. The long years of keeping life in my body by stalking the wildfowl that invaded the courtyard stood me in good stead now.

The limb to which I had attached myself was now flailing up and down, and I would surely have been dislodged in another moment; fortunately, though, another warrior had joined the fray. Past my head flew a massive inkwell of malachite, but its flight was a brief one, for it thudded home only inches from my own struggle. The sound of its meeting with a very solid surface was followed by an exclamation as that portion of the invisible opponent to which I clung swung suddenly downward. I was raked off on the rim of the desk and landed on the stone flags, my head so awhirl that for a moment I could only lie, limp and asprawl, coughing with body-shaking expulsions of air as a gout of dust billowed up to envelop me.

When I had blinked my eyes clear, I could make out a dark blot hovering in the air. That there was substance to what I had attacked I knew, and now, though the invader remained unseen, the splatters of ink betrayed both its presence and position.

Briser—I knew the strength of the great war-dog. Never before had I wanted him to rouse, as I found myself wishing; neither had I ever done what I did in the next moment. Moving belly-down so that I could see the hound's response, I raised my voice in such a caterwaul as should have brought all the castle awake and to arms.

The blotch of ink turned, dipping toward me, but it did not attack again. My princess leaned forward, too, and, in what seemed a single movement, she both seized the floating foolscap and straight-armed the space of air that was empty of all but the airborne stain. The edge of the paper snapped taut, but she got both hands on the disputed sheet. Her body tensed as she resisted the contending force, and her wide skirts swirled as she kicked out, meeting, as I had done, solid opposition.

The page came suddenly free, as whatever was facing us backed against the king's hound and fell. A hard crash followed, suggesting that a body of sizable proportions had made close acquaintance, unexpectedly, with the floor; the sound of the impact was followed by a moan.

Charlita thrust the parchment roughly down the neckline of her gown, then turned and caught me up while I was still ridding myself of the dust. Not turning her back on the dark spot, which lay almost at our feet, she began to retreat.

I was already considering what defense we might employ if we were to be matched fairly against this menace. Though it could not be seen without aid (or additions), we had, at least, managed to make its presence known. Now to its nothingness must be added a something that would render it completely visible. Had my charge heard my thought? No—surely not; her mind must merely be especially keen after its long rest. Yet this whisper reached me as she held me tight:

"More ink—or wine, perhaps." Then we were at the door.

Abruptly Queen Symma's embroidery frame shook. The stain rose upward once more into the air and moved away from man, dog, and desk. My mistress waited no longer but hastened from the library, brushing as she did so against one of the pair of door-guards who drowsed at their post. However, Charlita had taken only a quick brace of steps into the hall when she paused. Evidently she was not yet minded to leave the battlefield, for she turned back to the door, though she did not reenter. Loosing my claws from the now-battered lace of her bodice, she placed me upon the floor; then she moved to the nearer of the two sleeping soldiers.

"Guard you are, Sergeant Flors," she declared, "so guard you must."

With a push, she destroyed his balance, and down he went; a

moment later, his comrade joined him. The two now lay against each other and across the open doorway, where their bodies formed a considerable obstruction. Stooping, the princess made sure that the armsmen lay face up and as easy as they might.

"Flors and Winster. Be sure I shall remember this service."

She returned to me and made as if to scoop me up again, but I moved away on my own four feet, having had enough for the moment of floating aloft like What-Is-Its-Face.

"Kitchen!" Charlita spoke the word aloud, no whisper this time but an order for us both. Once more, my thought was in tandem with hers.

We had visited that part of the castle before in our search for waking life, and I recalled with amusement the sleeping cook and her cat, who had both been snoring lustily at the time.

Cook and Cat remained deeply a-dream when we returned. Pastry Cook still lay over the marble slab where he had evidently been at work. Various scullery maids and pot-boys lay slumped about the cavernous room where they had been stricken down at their labors for, though Head Cook might have been taking her ease when the sorcery struck, her underlings had been busily employed. But of actual foodstuffs none were to be seen.

And food we must have 'ere long. I felt the pinch of hunger, and I was sure that the princess did also, now that she was conscious and calling upon the strength of her body. But while I might quiet my belly by a stalk in the courtyard, whether any viands suitable for a human still remained in this place was another matter. Charlita was of the same mind, for she stood beside the cook's chair, surveying intently the appointments of the room. In a moment her attention had centered on the array of cabinets set against the walls.

Some time later, I sat on the broad expanse of a large table, cleansing a paw that I might employ it to remove some of the dust which had turned my cream fur a grimy gray. My charge had pulled up a stool and was seated at the opposite side of the board. Before her stood three small pots; the thick stoppers of wax that had sealed the vessels for so long now lay beside them on the polished wood. Having sniffed once and then again, Charlita inserted a spoon into the first pot and brought out a dollop of thick paste. She gave this lump a cautious lick, then waited. One hand still held the heaped spoon; the other was tightened into a near-fist around the amulet that had never left her neck since the morning of the fateful birthday whose close had seen her and all her world spelled asleep.

Having sensed no taint in what she had sampled, the princess nodded and opened her mouth wide for the whole of the spoon's contents. I wondered whether she thought of the nursery-verse about the queen who had gone to her own kitchen in search of honey when I smelled the sweetness of berries from her find. I was pleased that she had found such sustenance and hoped that I might shortly slip away to my own private larder.

Between raids on the preserve pots, Charlita drew forth from her bodice the creased parchment from the library and spread it as flat as she could in a square of sunlight that reached the table from an upper window. Now curiosity, runs the proverb, is a bane to my kind, rather than a blessing. I myself hold that, without questions, answers cannot be found.

But when the answers arrive *before* the questions . . .

My dampened paw shot out but did not come down upon that crumpled sheet. The girl was viewing it upside down but had not tried to shift it, which must mean she did *not* know—

My movement, though quickly aborted, had drawn her attention. She stared at me and then, to my astonishment, opened her fist so that the amulet it guarded could be fully seen. The talisman was not new to me, nor was it a recent arrival in this world. Such charms had been worn by the women of a royal house that lay so far back in time its very name was lost; even the land where that house held sway had been broken by a hammering sea and blasted by fire from the earth until it, too, had been forsaken and forgotten.

I stood. Though I knew that my gesture revealed a sacred and secret feline ritual (or did it? Cats, after all, *do* stretch upon occasion), I made the deepest obeisance my body could render, raising a purr of homage loud enough for the princess to hear—and an even more royal Lady.

"Great Bast, I, your kit, await your will. You have given into my paws the fate of this two-footed one—and I say that, though she may not sing in Your temple, she is yet worthy of Your care." Thus did my purr-prayer rise.

I saw the lavender of Charlita's eyes darken, her lips part as if she would answer me, but she made no sound. However, the amulet, which had been dangling from her fingers by its chain as she watched me, suddenly swung forward and touched my head between my ears.

"I . . . dreamed," she murmured, gazing into the distance. I believed she was speaking to me; then, when her eyes met mine in full focus, I was sure of it. "A dark enchantment was laid upon me—that I accept as a truth beyond denying. Now I also acknowledge that, having escaped its hold alone, I must act to aid those still ensorcelled."

My mistress fastened the chain about her throat and tugged her talisman forward so that it lay openly upon her breast. Then she glanced down at the parchment.

"And this writing contains the truth to guide us, Cobweb—is that not so?"

Was her action the answer I sought from Lady Bast? That I believed. Our patroness was a dealer in deep mysteries; indeed, neither the Daughter-of-Dark who had invoked the curse nor the Dweller-in-Light who, at the last moment of its pronouncing, had changed death for its gentle mimic, sleep, would dare raise eyes in Her presence.

Setting a forepaw on the foolscap sheet, I dipped my head in the accepted gesture of agreement used by the princess' own kind—a nod—and together we went forth from the kitchen.

The light had grown noticeably dimmer when we emerged into the hall that had brought us here; the patches of sun that penetrated the narrow, high-set windows were nearly gone. I could almost believe that the Dark Itself was rising against us. An odd stirring troubled the air at the other end of the corridor, but I could make out no shape distinctly in this half-light. If the intruder who bore the blazon of ink had come in search of us, it was still far behind.

We paused before an ironbound door that, strangely, had not had its bar-lock set. The portal groaned dolefully as the princess pushed it open, revealing the head of a staircase. The darkness grew denser as we descended, yet it never completely obscured our sight; perhaps my Protectress aided our vision and warded off blindness.

We traversed a lower hall onto which storerooms opened, then started down yet another flight of stairs. I heard Charlita's breath catch.

"Do we go into the center of the earth?" she asked in a near-whisper. I answered with a soft chirp, and she stooped to pick me up, then rested her cheek for a moment against my head.

Twice I caught the sound of footsteps, faint but steady, from behind—perhaps the creature we had already faced was indeed in pursuit. Yet I held to my hope of protection by the Lady Who carried the symbol of Life Everlasting in Her hand. Curiously, within me, and perhaps within Charlita also, the conviction grew that we were truly guarded by sure wards. The feeling persisted until the way we followed, which had been gradually narrowing, ended in an unbroken wall. I, however, had dealt with that barrier before, though the first time I had challenged it I thought I had failed, until—

I shifted in the princess' arms, and she understood and placed me on my feet before that blank surface. Its stones were a pale gray, a hue that seemed leached of all life. If despair could take a color, that chill hue would be its choice.

I set my paw to the wall. My claws scratched against the rough surface, though whether they left any record there I could not tell. Push thus, said my memory—and thus—and *thus!*

The door in the upper reaches of the castle had protested when we used it, but no sound came now. Before us, an opening expanded, its air illumined only by a dull gleam as of twilight. Silent ourselves, we passed within.

There was resistance—a power-ward of some sort had certainly been set here. My charge hesitated, but I caught the hem of her now-bedraggled gown between my teeth and used a force she could not resist to draw her on. She raised her chin determinedly and gathered her strength to advance.

It was a strange place we had entered. What we had reached was a bowl of stone held deep in the earth, but at first glance it seemed that we stood in a night-drowned forest. Trunks of trees arose on either side of a path leading forward, their branches interlaced to form a roof well above the princess' head. Strange rock formations with the look of plants ordered the trail; yet even they showed no color but the unbroken dusk gray—

—until my mistress moved forward. As she stepped through the futile defense of the ward, an awakening began around us. A spotting of rainbow-hued dots came alive on tree trunks, and on bone-pale branches and dead-looking leaves on ground-growth.

Faintly at first, but swiftly becoming stronger, sound followed—a flowing chant, both solemn and inspiring. We were surely approaching a shrine of power. As we set feet (and paws) on the path, the disks of rainbow radiance on the trees began to run together, melding into each other until they became so dazzlingly bright that we dared no longer raise our eyes to watch.

Time ceased to have meaning, and distance did the same; we seemed to cross a wide plain and to patiently keep to the track for a very long time. The end came suddenly as we halted at the foot of a second barrier that framed another stair—one so narrow that any castle dwellers who sought to use it must needs go in single file. Our eyes had adjusted to the light by then, for we could clearly make out the head of that staircase. But at the sight of what was displayed there, Charlita stood still, her hands braced rigidly right and left against the stone that walled the climb.

"The Scepter of Margalee," she said.

So—some portion of what was now legend but had once been history *did* remain. The House of Lud had given kings to Fallona, ten of them in direct descent. However, before those had come (it was rumored) rulers of a different bloodline, each of whom had, in turn, been greater than the humans over whom he or she had reigned.

But with the passing of years both the power and knowledge of the First Lineage had declined, and at length the House of Lud had triumphed after a red slaughter. The talents of the Firstborn had dwindled, then began to be viewed with suspicion. Archives were looted, and any information that might have restored tales to the status of truths was sought out and destroyed.

The handful of seers who had stood against the last Ludish ruler had withdrawn—

—until the casting of the Sleep-Spell! I had guessed that more than one of the old Great Ones had come forth again when I had been made the tool of good Lady Ulava, whose quick action had softened the malison against Charlita; now I knew my suspicion to be true. When is a curse *not* a curse . . .

A small bead of blood appeared on the princess' lower lip as she spoke, and her words, too, were bitten and spat out in anger:

"So—are we still to be pieces in a game played against our wills? We shall see!" Her body taut with rage, she began to climb the stairs, keeping her arms braced against the walls to move her upward the more swiftly. I followed as closely as I could.

And I in turn was pursued. The ink my charge had hurled at the library interloper had dried upon it but not faded. Whoever— or whatever—wore the sinlike stain was coming after us slowly; it did not begin its own ascent until we were near the head of the steps.

The princess used the momentum from her push against the walls to propel herself onto a platform that spread across a landing much wider than the stairs. At mid-point of that level space rested a block of un-worked stone over whose surface curled thick lines of some pure metal. Thrust deep into the rock by its point was the ancient symbol of the rulers of Fallona: the Scepter of Margalee.

Charlita stood gazing up at the length of chased and bejeweled silver; and, as she contemplated the rod that bespoke authority over her kind, I was aware of the presence of my own queen. With a leap, I sprang past the princess, voicing the claim-cry of the cat, and landed atop the stone that held the Scepter. Lowering my head, I set my mouth around a section of the rod where the wood was exposed, bit down hard, and held on.

Charlita reached forward to grasp the huge rock, intending to climb it, but a moment later she backed away with a gasp to stare upward. Immediately overhead, the Golden Key of Bast, by men called the Ankh, had sprung into being and now hung in midair above the scepter-bearing stone. In that moment, we were all frozen into place as surely as if chains had been cast about our limbs.

"NO!"

In the space of a single breath, the same word was shouted by three different voices; at the same moment, two different Powers struck at me. No, the attacking wills belonged neither to the princess nor to the one who appeared to be shaping himself from the very air as he stepped up next to her, his tattered left sleeve fluttering in crude pennons from the standard of his arm.

I could feel the air to both sides of me curdling into other shapes, but the blaze of the Sacred Key so dazzled my eyes that I could see only the princess and the young man beside her. He stood arrow-straight, and his dark hair was cropped as though he were prepared to don a helm of war, yet his belt did not even hold the sheath for a sword. A prince, it would seem, had come at last—and doubtless when he was needed least.

The youth had been studying my mistress closely, and the frown that had earlier bent his brows was fading. When he saw that he had caught Charlita's attention, he swept her the bow of the finished courtier, his left hand held before his heart but not quite touching the betraying blot. He smiled, and as he did so I judged that, though he was young, he already knew the worth of the policy "wait and see."

My princess, however, was not so ready to agree to what was certainly an offer of truce. She returned his smile, but with a meaningful glance at the stain.

"Your Highness . . ." The ingathering of mist to the prince's left had become solid, and the voice that spoke belonged to the serene and stately figure now revealed. This was Ulava of Fallona, so mighty a servant of Light with the ancient Gifts once common in her land that her very name was a title. Now she looked beyond the youth to me, holding her hand forth in respect and welcome—

—as another also hailed me, but with clawed fingers that raked the air in a gesture of contempt and dismissal. "Cat!" cried Urgal of Morh, the Great One of Dark power who had been born from the mist to the prince's right. "Think not to hold *that*—" she indicated the scepter, "—which is for your betters."

I did not relinquish the rod of rule to the Shadow-wielder, nor did I, in any way, deign to acknowledge her presence. Her skin, which sagged with age, flushed. Whatever power she had gathered down the years, she had never gained the ability to stop the ravages of time on her person. Neither had the Lady on her other side—Ulava, who had once been both sorceress and queen; but time had enhanced and not diminished her.

The Dark One set palms together, and her fingers began to move as though she would weave something from the air. With that action she also moved her lips, though nothing she uttered could be heard.

Ulava spared Urgal not a glance as she stepped forward to join the princess and prince. Join them she did, in more than one way. Placing a hand on the shoulder of each, she turned them so the youth faced the maid.

"Once done, ill done," she intoned, "twice done, well done. *Finished!*"

The pair might no longer have had any wills of their own. Prince No-Name-Nor-Nation and Princess Charlita of Fallona made not a move toward one another, but their lips met as if they were dreaming.

All about, the massive stone walls seemed to draw a deep breath; the castle itself was waking, as well as the people and creatures it held.

The palace might indeed have shaken off its sorcerous sleep, but Urgal, she who had called down the curse, was not yet defeated. I rocked back and forth, holding onto the scepter with all the strength in me and striving to work it loose from its free-standing position. I obeyed no actual order from the Lady of the Key, but Her will was at work. The gemmed rod shifted in my mouth-grip, tilted, and pointed at the enemy.

Suddenly I became a channel, as power that was neither mine nor native to my kind coursed through me. Shooting through my body up the scepter, it poured out the head of the rod and down, rained in a molten-gold flood over the last Priestess of Night, puddled, and rose about her twitching body. Urgal's wrinkle-wrung mouth opened in a soundless scream. Still further I turn-mouthed the scepter until its heavy ornate head swung floorward; and then a Force I *did* know made Herself felt. Down from My Lady's Life-Promise above shot a beam of white light to touch the rod. I could not choke back a cry of pain as Her lightning blazed through me up the scepter's length. The blast struck Urgal full on, and the Dark One staggered, fell, and vanished in a pillar of fire.

Thus ended what has doubtless become an oft-told tale: the story of a princess placed under an evil enchantment of sleep until a kiss awakened her and her ensorcelled folk, of a reckoning between Darkness and Light such as will occur many times again.

It was not given to me to know what happened—to learn whether my princess wedded her prince, then reigned with him wisely and well until Fallona rose to greatness once more in a "happily ever after."

No, my destiny lay in another direction and a different realm; for so great had been the demand of both the Powers of Light on my body that it could no longer remain in the mortal plane. But as I still held, exhausted, to the Scepter of the Great Ones, my eyes, which were closing to this world, opened to another. Above me, the glowing ankh became the figure of a Lady robed in light, a human woman with the countenance of a cat. Bending down, She gathered me into Her arms, murmuring to me of a new land and new life to come in Her service. And together, in joyous anticipation, we passed through that door to which Her symbol was, indeed, the Key.

FAIRE LIKENESS
Renaissance Faire (2005) DAW

The Renaissance Faire at Ridgewood had, within the past few years, become a national tourist attraction. The center of the festival was the castle that Margaret and Douglas Magin had made the focus of their retirement; and, though the fortress was somewhat modest in mass, it was, nonetheless, a castle. Leading to the pile was a lane, lightly graveled, that was lined on either hand by the "town": a collection of three-room cottages, each with a display area for handicrafts on the side facing the "street." Beyond the booths to lay and right lay wild land, where a growth of brush quickly gave way to woods. On the far side of the fortress was the famous Rose Garden—often put to service these days for weddings—and the tourney field.

Deb Wilson, my friend and sponsor at the Ridgewood Faire, was well used to these romantic surroundings. She not only displayed and sold articles made by herself and her classes in fine needlework, but also held seminars here. I had felt truly honored this year when she had asked for my help at her shop-booth during such times as she had to be elsewhere.

At that moment, though, I was beginning to regret my enthusiastic assent to be part of this year's faire, of which I was not a member. The heat clung to me like yet another layer of the archaic clothing in which I was already wrapped. Irritably, I pulled at the tight bodice-lacings of my "authentic" period dress, pushed at the heavy folds of the skirt. Deb was wearing a twin to my garment, save that she was allowed a touch of embroidery to enliven it, since her persona was that of a leading guildswoman. In addition, she was also a judge of correctly-chosen and constructed clothing, as Margaret Magin was a stickler for historical accuracy.

"Good day, me bonny wench! 'Tis a fine sight for the eyes that ye are."

Attempting to respond to this strange salute, I turned too fast and cracked an elbow painfully against a screen. Then I realized that the greeting had been meant for my booth mate.

The man standing by the supports for the counter we had not yet set into place was short—no taller than Deb, at least. He was also certainly no paladin come riding. His faire garb was the drab stuff of a very common commoner and looked as though it needed a good washing. Beside him stood two train cases lashed together so that one handle served both.

"Sterling! I thought you were banished!" My friend's jaw tightened in a set that suggested she wished her statement were truth.

The shabby newcomer grinned. "Well, now, Deb m'dear—let's just say that fickle Fortune beamed upon me again. And she continues to smile, for behold! She has given me a roost beside the beauteous needle wielder herself." He nodded to the right, where indeed another booth-cabin stood unclaimed. "And," he continued conspiratorially, indicating his double bundle, *"you're* lucky, too. I've a little something here that'll pull visitors aplenty in this direction."

Deb was flushing; this encounter was obviously no meeting of friends, as far as she was concerned. From a woman of usually even temper, such an attitude was puzzling. The needleworker turned a little toward me.

"This is Sterling Winterhue," she sated, as one person might call an unpleasant mistake to the attention of another. Then she gave a single curt nod at me. "Miss Gleason." The cold voice and bare-bones introduction were extremely unlike my friend.

"Yes sirree, ol' Winterhue hisself." The man pulled off his peaked cap, bowed awkwardly, and patted the top case. "Come with a real treasure. Gimme 'bout an hour to get set up; and then, Deb m'girl, you bring Miss Gleason over and get a preview."

"*Lemme alone,* Mark! Hey, mister—got any monsters this year?" The interrupting voice, shrill and willful, was that of a boy. Winterhue scowled, but only for an instant.

"So you like to see monsters, do you? Well . . ."

"Sir, I beg your pardon. Roddy—"

" 'Rod-dy, Rod-dy Rod-dy!' " the boy singsonged mockingly. "I don't hafta listen to you, you—cop! You been *no*-ing me all morning, and I'm gonna tell Nana!"

I had managed to push aside the embroidered screen that would shield one corner of the sales area and was now able to see the speaker. Very few Ridgewood residents would have failed to recognize that ten year old in spite of his page's dress: Roddy Magin, the pride of, and heir to, the castle.

The youth's companion was an archer, bearing an unstrung bow and a quiver of arrows across his back, but wearing on the breast of his jerkin a pendant in the form of a massive shield embossed with the royal arms of the court. A member of the security force, then. Just as I caught sight of the man's charge, Roddy threw a piece of pastry at him. The boy edged backward; however, he did not escape the hand that closed on his velvet-clad shoulder. He yelled and tried to twist free, but his guardian's hold failed to loosen.

As if the pair did not exist, Winterhue repeated to my partner, "Give it an hour, Deb, an' come along." With no further word he headed toward his booth, twin cases in tow.

Deb scowled openly after him. "I thought that man had been—" she began, then set her lips in a locking line.

The Magin boy now swung a kick at the archer. *"Lemme go, lemme—"* His protest cut off with a squawk as he was picked up and held fast by his much-tried chaperone, who growled: "Be quiet, you brat!"

For a wonder, the child obeyed, giving Deb the chance to finish what she had begun to say a moment before. "Doesn't court banishment still hold?"

"Not if it doesn't please the Magins." Mark's tone was dry.

Roddy turned his head sharply and snapped at the hand still restraining him. The security officer looked to Deb, shaking his head as the boy mouthed an obscenity and spat: "Nana'll get rid of you! Wait'll I tell her—"

"Wait till WE tell her," the archer corrected, controlling his temper heroically. "And we're going to do it right now. Sorry, ladies—" Giving a last nod, Mark set off down the lane, steering the pugnacious page before him.

Deb dropped onto a box, pushed a wandering strand of hair back under the edge of her frilled cap, and pulled her wristwatch out of the pouch at her belt. "Look at that—it's already eleven. I have to meet with Cathy and get the seminar leaflets. Don't wait lunch on me, 'Manda—I'll grab a burger or something on the way back."

I did not wish to make Deb late for her appointment, but I felt I *must* have some answers. "What was all that 'monster' business?"

Deb shook her head and picked up a tote that stood propped

against the cabin door. "I'll tell you when I come back," she promised, adding grimly, "I do hope Mark can get Margaret to put a tight rein on that little pest."

She was out of the shop before I had a chance to protest. I knew there was no use in simply sitting and thinking up more questions, but I was determined to see that my booth mate answered those that had already occurred to me when I could get her alone again.

I fetched a Coke from the cooler. My head ached, and I wanted noting more than to lie down on one of the cots. But rest, I knew, would not be sufficient to banish the disturbing thoughts that crowded into my mind; if I tried to relax, those would torment me even more. It was best to keep busy.

Regiments of thread packets had to be mustered out according to color, needles and other tools placed in plain sight. Books of tempting patterns required arranging, and some needed to be opened to a particularly intriguing design. As the display grew, I began to feel pride in my artistic ability.

When I broke off at last for a sandwich and another Coke, I glanced over to Winterhue's hut, but no sign of life was to be seen. Scents aplenty filled the air, however, chief among them the smell of barbecue from a cookshop down the street. The savory odor made me take an extra-large bite of my chicken salad.

"And where's the lovesome Deb, m'lady?"

I jumped. The packed earth and springy grass between the huts had deadened the sound of his approach, but Sterling Winterhue was back.

"She had to meet with one of the committee," I answered after a hasty swallow.

"And to see what brought me here." With this comment—and without invitation—the artist stepped into the outer section of the shop. He had removed the peasant's cap with its towering peak and, as he bent briefly over my display, the top of his head showed a few grudging strands of gray-brown hair that looked as though they had been painted across his scalp.

Suddenly he looked up, and even in the dim light I could see his eyes glint. "So—Guildswoman Wilson is willing to miss her tryst with Sir Sterling, is she? Well, now, mistress, *you* won't."

Before I realized what he intended, Winterhue strode up and put a hand on my arm. Nodding and grinning, he drew me out into the road, then laughed as he set me free.

"Think me a lusty rogue, do ye? Nay, I am not such. Also—" Winterhue gestured toward his hut, "—what I have to show is displayed in sight of all."

I shall never understand why, but, without a murmur of protest, I went with him.

We came up to the outer "shop" section of the artist's cabin. Its front now stood fully open and was further extended by a wide table that doubled the show space. However, what was displayed there seemed scarcely able to be contained even in so generous a frame. If a giant whose hobby was miniatures had taken the entire faire for his collection, Winterhue's Renaissance panorama would be that scene. Here, wrought to impossible fairy-scale, were the castle, the lane with its shops, the tourney field, the famous rose garden. But these settings, impressive as they were, were eclipsed by the inhabitants. Those were plentiful, and every person, from high to low, was an individual portrait, rendered with almost disquieting accuracy. In spite of the afternoon heat, I shivered, for I now knew who Sterling Winterhue was.

"You did the Lansdowne goblins!" I exclaimed. Late in the spring, a craft fair had been held at the castle, and at that festival, two disturbing life-sized goblin figures had been the main draw. They had been assigned a price that had astounded most viewers, but they had been purchased for that astronomical amount for—rumor had it—no less a personage than a screen director.

The sculptor nodded again. "Yessirree, that was me." He made a sudden predator's swoop upon the tabletop world and, scooping up one of the of the figures clad as one of the nobility, he lifted it to my eye level.

"Our hostess—and a fine lady she is."

The resemblance was unmistakable—this was indeed Mrs. Magin, clothed in the richest of court dress. Winterhue smoothed her full skirt of green satin; then, after patting her on the back with a forefinger, he leaned forward to insert her once more into the rose garden. There a stout, gray-haired doll in red velvet waited, using a silver-headed cane for support.

"Yeah, Court and Faire," the miniaturist stated as she positioned the figures. "This is going to be good PR for them both. And there are only a few more people to be added—"

My host reached under the edge of the table and pulled out a drawer. In that receptacle lay more images, each dressed in the garb of a different social rank of the past. Here was a country woman, there a glittering courtier.

"Are you going to sell these?" I asked. I did not have to give any of the small sculptures further scrutiny to be assured that they were works of art.

"Sell them? Yes, but kind of—backward." Winterhue's tone had lost the jovial well-met quality it had earlier held. "You want to appear here, you pay for it."

From the drawer, the artist selected another figure and held it up. This one was, as yet, bald of head and blank of features, but something was familiar—I drew in a breath as recognition struck. "It's *Deb!*"

"Just so," Winterhue agreed. "Our good needle mistress."

"But why—" I began, then stopped. I could not believe that

my partner had paid to have herself represented among the works of a man she so obviously disliked. I held out my hand, wanting to look at the poppet more closely, but its creator was already fitting it back into the case.

"Her doll's got to be done by tomorrow," Winterhue declared. "You might remind her of that, Miss Gleason." His hand still on the drawer he had just closed, the sculptor was now staring at me. "Gleason," he repeated. "Amanda Gleason, maybe? Wouldn't have thought you'd be interested in all this." He made a gesture that took in not only the table but our general surroundings. His stare grew more penetrating as he queried, "What do you think of it?"

In spite of the heat that had glued much of my clothing to my body, I felt a chill. "Do you intend it as a permanent exhibit at the castle?" I asked in a tone I hoped was calm.

"Right you are," Winterhue assented. "This display'll go into the main hall of the castle, and tomorrow CNN will be here to tape it for the news." Abruptly he changed the subject. "Ever hear from Jessie these days?"

If the image-maker meant to disturb me by that inquiry, he did not succeed.

"I believe she left town some time back," I answered.

"Hmph," he muttered. "Hope she'll have better luck wherever she lights."

Here was another question. How had Winterhue come to know the would-be mystic who had caused so much trouble for several of the Ridgewood citizens?

" 'Manda—" Deb's voice called. She had passed our cabin and arrived at that of the artist, carrying a covered basket whose lid heaved as though something within fought for freedom. Though she did not offer Winterhue the animated container, she spoke to him. "Margaret Magin wants you to include this. . . ."

" 'Zat so?" The sculptor asked casually. In another of those snake-quick strikes, he shot out a hand. His fingers did not encircle Deb's wrists; rather, they touched the lid of the basket for an instant, and that top settled quietly into place. Then he did reach for the handle, but Deb swept the container out of his reach.

Her movement bumped the lid askew so that we could see the basket's contents: a black kitten who, at the sight of us, opened its mouth in a silent mew.

Sterling Winterhue . . . Jessie Aldrich . . . I thought back to some nasty gossip from the past concerning the sculptor and the supposed mystic—rumors of so-called black magic and the discovery of a suspiciously dead cat. I was only guessing, but there was no question about the throbbing that had begun in my head, and which was growing worse with every breath I drew.

" 'Manda, you brought a camera—get it!" Deb had suddenly become a drill sergeant barking an order to a slow-moving soldier.

I hastened back to our shop, remembering where I had set the Instamatic on one of the shelves. As I reached for it, I could hear my friend's voice; she was speaking more loudly than usual, as if increased volume would make her words more forceful, so I was able to catch most of what she said.

"We'll take some pictures for you, Sterling," she was telling the artist when I emerged from the cabin. "Hallie's birthday is tomorrow, and this kitten is one of her gifts from Margaret; she says she wants it placed on Hallie's lap."

Winterhue did not answer immediately; Deb's take-charge tone and behavior might have put him into a state of slight shock. Not until I came up to his booth did he take a step toward the display table.

"Over there," he said, "under the pine tree."

By now I was close enough to follow that pointing finger. Hanging from the miniature evergreen was a swing, and the doll seated in it depicted a small girl who wore a puff-sleeved dress and had her hair caught up in a net of fine gold thread. This was Hallie Magin, Roddy's younger sister.

"So—" Deb nearly hissed the syllable; I could tell that her anger was barely suppressed. "You dared to use her—"

"And why not?" The sculptor's reply held something of his usual flippancy. "Our patroness wished it. All that witchcraft nonsense is over—and remember that the faire-in-small was Douglas Magin's idea to begin with."

Suddenly the basket tipped in my partner's hold, and a handful of black fur half jumped, half tumbled out. No sooner had it landed on the ground than it streaked into the brush behind Winterhue's booth and was gone.

Just as quickly, an expression that had probably been around since long before the Renaissance shot through my mind. Ramming the camera into a pocket of my skirt, I started after the runaway, but it had the advantages of youth, speed, and a good head start.

To my surprise, Deb laughed.

"Foiled!" She grinned, chuckling again. "Lucky for us the little thing's house trained; if we get some food, we can coax it back."

"That would be better for you." With this cryptic and somewhat sinister remark, the artist turned his back on my partner and placed both hands on the world-table. Under his careful urging, it gave way before him, sliding into the space at the shop front. Deb beckoned to me as she stooped to pick up the lid of the basket.

Back in our own private quarters, I settled myself on the edge of my cot. By now I felt thoroughly confused. Our neighbor's mysterious behavior was strange enough, and Deb's lack of effort to locate the kitten was another piece of the puzzle.

"You have got to tell me what this is all about," I declared.

Deb had bent over the cooler of food we had brought with us

and was probing among its contents. When she stood up, she was holding an oversized shaker that I knew contained her sea salt.

"Okay," she replied. However, her tone suggested that her focus for the moment lay elsewhere.

I had already had a good many surprises that day, but I was about to have another: Deb stepped to the nearest window and began to shake salt along the sill. Another sharp thrust of pain began above my left eye and headed inward, and I bit my lip to stifle a gasp, lest I interrupt the ritual. For ritual it was; I knew what she was doing, and I could guess why. She was now closing—according to Pagan belief—every opening in our temporary home that could be used as a means of entry by the Dark.

I have always believed that the needleworker's unique art flowered during her New Age research, which had, in itself, branched from her delvings into the past. As far as I knew, Deb was not a Wiccan, but she did accept a great many beliefs held by walkers of the Old Way. When, in the past, a group of us had been roused to action by the unethical conduct of Jessie Aldrich, my friend had been emphatically on our side.

My own interest in the early religion had been piqued at that time, but my convictions were too strong to allow surrender of the faith I had observed through my life. However, what I could accept, I did, and in no way would I question that which others felt to be true.

Deb's silence lasted so long I feared she did not intend to answer. At last, though, she set the shaker down on top of a box and seated herself on the opposite cot.

"Most of what I know about started at Hentytown over in Kentucky a couple of years ago. That was the first time the local Renaissance group held a faire, and they asked our people to give them tips."

Deb looked grim. "You know, after what we went through with Jessie, that fantasy has a dark side, and that, used for the wrong reasons, it can become truly evil. Well, Sterling likes to portray those unsavory aspects in his work. That kind of sculpture was never shown to the public, only to select customers; we always thought he made the shadow-ones to order. Anyway, he was still discreet about them.

"Then he brought a couple of boxed panoramas to Hentytown." Deb's mouth pursed as though she tasted something bitter. "It got around that he had a live monster in one of them. Our adorable Roddy, who'd been taken to that faire with his sister, broke into Winterhue's booth when the banquet was on; apparently another boy had dared him to. The kids took the box, but Hallie had followed them and they caught her. They were making her look at it when Mark Bancock found them."

Deb paused.

"What was in it?" I demanded.

"Hallie was screaming like a banshee, but she never would tell what she saw. Roddy and his friend claimed it was nothing really scary—just a scene of a girl in the woods at night with something looking at her from behind a bush. But the boys kicked it apart, so no one ever knew what it really showed."

My friend shook her head. "There was a lot of trouble; Sterling had done that box to order and had already taken a down payment. Nobody outside the inner Court knows what settlement was made to his customer, but it was said to have been a huge sum. Shortly after that came the nasty business with Jessie that I'm sure you don't care to remember—" (I raised a hand in a defensive gesture, wanting indeed to ward off those memories.) "—and witnesses said Winterhue was seen at two of her so-called Black Masses. The Court banished him; but apparently, after the craft fair here in the spring and that big sale he made with the goblins, Margaret Magin took him back into the fold.

"Now he's managed to interest CNN—they want to do a story and get pictures once his miniature faire is set up in the castle. That may sound like good publicity, but I keep thinking we're in for more trouble."

Perhaps more than you suspect, I thought. Then, hesitatingly, I told her, "Sterling showed me an unfinished doll he says is you."

Deb actually snarled. "Just let him try to use it! Margaret said he has to get written permission to do anyone's likeness in one of those things."

"Miss Wilson?" Deb was being hailed from the front of the store and rose to see what was wanted. I followed a few minutes later, after invoking the magic of two aspirin to banish the pain-demon who had taken up residence above my left eye.

The newcomers were a large woman and a boy who were wearing the coarse clothing of medieval villagers. "How do we look?" the matron was demanding of Deb as I came out.

"We're entering the contest as a family," she continued. "I'm Helen Quick, and my husband is Robert—he's playing the cloth merchant. Will we pass for a merchant's family?"

The boy, who plainly wanted to be elsewhere, shook free from the hold his mother had on his shoulder. "That guy with the little clay people," he said, pointing to Winterhue's display. "*He* liked what we had on—he said he might even put us in his table thing!"

Mrs. Quick's face flushed an even deeper red than the heat had already colored it. "Shut up, Mike!" she snapped, shooting a hostile look toward the sculptor's booth. "I've heard about him, and we sure don't want to get mixed up in *his* stuff! Well, Miss Wilson?"

Deb inspected the pair for a moment before she nodded and delivered judgment.

"Very good. Except—" she pointed to the child's footgear, "—those should come off, Mike. We're supposed to be in a small village. You might wear clogs in winter or bad weather, but you'd go barefoot on a day like this."

The boy's mother caught up her wide skirt to reveal simple black shoes. "Do I go bare, too?"

Deb smiled. "No, Mrs. Quick. For the wife of a merchant, you've chosen exactly right."

"Okay, then." With no more in the way of thanks, the matron stepped back into the street, pushing her reluctant son ahead of her.

I shook my head in disbelief as I watched them disappear into the crowd. "Are they all like that?" I wanted to know. It might be the needleworker's duty to pass on the authenticity of costumes, but it appeared she had a thankless task.

My friend laughed. "Well, there are enough like them to keep us in our places! Now that this faire has gotten important enough to draw the big media, we're getting twice the usual number of people signing up to do characters."

"Is Mrs. Quick in the SCA?" I inquired. "I don't remember her from last year." I knew some members of the Court, but I had never witnessed such rudeness from any of them.

"Not that I know," Deb answered, adding dryly, "If she's a newcomer, she may be an equally quick goer."

At that moment, the call of a horn rang out, making both of us jump.

"The parade is staring through town," Deb explained. "The Court will be making their entrance now; this is their first appearance all together." She gave a silent whistle of relief. "Glad I didn't have to be involved with *that*."

Afternoon slid into evening, bringing a welcome breeze as we finished our preparations. Several of our fellow "merchants" hung out lanterns. No such lighting beckoned passersby to the front of Winterhue's booth, but a dim glow in the back of the shop suggested that the artist might be busy there. Was he, I wondered, engaged in finishing the poppet that would link my friend to his miniature world, whether she wished to be so connected or not?

Deb's attention was also fixed on our neighbor's quarters. "Trouble!" she said tersely. "Not my affair, though—I refuse to get involved again." She made that statement as though repeating a solemn oath.

Turning away, she lit three lanterns, two of which were to be suspended outside, and a camp lamp of contemporary design (and greater power) whose use must be confined to the hut's interior. Next, she delved into a suitcase and brought out her second costume—that of the guildmistress—which she would be wearing to the banquet.

While Deb was dressing, I went down the street in search of the barbeque that had been teasing my nose all day. It was when I left the "tavern," supper in a bucket in my hand, that I saw the sculptor again. Unlike other merchants in the village, he had not changed his drab work clothes for more colorful and festive ones in preparation for the evening's activities, nor did he seem to notice me.

As I returned, I saw that my friend had two escorts waiting for her at the front of our shop. One was Mark Bancock, who was saying crisply to his companion, "If that kid tries to break into Winterhue's booth again, they'll have to lock him up. I've got no time to babysit the brat."

The other man was the first person I had seen in mundane clothing the whole day. Sighting me, he lifted a hand in salute, and I returned the gesture, recognizing an old acquaintance. Jim Barnes was the closest thing to a feature writer the modest Ridgewood newspaper possessed.

"Press on duty, Jim?" I asked teasingly. "Shouldn't you be wearing a town crier's outfit?"

He nodded toward the archer and returned my banter. "Nay, mistress—merely making the rounds of the crime scene with yon constable."

In the context of what I had seen and heard about our neighbor, the reporter's joke did not seem amusing. I certainly hoped that the already much-put-upon security man would not be forced to perform actual police duties.

" 'Manda . . ." Deb beckoned me inside to where she stood, well away from the shop door and the waiting men. When she spoke, her voice was hardly above a whisper. "Be careful, please. I don't like you being alone."

Such a warning was very unlike my friend, and I found it unsettling; I waited for her to tell me the reason for her concern, but she said no more. In fact, she seemed so eager to be gone that, as she stepped out and greeted her escort, I had only a moment to wish them an enjoyable evening before all three left.

After fixing the shop bell so that it would announce any visitors, I brought my supper out into the front portion of the booth. I ate slowly, watching the street.

Winterhue's hut was totally dark now; and indeed, all the world had grown gray, since the light of the period lanterns did not carry far beyond the fronts of the shops.

However, though the faire was shadowed, it was by no means silent. From the direction of the castle came a cry of trumpets, probably to announce the seating of the Court; then, more faintly, a burst of music followed, of the kind I had heard being rehearsed for several months. Light (albeit dim), and sound, and scent, too, had messages for the senses in the evening air. I was aware of incense burning, though not near; the night breeze brought no more than a hint. The unreal world that was the faire seemed to be waiting for something.

Having finished my supper—most of which, due to my

nervousness, had ended up in the trash—I returned to the inner room and took a paperback from my tote. Almost immediately I put it back again. Perhaps if I rested . . .

After a moment's struggle, I freed myself from the heavy skirt and the laced bodice that held me in the grip of an Iron Maiden and put on my Chinese cotton robe. On impulse, I pulled out several boxes and pushed aside a limp curtain to look out of one of our two windows at Winterhue's shop. Nothing moved there.

In the suspense stories I read for relaxation, a cold wind, or some equally disquieting phenomenon, always announces the arrival of danger. I, however, was simply unable to settle down. This was a strange feeling and one I had never had before; time might have ceased to exist.

The moon was favoring the faire tonight, and a bright beam carved a path between our booth and that of our neighbor. Without warning, something dropped from the air into that ray-path. Leaves and bushes rustled.

"Darn you, cat!"

The intruder from the woods could now be clearly seen: it was Mike Quick from the merchant family. The boy dropped to his knees to grab at a small black blot, but with a bound, the blot eluded him. Overbalancing, he fell forward, and his prey vanished into the dark.

"Sneaking around, eh?" A second, much larger shadow moved into the moonlight and pulled Mike halfway off the path in the direction of the artist's hut. "Well, I have a cure for *that*—"

By this time I was up, thrusting my feet into my shoes, sure I was hearing choking sounds from the merchant youth. When I looked out again, his captor was dragging the wildly-kicking boy toward the Winterhue booth, but the man halted abruptly when he sighted more movement at the trees' edge.

"Mike!" cried a second young voice. "You got that kitten yet?"

"You, is it?" the man roared. "You miserable little vandal, I'll have you now!"

His captor gave a forceful shove, and the Quick boy fell back again into the moonlit path. He did not get to his feet but scuttled for the safety of the wood on hands and knees.

Quietly as I could, I left my vantage point and moved to the front of the shop. Unlatching the outer door and loosening the alarm cord, I took up the flashlight we had set on one of the shelves. As I stepped outside, I almost echoed the leap of Mike's prey as a small furred body fastened onto the hem of my robe.

A rise and fall of words began, none of which I could understand. Tugging my robe free from the kitten's grip, I ran toward the speaker, who I did not think was addressing anyone in this world.

The chant cut off abruptly, and Winterhue (I could not see his face, but I knew it was he) spoke the merchant boy's name, making of its single syllable a drawn-out siren call: "*M–i–i–i–ke . . .*"

Hardly had he completed the word when the youth cried out. The artist moved onto the path to meet Mike, who was returning as summoned. The boy crawled back into the moonlight, body close to the ground, fingers crooked like the claws of an animal. Roddy simply stood to one side of the way, his mouth open as though he were screaming but making no sound at all.

I stepped up behind Winterhue, so that I, too, stood facing the boys. As I moved, the sculptor was lifting one arm; then he leaped toward them, and the moon caught the glitter of a knife blade as he raised the weapon. His other hand closed on a loose dark curl that lay over Roddy's forehead. Still the boy remained silent, his face a mask of mindless fear.

"No!" I cried. Snapping on the flashlight, I caught the three figures full in its powerful beam.

Startled, the sculptor loosed the lock of hair, twisting round so he faced partly into that light, and I clung to the hope that he could not see me behind it. Even his goblin figures had not worn such terrifying expressions as his own features now formed.

Stepping back from Roddy, Winterhue wheeled in a crouch, a soldier facing a charging enemy. The Magin boy made no attempt to rim as Mike Quick wormed his way up beside him; the older youth's mouth was working as though he were shouting, but he, too, was held by the spell of silence that gripped his friend.

"Drop that light, bitch!" the artist spat in my direction.

To my horror, my grip on the barrel of the flash was loosening. At the same instant, I felt a renewed pull at the hem of my robe: the kitten was climbing, but I dared not try to remove it, lest I lose control of the light, which I was now holding in both hands. I fully expected Winterhue to attack me and tried to edge backward, only to discover I was rooted there. I had no more power over my own body than the sculptor's small dolls—or the two large, living manikins who stood before me—had over theirs.

"I said, drop it—!"

A force that might have been an extension of the artist's will seized me, shaking me painfully, and only with great effort did I manage to keep hold of the light. The small cat had reached my shoulder in its ascent. Against the arm up which it was now making its way, its frail body weighed very little; however, it could interfere with any defensive move I might have to make.

Vicious laughter burst from the sculptor as he saw my predicament. I was sure he would reach out and take the flashlight easily from my helpless hands to complete his triumph; but he did not. What he did do was far more frightening.

For the second time he raised the hand holding the knife, but he did not strike at me; instead, he placed the blade between his teeth in the manner of a storybook pirate. From the breast of his jerkin, he brought out a poppet on which the moonlight seemed to center with added intensity. It was smaller than those he had shown to Deb and me, but it was unmistakably another portrait-figure. The head was still bald, but the features were those of Roddy Magin.

Returning the knife to his hand, Winterhue turned and twisted the weapon over the doll, as though seeking the most vulnerable spot to stab. Again he laughed.

"Needs a little trimming up—I was going to give him some hair, until you showed up, damn you! You've done enough already to spoil my plans with your bleeding-heart blabber in that letter to the paper about Jessie's animal sacrifice. Now, Miss Lady-in-Shining-Armor, you just watch old Winterhue, because he's going to show you a real artist's secret."

I could do nothing but obey in a body that had become an imprisoning shell. The kitten had settled on my shoulder, and its soft fur brushed my cheek as it shifted position. It was purring with surprising volume for its size, yet the vibration told not of contentment but of mingled fear and anger. And from that so-small source, power was expanding. Downward into my body it flowed, warming my arms until I once more felt the prickling return of life to my hands.

The sculptor moved the knife point closer to the head of the doll, aiming at one of the unblinking eyes.

"Easy—so very easy—to handle folk who come a-spying . . ."

That threat I head, but it was the last understandable thing the artist said. Yet again he spewed forth a series of meaningless sounds which, though discordant, had a rhythm to their flow. Winterhue took a quick stride to the edge of the light, revealing Roddy to my view. The boy was on his knees, swaying back and forth, his hands pressed over his eyes.

I tried to scream, but nothing came from my mouth. Then the rough tip of a tiny tongue flicked across my lips, and suddenly sound broke forth—no words I knew, but strange noises I had made no effort to form. The artist answered with cries that were loud enough to muffle my own, but still I continued. His fingers clenched as he tried to keep hold of the knife; even as I had fought to keep the flashlight steady earlier, so now he was struggling to retain his weapon.

It was the doll that fell though, thankfully, the knife did also a moment later. At the same time, the flow of Jabberwocky from my lips ended and I was free to move. Winterhue had gone to hands and knees to retrieve the blade, but only inches before his fingers, the thing was sliding itself away over the ground like a stray moonbeam.

" 'Manda!" a familiar voice cried.

"What's going on?" someone else called, followed by a chorus of other shouts to which I paid no attention; I had just achieved my goal of recovering the doll. Now, with Roddy's image in my hands, I started toward the boy himself. In that instant, the youth charged the still-kneeling sculptor—an attack I could see by the light that blazed from the poppet in my trembling hands.

Mark and two other members of faire security separated the youth from the object of his wrath, while Deb pulled the flashlight gently from my hands and held it steady. I became aware that the small weight on my shoulder was gone.

I felt completely bewildered by the events of the night—to such a degree that I could actually sympathize (a little) with Roddy Magin, who was crying with the force of a two year old and still struggling, in Mark's grip, to reengage his enemy. Winterhue, however, was no longer a threat.

That being so, there was something I had to do. I edged away from the light, though my friend tried to hold me, repeating my name in alarm. A few moments later, hardly knowing how I had come there, I found myself kneeling at the edge of the woods.

With one hand, I felt the ground until my fingers sank into a soft patch, then set about digging as a squirrel might open an earth pocket to hide a nut. Tearing off one of the ruffles of my chemise, I wound it about the doll, fitted the manikin into the hole, scooped back the soil, and flattened it.

Deb knelt down beside me. My friend no longer held the flashlight, so only the moon witnessed the "burial service" we gave the poppet, she pronouncing more of that unintelligible language over its "grave." I, meanwhile, sat rubbing my eyes, behind which had erupted a headache of migraine proportions.

Questions . . . so many questions. Who—or what—was Sterling Winterhue? The dolls he shaped—were they dangerously bound in some manner to the persons they represented, or was this fear only a dark fancy born of the torture in my skull?

I do not remember the ride to the hospital; once there, however, I know I was visited by dreams that left me weak and sick. When I finally began to rise from the utter debility and the pain that—I discovered later—had actually lasted for days, I made a decision about my experience. I had been drawn into the uncharted territory of the psychic realm, and I would not, in future, knowingly venture so, away from my earthly home. Never again—not I.

Before I was discharged from the hospital, my friend left town, having taken a position as a lecturer with a traveling exhibit of Renaissance needlework. She had visited me daily, but neither of us was comfortable with the other any longer. In the encounter with the sculptor, I had learned that the Deb Wilson I thought I knew was but a costume, like one of her period dresses, for the woman of power who had come forth that night. I found I did not even want to ask questions, though I had a daunting number of them to answer myself when the sheriff and a state trooper visited me. The most crucial query had yet to be posed, and not to me but to the organizers of the festival: Would there be another Ridgewood Renaissance Faire?

On the day I came home to a safe and sane life again, some-one was waiting at the door. This was one friendship I would not avoid, and my new acquaintance would ask no questions. Moon-shadow, the kitten, was the only piece of miniature magic I cared to own—or be owned by.

ABOUT THE AUTHOR

For well over a half century, Andre Norton was one of the most popular science fiction and fantasy authors in the world. With series such as Time Traders, Solar Queen, Forerunner, Beast Master, Crosstime, and Janus, as well as many standalone novels, her tales of adventure have drawn countless readers to science fiction. Her fantasy novels, including the bestselling Witch World series, her Magic series, and many other unrelated novels, have been popular with readers for decades. Lauded as a Grand Master by the Science Fiction Writers of America, she is the recipient of a Life Achievement Award from the World Fantasy Convention. An Ohio native, Norton lived for many years in Winter Park, Florida, and died in March 2005 at her home in Murfreesboro, Tennessee.

TALES FROM HIGH HALLACK

FROM OPEN ROAD MEDIA

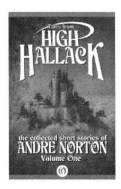  

Available wherever ebooks are sold

49717808R00208

Made in the USA
San Bernardino, CA
02 June 2017